Ni

Tom Barber

*****

Night Sun

Published: 13th March 2021

The Sam Archer thriller series
by
Tom Barber

NINE LIVES

26 year old Sam Archer has just been selected to join a new counter-terrorist squad, the Armed Response Unit. And they have their first case. A team of suicide bombers are planning to attack London on New Year's Eve. The problem?
No one knows where any of them are.

THE GETAWAY

Archer is in New York City for a funeral. After the service, an old familiar face approaches him with a proposition. A team of bank robbers are tearing the city apart, robbing it for millions.
The FBI agent needs Archer to go undercover and try to stop them.

BLACKOUT

Three men have been killed in the UK and USA in one morning. The deaths take place thousands of miles apart, yet are connected by an event fifteen years ago. Before long, Archer and the ARU are drawn into the violent fray.
And there's a problem.
One of their own men is on the extermination list.

SILENT NIGHT

A dead body is found in Central Park, a man who was killed by a deadly virus. Someone out there has more of the substance and is planning to use it. Archer must find where this virus came from and secure it before any more is released.

But he is already too late.

ONE WAY

On his way home, Archer saves a team of US Marshals from a violent ambush in the middle of the Upper West Side. The group are forced to take cover in a tenement block in Harlem. But there are more killers on the way to finish the job.

And Archer feels there's something about the group of Marshals that isn't quite right.

RETURN FIRE

Four months after they first encountered one another, Sam Archer and Alice Vargas are both working in the NYPD Counter-Terrorism Bureau and also living together. But a week after Vargas leaves for a trip to Europe, Archer gets a knock on his front door.

Apparently Vargas has completely disappeared.

And it appears she's been abducted.

GREEN LIGHT

A nineteen year old woman is gunned down in a Queens car park, the latest victim in a brutal gang turf war that goes back almost a century. Suspended from duty, his badge and gun confiscated, Archer is nevertheless drawn

into the fray as he seeks justice for the girl. People are going missing, all over New York.
And soon, so does he.

LAST BREATH

A Federal manhunt is underway across the United States. Three people have been shot by a sniper, and he's gone to ground somewhere in Washington D.C., his killing spree apparently still not over. As riots engulf the city and the manhunt intensifies, Sam Archer arrives in the city to visit his family.
Or so it would appear.

JUMP SEAT

A commercial airliner crashes into the Atlantic Ocean with hundreds of people on board. When another follows three days later, Archer and the rest of the team are assigned the case. At any moment, they know another plane could go down.
And to try and solve the case, Archer's going to have to go 35,000 feet up in the sky.

CLEARED HOT

A female CT Bureau detective and colleague of Archer's is shot in the head in an empty pool in Astoria. Archer learns she's been re-examining a strange case from seventeen years ago. On the morning of Tuesday September 11th, 2001, a FDNY firefighter showed up to work and committed suicide.

But no-one has ever figured out why.

TRICK TURN

At a pre-July 4th carnival in New York, an eleven year old girl is almost killed when a knife slams into a wall, missing her by a hair's breadth. No-one saw who threw the blade, but Archer and his NYPD team can guess why.

Her dead father was one of the most powerful mobsters in the city.
And someone seems hell bent on reuniting the girl with him.

NIGHT SUN

As Archer is sent to a federal prison to help transport an old foe to another facility, a situation erupts that leads to the escape of some other, extremely dangerous prisoners. One of them is an inmate with just six days left on his sentence.

But for a reason that quickly becomes clear, that's six days too many.

Also:

CLOSE CALLS

In a collection of three stories, familiar characters from the Sam Archer thriller series look Death right in the eye and don't blink first. Moments that forged the people they are today.
Moments they can never forget.
Their close calls.

HAND OFF

In this prequel novel, featuring two familiar characters from the Sam Archer thriller series, an investigation involving a dead famous athlete, another assaulted in a seedy strip club toilet and a vigilante going out at night delivering street justice draws the NYPD's attention.

Despite their junior status, Officers Matt Shepherd and Jake Hendricks are drawn into the case as quiet, unofficial investigators.

But also, as suspects.

For Isobel.

PROLOGUE

Vehicles were starting to back up on Pennsylvania's Interstate 90 highway, the hold-up caused by a roadblock ahead.

Using a finger to wipe away sweat from under his sunglasses in the early September heat, a PA State Police trooper stepped back from a gray GMC Acadia seven-seater and gave three fellow Staties a nod to let the vehicle proceed. The people carrier had to drive forward in a slow S-shape to negotiate two barriers placed thirty feet apart to block the road, but it performed the maneuver smoothly and as the car moved onto the open stretch of highway, the deputy waved at the next vehicle in line to roll forward.

Six troopers were stationed at this particular checkpoint, on a highway which entered north-western Pennsylvania from Ohio, snaked across the state on a fifty mile stretch of road and then passed into New York State, the border lying ten miles from their current position. Traffic was only clogged up on the lanes heading to New York, the fugitives the police were looking for considered highly unlikely to be going the other way. A similar roadblock had been set up south on the next closest highway, I-86, and helicopters had just started doing periodical sweeps of the spaces in between, with SWAT teams, other armed response and fugitive task forces on standby. Twenty six innocent people had been killed in the past two days across a number of states, including nine members of law enforcement. The suspects were wanted dead or alive.

The next car in line to be checked, a white Audi SQ8 with Ohio plates, came to a halt beside the lead trooper, a colleague standing slightly further back with the stock of a

Colt AR-15 rifle in his shoulder. The trooper taking lead inspection duty reached the driver's window and pointed down with his forefinger. The previous vehicle, the large GMC, had held a family of six heading up to Toronto for a vacation before attending a wedding next weekend, but this one only contained two men. The guy behind the wheel was in his mid-to-late thirties and wearing spectacles, a blue Wrangler shirt and jeans. 'Where you coming from?' the trooper asked.

'Columbus.'

The Statie bent slightly and looked past the driver at the other man in the car. This individual was dressed more formally in a dark suit and white shirt with no tie, and looked to be around the same age as the driver but olive skinned, dark-eyed and with thick dark hair pushed back off his face. The trooper eyed him silently. Photos of the wanted suspects had been distributed to all the checkpoints across Pennsylvania and had been appearing on TV for most of the morning. 'Afternoon.'

The man nodded, slowly chewing some gum. 'Trooper.'

'Hot day for a suit.'

'We've got the A/C running.'

'Where you both headed?'

'A conference in Syracuse,' the driver told him.

'License and registration.' The driver reached slowly into his jeans pocket; the sunglasses hid the trooper's eyes as they remained on the passenger, but the man watched his companion calmly as he pulled out his wallet and passed over his ID.

'May I go to the glovebox and retrieve the registration?' the driver asked.

The trooper nodded, studying the license. *Barrington Marsh,* the name read. He was about to ask the passenger for his ID too, but then heard whining coming from his right and turned to see a K9 sniffer dog on a leash indicating at the rear of the car. 'Pop the trunk,' the trooper ordered, keeping hold of the license. He walked around to the back of the vehicle, his fellow Statie with the rifle joining him from the other side, a third trooper approaching to cover the Audi with a Remington pump-action. The dog's behavior had caught their attention. 'Says they're heading to a conference in Syracuse,' the lead trooper told his colleague holding the AR-15.

'Conference for what?'

With the ID in his left hand, the trooper pulled up the lid of the trunk with his right and the dog showed even more interest. 'Step out,' he said, going back to the driver's door and opening it. 'You, stay there please, sir,' he told the man in the passenger seat, who remained where he was.

Barry Marsh did as he was asked and walked around to the rear of the vehicle with the trooper. They reached the trunk and stood there together, looking at the contents. The Statie pointed at six large, sealed cardboard boxes. 'What's inside?'

'Something which'll explain his reaction,' he said, glancing at the dog who was straining at his leash. The trooper nodded to his colleague, who slung his rifle over his shoulder and used a knife to slice the tape on the nearest box. He opened it, and the parted flaps revealed rows of cans and some foil packets, neatly stacked inside.

He took one out. 'Dog food?'

'I can leave a couple for your fellow officer, if you like,' Marsh said, nodding at the K9.

'Why you driving around with all this?'

'I'm a rep for a pet food company in Ohio. Conference in Syracuse tomorrow is for people in the industry. Biggest event of the year outside of the annual national forum in Kansas City. This is our new line of products.'

The trooper leaned in a bit closer, then straightened. 'Why does the car smell so strong? These cans are sealed.'

'I dropped one of the boxes loading it into the car. Guess a can must've split. Happens sometimes. Gives off worse in the heat.'

The trooper who'd opened the box cut the seal on another two, revealing one full of more cans and sampler packets, this time for cats, the other box full of dog food like the first they'd opened.

'You mind me making an observation?' the lead trooper told Marsh quietly.

'No. What would that be?'

'You seem nervous.'

'Not good around guns, Trooper. Never have been.'

'I understand. But can I tell you something else?'

'Sure.'

'Your friend in the front seat kinda looks similar to someone we're looking for.'

'That'd be one of the fugitives I've been hearing about on the radio?'

'Correct. Latest reports are they're in this area. And if he isn't who he claims he is, you don't have to say a word.' The trooper's voice lowered. 'All you'd have to do is give me an indication right now while he's sitting up there. He can't hurt you with us here. He won't even have a chance to get out of the car.'

'Is every driver who passes through this checkpoint getting that same advice?'

'Only the ones I got a feeling something ain't right with.'

Marsh smiled. 'Stephen's a lot of things but he isn't a thief and definitely not a killer. He works for the company with me. Has done for a couple years. We've gone on conferences like this before together.'

'Why's he wearing a suit and you aren't?'

'Said it saves him packing it. There's a meet and greet tonight and he'll be the one charming potential new clients.'

The trooper studied him for a moment longer, then nodded to his colleague, who went to the other side of the car and opened the passenger door. 'Step out please, sir.'

The man did as ordered and joined the group at the back of the car. As he stood there, the K9 sniffed at his shoes and suit pants but quickly lost interest and sat beside his handler, his eyes focused once again on the back of the vehicle.

'Mind if you open that jacket and we frisk you?' the lead trooper asked. The guy shrugged, turned and rested his hands on the roof of the Audi. The Statie with the AR-15 patted him down twice, before reaching into his pockets. He came out with a small wad of money, an Ohio driving license and a pack of gum.

'Sixty four bucks,' he said, counting the cash.

'If that's how much was stolen, your suspects need to rethink their business strategy,' the man said.

'Who said anything about money being stolen?' the lead trooper asked sharply.

'We've been listening to the radio. Heard what happened in Cleveland yesterday. Guessing that's why you guys are here.'

The trooper didn't reply, looking at his two fellow Staties who were carefully sizing up both men. They'd been instructed by their corporal when setting up position here less than half an hour ago to look out for traces of blood on clothing and under people's fingernails. Police in Ohio had put it out that the woman from the group of fugitives they were looking for had been shot so wherever she was, she'd be bleeding.

But they couldn't see any evidence of blood on either's man clothing or anywhere else. The horns of several cars caught up in the line along the highway sounded impatiently. After a few more seconds, the trooper passed Barry Marsh his license back, then nodded to his Statie with the AR-15, who returned the other man's license along with the cash and gum. 'Have a good day,' the trooper said as the two men climbed back into their car, the Staties already focusing on the next vehicle in line.

The pair reclipped their seatbelts before Barry navigated past the blocks, then he drove on towards the Pennsylvania-New York border, the long breaks in traffic meaning they had their side of the highway pretty much to themselves.

Once Barry Marsh had paid the toll and driven on for another ten minutes, the man beside him in the passenger seat looked behind to check there were no police cars following.

The road was clear.

He turned to face front again and checked a cell phone he retrieved from the center console. 'Take the next exit,' he told Marsh, who did as ordered. They drove down the off-ramp, then following more instructions, Marsh turned onto another quieter road, skirting around a town called Ripley. The passenger then directed them down a dirt track where there was no-one around. 'Stop here and pass me the keys.'

Barry did, his heart starting to race. 'I did what you-'

'Just do me a favor and pull those boxes back,' the man interrupted, exiting the car and going to one of the back doors. Marsh opened the trunk and did as asked, lifting the dog and cat food boxes out to remove their weight from the flattened rear seats. The passenger then folded the seats back up to full height and took away a blanket that had been spread across the two footwells.

It revealed a slim white-faced, red-haired woman lying there, holding a revolver and with dried blood staining her white shirt. There was a black holdall jammed into the space at her feet; the man with the fake ID took the strap and pulled the bag out before tossing it clear onto the dirt behind him. The zipper was open, blood having stained some of the stacks of bills and jewelry boxes it contained.

'*We made it?*' the woman asked weakly.

He nodded in relief, taking her handgun and putting it in the back of his waistband before reaching in to help lift her out. 'We're over.'

ONE

Almost seventy two hours earlier, inside a rehab gym at Johns Hopkins Hospital in Baltimore, Maryland, a blonde woman in her mid-thirties swayed as she stood up, two female physical therapists beside her with their arms braced ready to catch her. The woman had just risen from a wheelchair and was fighting to keep her balance, the muscles on her legs, hips and back trying to adjust to the unfamiliar demands on them.

'You can do this, girl,' one of the PTs said. 'Just like last time. Your body has to relearn the movements, but it's all there.'

The woman closed her eyes, taking hold of their shoulders as she focused, willing her nerve endings to make connections they hadn't needed to find in years, like searching for a signal in a desert where there was nothing but static.

Her right foot picked up on the frequency though, and she took a tentative step forward.

'Good! Again!'

Her left did the same, and she managed another, holding onto the two therapists to steady herself as a third pushed her wheelchair behind her. Then suddenly overwhelmed, her helpers felt her strength start to give out and took hold before easing her back into the wheelchair. 'I'm sorry,' the woman said, covering her face as a flood of mixed emotions hit her.

'It's OK,' one of the therapists said, rubbing her back and smiling. 'I'd be bawling my ass off.'

The woman smiled through her tears. 'I just feel like I'm going to wake up and find I'm dreaming.'

'You're not, honey. So let's try again.'

'This is unreal,' the woman's brother, NYPD Detective Sam Archer, said on a cell phone call as he watched the physiotherapy session through a window. At thirty two years old, he was a couple of years younger than the sister he was watching learning to walk again next door, but had the same dirty blond hair and blue eyes. They'd been born to an American father and an English mother, spending most of their childhood in the UK, and shared a similar duality in their character traits which meant their occasional clashes could be spectacular. Sarah's natural reserve could make her appear severe and slightly cold upon first meeting, but in fact that reserve hid a very sensitive, caring nature. In contrast, her younger brother was more friendly and outgoing, but both were as ferociously determined and just as resilient as the other. 'Shep, you can't be serious, I literally just got down here.'

'I know, I know,' Archer's investigation squad leader, Detective-Sergeant Matt Shepherd, apologized from their base in New York City. *'I wasn't gonna bother you but then I thought you'd want me to clue you in on this. Something's come up.'*

'I haven't seen my family in a couple of years.' He looked at his sister taking some more steps next door, a sight he'd never thought he'd see again. She'd been in the chair for half her life. It had definitely been a trip to remember so far and he'd only been in Baltimore for less than an hour. 'What's so important that it can't wait?'

'We just got a call from the Prisons Bureau. It's about Frank Lupinetti.'

Archer had been expecting something connected to Shepherd's six-person unit's duties in the Counter-Terrorism Bureau which he was a part of, but the mention of that name caught him by surprise. Frank Lupinetti was a former NYPD lieutenant who'd been convicted of second-degree murder among other charges of corruption and abuse of power, and as a result had been sentenced to twenty years in federal prison. The murder charges had him accused of being partially responsible for the death of nine people, including four fellow cops and a firefighter. One of the dead was a fellow Department detective of Archer's and Shepherd's, who'd also been a close friend. Lupinetti had sold out three other men on the stand with him by cutting a deal; unlike him, they'd never see a sunrise outside prison walls again. 'Something happened to him?'

'Repeatedly. He's been in general population since he went inside and other inmates have been trying to dice him up like you'd expect. Man's gotten stabbed on four separate occasions and he had his arm sliced open pretty bad last week. What you get for being an ex-cop and a first grade asshole. And for being unable to keep his big mouth shut, knowing him.'

'It'll be all of the above,' Archer said, remembering his run-ins with the man. 'But what's this got to do with us? He's under the prison system's care now.'

'His current warden is worried about his people getting sued if Lupinetti gets killed in their facility, so they've secured a transfer over to the federal pen at Lewisburg, in Pennsylvania.'

'Where is he now?'

'USP Gatlin in Virginia. It's in Lee County, bordering Kentucky and Tennessee.'

'Yeah, I know of it. Rough place. And what he deserves. We supposed to feel sorry that he's having a hard time in there?'

'No, but here's the shake; in his trip to the local hospital last week for his latest injury, he started claiming to prison staff who escorted him that he's got more dirt on some

influential people still in the NYPD. Heavy dirt. Wanted to talk to us about it, but refuses to say anything more until he's shifted out of Gatlin to somewhere else.'

'He's lying.'

'Maybe. But after the shitstorm when he and his friends got arrested last time, the powers-that-be here want him making it to Lewisburg in one piece. And enough people have heard him making these statements. Might look too convenient if something happens to him now.'

In the room beside the gym where his sister was taking another couple of steps, Archer could see where Shep's call was headed and closed his eyes. Baltimore was a lot closer to the prison in Virginia that Lupinetti was currently housed in than New York City. 'I've got to be stuck on a bus with the guy throughout his transfer?'

'Not a bus. With Lupinetti's history of getting attacked, Gatlin think our man might not even make it through a group transport unscathed so they've got him being taken solo. A Marshals squad have agreed to run lead on the extradition.'

'But?'

'But the Department want someone with a NYPD badge there to ensure he gets to Lewisburg alive. Franklin ran our offer of assistance past the Marshals Office, explained who you were and your link to the case; they signed off on it. Lupinetti helped murder someone we cared about, Sam. If it was one of us who died, I know Lucero would want to be there on the transport for us.'

'When's the transfer?'

'10am, tomorrow morning.'

'I'll need to hire a car. I took the train down here.'

'I put Marquez on it too and she set out an hour ago; tell her where you are and she can come pick you up. Area

around Gatlin has a few motels for visitors, so crash at one and be at the prison good and early to assist.'

'The Marshals don't mess around, Shep. Especially with cop killers. They really need us to babysit him too?'

'Lupinetti's information seems to involve some heavy hitters in the Department. If what he's saying is true and word's spread, any shot could be taken to stop him talking. Out there on the road would be a pretty good opportunity.'

'An ambush?'

'I don't know. What I do know is, Franklin's been told to have Lupinetti covered and kept vertical. I know you were tight with Lucero. If this shitbag is outside a prison wall, we owe it to her to have someone she'd trust making sure he stays alive to serve out every minute of his sentence. Plus we want to hear what he's got to say. The set up at Lewisburg makes it much safer than these other places he's been.'

Archer remembered spending time with his dead colleague, Diana Lucero, sharing a drink or three in an Irish bar as they watched rugby games from Europe together; her wild, frizzy hair and heavy Queens accent. Her smile and infectious laugh, and her work in the Bureau when they'd been involved in operations together. Shepherd was right. He did owe her that.

'I'll call Lis.'

'I'm sorry about this, Arch. Really. Once you get him delivered, take the full three days. I don't need either of you back until Tuesday.'

'Deal.' Archer hung up and looked at his sister as she continued the PT workout, knowing he was about to disappoint her, again. She took another step, something she hadn't been able to do for half her lifetime. This hospital was considered to be one of the founding institutions of modern American medicine and was regarded as one of the best of its kind in the world.

With what they'd achieved for his big sister, he could see why.

'You have to go already?' Sarah asked, looking at him in disappointment once her physio session had ended. Archer had called Marquez, who was making good time from New York City and said she'd be with him in a half hour depending on traffic. Those thirty minutes were almost up. Sarah was back in her wheelchair and looked tired but happier than he could remember seeing her; until he'd just broken the news that he had to leave.

'My sergeant needs my help with something down in Virginia. It can't wait.'

'We've got so much to catch up on. Did the doctor even explain-'

'He did, before my boss called. Do the girls know?'

'Not yet. I want to get stronger and then really surprise them.' Archer heard his phone ring again and saw Marquez's name on the screen. He picked up his overnight bag. 'I'll be back in the next couple months and we'll walk across the room together. Deal?'

She smiled, before opening her arms and hugging him as he bent down. 'I'll race you. I was always quicker on my feet.'

He grinned then said goodbye to the nurses and doctors who'd been helping his sister before leaving the ward. Marquez's call had dropped before he could answer, but Archer guessed it was because she'd already arrived; he headed out to the front in time to see a 4x4 Ford with NY plates pull up, the driver's window lowering to reveal his Latina colleague.

'What'd you do, break the land-speed record?' he asked as he walked over.

'Sounds like you wanna see Lupinetti again as much as I do,' Lisa Marquez said, as he threw his bag in the back before joining her up front. Five foot six with black shoulder-length hair and a Bronx native, she packed a punch, was an excellent interrogator and rarely missed a thing, the reason why Shep would have chosen her to accompany Archer. After he closed his door, he saw her looking at the name for the clinic. 'Department of Physical Therapy and Rehabilitation,' she read, knowing about his sister's condition. 'Did your sis hurt herself?'

'Not quite,' he said, buckling up. 'Get us back on the highway and I'll tell you.'

TWO

As Archer and Marquez left the hospital and began the drive south, inside the visitor room of their starting point tomorrow, United States Penitentiary Gatlin, a young dark-haired man just turned thirty years old was sitting on one side of a small table. Wearing the prison's orange jumpsuit overalls with a white t-shirt underneath, he was staring intently at an attractive woman sitting opposite him, who was fidgeting nervously as they talked. Her eyes were ringed with dark shadows, standing out starkly against her pale complexion.

'Five to six,' she said, looking at her watch. 'That's right, no? Or six to one. I will if you will.' She mussed her hair suddenly. 'I need to…to change this hair dye.'

'Or not. That's guaranteed.'

'Yes. It is.'

'Now's the time?'

She paused. 'I've wanted to since I was eleven. Will look sharp.'

A corrections officer standing near them yawned and wandered away, uninterested in what sounded like a dumb, inane conversation; he headed over to where some other inmates were sitting with their visitors instead. Very aware their every move was being recorded, but no longer in earshot of the guard, the Gatlin inmate leaned forward.

'*Are you out of your goddamn mind*?' he whispered, the woman returning his fierce gaze with one of exhausted defiance, this time his words making much more sense. She was red-haired, green-eyed and the same age as the man she was sitting opposite. His name was Nicky Reyes. Hers was Katherine O'Mara.

'It's a one-shot deal,' Kat told him quietly, her finger tapping nervously on the table. 'I'll never get this chance again. *We* never will. My people know what they're doing.'

'I've been locked in this cage for almost twelve years,' Nicky replied. 'Just before I can restart my life again, you come here and hit me with this?'

'The timing sucks. I know. But I can't keep going the way things are, Nick. I'm getting desperate. You must see that.'

'We can make it work when I get out.' He leaned closer. 'What you're telling me is crazy.'

'I got laid off again.'

He paused. 'From the diner?'

'Yeah, they canned me, five weeks in. I've got next to nothing to live on, and Blair and Alaina won't help. They won't even talk to me.' She closed her eyes. 'I pull this off, we're set for the rest of our lives. And I won't be stealing anything.'

'Listen to me,' Nicky said urgently. 'We'll find a way without you taking this kind of risk. Just don't try to do this.' He paused. 'Are you sleeping?'

'No.'

'Are you using?'

'No.' She looked at him, seeing the worry on his face as he looked at the exhaustion visible on hers. 'I'm trying, Nick. I'm doing everything I can.' After a jittery breath, she looked at him for a moment longer then rose from her seat. 'I'll get in touch once I'm out of Ohio. I'm ditching my cell so it can't be traced. Don't waste time trying to call me.'

'Stop and think,' he pleaded with her, keeping his voice low. 'You really figure they won't be prepared for this sort of thing?'

‘I’ve got no choice.’ He wanted to keep trying to talk her out of it, but she said a quick goodbye and left. Frustrated, he watched her go, knowing there was nothing else he could do from inside the prison and signaled to the guards he was done.

He was escorted back to his cell, the allotted hour of time in the yard for the prisoners following thirty minutes later. Nicky ended up sitting on some benches near the far fence, layers of chain link topped with circles of razor wire surrounding the prison, armed guards in the towers keeping watch. It was late summer, with fall to come, the seasons changing once again. He’d watched the leaves turn brown before snow fell and the dark nights of winter giving way to the light of spring for more than a decade in this place.

‘What’s wrong, kid?’ a voice asked, belonging to his cellmate who was sitting beside him. Nicky had been distracted ever since he’d left the meeting with Kat, where she’d given him far more information than the guard who’d been standing near them could have guessed. He looked up and realized his celly had been watching his back while he’d been distracted, a lapse you couldn’t afford in a place like Gatlin.

He made sure no-one was paying them attention or was close enough to listen, then told his cellmate everything he’d just learned from his meeting with Kat. The whistle went twenty minutes later, and the inmates began to trudge towards the door back into the prison, ready to line up before being taken to the chow hall. Nicky and his large, bearded companion joined them, keeping an eye on their backs as the COs led the line in.

The day’s visits were done, the site was secure and the prison’s routine continued the same as always, the sun starting to sink towards the horizon for the night to follow.

‘The doctor at Johns Hopkins told me my sister’s the sixth person they’ve had these past three months take their first steps after a severe spinal injury,’ Archer told Marquez, the two of them inside a Quality Inn motel room in the Lee County area a couple of hours later. There was a pizza box on the table, an old Tom Cruise movie where he played a paralyzed war veteran on the TV beside them. The irony hadn’t been lost on the two detectives eating their dinner.

‘When I was a teenager, I fell off a roof and almost broke my back,’ Marquez said. ‘Got away with it but had this weird tingling for a while afterwards in my lower back and legs. Went numb sometimes which scared the shit outta me, so I did my reading. I thought you couldn’t recover from spinal paralysis.’

‘You couldn’t. But the Johns Hopkins doc told me scientists just found an injured person’s dormant spinal column can be re-awoken by injecting a chemical solution. Binds to receptors or something, replaces transmitters that the brain releases in uninjured people.’ He laughed briefly and shook his head. ‘I think. I was trying to understand everything he was telling me.’

‘And it wakes up the spine?’

‘If I’m getting it right, yeah. Excites neurons and prepares them to coordinate lower body movement. Scientists then stimulate the spinal cord using electrodes. Sending continuous electrical signals through nerve fibers to the neurons that control lower body movement.’

‘Then?’

He smiled. ‘Rats they first tested it on regained the ability to walk. They were put on treadmills and the movement created some kind of sensory feedback. They were able to continue moving without any input from the electrodes. Body rewiring itself.’

Marquez dropped a half-eaten pepperoni slice back onto the torn off lid of the box, her face showing she wasn’t overly impressed with the pizza the area had to offer, before wiping her hands on a paper napkin. 'Now I see why you were pissed that Shepherd pulled you away to come do this. I'd have driven all the way back to Queens just to kick his ass.'

Archer smiled again. 'He's forgiven. He knew it was bad timing. And he knew I'd want to be here for Lucero.'

'How'd your sis get involved in the treatment?'

'Doc said she emailed the hospital almost ten years ago wanting to be kept informed of the latest research. When this study showed it was pioneering and going places, she was one of the first to sign up for human trials. Probably helped she was providing regular funding too.'

'That's crazy. How things can change.'

'Tell me about it. She deserves it.'

'So do you.'

Archer didn't answer. He was done with his food, and after seeing Marquez was too, he rose and picked up the box, putting the torn lid back to dump it all down the trash chute outside. 'Speaking of healing, sounds like Lupinetti's been needing to do a lot of that lately,' he said. 'You ready for a full day with him?'

'Let's just get him to Pennsylvania in one piece and get back home.'

'I'll see you downstairs at 8. Tell me how the movie ends.'

After the two detectives parted ways, Archer dropped the pizza box into the trash before going into his own room, darkness settled over a quiet, untroubled Lee County. Life going on in the area much the same as usual, just as at USP Gatlin.

How things can change.

THREE

'How far out are we?' Archer asked the next morning as he filled the tank on their police-issue 4x4 black Ford at a gas station in the local town of Jonesville. Marquez was leaning against the other side of the car eating a granola bar, a cup of coffee she'd just bought placed on the roof, some snacks for the road trip to come in a bag on the back seat.

'Eight miles, give or take.' The pump Archer was holding cut out so he replaced it on the hook before climbing back into the car, having pre-paid. He glanced in the rearview mirror and seeing there was no-one behind them waiting, opened a folder Marquez had brought with her from New York.

He looked at the photos showing the evidence of Lupinetti having been repeatedly attacked, the file put together by the Gatlin warden when he'd requested the transfer with the Bureau of Prisons. Three of the wounds had been long slashing cuts on Frank's torso, back and arm, the other showing a sharpened toothbrush handle prior-to-removal protruding from his shoulder-blade. It had been jammed into his body above the sleeve of tattoos with the NY Yankees insignia and other New York iconography, some new ink on his arm just above where he'd been cut consisting of some letters and numbers. Dates that meant something to him, maybe, or some bullshit code. There was an NYPD shield inked there too, an old tattoo, with the man's former badge number. The toothbrush wound looked like someone had used it as a bullseye.

‘Marshals say they want to be out the gate with him by 10:15,’ Marquez read from a text that had just come through on her phone.

Passing her the folder, Archer drove out of the gas station forecourt and back onto the road. ‘Hopefully he doesn’t get shanked again before we get there.’

If a person wanted to make their life inside a US federal penitentiary as difficult as possible, Francisco Matteo Lupinetti of Manhattan, New York would be a shining example. He was a former NYPD lieutenant, a cop killer with a tendency to run his mouth and having most of his life story inked on his arms, there was no way he could keep much of his past secret. After taking a deal and turning on some remaining guys he’d been working with during his years of corruption, getting twenty from the judge at the end of last year instead of forty or life, he’d known the ride ahead was going to be bumpy. But as Archer and Marquez had just been observing from photographs, he’d quickly found himself at the top of the list of targets from the first day he’d been incarcerated.

At USP Gatlin, the third location he’d been transferred to in just his first year of captivity, he was locked up with drug cartel killers, Somalian pirate leaders extradited to the US and even one of the assholes who’d plotted the 1993 World Trade Center bombing. But after Lupinetti had shown up, he’d bumped them all down to become public enemy number one. A lot of the other inmates hated the Yankees, hated cops and hated snitches, which made Lupinetti a triple hitter. The only way to make it worse would be if he’d also been sent down for messing with children.

His cellmate for the last few months ticked that particular box. ‘Bout time they shipped your ass outta here,’ the scrawny prisoner called Latham said from his bunk, a mean son of a bitch from some backwater town in Arkansas. He was eyeing Lupinetti who was standing near the open door of their cell, nervously tapping the leg of his orange jumpsuit pants with his fingers. 'Givin' me a pig for a celly. I never wanted that shit.'

'You raped your own niece and nephew, Latham. What does that make you?'

'Least I weren't a pig.'

Across the block, Lupinetti made accidental eye contact with a large inmate called Rainey, who he knew used to be the president of some major motorcycle club in Georgia with chapters all over the country. The man was standing in his cell, all their doors open for the time being, something permitted for one hour each morning; after they locked eyes, Lupinetti quickly shifted his attention elsewhere, then saw one of the access doors below get unlocked, two COs carrying shackles moving into the cell block.

They passed some metal tables and stools fixed to the ground, a few inmates sitting at them talking or playing cards. Lupinetti checked his watch again nervously.

His time to leave had come.

The correctional officers in Gatlin were accustomed to being heavily outnumbered by the prisoners, sometimes by a rate of twenty five-to-one or even higher, so being hyperaware was an important skill they all learned fast when they started working here. A chiropractor setting up business in the facility would have earned a fortune treating the crooked necks and backs from so many COs and inmates constantly looking over their shoulders.

But Gatlin's dangerous reputation was well-deserved and the guards also knew that despite being vigilant, things could turn south in an instant. Eye contact kept too long, someone saying the wrong thing, a perceived racial slur or just a prisoner's temper snapping could be the spark to set the place ablaze. The aftermath usually left broken skulls, slashed bodies or sometimes throats, illegal shivs slicing open flesh or slammed into necks or eyes.

The more experienced of the two COs sent to collect Lupinetti and take him out to processing before he was signed over to the Marshals' custody had checked carefully and was confident of a stable atmosphere as they walked into C Block, which was why the doors had been left open. No signs of trouble or tension. The boys had been well-behaved lately.

So he wasn't ready for the moment his partner was rushed from behind and stabbed in the back with a screwdriver stolen from the woodshop.

The sharpened Philips work-tool was buried deep, the inmate gripping him shanking him again several more times with it. The other CO was grabbed too before he could react, but instead of being cut was dragged back and spun around, a shiv held to his neck as he dropped the shackles he'd been holding.

'*OPEN THE GATE*!' the inmate holding him, called Hoffmeier, screamed at another CO inside the block's adjacent control room, the man jumping up from his seat beyond some protective glass.

'HOFF, DON'T DO THAT!' the CO shouted back, hitting the alarm as inmates suddenly started yelling, running out of their cells or going for hidden weapons as they realized an attack on the screws was going down.

'OPEN IT OR HE'S A DEAD MAN!'

The man in the box didn't move. Hoffmeier nodded to the other inmate called Kattar who'd jumped the first CO and he stabbed the man again who'd fallen to his knees, this time in the neck, the CO collapsing face down to the floor and spasming as blood spurted from the wound. Inmates cheered and yelled as the place started to erupt into chaos.

'ONE LEFT' Hoffmeier shrieked, punching the bulletproof glass with his fist holding the shiv. *'OPEN THE GODDAMN GATE!'*

Seeing his colleague dying on the floor, with the other man's life in his hands, the CO hit the button, and it started to slide back; some of the inmates immediately rushed through, leaving some bloodied footprints as they ran past the dying prison officer, two stopping to take his baton, cuffs and keys.

Up top, Frank Lupinetti watched this happen and also went to seize the opportunity to run, but was a second too late. His cellmate Latham suddenly threw his pillowcase over the former NYPD lieutenant's head, pulled it taut around his neck, then dragged him backwards as he started strangling him.

Just inside the front gate of the prison, Archer and Marquez had been handed back their IDs and told to proceed when a siren started to sound.

'*What is it?'* the CO with them shouted up to an armed guard in the tower, Archer and Marquez delaying moving off, waiting for the answer.

'*Riot just broke out in C Block*!'

'Is that where Frank Lupinetti's held?' Marquez asked the guard, who looked back at them and nodded.

'You both need to leave right now.'

'We're here for his transport!' Archer replied.

'Marshals already arrived. The entire site's gonna get locked down.'

‘We’re already in! Just let us get down there. Maybe we can help.’

They kept making their case with the CO for almost a full minute, who still refused to give them access, but then the guard was distracted by a laundry truck that was leaving the facility and heading towards the gate. He waved it down and the driver leaned out to show his ID as the guard from the booth who’d been going back and forth with Archer and Marquez headed to the rear, undid the latch and pulled it up. He disappeared out of sight, then a few seconds later dropped back down, relocked the door and hit the side of the truck twice, waving the gate to be opened again.

The truck sped off as Archer and Marquez waited for an answer, the guard turning back to them. ‘Alright, just go in! We gotta keep this gate closed!’

Archer immediately drove on towards the contained chaos ahead as the gate started sliding across behind them, hoping they could get to Lupinetti before someone in there took the chance to get their hands on him instead.

They couldn’t have known they were already too late.

FOUR

As Archer and Marquez approached the prison's main buildings, they saw a four-man team of US Marshals talking with corrections officers, all gathered in the area in front of the cell blocks. Archer swung the NYPD Ford into an empty bay and as the two detectives got out, the sounds of a severe disturbance became very evident despite the loud sirens, all the noise coming from inside the clearly-marked C Block with smoke already flowing out of a number of windows.

The prison COs who the Marshals were talking to were easily identifiable, wearing light gray pants and a similar shade shirt, their belts holding a flashlight, key clips, handcuffs and a can of pepper spray but no pistol. Like other prisons across the country, their uniforms also displayed their rank, the hierarchy similar to that of the military, and as Archer looked at the group, debating who to approach, an African American sergeant peeled off towards them having seen their car arrive.

'Who are you?' the man asked loudly to make himself heard over the noise.

'Here to assist with Frank Lupinetti's transport,' Archer replied, as he and Marquez showed their badges.

'Inmates attacked two of our guards who went in to collect your man,' the sergeant told them. *'Killed one, still have the other. We've got more COs in there and two of them just stopped responding on radio.'*

'So how do we get to Lupinetti?' Marquez shouted to him.

'He has to wait, right now we're in the process of locking down.' The sergeant motioned for them to follow

him behind one of the US Marshals' two black vehicles which helped block the noise of the sirens slightly, allowing them to hear each other more clearly. 'Last time this happened, eleven inmates got killed,' the sergeant told them. 'Their bodies were stacked up in the doorways like loose cigarettes to block us getting in.'

'How many prisoners do you have here?' Archer asked.

'1200, with 90 more over at a minimum-security satellite camp. But a lot of the boys in C Block know your man's history and that he's getting transferred this morning. You might already be too late. He's a major target.'

'We have to try to get him,' Marquez said, as the front gate opened again, a truck speeding into the grounds with the *Bureau of Prisons* logo on the side.

'Maybe he just ain't meant to make gray hair,' the sergeant said. 'Someone's gonna use this to get a piece of him.'

Archer looked over at the Marshals who were strapped up in vests and carrying weapons, the four men talking with the prison staff but clearly in no rush to try and extract Lupinetti. *He started claiming he's got dirt on some influential people still in the NYPD,* Shepherd had told Archer yesterday. *Powers-that-be want him making it to Lewisburg in one piece.*

'She's right, we have to at least try to get him out of there alive,' he told the sergeant, who took to his radio.

'Williams, you seen Frank Lupinetti in there?'

'Can't get a look right now, they're taking over the corrid-' The man swore and there was the sound of smashing and yelling. *'-ast we saw, they were chasing down Andrea and Abrams. We're trying to find them. Pena's dead. They still have Hannity!'*

'Back up's coming in, just hold on.' The sergeant left Archer and Marquez and jogged over to join the Gatlin captain, who was quickly explaining the situation to the riot response team who'd just arrived in the truck, the men listening as they started strapping on their gear.

'They're not gonna bother with Frank right now,' Marquez said to Archer. 'Got more important things to focus on.'

'So we need to find him,' he said, before approaching the Marshals. 'We want to try and get Lupinetti out,' he said, showing his badge. 'Could use your help if they give us permission to go in.'

'No way, guy; we're not taking one step in there until this is over,' their lead deputy answered. 'We're getting paid to transport a fugitive, not get involved in a riot.'

'It's your responsibility to get him to Pennsylvania,' Marquez pointed out, joining Archer.

'I'm not risking any of my people to save his crooked ass. The animals in there will swarm on anyone wearing a shield or carrying one. Let the riot control team cool it down. If he lives, he lives. I heard what he did to get sent down here. He dies, not a great loss, right?'

'It is if he actually has some information we need,' Marquez argued.

'That worth you going in there and getting cornered?'

The pair of NYPD detectives looked at each other, the sirens still wailing their repeated warning. The riot response team had finished prepping their gear and their leader was standing with the Gatlin sergeant who was liaising with their COs still inside. As the sergeant talked, he made eye contact with Archer and then Marquez before presumably explaining who they were. Marquez jogged over to talk to the riot team's leader and after she spoke to him for a few moments, Archer saw the man nod.

That was all he needed. He immediately went to the trunk of their Ford, opened it up and removed his Sig

Sauer from its holster, storing it before starting to strap on a vest as Marquez joined him. 'There'll be a lot of makeshift weapons in there, but you can't just start shooting folks,' the Gatlin sergeant warned, re-joining them.

'We won't,' Marquez said, as she pulled her pistol too and stowed it in the trunk alongside Archer's. The 4x4 was stocked for all sorts of situations, and vested up, Archer unlocked and opened a large inner compartment. The two detectives each took out a special twelve gauge shotgun with a yellow barrel and stock, before Archer withdrew a box of bean-bag ammunition. The shells contained lead pellets inside a small cloth bag and getting hit with one was like getting kicked off your feet by a horse, but it didn't kill you. The Ford was fully packed with lethal and non-lethal ammo, as well as two rifles, two more twelve-gauges and spare handgun ammunition.

'Don't let 'em get the drop on you,' the sergeant warned as they loaded the shotguns. 'A lot of the boys in C Block are lifers or doing bids close to it. Nothing more to lose. They'd love to brag they killed a cop.'

'You're planning to go in?' the Gatlin staff captain asked, coming over when he'd noticed the NYPD pair strapping up and loading the shotguns.

'Your role is to stop this thing,' Archer said, sliding a last shell into his twelve gauge and stuffing more into his pocket as Marquez did the same. 'Ours is getting Frank Lupinetti from here to Lewisburg with a pulse.'

'He's not gonna be sitting nicely in his cell doing a yoga pose waiting for you guys to show up. Could be anywhere in there right now.'

'We'll find him,' Marquez said.

'Take this,' the sergeant said, giving them his radio. 'I'll watch the monitors and guide you best I can. I'll try to locate him on the cameras to help you out.'

'We're not taking responsibility for you in there,' the Gatlin captain warned. 'Your choice to go inside. If you do somehow manage to find him, get the hell out again as fast as you can.'

Archer racked his shotgun, took the radio, and then without another word he and Marquez followed the riot control team towards the locked doors of the facility.

Inside the prison, the riot in C Block was following a scenario similar to a flooding ship, the water reaching a compartment and building pressure until the next seal burst. The inmates' way of breaking through to each new section was the same leverage they'd used to get the first door opened, another CO called Abrams acting as their currency. The sight of a sharpened shank held to his neck had given them access through three more doors and gotten the prisoners more sets of keys.

But while all this was going on, Lupinetti had been struggling with Latham, fighting for his life. His skinny celly had maintained the upper hand thanks to that initial element of surprise, despite being the smaller of the two men, and after a back and forth struggle Latham had managed to retighten the material of his pillowcase around Frank's neck and was doing his best to finish choking him to death.

As he felt unconsciousness looming, Lupinetti clawed behind him and with a wrenching twist pulled at the man's balls like he was trying to rip them free. Latham screamed and the pillowcase slackened. Lupinetti ripped the material away with his other hand, sucking in air, and gave his cellmate a few hard kicks while he was bent double, following up with a few more as he fell to the floor.

The former NYPD lieutenant staggered slightly, light-headed from lack of oxygen, and gripped onto the bedframe as he sucked in much-needed air, but as soon as he could see straight again he stumbled out of the cell.

Downstairs on the west-side approach to C Block, the first members of the riot control team were appearing, helmets and body armor in place, tasers and pepper spray ready. '*DROP THE WEAPONS*!' one of the officers shouted, all of them taking cover behind their shields as inmates hurled anything they could find, some of the prisoners rushing them, shouting abuse and taunts as they attacked.

Lupinetti went in the opposite direction and moved through the first door opened in the riot, past the pool of blood and the dead body of CO Pena lying on the floor.

Having followed the riot team through the main access door, Archer and Marquez were now inside the block and at the back of the group. The cell housing was to the right, but as the two NYPD cops made their way down the corridor, they saw just further ahead on the left was a room with a bank of screens inside, cameras providing full coverage of C Block.

'*Riot control are containing that area,*' the sergeant said over the radio. '*I can see you. You're good.*'

As the riot team went to war with the inmates inside the housing, the two NYPD detectives entered the room with the screens. 'Might be some prisoners disguised as COs or riot officers,' Archer warned the sergeant, seeing open lockers which he guessed would normally have held uniforms, batons and perhaps riot gear. 'The lockers in here have been stripped bare.'

Beside him, the monitors were good quality and Marquez searched them for Lupinetti, but it was almost impossible to pick him out in the melee with all the inmates wearing matching BOP-issue white t-shirts and orange jumpsuits. The former cop's tattooed arms were what she was looking for as a distinguishing mark.

'Can't see hi-,' she started to say.

'I think I just got him,' the sergeant's voice said over the radio. *'Check 14.'*

The two NYPD detectives immediately looked at the relevant screen, its number underneath, in time to see a figure running through the shot. Archer and Marquez watched him reappear in the next and tracked him to 15.

It was Lupinetti, and he was on his own.

'Where the hell's he going?' Archer asked the sergeant.

'Towards the laundry, looks like. I can guide you there. It's not far.'

Archer clipped the radio to his belt, lifted his shotgun's stock back to his shoulder and the two cops peeled out of the room to follow the sergeant's directions. As they turned onto the next corridor, the sergeant buzzed the door open for them. Marquez closed it again once they were through just as Archer saw a couple of officers coming towards them, wearing armor, helmets and carrying batons.

He took his finger off the trigger for the shotgun as he and Marquez continued towards the pair, but as they got closer, Archer noticed a splash of orange fabric visible where their uniform met their boots.

He'd just found who'd stripped the lockers bare.

Archer ducked as one of them suddenly swung his baton at his head, then threw himself back as the other did the same. Marquez, who'd been slightly behind her colleague, dropped her aim and blasted the first inmate in the stomach, sending the guy to the ground in a crumpled heap a second before Archer did the same to his friend.

The armor the pair were wearing took a lot of sting out of the non-lethal shells but the shots had still badly winded each prisoner and would leave one hell of a bruise. Before they could recover, Archer kicked their batons away, Marquez covering the hallway as Archer then dragged the two inmates one-by-one towards a pipe running along the wall. He locked a hand of each around it with his set of cuffs, then pulled off the men's helmets to reveal their faces; both were white boys, one with badly-designed tattoos covering his face, each still grimacing in pain and gasping for air like landed fish.

'I'll send someone to collect them,' the sergeant said over the radio. *'Keep following my directions.'*

Racking their shotguns which spat out the empty shells, the two NYPD detectives reached another door and after it buzzed, slipped through just as more inmates appeared in the corridor behind them, missing seeing the pair of detectives by a matter of seconds as the door closed.

Not far away, Lupinetti had almost made it to the laundry when he heard footsteps behind him. Swinging round, he saw it was the two guys who'd come at him with a blade the previous week and had turned his prospective transfer to another facility into a certainty. They were a pair from South Carolina each doing nine years for assaulting a police officer and stealing his squad car when smoked up on 'swamp glass' meth. Ever since they'd found out Lupinetti had been a cop, they'd been looking for a shot to get their hands on him.

'You ain't gettin' outta here, boy,' one of them hissed as they wrestled Lupinetti to the ground, before pulling the same shiv from his sock he'd cut him with eight days ago. He went to bury the weapon into Lupinetti's eye but the ex-cop brought his unbandaged arm up and the razorblade stabbed into the meat there instead, making him shout in pain. As the other inmate tightened his grip to help his friend pin Frank down and keep him still, he was suddenly

clocked from behind with the stock of a shotgun which sent him sprawling. The other inmate leapt up and spun round, but before he could move further a non-lethal shell to the sternum put him down too.

Lupinetti stared up in disbelief at the pair who'd just rescued him, the shiv still buried in his arm.

'You two?' he said. 'The hell are you doin' here?'

'Hi Frank,' Marquez said, grabbing him by his other arm as she and Archer yanked him to his feet. Lupinetti suddenly twisted and tried to headbutt her, but Archer had been ready for him to try something and snatched hold before hip-tossing him to the floor.

Despite his arms being hauled behind him and cuffed with Marquez's set of bracelets, Lupinetti continued to resist and in the struggle to contain him, the radio Archer had clipped to his belt was dislodged. The fall cracked the outer shell, but it was finished off when Lupinetti stamped on it accidentally as he kept fighting.

'Riot team is regaining control, sir,' a corrections officer informed the Gatlin warden who'd joined members of his staff in the prison's camera room/control center. The CO was right; the squad was making good progress into the riot, using seize-and-hold tactics, but they were employing non-lethal force while many of the inmates were looking to do just the opposite, meaning every inch of the block they won was hard-gained.

'I'm hearing two New York cops went in to find Frank Lupinetti?'

'I think they just reached him,' the sergeant who'd been guiding Archer and Marquez said. 'Got him somewhere near the laundry.'

'Can we see?'

'Someone's busted up the cameras in there so we lost them. I was leading the NYPD pair on radio, but communication just dropped too.'

'That ain't good,' one of the other COs said, as they saw two of their most violent inmates with makeshift weapons were one corridor away from where they thought the two visiting cops had just located Lupinetti.

'The hell are you two doing here?' Lupinetti asked again as he finally gave up struggling, his face pushed against the wall.

'You've got a cell date in Pennsylvania tonight,' Archer said. 'We're making sure you get there.'

'Take that thing out,' Lupinetti said, looking at the shiv buried in his arm, his hands cuffed behind him.

'No,' Marquez said.

'I know you hate me, bitch, but I'-'

'Think clearly, dumbass. We pull it clear, you'll start losing blood.'

'You're really gonna keep me shackled? Right now?'

'We'll watch your back,' Archer said, grabbing him by the collar and pushing him forward. 'Let's go.' But as they took him back towards the door in the corridor, Archer looked up at the camera.

The door didn't open.

'He on a smoke break or something?' Marquez asked, as Archer kept a tight grip on Lupinetti.

Two corridors away in another direction, Nicky Reyes' cellmate, the bearded, large motorcycle club president who Lupinetti had been housed opposite in C Block, was just moving past the chow hall with another inmate when he heard screaming from inside. It was a woman's voice.

‘Keep going,’ he told the prisoner with him, who was holding a rolled-up orange prison jump suit. ‘You gotta get to the cell right now.’

As the other man nodded and carried on, the biker moved into the chow hall to see six prisoners holding onto a blonde female guard called Andrea, two of them in the process of tearing her uniform off. A fellow CO of hers was lying on the floor bleeding from a wound to the stomach and he wasn’t moving.

The biker watched for a moment, then threw some keys in his hand aside and moved forward to grab two of the inmates, pulling them away.

‘*Wait your turn, Prez*!’ one of them snapped, fighting free from his grip. The other, however, made the mistake of swinging a punch at the big man, connecting with his jaw; a second later, Prez’s own fist crashed into the smaller inmate’s face and sent him spinning to the floor.

The biker saw a shank coming at the last second, and bent his elbow in across his torso like a boxer defending a body shot, but the hot pain that came from the weapon set him on fire and he started to lay into the group, three of whom turned on him as the others kept on tearing at the female CO’s uniform.

Archer and Marquez had decided to find another way out, sensing there must have been a good reason the sergeant hadn’t opened the door, and were just approaching the chow hall when they heard a woman screaming and the sound of a violent fight.

At the same time, at the end of the corridor ahead they saw the Gatlin sergeant who’d given them his radio appear at a locked exit, urgently waving them forward. *‘C’MON!’* he shouted.

Archer looked into the chow hall, then at Lupinetti with the shiv buried in his arm.

Next door, the scene resembled a lion being attacked by a pack of hyenas as the large biker fought a losing battle against three smaller inmates, the prisoner he'd hit still laid out on the floor, the female CO kicking and shrieking as she was held down by one guy, a second undoing her pants belt as fast as he could.

Suddenly the loud *boom* of a shotgun being fired echoed around the hall and the man restraining her was punched off his feet by a beanbag. The other one was hit a second later, another blast echoing, and the biker took the opportunity to put down two of his attackers when they turned to see what the noise was.

He looked over to see a blond man and black-haired Latina woman, both in bulletproof vests with *NYPD* printed in white on them, each holding a pump-action twelve gauge with yellow coloring on the stock and barrel. As the biker's last attacker thought better of it and decided to run off, the blond man moved forward and helped the shaken female CO to her feet, her shirt torn, blood leaking from a split lip and a cut on her head. The biker had already made eye contact with the Latina holding the shotgun, and kept his hands up as she racked the pump.

'Six o'clock!' he warned, and she swung round before firing, dropping another inmate who'd just run in. However, the prisoner had been holding a canister of pepper spray stolen from one of the COs, and the shotgun beanbag was enough to break the metal, the can erupting. Marquez took a nice dose of it to the face and she recoiled, coughing and stumbling as she followed Archer with the female CO back to the corridor outside.

Two riot control officers appeared and took the CO from Archer, hurrying her away down the corridor. *'GET ME*

OUTTA HERE!' Lupinetti begged; Archer undid his spare set of cuffs from a bar door handle they'd secured him to before entering the chow hall, then pushed him forward towards the exit gate. Archer grasped hold of Marquez's arm as Lupinetti hurried ahead of them and guided her until they exited the block, the pepper spray now taking full effect.

Turning, Archer heard the door lock again behind them and took some deep breaths while beside him Marquez coughed, cursed and wiped her eyes. He looked at Lupinetti, who was being held by the sergeant and another CO, the shank still buried in his arm.

They'd gotten their man out; not unscathed.

But still in one piece, more or less.

FIVE

Some prison riots across the United States in recent times had been known to stretch into several days, weeks or even months of standoffs between inmates and the authorities, but USP Gatlin's fast response and the decisive actions of their riot squad meant the officers had regained control of the notoriously rough penitentiary within the hour. Yelling and shouting was coming from other cell blocks, their inmates desperate to get involved, but they'd all been locked down as soon as the trouble started so the only thing those prisoners had been able to contribute was noise. Now even that was starting to die down too.

In the nearest parking lot to the front gate, there was a gathering of COs, riot officers and medical staff from the local hospital treating the wounded. Among the crowd, Archer was helping Marquez clear the effects of the pepper spray, tipping a bottle of water slowly into her eyes. 'Any better?' he asked.

'Not yet.' He continued to help her rinse her eyes, then waited as she blinked repeatedly trying to flush the chemical out, using tissues to blow her nose and wipe her face. The sergeant who'd assisted them walked over, passing Archer their three sets of handcuffs which had been retrieved. 'She doing OK?'

'Getting there. It's helping clear her sinuses,' Archer said, seeing the worst of the effects were beginning to ease off.

'Who said they needed clearing,' she retorted, looking at C Block through watery red eyes as they heard the sound of more shouting coming from inside. 'They still going at it?'

'Nah, just locked in their cells and pissed about it. They better get comfortable. They're going into 48 hour lockdown. Mandatory after any riot.'

'What were the casualties?' Archer asked.

'Two guards killed, three others stabbed. Six dead inmates found so far, fourteen more injured.' He nodded towards an ambulance where they could see the female CO they'd rescued being treated for some cuts to her face. 'And they were gonna rape and probably murder Andrea too. She's saying she wouldn't have gotten out without you two helping her. Thank you.'

Archer was about to reply, but then realized the significance of being given his cuffs back and looked around quickly. 'Where's Lupinetti?'

'On his way to the local hospital in Jonesville. Two of the Marshals went as an escort and they had him cuffed to the gurney. Don't worry. He's not going anywhere.'

'When we first arrived, you said collecting him set this whole thing off?'

'Pena and Hannity went to get him. Then it erupted.'

'Cells were open?'

'It's not supermax or twenty three hour lockdown. Inmates get free time in the morning to walk around. Things have been on the level in C Block lately, so we assumed they wouldn't be stupid enough to try anything. Things blow up here occasionally but it's normally inmates going at each other. Not at us.'

'Any way to tell when something bad is brewing?' Marquez asked.

'You start to sense when shit might be about to go down. Little clues. Older inmates'll start staying on the edges of the field during yard time, or in their cells even when the doors are open. Things go too quiet. That's when you need to start putting on body armor and calling the hospital. Someone's gonna get hurt.'

'But today?' Archer asked.

'No change in the static. C Block's had no trouble for a while apart from Lupinetti getting cut last week and we still don't know who was responsible. This blew up outta nowhere.'

'We're gonna get out of here and keep extra eyes on our boy at the hospital,' Archer said. 'He pulls a magic trick out of the Marshals' handcuffs, today's just getting started.'

'You go; I need more time to clear this, and wanna stay behind for a bit,' Marquez told him. 'I'll try and find out why collecting Frank looked to set this off. Seems like there might be more to it than just him being transferred out.'

'OK.' Archer returned to their Ford and moments later was driving towards the gate, as Marquez tipped her head back and had another go at rinsing out her eyes.

Inside C Block, roof lights were periodically flashing, breaking up shadows before casting everything into darkness again. All the suppressed anger, aggression and testosterone that had exploded into the riot had left a grim aftermath. Small fires that had been set with toilet paper, books and clothing had been put out and were now smoldering, scuff marks and bloodstains evident on the floor and walls. Riot officers still performing sweeps had just found two more inmates near the exit to the main rec yard, one of them with a broken arm, the other badly beaten and barely conscious. They were just being taken out to the front by officers to where the EMTs were set up when two COs reached the laundry and discovered the pair of prisoners who'd started the riot in the first place.

'God damn,' one of the COs said quietly, looking at the scene in front of him. There was no need to rush these guys out for treatment; they were dead, both with their throats slashed open and lying in a large, merged pool of blood. Whoever was responsible had also left a shiv buried in the second man's right eye. 'Gonna need a couple more body-bags for the laundry, Sarge,' he said into his radio. 'Looks like a snuff movie down here.'

'Who died?'

'Hoffmeier and Kattar.' He lowered the radio. 'Lighting this thing off didn't do them much good,' he commented to his fellow CO.

The sergeant had left Marquez outside to return to Gatlin's central control center, and after hearing the transmission, took a pen and then crossed the two men's names off a list pinned to a board, showing C Block's cell layout and which ones the prisoners had been assigned to. Their deaths would have to be investigated, but were deserved as far as he was concerned; not only had the pair been convicted of first degree murder almost fifteen years ago, getting put away for life for blasting a family of five apart with two sawn-off shotguns during a home invasion, they'd also killed two of his colleagues and started the riot.

'Williams, how you doin'?' he asked over the radio, while updating the tally of the injured and dead.

'Almost done with checking upper deck in C Block.'

'Gonna need a bag for Mendevev,' another voice said over the radio as Williams continued with his cell checks on C Block's upper tier, ensuring every man was accounted for before the two day lockdown punishment started. He wasn't carrying out the task alone, another CO checking cells below while some of the riot officers were positioned

around the debris-littered block in case of more trouble, waiting for checks to be completed. The housing was a mess of debris, strewn toilet paper and blood on the floor, the smell of burning lingering in the air.

Williams stopped at the next cell on his list, seeing the large biker from Georgia standing by the closed bars. 'You're bleeding, Prez,' Williams said, looking through the grille at the man's arm, the blood evident in the low light of the cell block.

'I'm good, boss.'

'Need to get it looked at,' he said, going to his radio.

'I said I'm good. I'm not going to sickbay with a scratch. It's fine.'

The CO held onto his radio for a moment, then let go. He liked 'Prez' Rainey; the man had never caused them any trouble and he'd also heard that the biker had intervened to prevent his fellow CO Andrea from being raped before the NYPD pair took over. Instead, Williams glanced at the big man's cellmate, who was lying on his bunk facing the wall with his thin top-sheet halfway up his back, his arm tucked under his head as he slept. 'Reyes, you alright?'

No reply came, just quiet rhythmic snoring. 'Ice in his veins, I guess,' Prez said. 'Trying to stay out of trouble until release.'

Williams nodded; Reyes wasn't a troublemaker either. He ticked them both off his list and continued down the tier.

'*Prez and Reyes present*,' he said over the radio, moving on, but then another voice cut in over the channel.

'Sarge, it's Anderson. I'm checking lower tier. We could have a problem.'

'What is it?'

'Can you list off the dead and injured again?'

In the control center, the sergeant read from his most up-to-date tally.

Inside C Block, the officer called Anderson stared at a two-man cell with a pair of empty bunks, bloodstains from where his fellow CO Pena had been killed still pooled on the lino twenty feet to his right.

'Oh Jesus,' he whispered, hearing the list while looking at the cell in front of him.

'What's wrong?

'It's the Loughlin brothers, Sarge. They're not here.'

SIX

Around eleven miles from the prison, the laundry truck which had driven out of the facility shortly after the riot had started was on its way back to the company depot when the driver got a call from his supervisor. He answered using the hands-free system, keeping his eyes on the road. 'Hello?'

'I heard a riot broke out in Gatlin. You make it out in one piece?'

'Yeah. Left after the alarms started going. Didn't hang around. Guards checked the truck at the gate.'

'How thorough?'

The driver paused. 'They had a good look inside. No extra passengers.'

'So where are you? What's taken so long?'

'Got held up at an accident, but on my way.'

'Get straight back here, keep the truck locked and we'll check again. Gatlin just called saying they've got a pair of inmates unaccounted for. These two don't sound like anyone you'd want as extra cargo.'

The driver ended the call and allowed himself to swallow. 'Good,' a voice from behind him said softly. A clump of the man's hair was being gripped in one thick hand, a crudely-fashioned shiv held to his neck with the other. There was a sliding panel connecting the front cab to the back and the truck had just got through the traffic build-up caused by the accident when the panel had slid open and the driver found a razor blade held to his throat.

Around them on either side of the highway were banks of trees with their leaves just starting to turn for fall, the nearest town a couple of miles away. The driver saw a car coming towards them and prayed the occupants inside would see what was happening, but the man holding the shiv to his neck slunk down out of sight while keeping a tight grip of the back of the driver's hair, the blade resting against his carotid artery. The car sped past, the laundry truck driver's hopes fading with it as he watched the vehicle disappear into the distance in his rearview mirror.

'Turn off here,' the voice instructed, the driver seeing a track leading deeper into their rural surroundings coming up on the right. He turned.

'Now go right.'

He did as he was told, until they ended up on a side track that cut a line between some fields of corn. The sun was shining and birds were chirping from somewhere. Everything normal.

'Engine off. Gimme the keys.'

The driver did as ordered, handing them backwards with a trembling hand, and a second later his throat was cut.

'What's happened?' Marquez asked a couple of COs, having picked up on a sudden stir of activity outside the prison's control center. The remaining pair of US Marshals still on site appeared behind her, also catching on that there was some sort of new trouble.

'Two of our most dangerous prisoners are missing,' the sergeant told her.

'*-working the laundry this morning, sir,'* one of the COs in C Block was saying over the radio to the Gatlin staff captain, Marquez and the pair of Marshals listening in. '*No sign of them down here. All we've got is Hoff and Kattar's bodies.'*

'Who exactly are these escapees?' the lead deputy Marshal asked.

‘They’re brothers,’ the captain told him. ‘Brooks and Billy Loughlin. Both four years into life sentences. Some of our worst and we’ve got a stacked roster.’

‘And they were tight with Hoff and Kattar,’ the sergeant added. ‘Or it looked like they were.’

‘What were the brothers sent down for?’ Marquez asked.

‘College student from Maine was driving back home for the Thanksgiving break,’ the sergeant explained. ‘Younger brother Billy saw her filling her tank outside Syracuse when he pulled in and decided to follow her. Rammed her off the road in his truck just over the Vermont State Line, kidnapped her. Kept the girl in his basement for almost two weeks, raped her repeatedly while a manhunt was underway.

‘Big brother Brooks found out Billy had her, felt only option left was to kill the girl and dump the body. They cut off her head, her arms and legs, then buried the separate parts around the area, thinking it’d be harder to identify the remains if only pieces were ever found, especially if animals finished her off. But a few days later a walker saw hair sticking out of some disturbed ground and sniffer dogs found some of the rest of the girl. Billy was already a prime suspect from the gas station video and having served time before. Both their DNA profiles came back a hit. Billy from the rape kit, Brooks from her clothing. And bite marks on her body.’

‘I remember this case,’ Marquez said. ‘It reached the major networks.’

‘The two of them had already served time down here at Gatlin, over ten years back. Billy was busted trying to set up a kiddie porn business up near where they live. He used his brother’s computer, so they arrested and charged him on it too, but their lawyer got their sentences reduced to a nickel. After they killed the girl, their defense tried to claim the brothers were both insane. Jury didn’t buy it, though Brooks almost pulled it off. He's smart but it wasn't enough this time. Kidnap across State Lines, rape and murder, on top of the first conviction? They were sent down for life with no chance of parole.'

'There was a laundry truck on pick-up this morning,' Marquez said. 'We saw it leave.'

'The gate would've checked the inside,' the sergeant said.

'They did, but it seemed pretty quick.'

'Call the depot and make sure the truck arrived,' the captain ordered one of his COs. 'You just said it yourself, Brooks is smart. If anyone could break out of this place, I'd put my money on that son of a bitch.'

'Already called ahead, boss. Local PD are heading there ready for a search when it arrives.'

'Cap, something's coming over the wire from the labor camp,' another CO said, holding a phone. 'Three of their inmates made a run for it this morning too. Pair of them were just found dead, but the other's still out there.'

'Who is he?'

'Craig Loughlin. The youngest brother.'

'There are three of them here?' Marquez said.

'Craig's not doing life like the other two, he's only in for a couple years for drug offenses,' the captain explained. 'Why he was out at the satellite camp. There's a lot of these Loughlins up there in New York State near Canada. Cousins, first cousins, second cousins, some marrying each other, all that weird shit. They've been responsible for a ton of crime in that area for years. Whole reason Brooks and Billy first got sent down to this place. Get them away from any family members pulling time in New York.'

'You get many escape attempts here?' Marquez asked, as behind her the two Marshals left to make some calls.

'Only had one successful breakout that I can remember. That was from the minimum-security camp where Craig just took off from.'

'How long til the guy was caught?' Marquez asked.

The captain glanced at the warden who'd just re-entered the room looking as troubled as his staff after being told about the missing men. 'Eight years.'

'Back again?' a nurse asked, inside a room at hospital's emergency ward in the local town of Jonesville. 'Didn't we see you just last week?'

'Wasn't exactly planning a return visit,' Lupinetti snapped, still in his bloodied orange prison jumps. 'C'mon man, can't you take these things off?' he complained to two hospital guards who were standing watching him as another nurse treated the wound. He rattled his hands against the sets of cuffs locking him to the bed as he spoke. 'I'm not gonna run.'

'Orders.'

'From who?' The New Yorker ex-cop's timing was impeccable; as the two words left his mouth, the door to the room opened and Archer walked in. 'Wonderful,' Lupinetti said. 'Thought I was done with you for the day.'

'All the thanks I get for saving you in there?'

'I had it covered.'

'What, the floor? You were kissing it when we showed up.' Archer turned to the hospital guards. 'Where are the Marshals who brought him here?'

'They just left to go back to Gatlin. Told us to take over. Something urgent's going on over there.'

'You can't get off my ass for ten minutes?' Lupinetti complained to Archer before he could press the guards for more details. 'I'm wounded, man. You saw what I got stuck with.'

'I don't care if you get struck by lightning, you're going to Lewisburg today. Marquez and I are gonna make sure you get there.'

'I can't leave, I'm injured,' he complained, both of his upper arms now bandaged.

'Is he OK to travel?' Archer asked the nurse, who nodded. 'There you go. When Lisa gets here, you can thank her for saving you too, or you can spend the journey to PA riding in the trunk.'

'You didn't save me,' Lupinetti replied, looking at his arm. 'You just made things a whole lot worse.'

On Route 58 twelve miles from the prison, a woman in her early eighties was driving home from an end-of-week visit to her hairdresser when she frowned and leaned forward, seeing something ahead on the road.

A large man was lying on the asphalt, another beside him waving her down, the two of them directly in her way. The man on his feet looked to be just as big as the one on the tarmac, huge and bearded, and was wearing a white t-shirt and sand-colored pants. The man on the ground was in a white t-shirt too, but bizarrely was just wearing boxer shorts and no trousers.

For a moment, the strangeness of the scene made her consider deviating around them and keep driving past, but her conscience won out. Before retirement she'd spent part of her working life as a court stenographer in Richmond, so was nobody's fool, but at that moment she was listening to the last thirty pages of an Agatha Christie audiobook so didn't have the radio on, which was currently giving a breaking report warning locals of the dangerous escapees just discovered missing at USP Gatlin.

That unfortunate choice was about to have consequences.

‘What happened?’ she asked, lowering her window as she pulled up.

‘Dunno, I just found him out here,’ the big man said, walking towards her quickly. ‘Think he’s got heatstroke or something.‘

The woman looked at the man lying in the road and reached into her purse to get her phone to call 911. She hadn’t noticed the stolen pants Brooks Loughlin was wearing didn’t fit properly, and she also didn’t see his hand come from behind his back with the blood-stained razor that had cut the laundry truck driver’s throat.

Her fingers never made it to the nine button and she’d never find out how the Agatha Christie book ended.

It turned out the killer was caught just before he could murder again.

SEVEN

'*Three of these brothers were locked up here,*' Marquez told Archer on her cell phone. '*Two in the main prison in C Block, the other at the minimum security camp. They all managed to get out somehow during the riot.*'

Archer was standing outside the front entrance to the hospital in Jonesville, having left the two guards with Lupinetti to take Marquez's call. 'What were they in for?'

'*Older two are on their second term. First stint was over ten years ago. Judge gave them a nickel for conspiracy to sell and distribute kiddie porn. Served it at Gatlin then, too.*'

'Five years? That's it?'

'*Their lawyer swung for the fences and connected, sounded like. But nothing any defense counsel could do their second time around. The middle brother Billy kidnapped and killed a college girl four years ago. Kept her in a basement for a couple weeks, evidence that he raped her repeatedly then dismembered and dumped her body under his older brother's instructions. And with his help.*'

'Jesus. The youngest one?'

'*Name's Craig. Doing two years for selling meth.*'

'All three have the entrepreneurial spirit, then.'

'*One way of putting it. Looks like he split from the work camp around the time we arrived at the prison this morning. The COs and riot officers are doing another sweep of the main facility right now to see if the older two are hiding somewhere or managed to get into another cell block. But it's unlikely; these guys are big men, Arch. Huge. The sergeant here told me the oldest brother Brooks stands six six and weighs three bills, and the other two are only a touch smaller. Hard to hide in a broom closet when you're that size.'*

'If all three of them did break free from two separate locations, this was no spontaneous riot.'

'That's for sure.'

'And if they're out there somewhere, from what you've just told me this county's got a serious problem on its hands.'

'Tell me about it. The staff here are quietly freaking out. They're contacting local police to call in more manpower and the Marshals just got ordered by their office to stick around and do whatever it takes to help find the fugitives. A couple of the COs think the two older brothers might've slipped out in a laundry truck.'

'The one we saw?'

'Yeah. Brooks and Billy were working in the laundry this morning and a pair of their friends were discovered with slashed throats a room away from where we found Lupinetti. Those two dead guys triggered the riot in C Block in the first place too, so I was told.'

Archer remembered the laundry truck passing them on their way into the prison this morning. He checked the time. 'If they got out in that vehicle, they've had an almost two hour head-start.'

'Company depot are trying to raise the driver. His supervisor said he spoke to him fifteen minutes ago, and the guy told him he was almost back.'

'Trying?'

'He's not picking up.'

'Jonesville, Pennington Gap PD and the Lee County Sheriff's Office are setting up roadblocks,' the USP Gatlin captain informed the warden, other prison officials and

Marshals inside the facility's control center. Everyone was on edge, waiting for news. Any escape of a lifer from a federal prison was a big deal but having these three brothers on the run was about as serious as it could get, with two of them being convicted sex offenders, rapists and murderers. The Marshals had authority to take over the manhunt, but were waiting to see if local law-enforcement could handle it first.

'Tracking dogs?' one of their deputies asked.

'On their way,' the Gatlin sergeant said. 'We need to get something from the men's cells for scent.'

'Send two of your guys to get the Loughlins' bed sheets and pillowcases,' the warden ordered the leader of the riot response team, the squad having remained on site for the time being in case they were needed. The man nodded and left the room quickly, a CO going with him to provide access and show them which cell.

'Williams, Anderson, any evidence of them getting out through the fence line?' the captain asked over the radio.

'*Checking perimeter but fence looks intact, Cap. No cuts or holes.*'

They used the truck, Marquez thought, having returned to the control room after her call with Archer and catching the latter part of the exchange; men that big wouldn't try to run on foot, they'd be too easy to spot and wouldn't get far, forced to rest regularly given their physical size. They'd need a set of wheels. Near her, the sergeant started to pass out some papers hot from the printer, the three brothers' mugshots on each page. 'Where are you standing on this?' the Gatlin captain asked the Marshals, as off-duty members of the prison staff who'd been called in started to gather in the doorway, taking a sheet each before leaving to return to their vehicles, the manhunt beginning.

'Our supervisor confirmed we're reassigned to the case, but you take the reins for now,' the lead deputy told him.

'These are your boys; figure y'all want to be the ones to bring them down. Just let us know what we can do to help.'

'911 call came in to local PD a minute ago, sir,' a CO said, entering the room quickly. 'Laundry truck's been found.'

'Where?'

'Down a dirt track off Route 58. Caller said the driver's had his throat cut up, but he's still alive.'

The CO stood back as the Gatlin captain and Marshals immediately moved past him, and moments later several vehicles sped out towards the front gate.

Marquez watched as they left. The prison staff's embarrassment and anger caused by the escapes was clear, but the additional concern when they'd discovered who exactly had broken out had created a charged atmosphere in the room. *Kidnapped a college student. Kept her in a basement for a couple weeks, raped her repeatedly then dismembered and dumped her body. Bite marks found on her remains.* What Archer had said on the phone was right. With men capable of that on the loose and no doubt determined to stay that way, southern Virginia's police authorities now had a major incident on their hands.

The Gatlin prison staff duty sergeant had remained behind, along with the other members of the on-duty COs, and the rest of the riot squad who were waiting for their two guys to return with the Loughlins' bedclothes. 'This pair of inmates who were found dead in the laundry,' Marquez asked the sergeant, walking over to him. 'They were tight with the Loughlin brothers, you said?'

He nodded. 'Hoffmeier and Kattar. Pair of degenerates doing life. Tried to rip off a mansion when they thought the family was on vacation, turned out they were still home. Did a good job redecorating the inside of the house with all five of them, using a couple of shotguns.'

Marquez looked at the camera monitors showing the locked-down prison block. 'The place is secure again right?'

'Yeah, C Block's gonna be like a closed bank vault for forty eight hours after this.'

'Before you do that, can I ask a favor? If it's safe?

'Depends what it is.'

'Can you show me exactly where Hoffmeier and Kattar's bodies were found?'

'Why?'

'I'm a detective,' she said. 'I get curious. The brothers escaped from the laundry. I might see something that could help.'

'Where the hell is he?' Billy Loughlin asked for the fifth time, back in his full prison orange jumps again and sitting beside his brother in the passenger seat of the car they'd taken off the elderly woman, whose body was now dumped in the corn several miles back near where they'd left the laundry truck.

'Think he's just gonna be standing out here with his thumb out?' Brooks answered, his seat pushed all the way back like his brother's to accommodate their size. They'd pulled up on the side of the highway beside another cornfield not far from Gatlin's minimum security camp. The old woman's blood had stained the seat, the wheel and the center console and although Brooks had wiped it down as best he could, the interior was still a mess. But it didn't matter; he'd dump the car soon enough for another. Their current ride wasn't what he was worried about, getting ahead of any impending roadblocks was, and he knew police would be setting them up real soon.

'We're wasting time,' Billy said, looking behind them anxiously. 'He might not have made it.'

'We gotta give him a chance. You want to just leave him behind?'

Billy paused. 'No.'

'We wait.'

Like the laundry truck driver earlier, both men saw a car speeding towards them down the highway; the brothers watched it approach silently, each still holding his shiv by their leg in readiness, but the vehicle didn't slow and it shot past them. Once the car was gone, Brooks and Billy relaxed slightly and it was then they saw their younger brother Craig finally emerge from the crops, blood and dirt staining the front of his prison jumps.

He sprinted towards the vehicle as fast as his bulk would allow, pulled open the back door and jammed himself inside, breathing heavily. Brooks was flooring it before he'd even shut the door but as Billy turned to talk to Craig, he swore when he saw police lights behind them in the distance. *'Shit, they found us*!' he said. *'We waited too long!'*

Brooks checked the rearview mirror and saw his brother was right; cruisers were coming up behind them, quickly gaining in their far more powerful vehicles. But as they watched, the police cars suddenly slowed and positioned themselves until they were parked directly across the road, ready to block any vehicles trying to head out of the area.

Brooks grinned as his two brothers whooped and high-fived each other, realizing they'd beaten the response.

'Told you we had enough time,' he said as they sped on down the highway, leaving the roadblock behind.

EIGHT

Frank Lupinetti's transfer out of USP Gatlin had been the only real task of importance early that morning at the federal prison, but with the riot followed by the discovery of the three Loughlin brothers' escapes, things had changed. The former NYPD lieutenant/cutting board for the other inmates had almost been forgotten for the time being, a long way down the list of concerns for the Marshals and prison staff, but not by the two NYPD detectives who'd driven seven hours south to escort him to his new home.

Archer had been put through to the warden at USP Lewisburg in Pennsylvania, another eight hours' drive north from where he and Marquez were now; the prison official had already heard about the incident at Gatlin but Archer was able to provide more details. *'Someone lit a fuse in there, huh?'* the warden said.

'Yeah, and I'm currently with an inmate who was supposed to be shipped your way today. I'd like to make sure he still gets there if you're willing to accept him.'

'The former cop. Lupinetti?'

'That's him. A colleague and I came here from New York to accompany the Marshals providing the transport, but they've got other priorities right now with these prisoner escapees. Frank's sustained a couple of minor injuries but we can still get him out of here and on his way to you before this has to be rescheduled.'

'Was he involved in starting this riot? Trying to stop himself being transferred?'

'Doubt it. He wasn't exactly clinging onto the bars to stay in Gatlin.'

'If the Marshals sign over responsibility and we clear it with the prison, a transport bus could extradite him here, Detective. They do it every day around the country. But you mind me asking, why so urgent?'

'Lupinetti was involved in the death of a friend of mine; she was a cop too. And he's been claiming he's got information on corruption involving people still wearing a badge in the NYPD, so we've been ordered to make sure he gets to you on his feet, not in a box. He stays in Gatlin any longer, we think that's looking doubtful.'

'I see.'

'It's probably all bullshit but we can't take that risk, and every minute this son of a bitch is outside prison walls, I want to be close by. He's responsible for a lot of people getting hurt and killed in his time. And he's slippery, Warden. We need him out of here and secured in your facility. Then we can question him and find out what else he knows. If it's anything at all.'

A pause followed. *'Like I said, I'll need to contact the Marshals Office and make this official. If they agree to sign him over, I'll see if there's a prisoner transport in the area and connect you to them. The Gatlin warden needs to ink the paperwork too. I know you're in a hurry to get Lupinetti out, but we have to follow procedure. He's a prisoner of the federal government.'*

'Thank you,' Archer said, ending the call and walking back into the hospital, saw the television was now showing the news. *Three fugitives escape USP Gatlin after riot,* the headline from the local station, WJHL, was telling viewers, providing the brothers' mugshots and allowing Archer to see each of them for the first time. The trio of Loughlins were all variations of the same theme; Brooks was starting to go bald, the sparse hair he still possessed straggling down his neck, but he wore a full beard. Billy had the same shade of sandy-colored hair which was also starting to thin and a similarly large beard to match; Craig had shorter hair with less of a beard and was clearly the youngest by a few years, but had the same mean, close-set eyes as his brothers. Marquez had said all three individuals were the size of a barn door so alone, each was a problem; together, they'd be formidable. But they weren't Archer's issue right now. The man who'd murdered his friend was.

The Lewisburg warden came back fifteen minutes later, having spoken to the Marshals Office for Virginia's Western District who'd confirmed they were more than happy to let someone else take Lupinetti. Archer was then connected with an extradition agent supervisor who worked for one of the transport companies the PA prison's boss had provided details for, tasked with picking up and delivering prisoners around the country.

'How bad was this inmate hurt?' the man at the other end asked.

'Not bad enough not to travel.'

'Any chance the local jail could do a courtesy hold until morning? We can try to help you out, but this isn't like delivering a pizza, man. I could arrange for a bus to swing by before 10 am tomorrow.'

'I checked. The cells are full. They're having to house spill-overs from another prison across the county. USP Lee.'

There was a pause. *'We've got a transport forty something miles east of you. I'll give them a call and see if they'll detour to come pick you and your prisoner up. You said you were at the hospital?'*

'At Jonesville. Yes.'

Marquez was back inside C Block at Gatlin in the laundry area and was looking at the drying blood that had pooled and stained the floor to merge into one large puddle. The bodies of the two instigators of the riot, Hoffmeier and Kattar, had already been transported out along with the other dead from inside the prison. They'd be in the county morgue tonight lying on shelves alongside the two COs the pair had helped murder when they'd set all this off.

'You come across Hoff and Katt when you were looking for Lupinetti?' the Gatlin sergeant who'd reentered the block with her asked. Two riot officers were standing behind them, providing an escort just in case of more trouble.

'Didn't quite make it this far. Any word yet on who killed them?'

He shook his head. 'Some of the inmates might know, but we won't find out until an investigation starts. Even then they most likely won't tell us shit and the camera covering this area went dead too. The Loughlins probably knocked it out, but we'll have to check the others and see who we can ID down here around the same time.'

'It had to be the brothers.' As Marquez was speaking, she looked around; her eyes settled on one of the empty laundry baskets and she walked over to it. She checked the locks were on the wheels, then gripped the rim. One of the riot officers saw what she was intending to do and moved forward to steady it. Using him for support, she stepped up and inside the large basket then crouched down out of sight.

She fit easily.

'Brooks and Billy are a lot bigger than you, girl,' the sergeant told her.

'You're over six foot. You try.'

They swapped and the sergeant found that he fit pretty easily too, the flexible basket designed to take large bundles of clothing.

‘And some of these would be placed in the back of the truck?’ she asked.

He nodded. ‘Pick-up takes about twelve of them at a time.’

‘So a large man could squeeze in and cover himself.’ As she steadied the basket while the sergeant climbed back out, Marquez glanced again at the large pool of drying blood and caught its metallic scent mixing with the other unpleasant odors, the lingering smells of burning and dirty laundry making the air sour and acrid. She thought of the hundreds of caged prisoners in the same block with them right now, many responsible for some horrendous crimes, walking proof of how dark and dangerous the human animal could be.

For an instant she imagined the inmates’ doors opening again and the four of them here standing in the laundry, trapped.

‘Thanks for showing me,’ she said. ‘Let’s get back outside.’

As they passed through the last gate, the sergeant relocking it behind them, the guard called Anderson was waiting. ‘Got more details from the work camp. One of the three prisoners who made a run for it got a set of opened handcuffs buried in his neck; the other got hit over the head with a rock. Craig Loughlin just boosted himself up to a double murder charge.’

‘Maybe he felt left out,’ the sergeant commented. As he, CO Anderson and the riot officers pushed for more details, Marquez’s phone rang. It was Archer.

‘What’s the latest?’ she asked, parting from the group.

‘I’ve set up a transport with the warden at Lewisburg. Lupinetti’s out of here in the next hour.’

‘With who? A private company?’

'Yeah. I called Shep and he did a background check. The company are legit; perform transfers like this all over the country every day. They're detouring here to get us, but we need the release paperwork from the prison. The Virginia Marshals Office already sent over signed approval.'

'Figured you'd make something happen. I'll get it inked and be there soon as I can.' Hanging up, she saw an ambulance loading up two injured riot officers then caught sight of the warden exiting the control center and ran over to intercept him.

'Don't get cushy,' Archer said, stopping in the doorway to Lupinetti's room, the former NYPD cop still cuffed to the bed. 'You're gonna be rolling out of here before the end of the hour.'

The remaining color drained out of Lupinetti's face. 'You can't take me back to Gatlin. I won't last another night in that place.'

'You're not going back there. He been causing you any problems?' he asked the hospital guards.

'Just earache.'

'He'll be gone shortly. If he tries anything, shoot him,' he told the guards before heading out again, ignoring Lupinetti's parting comment.

He waited out front and fifteen minutes later an ambulance swung into the space outside the hospital. Marquez stepped down from the front seat, holding a folder.

'That was fast,' he told her. 'You get his signature?'

She nodded. 'With the Loughlins out there, the prison wants one less thing to worry about and are pleased for Frank to be someone else's problem. The warden confirmed everything with Lewisburg. When he was signing the document for me, he got a call from one of his guys out on Route 58 where the laundry truck was dumped.'

'And?'

'Back was opened up, driver slumped over in the cab with his throat cut open. Bunch of footprints around the vehicle. Brooks and Billy Loughlin are big guys, so must have tucked themselves up in a couple baskets like they were piking off a diving board. The sergeant and I checked to see if they could fit and we think it's possible. The COs at the prison can't figure out any other way they could've got out.'

'Through the laundry? How did that CO at the gate not check properly?'

'He looked pretty distracted with everything going on. Sirens going off, the guy shouting down at him from the tower and us showing up too. He can't have done a proper search. Wouldn't wanna be in his shoes if turns out that's how they escaped.'

'Search teams using dogs yet?'

'Not gonna work. The brothers' jumpsuits were dumped outside the truck and drenched in bleach. They poured it all over the back and cab too so the K9s can't get a scent. The guards who went to their cells found their sheets and pillowcases were soaked in the stuff too. Like we agreed earlier, this was carefully planned.'

'Least if the brothers are on foot, they can't have got far.'

'Officers found blood spatter further up on the highway near the turn off to the track where the truck was left. Just located an old woman's body dumped in the cornfield. The Loughlins must've flagged her down and stolen her car.'

'Which means they could already have beaten the roadblocks,' Archer replied. 'And be out of Virginia too.

We're not far from Kentucky, Tennessee and North Carolina.'

'Staff at Gatlin think Brooks and Billy would've waited for Craig; he didn't break out at the same time to run by himself. He'd need their help. But he'd also have needed time to get to where they were, which would've slowed them down.'

'So they might still be in the county.'

'Let's hope so.' Behind them on the wall inside the hospital's entrance, the TV was showing the mugshots of the escapees again and the two detectives stepped inside to watch the live report. 'The sergeant told me the two prisoners found dead in the laundry at Gatlin used to run with the Loughlins,' Marquez said to Archer. 'Looks to me that the brothers used them to get the riot started and then killed them before hiding in the back of the truck. I'll bet the two who died thought they were getting out too, otherwise why help?'

'But Brooks and Billy would know there'd be way more chance of getting past the gate with only two of them in the back instead of four,' Archer replied. 'And Craig must've used the two guys at the labor camp to get out before killing them too.' He thought about the escapes. 'What about the laundry truck driver? Think the guy was involved the same way and they double-crossed him?'

'Don't know, but he's on his way here.'

'He's still alive?'

'Barely. He had his neck padded up and bandaged when EMTs reached him. Cell phone lying in the dirt beside him.'

Archer frowned. 'Who applied the field dressing? Same person who called it in?'

'No-one was at the scene when law-enforcement got there. Maybe someone saw the Loughlins running back to the main road or something. Got curious then found the truck. Patched him up best they could, used the driver's own phone to dial 911.'

'And didn't want to stick around after making the call?'

'Might've been scared that whoever did that to the driver could come back.'

As they talked, the pair saw an ambulance pull up and medical staff run out to the vehicle. 'Time to get out of here and let local law-enforcement handle this,' Archer said, as they both headed back into the hospital to fetch their prisoner. 'The brothers aren't our problem. Let's focus on the one who is.'

But as the two detectives walked down the corridors and arrived at Lupinetti's room again, they found the bed empty. One of the two guards was standing outside the bathroom door which was shut. There was no sign of the other.

'*Time's up, Frank*,' the guard said, knocking on the door when he saw Archer and Marquez reappear. 'Pull up your pants and get out here, man.'

'You uncuffed him?' Marquez asked quickly.

'Said he wanted to use the john before the bus ride. There's no window in there. It's cool.'

The guard realized immediately from their reaction that he'd made a big mistake. Archer brushed past him and tried the handle but it didn't open; Marquez dropped down and looked at the gap under the door but couldn't see any feet.

'*Break it!*' she said, making room for Archer to step back and ram the door. He smashed it back on the second attempt.

Frank Lupinetti was gone.

Up in the crawlspace five rooms down, Lupinetti was working his way along as fast as he could when he stopped and as quietly as possible, removed another slat to check below.

Peering down cautiously, he saw the bathroom was unoccupied, so he quickly lowered himself onto the toilet before slowly opening the door. The room it belonged to was also empty so he headed swiftly for the door then eased it open.

He couldn't see anyone in the corridor so he slipped out and started to swiftly make his way towards where he remembered the ambulance had brought him in earlier. But as he passed another room he stopped, seeing the elderly male occupant was asleep, his head and one leg heavily bandaged.

As he looked in at the patient, Lupinetti heard a commotion coming from the room he'd just escaped from, so cut inside before closing the door quietly. He went quickly to the closet where he found the guy's clothes, and slid a pair of jeans off a hanger, but as he pulled them on, saw something even more useful resting on the table beside the man's bed.

Marquez had drawn her pistol and started to quickly check all the rooms in the ward, unknowingly heading away from the room Lupinetti was in, while Archer climbed onto the basin in the bathroom and pulled himself up so he could see into the crawlspace, having immediately realized how their prisoner had fooled the guard and gotten away.

There was light coming from a space a few doors down. He dropped back, drew his Sig Sauer and started to check each room. In the fourth, he found a man with a bandaged head and injured leg fast asleep.

But the locker in the room was open and so was the window.

To make sure, Archer checked under the bed and had just cleared the bathroom when the guard who'd allowed Lupinetti to escape appeared in the doorway. 'Search the other rooms just in case and warn the front desk!' Archer told him, as Marquez joined them. 'I think he already got out,' he told her, looking at the open window.

Marquez reached it first and climbed out, jumping to the ground below as Archer followed a second later.

In his prison jumpsuit top and stolen jeans, Lupinetti was now just ten feet from the front gate when he heard running footsteps behind him.

'*STOP!*' a familiar voice yelled.

He looked back and saw Archer bearing down on him, Marquez a few paces behind. In desperation Frank turned, intending to keep running, but caught his foot on an uneven concrete slab and fell.

Archer stopped and raised his pistol double-handed, lowering his aim. 'You move, I'll put one through your knee, Frank,' he warned, and Lupinetti sagged, knowing his brief bid for freedom was over. Marquez ran up and pushed the attempted runaway down to the ground before cuffing him again. As Archer holstered his weapon and moved forward to help haul him back to his feet, a black and white bus turned off the main road and swept past them before stopping at the entrance for the hospital.

Lupinetti's transport to Pennsylvania had just arrived.

NINE

The bus was a Ford E350 with *US Extradition Prisoner Transport Unit* printed on the side, the company's circular insignia beside the lettering. Five minutes after arriving at the hospital, the driver was standing outside the vehicle with Archer and Marquez while another agent inside kept an eye on the passengers.

'You got this approved pretty late in the day,' the driver told the two detectives. 'Don't normally add pick-ups this short notice. Your guy must be a real piece of work.'

'Oh, he is,' Archer said, as he and Marquez looked through the glass at Lupinetti; even from outside, they could hear him arguing with the agent on-board as the man double-checked his cuffs and the chain they'd been secured to, which was fixing the ex-cop to a metal bar positioned under his seat. The jeans he'd stolen from the hospital patient asleep in the bed during his brief escape attempt had been returned, now replaced by his orange prison pants again. 'We're here to help keep an eye on him.'

'The warden passed that on, right?' Marquez asked.

'Yeah, but afraid I've only got one spare seat. We're picking up a full house tonight.'

'We've got our Department wheels here,' Marquez said to Archer. 'Why don't we just follow in that? No reason to stick around town anymore.'

'It wasn't running right when I brought it over from Gatlin earlier,' he replied. 'I think something's up with the engine from the journey yesterday.'

'For real?' She paused. 'I did push it kinda hard once I was out of New York. I was pissed. Frank has that effect on people.'

'We can't risk it breaking down on the way.'

'If it does, we ain't stopping to wait for you,' the bus driver said. 'Can't hang around in the backass of nowhere until AAA show up.'

'So should we split up again?' Marquez said to Archer. 'One of us stays and gets it looked at. Other takes the bus?'

'I'll go, if you're cool with it,' he replied. 'You got pepper sprayed earlier. Take a few hours to rest up.'

'You don't mind?'

'Looking forward to it,' he said dryly as they both heard more profanity and complaining coming from the bus.

'Sure you wanna come?' the driver asked. 'We're not picking up choirboys on the way. They might hear what happened at Gatlin and start getting ideas. These rides can wear you down.'

'Then it could help having an extra pair of hands.'

The extradition agent shrugged. 'Up to you. I got the room but I need to get rolling. Roadblocks are gonna hold us up some and these boys have to be delivered before the sun comes up. We're on a schedule.'

'I'll pick you up tomorrow in PA,' Marquez said to Archer. 'Or the day after if the car needs overnight attention. I'll clear it with Shep and tell him what we're doing.' He nodded and they bumped fists. *'Keep a close eye,'* she said quietly, looking behind him at Lupinetti in the bus, who'd finally quietened down and was watching them instead. 'You know how he is.'

Archer nodded. He jogged over to the Ford and collected the bag containing his belongings before tossing her the keys, and then stepped up onto the bus, the driver having restarted the engine and now waiting for him.

'*Yo, you forgot something,'* Marquez suddenly called out. She ran back to the NYPD car and collected an item from inside. When she returned, Archer saw it was a blue can of Pringles she'd bought at the gas station earlier that morning. She threw it up to him. 'Dinner. Don't want you getting hungry.'

He smiled and held the can up to thank her as the door closed, and moments later the transport started the slow turn out of the hospital parking lot.

Along a rural road towards the western edge of the State's border with Kentucky, a local fishing enthusiast had just arrived home from a day out at the Powell River, making the most of the dying days of summer. Relaxed after the hours he'd spent casting a line, and looking forward to a shower before he headed into work at a local bar, he was just unlocking his back door when another, moving shadow appeared on the wood in front of him.

Craig Loughlin hit the man over the head with a piece of firewood so hard that it killed him with one blow. The fisherman smashed into the door and collapsed, dropping his tackle box and line as the youngest Loughlin watched him go down, knowing he was dead; he'd wanted more of the adrenaline rush he'd felt when killing those two dumbass prisoners earlier when they broke free from the labor camp, and understood more now why his brothers had done what they did to that college bitch four years ago. It had sent Craig higher than any drug he'd tried in his life, and that was more than a few.

Brooks and Billy emerged from the shadows behind him, all three men still in their bloodied and dirt-stained white t-shirts and BOP orange jumpsuits; they kept watch as Craig finished unlocking the door then the older two carried the dead fisherman into his home, the car they'd followed him in abandoned on the other side of the road.

They paused, waiting for an alarm, but everything was quiet. Brooks kicked the door shut before he and Billy dumped the body on the floor, then they hit the lights and started to look around. Craig went straight to the kitchen, snatched a box of Ritz crackers off the side counter and started shoveling the contents into his mouth. Billy joined him, opening the fridge door and taking out a two liter bottle of Pepsi before drinking from it and belching loudly.

As the pair began to stuff their faces with whatever else they could find, in the main room Brooks turned on the TV and clicked until he reached the local news on Channel 11. '*We famous*?' Craig asked through a mouthful of crackers.

'Local celebrities,' he said, seeing their mugshots. 'Bag up anything we can take in the car, especially food and water. Look for money too.'

His brothers found some plastic bags and started filling them with supplies, continuing to chow down as they worked. Meanwhile, Brooks looked at his prison jumpsuit, stained from the old lady's blood when he'd sat in the car, and headed upstairs. After he double-checked each room to make sure they really were alone, he went into the main bedroom and used the landline to call a number, the first three digits 315, the area code for north central NY State.

'It's Brooks,' he told his cousin, Cusick. 'We made it out.'

'I heard. Bet you boys are celebrating.'

'Not yet.'

'The plan was Monday. What happened? Why'd you pull it forward?'

'Things changed.'

'Didn't go quite the way you intended though, huh?'

'How'd you know?'

'I got some information for you,' his cousin replied, as Brooks listened.

As Marquez walked back into the Jonesville hospital and looked up local mechanics and auto-shops on her cell, knowing it was going to be hard to get the Ford looked at this late on the Friday before Labor Day weekend, an update came onto Channel 11 concerning the prison escape.

Local woman found dead off Route 58, Gatlin prison escapees lead suspects. Marquez glanced around for a remote but not seeing one, moved closer to the TV before manually bumping up the volume. *'-discovered in one of the cornfields off the highway,'* the lead deputy Marshal who'd been at the prison earlier told the media. Looked like they were going from being bystanders in this situation to taking the lead now murder outside the walls had occurred. *'She has no identification on her so we still have no clue of her identity, but if anyone in the local area hasn't heard from a loved one matching her description, please call local police immediately. She is gray-haired, looks to be in her 80s, five foot two-'*

'C'mon, man,' Marquez muttered. She already knew about the woman's murder so it was no surprise, but still sickening. 'Killing an eighty year old woman?'

'No shame,' a voice said, and she saw one of the hospital guards had walked up, watching the report too. Marquez didn't answer. 'Sorry we screwed up with your prisoner,' the man apologized. 'I went to take a leak while AJ stayed with him in the room. Your guy didn't seem like he was gonna run.'

'We got him back and he's gone. Don't worry about it.'

He nodded but then looked back at the TV. 'Lady must've called the cops when she found the truck and they killed her for it. What you get for being a Good Samaritan. World ain't fair.'

The bartender Craig had killed was a good foot shorter than all three Loughlin brothers and much slighter; upstairs, Brooks swore as he tried to button one of the man's shirts in vain, tossing it aside before raiding the rest of the closet. Inside the bathroom, Billy was now shaving off his beard on his brother's orders, using an electric razor he'd found charging in a socket. Tufts of hair fell to the basin and floor.

'*Don't buzz the dome yet,*' Brooks called through to him.

'Why not?'

'Need to save it, case we gotta change appearance again later.' Brooks tried to pull on a pair of Levi's, but there was no way they were going to fit either. He gave up and yanked the jeans off before throwing them on the floor just as Craig appeared in the doorway, looking very pleased with himself.

'Dead man had thirty two bucks in his wallet,' he told them.

'Cards?' Billy asked.

'Leave 'em,' Brooks said. 'Same as the cell phone. Too easy to track.'

'TV says there are roadblocks all over the county.'

'They'll have them up on the interstate soon. We needed to get out of Virginia twenty minutes ago.' Brooks grabbed a John Deere cap that had been hanging on a hook in the closet and threw it to Craig, taking a cold weather beanie for himself and pulling it over his head.

'Before we go, you gotta see something,' Craig said, still grinning. His obvious excitement got his brothers curious so they followed him back down the stairs and then to the basement.

A gun safe was positioned against the wall, the keys hanging from the lock, the door open. The interior was packed with shotguns, rifles, all sorts of handguns and boxes of corresponding ammunition.

'*Oh baby,*' Billy whispered.

'We struck oil, boys,' Craig said, taking a rifle from the rack and lifting it to look down the sights. Without delay, Billy dragged a backpack from one of the shelves, tipped out its contents and then started to load it with ammunition and the guns.

'We're back on the road in the guy's truck in five minutes,' Brooks ordered, as his brothers stripped the shelves of weapons. In the meantime, an old coiled hose had drawn Brooks' attention in the corner of the room. He hooked it under his arm, then took a handheld power drill and box of nails, before heading back up the stairs.

True to his word, five minutes later the three fugitives were driving away in the dead bartender's car, the vehicle loaded with food, water and enough guns and ammunition for them to be considered a roaming militia. The three sibling escapees were already ahead of Lee County's various police authorities.

But any law-enforcement at the State border who tried to stop the car were now going to pay a very heavy price for getting in the brothers' way.

TEN

The prisoner transport had been on the road for almost two and a half hours since its pitstop in Jonesville to collect Lupinetti and dusk was beginning to steal over the highways, the shadows starting to lengthen. Archer, the driver and the other extradition agent had been engaging in some sporadic conversation; he'd learned their last names were Spencer and Harrington, and they'd been doing the job for three and four years respectively. The men had shared some of their history but took care not to reveal any personal details that could be overheard by the small group of prisoners sitting in the back.

'Can never know what the boys we pick up might be planning,' the agent tasked with watching the passengers, Harrington, advised Archer quietly, taking a few Pringles from the can the NYPD detective offered. 'Three of our agents got killed on a transport two years ago.'

'What happened?'

'Lifer being taken to Forrest City from Petersburg picked his cuffs, then stabbed an agent in the neck with one of the metal arms on the bracelets. Stole the man's gun, shot the other two on board. Took four days for police to corner him. He went down firing.' The story made Archer think of Craig Loughlin and his escape from Gatlin's satellite camp earlier that morning, using the cuffs in the same way to rip open a man's throat. He had more questions, curious about the extradition agents' line of work, but as they drove deeper into Kentucky, he noticed both men started to quieten as they approached their next pick-up, so he did the same.

Leaning back in his seat, he glanced at a TV monitor fixed to the dash which showed a four-way split shot from a camera positioned in each corner of the bus's interior, focused on the prisoners. He could see and vaguely hear two of the three inmates back there chatting; to be more accurate, one was doing all the talking, the other forced to sit there and listen. From what Archer could catch, the conversation was revolving around a visit the prisoner had made to a brothel down here in Harlan County when he was nineteen, the man giving the experience a five star review. He'd also tried unsuccessfully to engage with Lupinetti earlier which Archer had noticed, but after a response containing a four and three letter word, both prisoners had taken the hint to leave him alone.

The storytelling dried up however, when the bus started to approach a huge federal facility. The prison had the same sterile concrete look as USP Gatlin, faceless gray buildings with thick coils of razor wire on top of tall fences and armed guards in towers beside large spotlights.

'Welcome to Big Sandy,' Spencer told Archer, as the other agent picked up his shotgun. The bus stopped as credentials were checked; Spencer waited while a guard called it in on his radio for confirmation, then the gate slid open after a *buzz* and the vehicle drove forward into the prison.

Once they'd completed a slow loop and drew to a halt, Archer followed Spencer off the bus to take the opportunity to stretch his legs while Harrington opened up a reinforced grille separating the back seats from the front area, the three guys in there safely shackled and restrained.

'How many on the pick-up?' Archer asked Spencer as they waited outside.

He checked his clipboard. 'Four.'

'Does the form tell you what they're serving time for?'

'Make sure we find out after our guys got killed on that Forrest City botch. Tonight we got a serial rapist, pair of lifers serving out murder bids and another who got twelve years for narcotics. One of the two killers executed a couple homicide detectives in Atlanta.' He paused and shot Archer a glance. 'You seem like a guy who's got some experience.'

'Some, yeah.'

'But not been stuck on a prison transport bus for hours?'

'No. This is a first.'

'Word of advice, don't relax. Don't matter how calm things feel, these boys are always looking for a way to punk us out or try to escape. If one of us gets killed, what's the judge gonna do, add on another life sentence? They got nothing to lose.' As he said the last few words, a metal door opened with a quiet creak and the jangle of shackles could be heard seconds before the four prisoners appeared.

Two were white, one was black and the other Latino; the first two shuffled their way onto the bus without a word. Archer saw that one of the white boys looked unusually pale in the harsh spotlight, his hair damp with sweat, but he didn't cause any problems, eyes lowered as he was led past. The Latino glanced at Archer and then the driver as he passed by, the man with a prominent brow pocked with scar tissue and a straggly goatee trident-style beard. Trying to guess which one was the rapist, the kidnapper and the murderers was like a macabre version of the mystery board games Archer had played as a kid.

Then seeing the last prisoner, the second white guy, Archer had a feeling he was one of the latter. The man was enormous, possibly even bigger than how the guards at USP Gatlin had described the Loughlin brothers, his knotted, bunched-up neck and wide upper chest an entire canvas of one merged-together dark green tattoo.

He stopped a few feet out, and although the guards tried to keep him going, he wouldn't budge, instead weighing up the men who would be transporting him for the next few hours.

Archer saw the man's eyes pick up on his NYPD detective's badge.

'We gonna have to use a taser or hog tie you, Briley?' one of the guards asked. 'Make it easier for all of us, get your ass on the bus. Right now.'

The giant looked at the guard who'd spoken for a long moment, but then ended up doing as he was told and was taken onto the vehicle before being locked in place. The talkative prisoner already inside went very quiet when he saw the huge Big Sandy inmate, who was put in a seat across the aisle from him.

Once the Sandy guards stepped off, Spencer handed his clipboard to one of the COs. He signed the paperwork, passed it back and the bus driver thanked the correctional officers before stepping back on board. Archer had already noticed the Sandy guards visibly become less tense once the huge inmate was on the bus and shackled in place.

'Remember what I said,' Spencer said to Archer, as he restarted the engine. 'Don't relax.'

Back in Jonesville, VA, as expected, Marquez hadn't managed to find any mechanics or auto-shops open until morning, being a more rural area and not the crazy, 24-7 city she was used to; so with nothing else to do but wait for the Ford to be checked out once the sun came up, she updated Archer with a message then decided to stick around at the hospital for the time being instead of going back to the motel.

In the waiting area, the local news on the TV was still covering the discovery of the elderly woman found dead off Route 58 but they hadn't released her identity yet. Perhaps they still didn't know it. Marquez watched as one of the Channel 11 correspondents reported live from a roadblock near the Kentucky border as State troopers checked cars one at a time behind him, other armed members of local and state law-enforcement visible in the background wearing protective vests and holding rifles or shotguns or with dogs on leads.

If the three Loughlins had managed to link up, and Marquez knew there was every likelihood they had, they'd be a chilling prospect to deal with, especially if they could get their hands on weapons heavier than a shiv, rock or a set of handcuffs. Two of them had been four years into life sentences for what they'd done to that college girl, and Marquez recalled the pool of blood inside Gatlin's laundry belonging to a pair of inmates who had supposedly been friends of theirs. These brothers clearly had no problem killing anyone and would be ruthless in their determination to avoid recapture. With them free, no-one out there was safe.

She approached the nurse's station near the emergency ward and showed the woman working there her badge. 'The laundry truck driver who was brought in,' she said. 'The one with the cut throat. Know how he's doing?'

'He's still alive. Heard the blade sliced across his vocal cords, but didn't sever his windpipe. The doc's with the man's wife and kids right now. Give 'em some time to be told what the situation is, then I can find out more.'

Marquez nodded then checked her watch as she walked away, thinking of Archer on the bus wherever it was right now. Maybe due to the unexpected events of the day, maybe due to experience or perhaps just due to tiredness, that cold sense of unease that had crept over her inside the Gatlin laundry had come back to settle in her gut.

She took out her phone to message him, but then hesitated and put it away. If there was an issue, he'd let her know, and she had nothing new for him right now. She returned to her seat.

But that uneasiness wasn't going anywhere in a hurry.

'*Yo fat boy, stop at the drive-through, I want a milkshake,*' the black inmate from Big Sandy called out as a couple of the others cackled with laughter, the bus now out of Kentucky and pushing on up through West Virginia on the I-77 highway. Up front, Archer was choosing to watch the monitor rather than face the prisoners and give them something to work with. Lupinetti was his responsibility and focus, not the others, and was the only one he was keeping an eye on for the time being. The former cop had already tried to escape once tonight. *'I remember you from our last trip, Agent Spencer,'* the black Big Sandy inmate continued from the back, trying to rile the driver. *'I see you wearin' that wedding ring. I got brothers who can go visit yo wife when you're out on the road. They'll take care of that bitch. Just tell us where y'all live.'*

Spencer carried on driving, no change of expression to indicate that he'd heard the prisoners comments.

'*Who are you, beautiful?*' the voice continued; Archer looked at the screen and saw Lupinetti turn to the man on the monitor, talking to him. '*You a cop, huh? Homeboy's saying he killed one of your friends. Your bitch-ass must suck at what you do.'*

Archer leaned back in his seat, stretched his legs out and ate more Pringles. Spencer glanced at him and chuckled when he saw the NYPD detective's lack of reaction. 'Took me a while to get used to their bullshit,' he said. 'You seem like a natural.'

'I was the younger brother growing up. No-one knows how to get under someone's skin better than us.' Archer looked out of the windshield ahead, tuning out more insults coming from the rear of the vehicle and thinking back over this trip. He and Marquez should've seen Lupinetti delivered and be on their way back to New York City by now, but from past experience he might have known it wouldn't turn out to be so simple; his life rarely was. But then he thought of his sister managing to take those steps at Johns Hopkins yesterday, and smiled. Aside from riots, prisoner escapes and being stuck with Frank Lupinetti for hours on a bus, the trip away from New York hadn't been a total wash yet.

'Do your pick-up stops change journey to journey, or is it always the same schedule?' he asked Harrington.

'Varies, but we often get prisoners from Gatlin and Big Sandy on the same ride. Sort of guys these places house means inmates need to get transferred in and out a lot. For their safety, and others.'

'You always take the same route north on this highway?'

'Unless there's good reason not to,' Agent Spencer said from behind the wheel, overhearing. 'We stick to 77, the main routes and other turnpikes. Get stuck down a dirt road in this thing, we're stranded with these guys and unless we call local police, back-up might take time to reach us.'

'*Yo, Agentman, look at this,*' a voice called from the back. Archer and Harrington both turned and saw the pale-looking smaller white guy from Big Sandy was slumped against his window. His eyes were open but glazed, sweat on his brow glistening in the low light of the transport. He'd looked bad when he'd first shuffled onto the bus but now seemed even worse.

'What's his deal?' Spencer asked, checking his rear-view mirror. Harrington went through their paperwork for the ride and found the man's file.

'Doing twelve for narc offenses,' he told Spencer and Archer. 'Rehabbed for heroin but a lot of these guys score it or other junk to tide them over on the inside. *Gallagher, when's the last time you used?*'

The man didn't reply, still sagged against the window.

'I've seen this movie,' Archer said. 'We open that gate, he shanks you and they end up crashing this bus. We die or near enough and Tommy Lee Jones gets deployed to find the prisoners.'

'If Gallagher's passed out or in a coma when we deliver him, it's gonna be bad for us. Help me out here. Watch them.' Harrington stowed his shotgun then opened the gate, the inmates quietening down as the space between them and the outside world suddenly shrank.

Pulling his Sig Sauer but keeping it out of sight, Archer sensed the atmosphere shift in the bus. None of the prisoners moved as the guard went down into the bus towards Gallagher, who was still hunched against the window.

'Try something, I'll make sure they give you a real warm welcome at Gilmer when we get you there,' Harrington told him, seeing the guy was still conscious.

'I won't, bro,' the man whispered.

Harrington examined him up close. 'Told you,' the black inmate who'd called out said, as the agent turned Gallagher's arms over, examining the marks.

'When's the last time you shot up?'

'Couple days.'

Two of the inmates were eyeing the open grille, two more Harrington and the keys on his belt, but as he kept watch on them, his pistol in his hand behind his leg, Archer's eyes lingered on Lupinetti for a moment. The former cop wasn't looking at what was happening in the bus which was unusual enough, watching the darkened landscape pass by outside instead, but then Archer caught his expression in the reflection of the window; he was looking pleased about something.

Frank's face reverted to its usual blank expression as he sensed Archer's eyes on him, but too late; the NYPD detective had seen it.

A man stabbed twice in one week, his escape attempt from the hospital foiled and now being taken to a new high security federal prison to serve out another nineteen years of his life.

What did he have to look so happy about?

With fatigue beginning to take over, Marquez still hadn't had received an update on the laundry truck driver's condition, so deciding her day was finally done, was about to leave the hospital for the night when she saw a nurse walk up to the station and overheard her ask if a cell phone had been handed in.

'Someone lost a phone?' Marquez asked as she passed, her instinctive curiosity surfacing again.

'Just one of our patients,' the nurse replied.

The NYPD detective turned away but then stopped. 'Which room is he in?'

'17. Why?'

The number immediately rang an alarm bell in her mind. 'Show me,' Marquez said. She followed the nurse and stopped when she reached the room in question.

The window in room 17 was the one Frank Lupinetti had gone out through when he'd tried to escape. *But we frisked him*, Marquez thought. *He didn't have a cell on him.* His hands were also cuffed on the bus right now, which meant even if he'd decided to try and hide the phone somewhere much more uncomfortable than a pocket or in his sock, he wouldn't be able to get it out.

As the nurse looked at her, wondering why Marquez was so concerned about a patient's lost phone, the NYPD detective turned and walked swiftly out of the hospital until she stopped outside 17's window. She then followed the path Lupinetti would have taken, ending up in the exact spot where she and Archer had stopped him just before he'd had the chance to get through the gate and to the road.

She looked all around her, but couldn't see a dropped phone. She tracked back towards the hospital building and started again, this time more slowly. She followed the path again, using the flashlight on her cell to illuminate the sections of the path further out than she'd checked before.

She found it on the second trip. There were embankments lined with trees in the parking lot carpeted with bark chippings, just off the track Lupinetti would have taken, and a cell phone was jutting out of one of them, only a sliver of the screen catching the moonlight with the rest buried under the chips. Marquez saw the screen had been smashed, pieces of its protective cover ground into the concrete a foot away, but it seemed hidden too particularly to have been dropped accidentally.

To her, it looked like Lupinetti had stamped on it before attempting to quickly hide the device.

She picked the phone up with her sleeve, and tried to turn it on but no luck. Before she moved to take it back inside, her eyes shifted to the window.

He'd stolen a phone but hadn't taken it with him.

Why?

'He's cold as ice,' Harrington told Spencer behind the wheel, having come back to the front of the bus, the gate relocked, his keys still clipped to his belt and his shotgun back in his possession.

'Better call ahead to Gilmer and see if they can get a nurse or doc ready to give him something,' Spencer said, as Archer kept his eyes on Lupinetti. 'Most likely be methadone, right? For heroin treatment?'

As the two extradition agents talked, Archer was barely listening, still thinking about Lupinetti's self-satisfied smile. It was the same expression he'd seen on the man's face during the operation last year in New York City when Archer's friend Diana Lucero had died.

When Lupinetti had known something the people around him didn't.

'It's not working,' one of the nurses told Marquez, having retrieved a charger for the phone. The NYPD detective tilted it and saw the small hole she was looking for.

'Can you score me a safety pin?' The nurse left and came back with one a few seconds later. Marquez used the end to open the cradle where the SIM card was held and opened her own cell the same way. She swapped them out, then switched her phone back on.

'Pin number required?' the nurse asked. Marquez shook her head; the guy recovering in room 17 didn't seem to have activated one, which she knew happened sometimes with older folk given these kinds of phones by family members. Once it had loaded and her phone recognized the storage on the SIM, she went to *Call History*.

The previous six numbers dialed were all named contacts, but the most recent number was unsaved. Marquez turned and went into the man's room. 'When was the last time you used your phone, sir?' she asked the guy lying in the bed.

'This morning.'

Marquez's eyes were fixed on the time of the last call. Outgoing, not incoming, at 5:42pm. The area code for the call was 315, which she knew very well was for upstate New York.

So Frank Lupinetti had called someone up there.

She was staring at the screen, wondering who that could be, just as Archer and the other passengers on the bus were about to find out.

ELEVEN

On the I-64 highway, almost halfway to their next stop at FCI Gilmer and currently outside Charleston, West Virginia, the extradition bus had just passed through a traffic build-up after having been delayed by an accident for almost ten minutes. As they moved clear, passing another vehicle apparently broken down on the verge with its hazard lights on, Archer was glancing behind him to take another look at Lupinetti when they began to approach a long low bridge, the Kanawha River running not far below.

'Search for your boys might be spreading out,' Harrington said, tapping Archer on the shoulder, who turned to see what he was talking about. As the large steel girders of the bridge passed either side of the bus, Archer saw a WV State Police cruiser parked across the far end of the bridge ahead, a navy blue Chevy Impala with a gold-colored roof.

It was straddling the two lanes, clearly expecting them to stop. The queues from the incident ten miles back down the highway had thinned out traffic significantly, so the bus currently had nothing ahead between it and the end of the bridge.

'Slow down,' Archer said, rising from his seat. 'Stop back here if you can.'

'What's wrong?' Spencer asked, as Archer focused on the road ahead. He would have expected to see troopers either standing outside or at least sitting inside the vehicle, but there weren't any.

Then as Spencer started to brake, the headlights illuminated something snaked across the road.

As Archer shouted a warning, there was a loud *bang* and the heavy bus started to veer out of control. The extradition agent stamped his foot harder on the brake, throwing everyone forward as the vehicle slewed across the two lanes, only stopping when it hit the low concrete wall which intersected the bridge. '*The hell was that*?' Spencer asked, as the inmates in the back started cussing them out. Gallagher had been smacked into the seat in front when the bus had braked and was now looking even worse than he did before, bleeding from a cut to his forehead.

With the road behind them momentarily clear but the State Police Impala blocking off the way ahead, Archer pulled his Sig Sauer and crouched low as Harrington joined him, pumping his shotgun. Over the dash and illuminated in the bus's headlights, Archer saw now they were closer that the police cruiser ahead was damaged.

And he could also see what looked like blood, spattered across the windshield.

The extradition bus's own windshield was suddenly partially shattered as a muzzle flashed from behind the Impala, and Agent Spencer was cut through by three bullets fired in quick succession, another few missing him but smashing out more glass at the back of the bus. The prisoners saw the agent get hit but rather than start hollering, most of them ducked down as self-preservation kicked in, a few starting to fight to try to get free from their handcuffs and chains. Archer kept low and moved closer to Spencer, seeing the man was still alive but not for much longer. Then another burst broke more of the windshield, forcing Archer down lower and spraying him with shards of glass, but two of the bullets hit Agent Harrington in the back of the head as he'd turned to check the prisoners were still secure, the shots killing him instantly.

As Harrington dropped, Archer gripped Spencer who was held in place by his seatbelt, blood leaking down onto the floor as the prisoners started shouting to be released, but while holding him he felt the extradition agent sag against him and go limp. As he turned to look down the bus, now after only a matter of a few seconds the last member of law-enforcement on board, Archer realized Harrington had fallen backwards near the inmates and the rear gate was still open from their checks on Gallagher.

The dead agent had landed near the foot of the Latino with the wispy goatee beard who was frantically trying to reach the shotgun with his shackled foot. Archer caught the grip of the 12 gauge and pulled it away an instant before part of the bus's front door was blown apart by the shell from another shotgun, Agent Spencer's dead body taking a flanking shot.

Someone had moved forward to assault the bus, and a hand reached in to pull the door open.

'*COP ON BOARD*!' Archer recognized Lupinetti's voice shout from the back, just before the NYPD detective pulled the trigger on the twelve gauge. Whoever was out there ducked as the shotgun blasted glass and metal into the air, and Archer racked the pump before firing again through the windshield, the figure abandoning the attempt to board the bus and scurrying for cover instead.

As the individual retreated, Archer caught a glimpse of a huge man wearing a white t-shirt with orange prison jumpsuit pants. He fired again, more in an attempt to dissuade whoever it was from having another go at approaching the bus rather than in an expectation of hitting him, and watched for a moment to make sure no-one else was going to attempt to get on board, then hearing a noise behind him, swung round to see the black inmate from Big Sandy scramble out of the rear window smashed by the bullets that had killed Spencer. Archer realized the Latino convict who hadn't quite got hold of the shotgun must have managed to unclip the keys from the dead extradition agent's belt instead, and had released himself in seconds before throwing them to the black inmate on his way out.

As another prisoner started to free himself, the one who'd been talking nonstop since they'd left Virginia, Archer ran down the bus but was slammed off his feet by the giant called Briley who'd just successfully removed his leg shackles. These guys had worked incredibly fast, just as Spencer had warned earlier, always waiting for an opportunity. While Archer was bulldozed onto one of the empty seats and tried to fight off the giant, the next inmate with the keys undid his shackles and threw them at Lupinetti, the remaining prisoners shouting at him to pass the set over.

Flashing red and blue lights suddenly lit up the back of the bus as a police cruiser pulled up on the bridge behind them, but Archer was too busy to notice; he'd dropped the shotgun when he was hit and had pulled his Sig, but Briley had him pinned to one of the seats and was bending his arm slowly, forcing the gun towards Archer's head. The prisoner was so strong there was nothing Archer could do to stop him, and he realized the guy was going to put the gun to his head before pulling the trigger. *Executed a couple homicide detectives in Atlanta,* Spencer had said about one of the pickups from Big Sandy. Archer had just found out which prisoner that was likely to have been.

'Night night, piggy,' the guy told him, but Archer suddenly stopped resisting with his left hand, then snapped his head up a split-second before the gun fired, the bullet missing his skull by a hair's breadth and going into the floor of the bus instead. Before Briley could react, with his free hand, Archer buried his thumb deep into the man's eye. As the giant screamed and dropped the pistol, Archer grabbed the twelve gauge on the floor beside him and rammed the stock into the convict's head several times, putting him down hard.

The Charleston city police cruiser that had stopped behind the bus had been returning to patrol from the accident scene and traffic buildup further back down the highway, but instead, the officer inside had just found himself unexpectedly caught up in the assault on the prison transport on the bridge.

A civilian vehicle had also arrived just ahead of him, now trapped between the cop's cruiser and the bus, but before the lone patrolman inside the cop car could reach for his radio or weapon, he came under fire from a vehicle with Virginia plates that had just screeched to a halt behind him. He was immediately killed; the VA truck had been the vehicle the bus had passed back on the highway, apparently broken down on the shoulder.

Unknown to Archer at the time, Craig Loughlin was the driver.

Leaving Archer to fight a losing battle with the monster inmate from Big Sandy, Lupinetti jumped out of the broken window at the back of the bus, having thrown the keys on the seat beside Gallagher as the other two inmates still secured yelled for them. He fell as he landed, hearing a gunshot followed by a shout of pain on the bus and smiled, knowing it had to be Archer. He got back to his feet but before he could take off, his NYPD nemesis landed on the broken glass beside him, shotgun in hand and still very much alive.

Archer ducked under a wild swinging backfist before smashing the stock of the twelve gauge behind Lupinetti's ear, dazing him; he then pulled him back against the rear of the bus, using it as protection while giving himself a chance to catch his breath and figure out what to do next.

Three cars were now lined up behind the bus stopped at an angle across the road. A civilian Subaru which had been unfortunate enough to have been travelling behind them was the closest; the vehicle hadn't taken any gunfire, its terrified driver huddled inside, but Archer saw the second in line, a Charleston city police cruiser, had been hit, an officer at the wheel slumped against his door. It looked to have been shot at from behind, some of the front windshield blown out onto the hood, which meant whoever was responsible for this attack had people on both sides of the bridge. He saw the door to the car farthest back in line was open but there was no sign of the driver.

But it was then that Archer also became aware of the smell of gasoline, and saw the coiled snake lying across the road responsible for blowing out their tires was actually a hose with dozens of large nails drilled through it. The hose had got caught up under the vehicle and Archer guessed the nails being whipped around underneath had ruptured one of the bus's fuel tanks.

Gasoline was now leaking out onto the concrete around them, and he and Lupinetti were standing right in the middle of the growing pool. Keeping a tight grip on his prisoner, Archer edged to the side of the bus and risked a glance around it, seeing two large men moving his way.

He recognized them immediately as Brooks and Billy Loughlin, still in their Gatlin jumpsuits and white t-shirts. Using the bus as cover, Archer retreated, dragging Lupinetti with him towards the first car, worried that a muzzle flash from his own weapon could ignite the gasoline and send the bus, and them with it, skywards. Running turned out to be a wise choice; the result of a shotgun blast moments later created sparks on the asphalt which set the gasoline on fire, just as Archer had feared.

Two remaining inmates on board were still secured, but from his position behind the car, Archer saw Briley tumble out of the back window, followed shortly after by Gallagher who'd somehow found the strength to free himself. They both landed in the flaming gasoline which set their shoes and lower jumpsuit pants on fire; the pair each batted at the flames, then realizing almost simultaneously they were fighting a losing battle, both ran to the edge of the bridge before hurling themselves off into the dark water below, flames creeping up the legs of their jumpsuits as they disappeared out of sight.

The other two still trapped on the bus weren't so lucky. Flames pooled out and spread under the bus, and within seconds it was consumed by an explosion; the force of the blast knocked both Archer and Lupinetti to the concrete, despite taking cover behind the car. As they recovered, Lupinetti started struggling to escape Archer's grip again, but while the NYPD cop fought to overpower him, he caught sight of Brooks and Billy giving the bus a wide berth and heading straight for him and Frank, both men holding weapons up ready to fire.

Archer abandoned his efforts to overpower Lupinetti and rolled back behind the civilian car as a shotgun blast disintegrated the wing mirror above his head. He pumped his own twelve gauge and dropped down to look under the car in time to see Billy waving Lupinetti forward to join them. Frank passed the giant figure of Brooks who was advancing towards Archer, holding a rifle, but the oldest Loughlin brother suddenly stopped and ran to his right.

In that instant, Archer remembered the empty car back down the bridge, and also that he hadn't yet seen the youngest Loughlin. He swung round in time to see Craig had stalked down the bridge, his prison overalls stained with dirt and dried blood. He was already raising a rifle, but Archer was faster than the escaped convict could ever have expected and threw himself across the concrete as bullets hit the civilian car instead of him. A blast from

Archer's twelve gauge a second later hit Craig before he even had time to realize he'd been outmatched, and this time the NYPD detective wasn't firing a non-lethal beanbag; the shell punched through the convict's blood-stained, dirty white t-shirt a second before he collapsed to the road.

Further up the bridge, as Billy ran back to the shot-up trooper cruiser with Lupinetti, unaware his kid brother had just been shot, Brooks watched in horror as Craig went down. Before he could react, there was a second explosion from the bus as another tank ignited, knocking him to the ground.

Knowing the shotgun was either out of shells or close to it and that he was still outnumbered three to one, Archer decided it was time to split. As they'd approached the bridge in the transport bus, he'd seen it was relatively high above the water.

But he hoped not high enough that a fall would kill him.

Keeping low, he ripped open the driver's door of the car he'd been using as cover and pulled the terrified man out. 'Can you swim?' he asked the guy, not waiting for the answer as he ran him towards the concrete barrier running the length of the bridge.

The answer was irrelevant anyway.

As Brooks got back to his feet, he was just in time to see the guy who'd just shot his brother disappear from sight as he and another man jumped off the side of the bridge.

He climbed over the barrier, ran across the opposite lanes which were now completely empty of traffic after approaching drivers had seen the attack on the bridge and reversed quickly out of harm's way, but it was dark down there and he couldn't see much.

Apoplectic with rage, Brooks started blindly firing bullets into the water below. As the magazine clicked dry, he went back across the central median then ran towards Craig. It was only then he saw he was still moving. He dropped to his knees beside him as Craig writhed in pain, coughing up blood, the front of his dirty t-shirt becoming increasingly soaked in it. Brooks looked to his right as he heard someone running towards them and saw it was Billy, who'd now realized what had happened.

'Hold on, baby brother,' Brooks said. 'Just hold on.'

Craig coughed a few more times, then went slack in his arms.

The first of the USP Gatlin inmates to go down since the breakout.

He'd lasted less than twelve hours.

TWELVE

Two hours earlier, Friday night traffic had been running smoothly over the Kanawha River Bridge in both directions, with people getting out of the city of Charleston for the Labor Day weekend or heading in from out of town. But now each of the two lanes both sides of the central median were closed off, vehicles further back being rerouted. The bridge was completely sealed as troopers set up armed roadblocks on each side, the extradition prison bus still burning and surrounded by firefighters working on extinguishing the flames. Water sprayed off the vehicle, reflecting the color of the flashing lights close by.

A lead deputy from the US Marshals district office in Charleston had just arrived with members of his team. They'd liaised with their contemporaries in southern Virginia who were now overseeing the manhunt for the Loughlin brothers, a situation that was escalating fast. The three fugitives were not only responsible for a batch of fresh murders but their actions had allowed several high-risk prisoners to escape from the bus and also caused the death of the two still trapped on board when the transport exploded, as well as the two extradition agents and three members of law-enforcement. The need to locate and apprehend the runaways as soon as possible had become an urgent necessity. 'How many got out?' the Marshal deputy asked a State trooper, looking at the burning vehicle.

'Five. Cop from New York who was on the transport gave us the details.'

'New York? The hell is he doing out here?'

'Helping escort one of the prisoners who used to wear a NYPD badge, apparently. Guy escaped and took off with the two remaining Loughlin brothers.' He looked at the scene around them, then back at the deputy. 'They shot a local PD officer and two of our people. Stole their cruiser and set it up down there across the road to block it off.'

'Where's this cop from New York?'

The trooper nodded at a sodden Archer wrapped in a borrowed blanket standing further down the bridge as he stood looking at the bus. 'He ended up in the Kanawha?' the deputy asked.

'Probably the only reason he survived.'

Dripping wet from head to toe and hugging the blanket close in an effort to warm up, Archer turned when he realized a gray-haired man wearing a Marshals badge on a chain around his neck had approached and was saying something to him.

'What was that?' Archer said.

'-said, I heard you were on the bus?'

Archer nodded and let go of one side of the blanket to shake the Marshal's hand, as well as that of another deputy who'd joined him. 'Sorry. My gun went off right next to my ear. Can't hear too well.'

'They fished you out?'

'With the driver of the Subaru,' he said, nodding at the car of the unfortunate local who'd been caught in the crossfire. 'Jumped off with me. He's been taken to hospital to get checked out.' Luckily for Archer there'd been no sign of his new friend from Big Sandy, the cop killer Briley, who'd gone off the bridge before them.

'They didn't want to take you in too?'

'Yeah, but I told them I'm fine. Subaru driver was too I think; just suffering from shock.'

The deputy was looking at him curiously. 'Accent of yours ain't exactly from Brooklyn.'

'Long story.'

'They hit you hard man,' the other Marshal said. 'These Loughlin boys didn't have long to plan this. They've only been out of Gatlin for what, twelve hours?'

'Paid a heavy price for it though,' Archer told him. 'That's the youngest brother over there.' He nodded down the bridge and the Marshals saw Craig Loughlin's body still lying where he'd fallen, covered with a sheet but left in place until all necessary photographs had been taken. Archer could see glimpses of orange under the sheet. The man hadn't been gone from prison long enough to even change out of his BOP clothes.

'These boys busted out of a federal house just to hit this bus and break free more guys who they didn't know?' the lead deputy said. 'That sound right to you? Why not just keep running.'

'They know Frank Lupinetti,' Archer said. 'When we found him this morning during the riot, he was close to the laundry. It was where the brothers escaped from.' Archer looked back down the bridge at the flames being extinguished. 'Been thinking about it. My guess is, he was supposed to get out of the prison with them but he was too late and the truck left without him.'

'I heard he used to be a cop,' the other Marshal asked. 'They that desperate for his company? What's their end?'

'Haven't worked that out yet.' Archer wrapped the blanket tighter as he shivered, trying to ward off the night chill.

'Any idea how'd they know he'd be out here?' the lead deputy said. 'Our people in Virginia said this isn't the transport he was supposed to be on.'

'Hospital guards at Jonesville where he was being treated screwed up and let him slip out of custody before we re-apprehended him. I borrowed a cell phone just now to call a colleague who's still there. She told me a phone had gone missing belonging to a guy in the room Frank escaped out of. Last call on it was to an unlisted cell in upstate New York. 315 area code. The Loughlins have friends and family everywhere up there. It's home turf.'

'So Lupinetti told someone he was gonna be on the bus heading this way tonight?' the assisting Marshal said. 'And whoever that was, they found a way to relay it to the Loughlins?'

Archer nodded. 'The two agents who were on board told me these buses follow the same route most of the time. Big Sandy, to FCI Gilmer, going up I-77, taking the 64-exit and going over this bridge near the State capital. Prisoners know the journey well enough from back and forth transfers.'

'How you think they timed it so well? What did you see?'

Archer nodded back at where Craig was lying. 'Youngest brother came at us from the south side. Think they picked us up on the interstate in a car they'd stolen, and rode ahead to look for an ambush point. Traffic was backed up down the highway from an accident. Gave them the perfect opportunity to kill the troopers they came across whose car they stole to block the road. Then Craig must've doubled back and been waiting for us on the highway, pulled off to the side with his hazards on like he'd broken down. They knew we were coming. Drew us into a chokepoint on the bridge then cut off both ways out.'

'So you took one prisoner down, but he's been replaced by four more.'

'Way today's been going, I'm afraid.' The Marshals headed back down the bridge to talk with a Charleston PD lieutenant who'd just arrived along with some more State troopers waiting for directions on the manhunts, the men and women visibly shaken by the deaths of their colleagues. Archer knew what that felt like, remembering what Lupinetti and his friends had done to Lucero.

Up above, a police chopper had started to hover over some woodland half a mile away, searching with its spotlight. He was sure that like near Gatlin, K9 tracking dogs would be out there as well. 'APB went out to all units for the brothers and your man in the stolen trooper Impala,' a city cop who'd loaned Archer the blanket said, joining him. 'But the other prisoners most likely are still on foot. Should be easier to find.'

'Not if they make it into the city,' Archer said, looking at the lights of Charleston beyond the bridge. It wasn't a big metropolis by any means, but it had plenty of places to hide, people to take hostage and vehicles to steal.

The assisting deputy Marshal returned. 'We're warning local counties and putting out alerts, but the chief asked if you'd stick around for a few hours,' he told Archer. 'Our people in Virginia are gonna want to know exactly what happened here in detail. You're the only one who can tell us.'

'Whatever you need. But I'm going back on Lupinetti's trail as soon as it's picked up again.'

'We'll find him along with those two brothers.'

'Maybe, but he was my responsibility. This doesn't end until I've got him back in a prison cell.' Archer remembered Spencer and Harrington getting hit with rifle and shotgun fire from the Loughlins, his two companions on the journey who now wouldn't be going home to their families tomorrow morning. *And I'd like to run into Brooks and Billy again too while I'm at it,* he thought.

The Marshal nodded before walking off as Archer checked the time. Just past 10pm. 'Dispatch wants us back in town and patrolling in case some of these boys show up looking for cars, weapons or supplies,' the local female cop told him. 'I'd better get rolling.'

Archer's wet clothes were clinging to him and he felt chilled to the bone. 'Mind if I hitch a ride?'

He was going to leave his cell number with the US Marshals, but after discovering his phone was out of action after its dunking in the river, they gave Archer a card instead with a number to call in an hour or so when he could find a phone to check for an update. The female cop gave him a lift into the city, but despite a quick drive around, couldn't find any clothing outlets still open at that time of night; with his bag of spare clothes torched on the prison bus, it meant the sodden NYPD detective was just going to have to wait until morning.

His shivering was burning up energy and had left him starving. He hadn't eaten anything apart from some Pringles since he and Marquez had left the motel earlier that morning, so the Charleston cop dropped him at a diner in the city that closed late. Draped in the blanket, he attracted the curious attention of the server and few other customers as he took a seat at the counter, but they soon turned back to their meals. Archer's own attention went to the TV as he ordered the first things he saw on the menu, a grilled cheese sandwich, fries, chicken soup and hot tea.

Spencer and Harrington were still on his mind; he'd learned a bit about their lives during the journey and had liked both of them. He remembered the taunts aimed at Spencer about his wife. Both agents had been doing an important job and by requesting the transport, Archer had involved them in this situation; now they were dead, their families due to receive the knock tonight. Archer also recalled Frank's smug expression, reflected in that dark window.

He'd known something was going to happen.

The two agents' deaths, the Loughlins' actions, Lupinetti's escape and his plunge into the Kanawha had left the cold, damp NYPD detective tired and thoroughly pissed off. Once his meal arrived he ate quietly, watching the TV screen as Statewide news reported live from the scene on the bridge, the crew as close as they could get to make their report. *The Gatlin Four*, the Loughlins and Lupinetti were now being called, considered a separate group and being covered independently from the other bus escapees. Archer ran his eyes from left to right across the mugshots on the screen. The three Loughlin brothers, all rotten to the core, the remaining two sure to want to get revenge for taking down their youngest.

Lupinetti will tell them who you are. Where to find you.

Bring it on, he thought. He continued to watch the TV while finishing his meal which was warming him up and helping to improve his mood very slightly. Getting a report of the incident out there so fast was also good; millions of eyes were more effective than just those of the police.

'Want another bowl, man?' the server asked, seeing the soup was gone. 'It's on the house. We got half a pot left. Looks like you could use it.'

Archer raised a smile, wrapped in his blanket. 'What gave you that idea?'

As the young man took the bowl and refilled it, the local news report linked to one from WJHL back in Lee County, giving updates on the situation there; Archer started to think about the others killed by the Loughlins today. The firearms the brothers had been using on the bridge might've come from the troopers whose car they'd stolen, but they had to have been armed before that; the windshield on the Impala had been shot up. Someone could've delivered guns to the fugitives, but he hadn't seen anyone else helping them out on the bridge. The most likely scenario was they'd broken into someone's home and stolen them. Southern Virginia was hunting country. And meant there was possibly another innocent victim missing some weapons and ammo.

So, in half a day, they'd murdered four inmates in their respective escapes and caused another three to die on the bus, shot three cops, two extradition agents, and there was that laundry truck driver who most likely had died too by now, the man having been left clinging to life by a thread and only because the brothers had made a mistake by not cutting his throat deep enough. Archer also then remembered the elderly woman who'd called 911 to alert them about the truck, killed by Brooks and Billy for her trouble and more importantly to them, her car.

The server brought back the bowl of soup and a fresh refill of tea as the elderly woman's fate stayed with Archer. He thought about that particular scenario some more. A Virginia State trooper had just said on the TV that blood had been found on the highway, but Marquez had mentioned earlier that the truck driver had been discovered by first-responders with padding wrapped around his neck.

So the old woman got out, found the injured driver, strapped his wound, called 911 then went back to her car and was stabbed? Archer envisaged Brooks and Billy Loughlin lying in wait in the cornfield for an approaching car they could hijack, before stepping out and flagging her down. They wouldn't have let her help the driver and definitely wouldn't have given her time to call the cops.

He took out his cell and tried to turn it on, but the device still wasn't working. As he started looking at ways to take it apart to give it a chance to dry out, the Charleston PD cop who'd dropped him at the diner walked in and approached his seat, a folded pair of jeans, a shirt and sweater in her hands. 'These are my husband's,' she said, passing Archer the clothes. 'He's got a couple pounds on you, but they'll be better than what you're wearing until morning. Don't want you getting sick.'

Archer was surprised by the gesture. 'He's OK if I borrow them?'

'Says they're old, so you can throw 'em out when you're done.' She smiled. 'I've been looking for an excuse to get them out of the dresser for a while.'

Archer looked at the sweater, which had the Virginia Tech University logo on it. 'Thank you.'

The cop nodded then turned to the server and passed over a thermos. 'You do me a favor and fill that up, sir?'

'You got it.'

Archer's thoughts were still with whoever had made that call about the laundry truck driver, and he caught the server before he headed to the coffee pot. 'There a phone here I could use?'

'911, what's your emergency?' the recorded call said. The female cop had become curious when Archer had told her what was on his mind, interested to hear the outcome, so had decided to wait while the server brought over a cordless landline.

Having quickly changed in the men's room into the officer's husband's jeans, t-shirt and old gray college sweater, Archer had the call on low speakerphone setting so she could hear too. He'd dialed the CT Bureau back in New York, who at his request had contacted Jonesville PD in Virginia near Gatlin prison, asking if they could hear a cut of the 911 call from earlier that day when the laundry truck had been found. Jonesville had called Archer back and were playing him the recording he'd asked to hear.

'I'm on a track off Route 58. There's a laundry truck here. The driver's been stabbed,' a voice said. *'He needs medical attention immediately. Get here fast.'*

‘So it wasn’t the old woman who made the call,’ Archer said quietly, hearing the operator asking more questions but the caller not answering. ‘No-one thought to check the recording, but you just heard. A guy called the 911 operator. Not her.’

‘A passing driver, maybe?’

‘Who stopped, found the driver choking on his own blood, wrapped his neck up as best he could, phoned the local police then left before they showed up?’

‘Might’ve been scared whoever did that to the driver could reappear and cut him up too,’ she suggested, echoing what Marquez had said back at the hospital in Virginia before Archer left. ‘Or he didn’t wanna hang around to answer questions.’ She paused, thinking. ‘Maybe he’s got a record or something.’

‘*The call came from the truck driver’s cell phone,’* the Jonesville dispatcher said, hearing the two cops exchanging ideas.

‘Could you connect me to USP Gatlin if possible, Miss?’ Archer asked, the Charleston PD cop’s last comment moments ago sticking with him.

‘Sure, but they might be too busy to talk.’

‘They won’t be if they hear what I have to say. But I need to speak to them right now.’

THIRTEEN

'C Block's under lockdown right now,' the corrections officer called Williams told Archer impatiently, still on duty after a brutal day and one of three COs currently in the control center at USP Gatlin. 'We haven't even had time to wipe the blood off the floor and walls yet.'

'I'm just asking for another headcount. It's important.'

'That was done already, after the riot team took back control.'

'With cells closed?'

'This isn't *Escape from Alcatraz*, guy. We make sure we see more than just the top of a head. Protocol is forty eight hours locked in their cells after a riot; no meals, no yard time, no contact with the outside world. These sons of bitches don't deserve anything less after what they did today. They killed two of our guys. We go easy, they'll start thinking we're slipping, then they'll pull this shit again. I'm not gonna be the next one ending up in a box.'

'I get it. I'm not suggesting you go light or even talk to them. Just tick off each man in his cell. There's a good reason I'm asking.'

'Apart from Brooks and Billy, everyone who wasn't killed today is accounted for. We don't screw up count. There's too much at stake if we do.'

'Who's on the line?' the captain of the corrections team asked, walking back into the control center holding his cell phone. He'd been in close discussion with the Marshals Office and various police agencies across southern Virginia for most of the last hour, the groups not sure whether to halt their searches after confirmed sightings of the Loughlins had been made on the bridge over in West Virginia a state away.

'One of the cops from New York who was here earlier.'

'The Marshals just told me he was on the prison transport when it got hit outside Charleston,' the captain answered.

'It got ambushed?' one of the other guards, Anderson, asked in surprise.

'Yeah and your man there capped off Craig Loughlin,' the captain said, taking the phone from Williams. 'Cap here. I hear it right that you took down the youngest brother?'

'Yeah, but not the other two unfortunately. Brooks and Billy broke Frank Lupinetti free and four other prisoners who were on the bus made it out too. I'm gonna be after Lupinetti again as soon as I get a lead but right now, I think I can help you.'

'How so?'

'I strongly suggest you run another count in C Block. I think you could be another man down.'

'That's impossible,' Williams muttered, able to hear what Archer was saying. 'I told him, we already did a check earlier.'

'A quick recount with inmates looked in the eye and accounted for,' Archer said to the captain. '*I wouldn't waste your time if I didn't think it was necessary.'*

It had been almost eleven hours since the riot had been brought under control. Most of the inmates locked back inside C Block had quietened, resigned to the punishment of being stuck in their cells without food for forty eight hours, when the doors below opened and three COs walked into the block with the captain, riot officers behind them carrying shields and batons.

This happening after a disturbance or a riot was very unusual. On the upper tier, Prez raised his head off his pillow, then climbed out of his bunk and went to the door.

'One drop of bullshit from anyone, you go to the SHU for a month,' the captain warned loudly, his voice echoing off the walls, and the noise which had started to come from some of the cells subsided. Beside him, Williams and Anderson both glanced at the dried blood on the floor and then at the Loughlins', Hoffmeier's and Kattar's empty cells as they passed.

Two escaped, and two dead.

'Open up ground tier north,' the captain ordered into a radio. As the cell doors were unlocked and the old-school grilled bars slid back, Anderson and Williams each brought up a shotgun to cover the line, the riot officers standing alongside them ready to crush any attempt at another uprising. 'Step out! All of you.'

The inmates did as they were ordered, some with minor injuries, some of them glancing around warily wondering if an unsanctioned revenge beatdown was about to take place. Most of their attention was focused on the two armed COs behind the captain holding the shotguns; firearms were rarely brought into the block, so the fact they were now was a clear demonstration the staff weren't taking any chances.

The third CO who'd been in the control center with Anderson, Williams and the captain went down the line with a checkboard, ticking off the prisoners one by one. As he passed each man and checked them off, he ordered them back into their cells. 'Lower tier set, Cap,' the guard said when he reached the last inmate. 'All accounted for.'

'Told you this was a waste of time,' Williams muttered, holding his twelve gauge.

'Close the cells,' the captain ordered over his radio, the doors sliding back into place. The team checked the other lower side, all the prisoners ticked off there too, then once their doors were relocked the group moved to the upper tier. The cells on the south side were opened first and the inmates stepped out.

Once again, the guard went down the line with his clipboard, ticking each man off his list. 'Cap, we're a man down,' the CO said, stopping. 'Where's Pugh?' he asked the cell's remaining inmate, as his captain joined him.

'Got shanked.'

'Did Pugh get hurt in the riot?' the captain asked his COs below.

'Yeah, taken to Jonesville,' Anderson confirmed. 'They're housing him at County until lockdown's-'

Then he stopped talking.

His eyes had locked onto a couple of inmates towards the end of the upper southside tier, who he could just see from his position a level down. The captain turned to see what had caught his attention, and after following his gaze walked down the line quickly, stopping near the end of the tier.

He reached the two prisoners in question who were standing nonchalantly outside their cells, looking the CO and captain in the eye.

The prison staff were focusing on the smaller of the two men, who was grinning back at them.

At that moment, with USP Gatlin staff realizing they'd all made a very serious mistake, a young couple driving a country road north of Charleston in West Virginia had just been flagged down to help a guy standing beside a State Police Impala with its hood up, the car blocking the road.

Unlike the elderly woman back in Lee County who'd been listening to an audiobook instead of the news, the boyfriend and girlfriend were aware from updates on their phones, as well as the radio, about the attack on the bus back on the Kanawha Bridge and the missing fugitives in the area. The man standing by the broken-down Impala ahead was wearing a trooper's forest green uniform, but the shirt was open and revealed a stained white t-shirt stretched tight over a large barely-contained belly; he looked a mess, wasn't wearing a campaign hat and was sporting a large unkempt beard. And when the couple stopped just behind the cruiser, they saw he was wearing white sneakers, not boots.

The driver was no fool. As he went for the glove compartment, which contained a concealed-carry lightweight compact revolver, he was flanked by Billy Loughlin who'd emerged from behind some trees with a rifle, and just as he took out the Ruger .357 the driver was unceremoniously shot in the head. His girlfriend screamed as he rocked from the impact and went limp, high velocity blood spatter and other matter spraying over her as the gun clattered out of her boyfriend's fingers to the floor. She continued to scream, staring at her dead partner in shock, so didn't see Brooks arrive outside the car. He ripped open her door, dragged her out and quickly broke her neck, this time making sure he did the job properly unlike with the laundry truck driver whose survival he'd heard about on the radio.

Billy pulled the man's body out too and the brothers dumped the couple in the bushes out of sight of the road while Lupinetti stood on the side of the road with a handgun, keeping watch. Brooks had squeezed into the trooper's stolen clothes a couple of minutes ago to make the stop more convincing to an oncoming driver, but he quickly swapped them back for his XXXL BOP jumps again now the job was done. The man they'd just killed had been larger than the skinny fisherman the three Loughlins had taken down at his home in Virginia earlier, but still was nowhere near big enough for his clothes to fit either of the two brothers.

Brooks whistled to Lupinetti and waved him over before throwing him the man's jacket. The former NYPD lieutenant tried it on then went into the bushes where the guy had been dumped and stripped him, pulling on his shirt and jeans before putting the jacket back on. He was pleased to ditch the prison overalls he'd been wearing despite the fact the shirt was now stained with blood and other gunk. That didn't overly bother him; he could cover the worst of it with the jacket. He also discovered the man's boots were only half a size bigger than what he wore too. Things were starting to look up.

In the meantime, Billy had transferred their bags of guns, ammo and food to their new ride, keeping a sharp eye on the road as he did so. Once Brooks pocketed all the cash he could find in the woman's purse and man's wallet, totaling a hundred and fifty three bucks, he re-joined Frank by the police vehicle and they rolled it off the road and down a bank, the Impala gathering pace until it hit a tree. They returned to the dead couple's car and climbed inside, Brooks scooting the driver's seat back as Billy did the same on the passenger side while Lupinetti took the back. Billy picked up the dropped compact .357 and inspected it before stuffing the small gun into his waistband as his brother found an old roadmap in the glovebox, taking advantage and using it to doublecheck the direction they'd need to take.

'How far's the drive?' Lupinetti asked, still holding onto his pistol and keeping his eyes on the empty road. Neither brother answered as Brooks stared up from the map at the road ahead, the car not moving. Billy glanced at his older sibling, who'd been unusually quiet since they'd escaped from the bridge.

Looking at them both in turn, Lupinetti could guess why.

'The guy who shot him is a cop,' he ventured quietly. 'His name is Sam Archer. I can help you find him.'

Brooks looked at him in the rear-view for a few moments, and Frank felt his stomach tighten. But instead of replying, Brooks passed the map to Billy and they moved off, planning to stick to the backroads while heading north. The upcoming journey would take them a while longer but that didn't matter; they had all night.

Their destination was around seven hours away and they just needed to be there by 11 o'clock the following morning.

'What's the problem?' the warden asked, striding into C Block to meet the captain who'd called him, saying it was urgent. The captain led him back up to the upper south tier and headed towards two inmates who'd been near the end of the line, all the other prisoners now locked inside their cells again.

'His name is Freddy Janks, sir,' the captain said, Williams and Anderson flanking the grinning inmate. 'He's one of the guys from-'

'This is my prison, Captain. I know who he is. So what's he doing here? Last I heard he was in the SHU from the psych ward for biting lumps out of another inmate.'

'He was.'

'What's your point? Someone must've let him out during the riot and he hid under a bunk or-'

Then the warden understood and his expression changed.

'Where's the man who was meant to be in this cell?'

'He isn't on the list of the dead or inmates taken to hospital or County, sir,' the captain replied, looking at Prez Rainey standing beside Janks. 'We've got another escapee.'

FOURTEEN

Marquez had stopped by USP Gatlin one last time to get a photocopy of Lupinetti's paperwork for Shepherd before heading back to the motel when she heard the COs radios lighting up, the captain reporting they had another missing prisoner after a recount of C Block.

'He's gone and nobody noticed until now?' she asked the sergeant who'd helped her and Archer extract Lupinetti earlier in the day, walking with him to their control room. 'How'd he'd pull that one off?'

'You tell me. God dammit, we completely missed it. If it hadn't been for your partner, it would've been hours before we noticed.'

'Archer? How the hell did he know?'

'Again, you tell me.'

'Who is this new escapee? Don't tell me the Loughlins have another brother.'

'No, his name is Nicky Reyes,' the sergeant told her as they approached the door to the control room. 'Thirty year old from Cleveland, in for manslaughter. We're checking every place we can think of in the block but the guy's vanished.'

'Go back and trace Reyes' movements on the cameras from when the riot started,' the captain ordered a pair of COs, having returned to the control room just as Marquez and the sergeant arrived. 'Where's Janks right now?'

'On his way back to the SHU, like you ordered,' a CO told him.

'Take him to one of the meeting rooms instead. We're gonna talk.'

'Guy's a fruitloop, boss,' the sergeant beside Marquez said. 'Questioning him might take weeks, cutting through all his bullshit. Prez could be an easier nut to crack.'

The captain saw his point and nodded. 'OK, get him over here. I want visitor records checked too. See who Reyes has been speaking to recently, get on the horn to local authorities and tell them the search in Lee County is back on.'

'Prison's saying they did a cell count after the riot, and definitely saw an inmate lying in the missing man's bunk,' Archer explained to the Charleston PD cop, both of them still in the diner a state west of USP Gatlin. He'd been called back by the federal facility and told his suspicions that another prisoner was missing had been correct. 'Assumed it was him, didn't even think to check the SHU too for absent inmates because it wasn't affected in the riot.'

'What's SHU?' the diner server asked, listening avidly from his side of the counter.

'Secure Housing Unit,' the Charleston cop replied automatically before realizing who she was talking to. 'How'd this guy get out of there and into the missing man's cell?' she asked Archer.

'Yeah, how'd this man escape the SHU, Lis?' he asked Marquez.

'A couple of the COs' keysets were lifted in C Block when things went crazy. Someone must've let Janks out but only him. And the staff are saying psych ward inmates here wear green jumps to differentiate them. Janks was a proud owner, but he'd changed into orange by the time count happened.'

'So he was covering for Reyes in his cell.'

'Looks that way to me. The CO who checked the cell said he saw the guy asleep lying with his face to the wall. The imposter's a similar build and is dark-haired like this man Reyes, so the CO didn't think anything of it. Reyes' cellmate is being brought out for questioning. Some motorcycle club president. He definitely knows something. Getting him to talk is probably gonna be another matter.'

'Pretty hard to claim he was oblivious,' Archer said. 'There's been a different guy in his cell for the last twelve hours.'

'Staff did a prisoner count at breakfast first thing and Reyes was ticked off, so he was definitely still on site then. He must've got out during the riot.'

'What's the man doing time for?' Archer asked.

'*Manslaughter. Twelve years. Killed a guy at a party when he was seventeen.'*

'Good going, Prez, you just got a load more time tacked onto your sentence,' the Gatlin captain told the biker who'd been attacked in the chow hall earlier in the day; the door to the meeting room was shut behind them as the large bearded man was pushed into the seat by Williams. 'You helped your celly break out.'

'Can't see you proving that one, boss.'

'Think it's gonna be hard? You've had Freddy Janks in there since lockdown started and didn't happen to notice?'

'What should I have done, called for room service? Some of the boys have been yelling in there for hours and y'all been ignoring them.'

'So you knew Janks was in Reyes' bunk?'

'No, I didn't. He was up top and was there with his back turned when we were all shut in the cells again. After the riot was done I laid down, didn't say shit to the kid and the guy didn't speak to me either. I didn't know it was Janks until you opened us up for a recount.'

'So he somehow teleported from the SHU, ended up in your celly's empty bed wearing orange jumps and you know nothing about it?' Prez didn't answer. 'The Loughlins have started a killing spree already since they got out. Three of the men they've murdered were law-enforcement and two were extradition agents on a bus Brooks and Billy sent sky-high. We prove you helped the brothers as well as Reyes in this, it'll add a nice heap to your sentence. You're still ten months from release. I'll see to it you get another ten years, you don't start talking.'

'You think me and those kid-molesting farmboys were suddenly cool with each other and I helped them break out? You know we avoid each other like we're allergic. They stay outta my way and I return the favor.'

'I know how you are with Reyes. He's like your little brother in this place. You and him always stick together. You might not give them a hand, but you'd sure as hell help him.'

'If he was planning something, he didn't tell me.'

'Take him to the SHU,' the captain told Williams. 'Hell's Angel here can take a cell next to his buddy Janks, since you two seem to like being so close.'

Prez's attitude suddenly changed. 'You got no reason to send me there.'

'Some of our boys might be loose on society right now, but you still belong to Gatlin, Rainey. Maybe peace and quiet in there for a few days'll make you think twice about lying to me.'

Marquez was standing outside with other prison staff when the door opened, and although she'd missed Prez's arrival, she was there to see him being taken out again. She immediately recognized the man from the chow hall earlier, when she and Archer found him being attacked by some of the other inmates. The same one who'd warned her she was about to be rushed from behind.

The biker glanced her way before he was given a push to get him moving and he shuffled forwards. 'Anything?' one of the COs asked the captain quietly, who'd just walked out of the meeting room behind Rainey.

'No, but time in the SHU will soften him up.'

'The manhunt for his cellmate's just starting,' Marquez replied. 'You shut him away and wait it out, could take days to get any information, right?'

'I'm just putting some pressure on. Few hours in there, Prez'll give us something.'

'He doesn't seem like he'd get spooked by some time alone.'

'Only other stint he's pulled in solitary before, his daughter died and he didn't find out for a week,' the captain said. 'My predecessor ran the show then, not me,' he added, seeing the look on her face. 'But that place holds bad memories for him. He won't want to be back in there.'

'What's he locked up for?'

'Trafficking guns across State lines,' the captain replied, before the door ahead reopened and one of the guards who'd been transporting the MC president jogged back.

'Said he's ready to talk.'

'Told you,' the captain said to Marquez. 'That was fast. Bring his ass back.'

'Not to you, boss.' The CO nodded at the female NYPD detective. 'He wants to speak to her.'

'What? Why?' the captain asked, just as surprised as Marquez by the request.

'Didn't say. Do you know him?' the CO asked Marquez who shook her head.

'Never seen him before today.'

'So why's he asking?'

'Maybe he's got a crush. Who cares; we can listen in,' another CO said. 'He starts spilling, who gives a crap who he tells it to in the room?'

'But how would he have a crush on her?' the other officer said. 'He doesn't even know who she is.'

'We crossed paths in the chow hall during the riot,' Marquez said. 'Looked like he was trying to save Andrea from being raped.'

'Or he was fighting others off to have first shot at her,' the captain countered.

'He's wasting time, Cap,' Williams said. 'Just doesn't want to go into solitary.'

'Must be worth a try?' Marquez suggested. 'I'm gonna leave soon but happy to help while I'm here.'

'Her colleague's the one who pushed for another cell count too, Cap,' the sergeant said, nodding at Marquez. 'We wouldn't have checked for two days if he hadn't prompted it. Reyes could've been in Cancun by then.'

'Archer also took Craig Loughlin out of the equation,' Marquez added. 'I'd say he did you another big favor there.'

'Fine, bring him back,' the captain said. 'We're burning moonlight here. Make it fast.'

A couple of minutes later, Rainey was sitting opposite Marquez in the interview room. 'Your celly can't be found on site,' she said. 'Looks like he's been gone for hours.'

'Seems he has.' On his way back to the room, she'd been given his full name. Kevin 'Prez' Rainey of Macon, Georgia; she guessed he was around forty five years old, an imposing man standing around 6'3 or 6'4 with dark brown hair and brown eyes, a gray-flecked beard and faded tattoos on his arms. She noticed a fresh cut across his right forearm, most likely from the fight with the attempted rapists in the chow hall.

'You help me out with Reyes, we can get that cleaned and stitched up,' she told him, looking at the injury.

'You and your friend could've ended up as hamburger meat this morning, coming into the block during the riot.'

'That why you agreed to talk to me? Because you think I helped out?' Rainey didn't answer. 'If it is, help me get your celly back safe before he gets himself hurt or killed out there.'

'I told the boss already. I don't know anything about what the kid had planned.'

'So if staff check the cameras frame-by-frame, we won't find you taking keys off one of the guards and getting Janks out of the SHU?'

'The cameras were broken down there. Smashed, I heard, when all the shit snapped off.'

'How convenient.'

'Wasn't it. I've been in here for fourteen years and I got ten months left. I'm not looking for more time or trouble.'

Marquez paused. 'Two State Police troopers and a local cop were killed on a bridge in West Virginia an hour ago. A prisoner transport was ambushed.'

'I heard. Cap mentioned it.'

'The Loughlins were responsible. If your celly was involved-'

'He wasn't.'

'You're so confident?'

'Not something he'd do; but those rednecks would. Billy's about as smart as this table but he's a mean SOB and murdering means nothing to him. Brooks is the clever one; he's the more dangerous of the two.' Rainey was curious. 'They hit a prisoner transport, huh?'

'Yeah, and some of the inmates on board escaped too. The brothers took Frank Lupinetti with them but my colleague shot Craig Loughlin. Killed him.'

'Your friend the same one from the chow hall?' Prez asked. Marquez nodded. 'Brooks and Billy ain't gonna forget that. He better be ready.'

'He can handle it. But three cops died out there. If State Police or federal agents corner your celly and he won't surrender, it doesn't matter if he wasn't at the bridge, he still broke out of here. They'll even the score real quick.'

'Like your guy, he can handle it. He's made it through his time in this place. Ain't an easy thing.' Before they could continue, the door to the room opened and the captain walked in, carrying a laptop with a memory stick attached, the sergeant and CO called Williams with him.

'We just looked at the visitor logs, Prez,' the captain told him. 'Reyes' sister came to visit him yesterday. Burned this off from the cameras.' He turned the laptop, so Rainey could see the video. Marquez watched too, seeing Nicky leaning across a table and talking agitatedly to a young woman with reddish hair who also looked stressed and anxious. 'What did they discuss?'

'Look like I was there?'

'She helping him on the escape?'

'I said already, I don't know, Cap.'

'Tell us.'

'Tell you what?'

A frustrated pause followed. 'You done here?' the captain asked Marquez. 'Or is he just wasting time?'

'We're done,' she said, looking at the biker and trying to work out why he'd wanted to speak to her. He kept a good poker face but she was certain he knew a lot more than he was telling. However, they couldn't make him talk. 'He's all yours.'

FIFTEEN

'We just got Gallagher, Chief,' a US Marshal from the West Virginia Charleston Office told his boss on a call, less than two miles from where the bus had been ambushed on the Kanawha Falls Bridge. The inmate who'd been sick from drug withdrawal on the extradition transport was marched towards a waiting police car, sniffer dogs barking as he passed. 'Found him hiding in a shack down the riverbank, soaking wet from the river and shivering, looking like a bag of freeze-dried shit.'

'He was always gonna be the easy capture. Cop from the transport said the guy looked halfway dead before the ambush.'

More barking suddenly came from deeper in the woods, and the Marshal, officers and everyone with them immediately started heading in that direction as Gallagher was driven away.

'Are they saying if Nicky Reyes had been acting any differently than he normally does lately?' Archer asked Marquez, still on the diner's landline with the local cop beside him, the woman too interested in this latest development to leave just yet. Lupinetti was Archer's main draw but this other man's escape had caught his attention, particularly as Archer had called it, and with Marquez still at the federal prison, she was best placed to provide answers. Reyes had escaped the same day as the Loughlins and Frank; there might well be a link or some indication of cooperation there.

Find the guy and he could maybe also find Lupinetti.

'Staff say no. Man keeps his head down, never caused them much trouble besides getting in a couple scraps over the years. But he had a visitor yesterday, the last before the Labor Day weekend. Records have her down as his sister but take a look at the message I'm just sending over.'

'Don't, my phone's still busted.' He saw the Charleston officer reach into her pocket and offer hers. 'Send it to this one instead,' he told Marquez, before relaying the cell number.

When it arrived, he opened the message and saw the scanned photo of Reyes' visitor's driving license that the prison had stored. 'They don't exactly look related,' he interpreted, showing the officer and looking up at the diner's TV. Reyes' mugshot had gone out over the networks, Gatlin having got his profile out immediately to join the others, and although it wasn't currently displayed, Archer had seen the image a few minutes ago. Reyes had olive skin and dark hair with brown eyes to match, an indication of a Spanish heritage that matched his surname. The woman, with the name *Katherine O'Mara* on the ID Marquez had just sent, had Irish red hair, pale skin and green eyes.

'Different last names too,' the officer beside Archer noted.

'She might be married, or they share one parent and not two. Or they're adopted. But apart from this chick, they told me Reyes hasn't had any other visitors for the last eight years. She seems to be the only person he's got any real connection left with on the outside.'

'Hold on, Lis,' Archer answered, seeing the time. 'I told the Marshals from the bridge I'd call them about now. I'll see if they've got anything more on Frank while you're on the line.' He rested the receiver down and picked up the officer's phone. 'That OK?'

‘Long as I can listen,’ she said with a smile. He took the Marshal’s card off the counter, where he’d placed it beside his damp wallet and phone, and called him on speaker. All the other diners had paid and were already gone, just the server and the two cops left. ‘It’s Archer from the bridge, Deputy. What’s the latest?’

‘We just got prisoner Gallagher on his way to custody. Others still missing.’

‘Nothing on the brothers or Lupinetti?’

‘We might have something. State troopers lost contact with a roadblock almost an hour north of here. Arriving units just found someone blasted their way through. Four more troopers dead.’ Archer closed his eyes. *‘That kind of firepower, not a stretch to guess who mighta been responsible.’*

‘Still need me to stick around?’

‘Not as long as we can still raise you.’

‘My phone should dry out soon. I’ll check in if not. Thanks.’ He ended the call and picked up the landline. ‘You hear that?’ he asked Marquez.

‘I did. Murder across state lines. This case is getting bigger by the hour.’

‘And Reyes is now out there somewhere too.’ Archer was intrigued by the man’s involvement and glanced up at the screen as his prison mugshot was shown again. ‘Kat O’Mara’s license says she lives in Cleveland.’

‘That’s where Reyes grew up. Prison staff informed the Marshals about his escape and they’re directing some of their people to her home to keep her under surveillance in case he shows up.’

‘He seems too smart for that.’

‘He broke out of here somehow without anyone noticing. Tell me about it.’

'I don't think sending Prez to the SHU is gonna work, Cap,' the sergeant reasoned at Gatlin, Marquez catching their exchange. 'And we need the extra cells for the boys who attacked other inmates. Let's throw him back in C Block. He's gonna be under lockdown anyway.'

'Whatever, just get him out of here,' the captain snapped, the discovery of Reyes' escape the final kick in the groin for the day. A riot, two dead COs, four prisoners on the run and a growing number of dead law-enforcement and civilians as a result, all technically on his watch.

Marquez watched as Rainey was led back towards C Block by a couple of the riot officers and CO Anderson; this time the biker club president didn't make eye contact with her. 'Reyes must have lost part of his mind in here,' the sergeant told her. 'Six days to go and he bolts. He just added another five to ten years at least once we catch him.'

Marquez was still observing Prez being walked away, but then looked at the sergeant in surprise as she caught what he'd just said. '*Six days?*' she repeated. 'Reyes only had six days left on his sentence?'

Beside the sergeant, CO Williams nodded. 'Twelve years in here, and he was being released on Wednesday. Guess he's not as clever as everyone thinks he is.'

Beside Archer, the Charleston officer in the diner had just received a call from her dispatcher and turned to pick up her filled thermos. With the fugitives still out there in the area, she had a long night ahead of answering usual callouts, as well as assisting in the searches if required. 'Good to meet you, man,' he told him quickly, shaking his hand. 'Hope you catch your guy.'

'I will. Thanks for the clothes and letting me use your cell.' The officer then left, meaning Archer and the server were now the only people in the diner.

‘TV said that guy’s from Ohio,’ the server asked. ‘Why’s he serving time down in Virginia?’

‘He was found guilty of a federal crime,’ Archer explained. ‘Means you can get transferred to any federal facility across the country. State crimes get you locked in a state pen for your sentence.’ He checked the time. ‘You know if there’s somewhere I can rent a car around here?’

‘You’ll have to wait until morning, man. Hire places would’ve shut hours ago. We got a few hotels in town that you could crash at.’

‘Sleep’s gonna have to wait.’ Archer thought for a moment. ‘Where’s the nearest airport?’

‘Yeager. About a twenty five minute drive.’

‘I might still be able to get a car there. I’ll give you forty bucks if you give me a ride over.‘ Archer looked at the contents of his wallet, spread out on the table to dry, and found another ten dollar bill stuck to his driving license. He peeled it off. ‘Make that fifty.’

The guy took him up on the deal and closed up as Archer used the landline before they left to doublecheck the rental company at Yeager was still open. The place shut at midnight so he booked a vehicle on his credit card and forty minutes later, Archer walked across the parking lot at the airport and climbed into a black Cadillac ATS. Refueled with food, in dry clothes but dog-tired from the day and still half deaf in his right ear, he keyed the engine, turning on the radio to hear the latest news updates.

Nicky Reyes’ escape was the hot news, Craig Loughlin’s replacement in the *Gatlin Four* as they were now being referred to. As Archer listened to the report, turning it up so he could hear clearly, he glanced at the time on the dashboard.

It was 11:51pm; Reyes had won himself half a day to get out of Virginia before the guards and State Police got wise to his absence, but Archer was convinced he was the guy whose voice he'd heard in the 911 recording concerning the laundry truck driver. No-one aside from possibly his cellmate had known Reyes was out of the prison at that point.

But he'd jeopardized all that to try and save the truck driver's life?

Archer had also called Marquez from the server's phone on the way to the airport to brief her on his plans and it was then she'd informed him about how much time Nicky had left on his sentence. Breaking out of federal prison six days before the end of a twelve year bid, then calling an ambulance for a driver who'd got sliced up in the breakout. It made no sense.

However, as mysterious as the guy's motivations were, Archer nudged thoughts of Reyes' escape to the back of his mind, refocusing on Lupinetti. He tried to power up his cell again, but it was still dead. Tossing it onto the passenger seat in the hope it would eventually dry out, five minutes later Archer was pulling onto the highway and settled in for the dark drive ahead, keeping the radio on for news updates between music tracks.

Frank was with the Loughlins, and the roadblock that Archer heard had been shot to pieces was north on Route 68, not far from the I-77 highway and a few miles from the Ohio border.

The brothers and Lupinetti seemed to be going north, not east.

So that was exactly where Archer was heading too.

SIXTEEN

Marquez had returned to the Quality Inn where she and Archer had stayed the previous night, driving the still-defective NYPD Ford cautiously, guessing it was most likely her fault the car was playing up; she'd been more than annoyed at the prospect of having to see Frank Lupinetti again when she'd first set out from Queens at Shepherd's request yesterday, and had taken her frustration out on the gas pedal, pushing it hard on the highway on her way to pick up Archer. She'd offer to pay for the repair herself first thing tomorrow if it turned out to be something she could have been responsible for, but her punishment was to be stuck here for the night.

The riot, lockdown and search for fugitives in the area meant a few Labor Day weekend bookings at the Inn had been cancelled at the last minute, so it had been easy to extend her stay. She walked back into the same room she'd used the night before, kicked off her shoes then poured a travel-size bottle of tequila into a plastic cup she found in the bathroom, dropping a cube of ice into it from a small container she stepped out to fill from the machine down the corridor.

Clicking on the TV for some background noise, she then sunk into a chair, the network this time showing an old Clint Eastwood flick. The local news on Channel 11 would be running fresh updates on the manhunts but she wanted a brief respite from the day's events. As she drank some of the mezcal and watched Clint get into a barfight, she realized she could still smell the prison on her clothing and in her hair. Undressing, she took a shower and after changing into a fresh t-shirt and jeans, bit into a plastic-boxed quesadilla from the hospital's cafeteria that she'd bought before leaving.

She was just starting to dry her hair when she heard her cell phone ring. 'Ethan, I've had the day of days, man,' she told one of the Bureau analysts after answering, his number from his desk saved to her phone and showing up as the caller ID. 'I'm not in the city right now. Can it wait?'

'I've got a guy on the line saying he wants to talk to you. Said you two spoke earlier about a riot inside Gatlin prison? He says you'll know who he is. You met in the chow hall first thing this morning.'

Back inside his cell, Prez took another careful look along the upper and lower tiers, C Block dark now with no sign of any COs. The second cell count and discovery of Freddy Janks had disrupted the lockdown but the prisoners had settled in again, waiting for the long hours to pass until they could shower, get fed and be allowed back out into the yard.

However, Prez wasn't resting up so easily; with the man who'd been his celly for almost twelve years missing and with him claiming no knowledge of Reyes' escape, he knew the guards, warden, federal agents and other investigators who'd be at Gatlin tomorrow weren't done with him by a long stretch.

'Rainey?' Marquez asked, the surprise in her voice evident.

'Loud and clear,' he said quietly, his contraband smartphone in his hand. The phone had been smuggled in almost three years ago; ever since his daughter had died without him knowing during the time he'd been stuck in the SHU for a week, Prez had wanted the ability to communicate with the outside world whenever he felt like it and for people out there to be able to contact him. It made providing leadership for his brothers in the motorcycle club easier too, rather than having to wait for scheduled visits with COs present who tried to overhear what was said. He wasn't the only inmate who had a phone either. Most were found; some weren't, and he was one of the lucky ones.

'How'd you know to call my division in New York?'

'Saw your badge when we sat down to talk. Had Counter-Terrorism Bureau on it.'

'Someone's gonna hear you.'

'Think you're the first person I've called from in here?' he whispered, going to the back of his cell and stepping behind a sheet from the empty top bunk that he'd hung up to dampen the noise of his voice. 'Long as the screws don't come back, we're straight.'

'Why are you calling me?'

'I think those pendejos in the chow hall earlier might've had me pretty good, but you and your friend took care of that. Means I owe you. That's the code in here.'

'C'mon man, don't try me. When we talked earlier, your mouth was closed tighter than two homies who grew up on the same block.'

'In front of the cap and other COs, yeah. But just because I'm locked up don't mean I don't have honor, lady. You got an opportunity here. I'll give you some answers if you still got questions.'

'What's your benefit?'

'I got time to pass. And you earned some more information than the screws.'

A pause followed. '*Your missing celly seems clever, but no-one with a functioning brain would be dumb enough to break out so close to their release. He only had six days left, right?'*

'That's right.'

'He just earned himself another load of time back inside when he gets found. Might even have reset the clock on his bid.'

'He had his reasons.'

'Was he in danger?'

'We all are, in here.'

'But he couldn't stick around until next week? After surviving almost twelve years?'

'Correct.'

A pause. *'Can you tell me when he started planning this? A month ago?'*

'Sooner.'

'A week?'

'Sooner.'

'Three days?' Marquez asked, Prez hearing the rising incredulity in her voice.

'Sooner.'

'Jesus, Rainey, a day?'

Prez didn't answer. Silence as confirmation.

'If you're not leading me, he worked out a way to break out of a high-security federal prison over the course of a single night?'

No answer.

'He had a big head start on us. I don't think he's even in Virginia anymore. You won't be betraying him or his friends if you tell me how the hell he managed that.'

'The Loughlins ain't his friends, lady. They've wanted a piece of him since the first day he got here.'

*

Eleven years, three hundred and fifty nine days ago, the journey from the Cuyahoga County Jail in Ohio to USP Gatlin took a slow, nerve-wracking nine hours, the bus transporting the prisoners similar to the one Archer would travel on years later.

Nicky Reyes had been on some long road trips before, most of them with his father when they used to go camping all over the Midwest on weekends to escape the rough neighborhood they were living in, but he'd never been scared on one before. And when the eighteen year old saw the gun-towers, razor wire, pale gray walls and huge fences of his new home for the next decade, the triviality of any other problems he'd thought he had hit him like a shotgun blast. Many convicts who made it through sentences in state or federal prison would boast that they were never afraid, but arriving at Gatlin that afternoon was the most frightening thing Nicky had ever experienced in his eighteen years. Until later on that night.

Once the bus stopped, he was led out with five other inmates before instructions were barked at them. 'Stop at the sally port!' 'Address me as *sir*!' 'Strip down*!*' 'Get moving!*' He hadn't seen any other prisoners in the yard when they'd arrived but Nicky heard shouting and catcalling coming from cells in the blocks nearby, indicating they knew a busload of new guys had just shown up.*

Taking off his county jail jumps, Nicky watched them get swept up and collected by the guards, and he stood there naked alongside the other new prisoners, the floor icy under his bare feet. He was the youngest of the line-up; the guy next to him looked a couple of years older and Nicky had noticed him starting to shake throughout the last hour of the ride here. 'Ah Christ, don't piss on our floor!' one of the guards said, Nicky seeing urine streaming down the inmate's leg, and as it pooled out, some of the liquid reached his cold left foot.

At that point, Nicky retreated to somewhere inside his head, trying to find an escape from the complete lack of dignity, the ammonia smell of urine, the fast beating of his heart and the fear that he was trying to keep concealed and prevent from paralyzing him. But there wasn't anywhere to hide except just to draw into himself like a terrified animal caught in a cage. He was checked for contraband in every major orifice and then was unceremoniously handed a set of prison-issue boxers which he pulled on quickly. Next thing he knew, a hard-faced woman with a cloud of red hair and who reeked of cigarette smoke was asking him questions while she filled out a form; then he was given his jumpsuit, basic canvas shoes and marched through the prison into C Block towards his waiting cell.

As he walked through a torrent of jeers and profanity from the other cells, Nicky was just relieved he'd been given the pair of boxers, not marched in naked like he'd seen in some movies. He was led to a cell on the upper southside tier, pushed inside and five seconds later, the grilled barred door slid closed behind him.

His mouth was bone-dry; he tried to swallow, but couldn't. He turned and saw a dark-haired bearded man lying on the lower bunk, reading a magazine. He had tattoos on his arms and was much bigger than Nicky.

'Welcome to prison, kid,' the man said nonchalantly, turning the page on his magazine.

Gatlin C Block's newest and youngest resident only managed to force down a mouthful of food at chow, sitting alone, and was still awake at midnight when his cell door was unlocked and then quietly slid open on its greased hinges.

Turning his head, Nicky saw two figures illuminated by the moonlight coming in through the cell's window. One of them was around his size, the other enormous, and he could see they both had their eyes on him, the smaller one holding something made of fabric that was dragging on the ground.

'Wakey, wakey,' the bigger one said, stepping into the cell. But then a voice quietly spoke from the bunk below.

'Lay a finger on him and I'll break every bone in your hand, Billy.'

'Stay out of this, Prez,' the giant answered, as Nicky backed up on his bunk in terror. 'We get to pop his cherry.'

'One more step into the cell, I'll kill you both.'

'You ain't serving life, Rainey. You're talking real big for a guy who got busted moving around Tec-9s and-' But before Billy Loughlin could speak further, the man in the bunk below Nicky was on his feet and had him up against the wall, a sharpened pen pushed against his neck. The smaller man holding the scrunched-up garment of clothing dropped it and moved forward, but Nicky's cellmate pressed the shiv harder, eliciting a panicked gargle as he drew a stream of blood from the shiv.

'Want to explain to Brooks how you got his little brother killed, Hoffmeier?'

'Let him go.'

'We stay clear of each other,' Prez told Billy. 'That's always been the deal. Now it includes anyone I share a cell with.'

'You claiming him?'

'You sure as hell ain't.' Prez hauled Billy to the door and shoved him roughly onto the tier before grabbing Hoffmeier and doing the same, kicking out the garment the latter had been carrying. Prez glanced down and although he couldn't see any of the COs, knew immediately which one was likely to have opened their door. The two men slunk off back into the dark cell block, taking the article of clothing with them, as Nicky looked fearfully at the big man who'd just protected him. The guy turned and tossed

him the shiv. 'You got first watch, kid. Wake me up in a couple hours and I'll take over. They might be back.'

Nicky's first night in prison was the longest of his life. He didn't wake the bigger man so had stayed up until the pink early morning light of dawn started shining through their window, holding that shiv and waiting for the two inmates to return.

They never did.

*

In Cleveland, the woman who'd visited Nicky at the prison, his sister according to visitor records, had just arrived at her home in the westside Clark-Fulton neighborhood and took out her keys as she walked up to her door. Federal deputies watched her every step from various concealed positions; they'd been on her for several hours.

'Keep eyes on the street. Be ready for an approach,' an Asian American US Marshal from their Cleveland headquarters instructed over his radio, sitting some distance down the street in an unmarked car. 'Guy escaped from Gatlin ten hours ago. He could be in Ohio already.'

'She looks edgy.'

'I would too, living down here.'

Kat O'Mara glanced around the street as she opened her door. The deputy was right; she did look anxious. 'Chief wants us staked on the place all night,' the lead Marshal said into his radio once she'd gone inside and closed the door. 'And the phone tapped first thing tomorrow morning. Virginia's saying this guy Reyes has got no other contacts on the outside other than this chick.'

'We'll need a warrant for the tap.'

'Chief'll get that and then we'll get Reyes. He'll try to raise this girl. Clear as day.'

*

'Why didn't you wake me?' Prez asked Nicky the morning after that long first night, as the inmates were waiting to be released from their cells for breakfast. Nicky had already returned the shiv, his cellmate secreting it behind their basin.

'You did enough. Why'd you step in like that?' he asked in reverse.

'Wanted a full night's sleep.' Nicky knew that wasn't quite the whole truth and smiled at the bigger man. 'Don't look at me like that, kid.'

'Like what?'

'Like you owe me one. Don't let the animals in here ever see that. You can't show any weakness in this place. Wrap those feelings up, lock 'em in a box and save it for when you get out.'

The smile gone, Nicky looked out at the lower tier, and saw the two men who'd come for him in the night standing near the bars in their cells, watching him. 'What's to stop them coming back tonight?'

'We'll take shifts until I can talk to the sergeant. He's got a Triumph I helped repair for him so he owes me. Couple of the COs can be bought like you saw last night, but they won't risk getting caught. Most of them are OK.'

'What are you in for?' Nicky asked, as the doors opened. 'Guy last night mentioned moving around g-'

'Two places where you gotta have eyes in the back of your head,' Rainey told him, ignoring the question. 'Chow hall and the showers. Don't hang around. Eat fast and shower faster.'

The truth of the biker's warnings became evident very quickly; within ten minutes, in fact. The two inmates from the night before came for Nicky again at breakfast and this time they weren't looking for love.

The eighteen year old was in the food hall with a tray, almost at his turn at the front of the line, when he saw the closest CO who'd been watching the prisoners suddenly turn away. Nicky had noticed during dinner the previous night that there were only four of the guards on duty in here, with about a hundred inmates. His cellmate's warning rang in his ears. The CO had turned his back for a reason.

Someone had left a large metal wheeled container used to transport empty trays just ahead of the line. Its polished end was facing Nicky, allowing him to see what was going on behind him, and in the container's dull reflection, he picked up the two inmates from the previous night, Derek Hoffmeier and Billy Loughlin, as they stepped out of the line and started moving towards him. He knew he was in trouble and this time was going to have to fight them off on his own.

His eyes darted around quickly, to anything within reach that he could use. One of the inmates working the other side of the counter, placing packets of oatmeal, slices of bread and packets of grape jelly and margarine onto trays, had a drink beside his hand. From his time in the county jail back in Ohio, Nicky recognized it as a 'prison latte', a carton of milk stuck under a faucet of hot water before instant coffee and maple syrup was added. Hot, sticky liquid. Nicky saw steam coming out of the opened carton, which told him it was freshly made.

Lunging forward, he grabbed the milk carton and in one swift turn slammed it up into Billy Loughlin's face just as the man was about to rip into Nicky's torso with a shank. The latte wasn't hot enough to cause serious burns, but the shock of a face-full of hot milk, coffee and syrup was enough to stop the huge man for a moment. In that following second, Nicky gripped his tray and smashed it into Hoffmeier's chin, repeating the action with Billy

Loughlin before shoving them both back. Billy fell into the other inmates who pushed him away as he wiped his eyes, still unable to see. Prisoners started to shout as the fight caught the attention of those already sitting down, but before the two men could hit back at Nicky, more COs joined the other others in the hall and ran forward to separate the three inmates, taking them out of the chow hall.

It had cost him breakfast, and he was starving after barely eating the night before, but Nicky felt like he'd made a statement and knew the whole of the block had seen it. On his way back to his cell, he glanced into the open cells on the north side, and saw the garment that had been in Hoffmeier's hand last night, dumped on the floor: a dirty, blood-stained white dress.

The sight of how ludicrous it looked there made him smile for the first time since he'd arrived here yesterday.

But then it occurred to him what they'd intended it for.

*

A small pool of condensation had suctioned Marquez's tequila to the desk in her motel room. She felt as cold as the ice inside the glass. 'Do I wanna know?' she asked.

'Billy, Hoff and sometimes Kattar used to have a tradition to welcome the new boys,' Prez told her. *'Back then, any fresh meat who caught their eye had the dress pulled on before they were raped on their first night. Sometimes, it happened every day to the same new fish for a couple months.'*

Without looking at the cup, Marquez pulled it off the desk and took a mouthful before setting the drink back down. 'But not to Nicky.'

'*No. What he did to Billy at chow that morning dictated terms between him and the brothers. That shit's never changed since.'* Still listening closely, Marquez rose to pour herself the second of her two mini tequila bottles, brought down with her from New York in her bag. '*Billy targeted the kid just like he had others since he'd been inside, but Nicky fought back, which Loughlin junior wasn't used to. Humiliated him in front of the whole cell block.'*

'Did he come at him again?'

'He tried. I kept an eye out and after a while he and Hoff gave up and focused on the other new guys instead. Billy and his brother both got released, so we thought that was the end of it, but then they ended up right back here again four years ago, this time for good. I wasn't surprised. Half of all the guys in the country who ever end up in prison end up getting sent back down at some point after they get out.'

'Their beef with Reyes wasn't just forgotten, I guess.'

'*Right, and something had changed with those two. They were real bad before, but once they killed that college girl? After that it's just numbers; can't get punished any worse than what the judge already gave them, apart from the needle. You get what I mean?'*

She did, aware before she'd been sent down here of Gatlin's rep as one of the most dangerous federal prisons in the country. An average of more than ten prisoners died prematurely in the facility every year and not all of them committed suicide. From what Prez was saying, Brooks and Billy were responsible for some of the deaths.

'Brooks didn't have anything personal going with the kid, he just took against him after he made a clown of his brother, and that family never drops a grudge. Any chance they could get they'd have cut him open, but Nicky learned fast. Made sure they couldn't get a shot. But right now if Brooks and Billy find out he used them to get out of here, they're gonna want more than to pop his cherry.'

'So he used them,' she said, noticing the detail Prez had let slip. 'Tell me how he busted out.'

'Not yet.'

'At least tell me why.'

'Why'd you think? To be free.'

'Bullshit, Rainey, he'd be a free man in less than week. Made it almost twelve years and he couldn't do another six days?'

'Call me tomorrow night and I'll tell you.'

'I thought you said this conversation squared us away?'

'I got time to kill and no-one else to talk to right now. Hit me up at 1pm. You work out how he got out of the prison, I'll tell you why he did it.'

SEVENTEEN

'*Police picked up two more guys from your bus last night,*' she told Archer the next morning, who was using a prepaid disposable phone he'd just bought at a gas station a few miles south of Cleveland, Ohio. His rental car from the airport last night was parked in a rest spot away from the pumps, now with a full tank. He was also realizing that people almost always held their phone to the same ear, including him, and had been forced to switch to his left thanks to his Sig Sauer going off an inch from the right. '*A black guy from Big Sandy and someone from USP Lee who they can't get to shut up.*'

'Yeah, he was making everyone's ears bleed.' Archer opened a canned energy drink and took a sip before placing it on the roof of the car. 'What about Nicky Reyes? He's the only one no-one has seen since this all began.'

'The roadblocks that Highway Patrol and other authorities set up haven't scored anything. He might still be down here in southern Virginia for all we know. Waiting for things to settle.'

'He gave himself a huge head start to get out of the area. Someone smart enough to break out of federal prison without anyone noticing wouldn't be dumb enough not to use that time effectively, right?'

'Well, his anonymity's about to end. His photo's on the news in Ohio this morning, same as all over West Virginia, Kentucky, North Carolina and Tennessee. But everyone here's assuming he's heading for Cleveland to meet the girl who used to visit him in prison.'

'Not if he's as bright as he appears to be.' Archer had called the Marshal deputy from the bridge again earlier, using another gas station's payphone when he was just over the WV-Ohio State Line, and had learned there'd been two suspected sightings of the Loughlin brothers and Lupinetti during the night. The first hotline call came from outside Canton, the other two hours later further north on a road outside Akron by a trucker who thought he'd seen them in a car waiting at a red light. Archer had checked a map he'd bought in the rental office at the airport and saw if the sightings were accurate and the brothers and Frank kept following that path, they'd be arriving in Cleveland sometime this morning. If that was a coincidence or not, he wasn't quite sure yet. But something about this felt peculiar. 'Any fresh tips on the brothers and Frank?'

'Nothing yet. Looks like Brooks and Billy have managed not to kill anyone for a few hours, so no idea where they are right now.' Archer walked across the gas station forecourt to the window and saw the TV on the wall inside was playing an episode of some soap opera. The clerk working the counter was about to ring up a trucker buying some coffee and a sandwich when Archer showed his badge and pointed at the television.

'*News*?' he mouthed. The guy understood and changed the channel. Archer watched until the four fugitives' photos flashed up, Craig's photo replaced with Nicky's. 'Reyes looks pretty young, Lis,' he said, looking at the newest addition to the line-up. 'Taking another look at his mugshot on the TV.'

'They're using the photo from when he first went into prison. Not like he's needed a new driving license for the last twelve years or anything. Guards say his hair's grown out some and his face has matured, obviously.'

Archer nodded. Hard time would put years on a man's face; especially somewhere like Gatlin. 'That'll come in useful for him. And I get why Reyes might be heading to Cleveland,' he added, looking at the screen one last time before returning towards his car. 'But if we're right, what's the sudden draw in the city for the other three?'

'No idea,' Marquez replied, speaking to Archer from an auto-shop she'd sourced in Jonesville, watching as the NYPD Ford was examined. She'd already made sure to secure the compartment holding the weapons in the trunk. 'I can't get a clear view on a lot of this.'

'How'd that laundry truck driver make out?'

'He's hanging on. I called the hospital soon as I woke up first thing. Whoever out of the two Loughlins cut him sliced his vocal cords but missed his arteries. He was at death's door and about to start knocking but looks like our man who called 911 and wadded jumpsuits to his neck saved his life.'

'Reyes. It must've been.'

'Wouldn't have been the Loughlins, that's for goddamn sure.'

'Do we know yet how Reyes broke out?'

'I'm working on it,' she said, glancing at her watch and remembering Prez's deal: if she figured out how the man's celly escaped, he'd tell her why he chose to do it so close to release. That information could prove very useful to investigators trying to catch all the fugitives, so she intended to keep the conversation going for the time being. She suspected he wasn't talking to her just because he was bored, but was using her to try and find out what the police currently knew; two could play that game.

'How's the Ford?'

'Dunno, hang on. *How long's it gonna take*?' she called out to one of the mechanics working on the NYPD vehicle.

‘Couple hours,’ he said, stopping to walk over as he wiped his hands on a rag. ‘You got an issue with the fuel pump. We gotta do some work then hook it up to a tablet to clear the fault.’

‘I’m gonna leave and come back if that’s cool.’

‘Sure, write down your number,’ he said, taking a clipboard off a table and pinning a sheet onto it. ‘I’ll hit you up when it’s ready.’

‘It’ll be good in a couple hours, Arch. I’ll call you back.’ She scribbled down her number, then handed the board back. ‘You know where the local police impound is?’ she asked the mechanic. He did, and ten minutes later she was in a cab heading over there, wanting to see if they’d let her examine the laundry truck found off the highway yesterday.

You might find something useful that could help the case, she tried to tell herself, but really it was because she was extremely curious about how all this had played out. There was a reason she was considered a top-tier detective; when something caught her attention, it really took hold, and she didn’t drop it until she got answers. Right now, she wanted to know one thing.

How the hell Nicky Reyes had managed to get himself onto the truck and out of the prison without being seen by either the Loughlins or the prison COs?

‘If Lupinetti thought he had it bad before, he better just wait until we catch him,’ Shepherd told Archer, who’d called him in New York City straight after speaking to Marquez. *‘He couldn’t be held responsible for when these brothers attacked the bus on the bridge, but he was right there with them when they blasted their way out of the State and killed more troopers last night. They left a roadblock on one of the routes leading out of West Virginia in shreds. Everything shot up. It was a massacre.’*

'I still don't know Frank and those two got so friendly.'

'He must've promised them something to keep himself alive in Gatlin. And be significant enough for them to take the trouble to get him off that bus. The two brothers don't seem the philanthropic type so he'd need to earn his way. Whatever the reason, the Marshals called earlier. Wanted any possible contacts Lupinetti might try to reach here if he comes this way.'

'Could be a few he hasn't pissed off or double-crossed. He lived in New York his whole life before he got busted.' Archer had suffered enough of the energy drink and threw it into a trash can nearby. 'The deputies tell you what they're doing right now?'

'Laying traps. The Loughlins are from a town called Red Creek not far from Syracuse so police upstate have been warned to keep a close lookout. The Marshals' office in Cleveland has had people on Nicky Reyes' sister's place all night. They snare the guy, he could give up where the Loughlins and our man Frank might be heading. Seems like they're all involved in this escape somehow.'

'The sister had any visitors?'

'No-one all night, they said. Not even her roommate showed up.'

'If the girl has a job somewhere, Reyes could try her there if she's working today.'

'Let the Marshals handle her, Arch. Reyes isn't our problem, Lupinetti is. Your assignment's still to get him back alive, but these brothers seem the type to go down shooting. Federal deputies and local cops won't care too much if Frank catches a bullet and gets killed too. If you and Lisa can get to him first, more of a chance we can stop him getting himself toe-tagged.'

'I just arrived in Cleveland. I'll set up in the city and wait for another sighting. They might be bypassing here to peel west to Michigan or east to Pennsylvania. But I'm on a prepaid, boss. Take down the number.' He read it out from the packaging still sitting on the passenger seat.

'*Dried out yet after your dip in the river?'*

'Just about.' Archer looked down at his slightly too-big sweater with the Virginia Tech University logo on the front. 'But I've ended up looking like a college grad.'

A brief chuckle came down the phone. *'What you talking about?'*

Archer smiled. 'Not important. I'll be in touch,' he added before ending the call. With law-enforcement across numerous States searching for the fugitives and time of his own to kill until another sighting of Lupinetti came in, the prospect of a hotel room with a hot shower was very tempting. But as he got back into the car, Archer looked down at his borrowed clothing then at his own still-sodden jeans, sweater and jacket screwed up in a plastic bag in the passenger footwell.

One more stop needed to be made before he found a hotel. 'You owe me a new set of clothes, Frank,' he muttered, before starting the engine and pulling out of the gas station to head onwards into Cleveland proper.

EIGHTEEN

On the westside of the city in Clark-Fulton, two men in Spectrum uniform were standing outside Kat O'Mara's residence.

'*Hello*?' one of them called, knocking loudly on the door for the third time. He stepped to the side and cupped his hand as he put it on the glass, shielding his eyes from the reflection as he peered inside. Having repairmen show up unannounced to check the phoneline a day after someone you considered family went missing from federal prison was a pretty damn obvious tell, but the Marshals had managed to get the apartment's electricity shut off by the provider. O'Mara and her roommate had been late on payments before, so there was a chance it could pass unquestioned.

'She might be asleep,' their lead deputy ordered over their earpieces. '*Try agai-*'

'*Yo man, shut that shit up!*' a neighbor called, leaning out of a window next door to yell at the two men. '*It's the weekend!*'

'Austin, you didn't see this girl leave?' the Marshal who'd been knocking asked, turning his back so he could speak into his sleeve mic while his partner apologized to the irate man next door to try to calm him down and avoid attracting unwanted attention.

'*Yeah, I just forgot to mention it,*' their team member who'd been on stakeout all night replied sarcastically, having assumed the role of a homeless drunk slumped against a wall down the street for the past ten hours. *'The girl hasn't left and I haven't seen her roommate.'*

'Well if she isn't inside, she must've slipped out somehow without you noticing.'

'Or she's in bed with a hangover.'

'Or she's seen the news about Reyes and will guess she's under surveillance. Won't answer.'

'Just try again,' their lead ordered. The undercover deputies knocked again, still with no response from Kat's apartment, so one of them used a lock key to get the door open and the pair moved inside, closing it behind them quickly.

After a quick check around, one of them got back on his radio. 'She's not here, Chief. Neither's the other girl. Name's Erica Till. We ran her ID and she's got a criminal history too, same as Katherine O'Mara. Served two stints inside ORW for burglary.'

'We gotta find O'Mara. Reyes is gonna try and raise her. She's all he's got outside the prison walls, so plant the bugs and get out.' As one of the deputies unpacked their gear and started installing listening devices and cameras in case she came back or Reyes turned up, the other took a closer look around the place.

He found the back door was unlocked and swore; it opened onto a very narrow alley which a slender woman could easily slip down, with a tall fence at the end that could be scaled too with some effort. The Marshals had only had coverage on the front, not thinking anyone could squeeze out the back way, but it appeared they'd been wrong. Looking around, the deputy noticed something else too: the kitchen cupboards and fridge were almost completely empty. It meant either Katherine O'Mara and her roommate ate out a lot, which living in this area on what must have been a small income wasn't likely, or something else. He checked the closets in the two small bedrooms and saw both were also pretty much cleared out too, confirming his suspicions.

Apparently the two women weren't planning on coming back here again any time soon.

Over on the eastside of town, in the inner-ring city suburb of Cleveland Heights, a black and white CHPD squad car was parked on the side of the road, the two officers inside each eating a breakfast burrito one of their wives had made for the pair, when there came a tap on the window.

The cop in the driver's seat turned to find himself looking at a man wearing a jacket, jeans and sunglasses. '*Officers, can you help me out with somethin'?*' he asked, his voice muffled by the closed window. The officer lowered it.

'What's wrong?'

'I gotta get into my business this morning but there's some bum drunk off his ass who won't let me get to the door. Think if I keep tryin' to get past, he's gonna start throwing hands.'

The pair immediately put their food down, got out of the car, and followed the individual down an alleyway. Being a possible minor disturbance not yet confirmed, they didn't radio anything in to Dispatch. 'Where is he?' one asked.

Instead of answering, Frank Lupinetti stood to one side as Billy Loughlin stepped out from a doorway and shot one of the officers in the face with the concealed carry revolver he'd collected from the West Virginia couple they'd killed last night, using his prison jumpsuit top as a rolled-up suppressor to muffle the sound. Brooks emerged from behind a dumpster at the same time and broke the neck of the other as fast as he'd killed the woman passenger the previous night.

Once the two cops were splayed out on the ground, Lupinetti turned to keep watch on the mouth of the alley as the Loughlins started stripping the pair. Billy sucked in his stomach less than a minute later to try and zip up the first cop's pants, already wearing the shirt with the buttons open. 'How we fatter than them and we been in the joint for the last four years?'

Brooks didn't waste time replying as he pulled on the other cop's overshirt; it didn't quite fit either, but no-one would see that with them riding in the squad car. With their uniforms removed, the two cops were left dumped face down in the alley. Billy finished adjusting and fixing his belt, as his big brother checked the magazine on the Glock taken from one of the dead officers before slotting the pistol into his holster.

'Move the rest of the guns into the cruiser then follow us,' he ordered Lupinetti. The ex-NYPD lieutenant turned and ran back to their car as the two Loughlins dragged the dead cops' bodies out of sight behind the dumpsters, then returned to the police vehicle. As they got inside, Lupinetti pulled up behind them in the car they'd stolen from the couple in West Virginia late last night; he glanced around to make sure there was no-one observing them, then quickly transferred their stockpile of weapons and ammo from the truck to the squad cruiser.

While Billy took one of the rifles, double checking it was loaded before doing the same with a shotgun, Brooks used the squad car's screen to draw up a map of downtown, looking for a certain cross-street. He found it, checked the time then moved off, Lupinetti following behind in the other ride.

It was just coming up to 11am.

As the Marshals were in the process of bugging Kat O'Mara's home in Clark-Fulton, and the Loughlin brothers were driving through the city streets in the stolen squad car with Lupinetti following close behind, Archer was just taking some clothes up to the register of a downtown store.

And at the same time all this was happening, an armored truck on its way to the downtown Morningstar bank in the city's Public Square stopped at a red light on East Superior Avenue. Waves of morning traffic often ebbed and flowed, and there weren't as many vehicles around on this holiday weekend, so only a few cars were currently positioned at the intersection. The driver in the armored truck was drumming his fingers on the wheel as he listened to a Doobie Brothers song on the radio, his partner keeping an eye on the street while he drank coffee.

A small team of construction workers were working on a site beside them, only ten feet or so from the intersection. A pear-shaped wrecking ball hanging from a small crane and attached to a lifting hook was positioned facing a building, its steel rope already having pulled and locked the ball in place towards the cab. One of the workers was sitting behind the controls.

'Wake up,' the truck driver said, stopping tapping the wheel to *What a Fool Believes* to lean on the horn instead. The car in front hadn't moved off at the green light, but because they were focused on the vehicle in front, the two men didn't notice the crane beside them start to turn.

The driver and passenger were both just starting to get suspicious when the wrecking ball was released.

It swung down fast towards the armored truck, the intersection in a final moment of quiet.

Then the three-ton ball smashed into the side of the vehicle, and any sense that this was going to be a normal Saturday morning was obliterated.

NINETEEN

'Mind if I use the changing room?' Archer asked the cashier in front of him, who'd just rung his purchases up and passed him a receipt for a new pair of jeans, t-shirt, boxers, socks and black sweater.

'Sure.' She took the bag back and clipped off the price-tags on the clothes. 'Just keep the receipt in case you get stopped at the door. Don't want anyone to accuse you of stealing,' she added with a smile.

'Me neither. Thanks.' He walked back across the store and went into a private stall before closing the door. He was grateful to the Charleston cop's husband for providing him with his current set of clothes, but the new items were fresh off the rack and fit much better. He swapped what he was wearing, re-tied his brown Timberlands which had just about dried out, bagged the old items, then making sure he had the receipt he exited the store, raising a hand to the woman at the checkout as he left.

He dropped the old clothes in a trash can and returned to his rental parked beside a meter. But just as he was reaching for the door handle, he stopped and lifted his head.

The sound of harsh bangs could suddenly be heard echoing from somewhere in the distance.

He might have been dressed much like other men on the street, but the wealth of experience Archer had gained over the years since he'd been a cop meant that unlike them, not only did he recognize the noise that had others looking around uncertainly.

But he immediately reacted to it.

Ninety seconds earlier, around the time Archer had been paying at the checkout, the force of the released wrecking ball had knocked the armored truck on E Superior Avenue off its wheels and straight onto its side, the two men sitting up front hurled sideways in the cab with only their seatbelts saving them from serious injury.

The ball jangled and came to a shuddering stop on its steel chain, most of its force from the downswing delivered into the heavy truck. The three individuals who'd appeared to be working on the construction site beside the road abandoned what they were doing, each pulling a fully-loaded M11 9mm auto from where they'd had the firearms concealed and ran forward, keeping their sunglasses and hardhats on to mask their identity from cameras and passers-by. One of them went to the cab of the truck just as the two dazed individuals inside were starting to try and release themselves from their seatbelts; he pulled the pin on a smoke grenade and dropped it in through the broken window before the pair inside could reach for their sidearms or the radio to call it in.

As smoke started to fill the cab, a large silver Hyundai swung onto the street and reversed up to the truck, a slender figure in a ski-mask behind the wheel. At the same time, another female leapt out from the car that had been stalling at the green light in front of the armored vehicle, but rather than a firearm, she was carrying two rolled-up holdalls and a chain. As smoke poured from the toppled truck's cab, coughing and sputtering coming from the two disoriented men inside, she looped and locked one end of the chain to the already-damaged rear doors of the truck, before fixing the other to the rear of the Hyundai that had just pulled up.

Once it was secured, she hit the back of the car twice and the driver floored it.

The chain snapped taut and with the tires spinning to gain traction on the asphalt, it ripped the rear door of the truck further open. The men who'd been posing as construction workers had separated on the street with their submachine guns raised, covering the other vehicles that had either stopped or were frantically backing up, a few people on the sidewalks braving it out to film on their phones, the more sensible ones running for safety.

The woman who'd attached the chains went to the back of the truck, carrying the two empty holdalls, but then encountered a hitch; she was no bigger than about a hundred and forty pounds, but even so, the hole wasn't quite big enough for her to squeeze inside.

The driver of the car saw the problem and put her foot down harder but the door wouldn't snap free or open any wider. *'What's taking so long?'* one of the construction workers yelled.

'I can't fit!'

The driver of the car got out and ran towards the truck; she was slighter than the other woman and after taking the bags and a flashlight from her, managed to slide through the small gap. By now some of the people who were witnessing the attack were using their cell phones to make calls to police rather than film the scene. The thieves had chosen this specific spot to hit the truck to give them various options at the intersection for their escape, but the seconds until the cops responded to the emergency calls were ticking by fast.

Inside the truck, Kat O'Mara was using the flashlight to rapidly check the numbers on the deposit boxes that had been stored inside. She found one that she wanted and quickly dragged it into one of the holdalls, then frantically started to search for the other.

'*WE NEED TO GO!*' she heard a voice shout from outside, her hands shaking from adrenaline as she tried to find the second and to her, most important box. They'd been stacked in numerical order but when the truck had been knocked over, the boxes on one side had been dislodged and were now strewn haphazardly all over the floor.

Then with a gasp, she found what she was looking for. Shoving it into the remaining bag, she made her way to the back of the truck, but a sudden outburst of gunfire and screams stopped her before she re-emerged into the daylight.

That first harsh burst of gunfire was what Archer had heard, and it was only when he'd jumped behind the wheel of his rental and instinctively started driving in the direction the noise was coming from that he remembered he wasn't in New York City and was an outsider in Cleveland, badge and sidearm regardless. However, that didn't deter him, particularly considering who he'd come to the city to find, and he kept going, following the sound as more gunfire echoed around these unfamiliar streets.

There were five people involved in breaking into the truck, and as she peered out of the crippled vehicle like an animal caught in a trap, through the smoke Kat O'Mara saw her four fellow thieves get cut down by two huge police officers who'd arrived at the intersection in a black and white CHPD squad car.

In horror, Kat saw the four fallen robbers getting hit again repeatedly; execution shots. The cops were using a shotgun and rifle, and all she had was a revolver in her pocket. Smoke from the grenade inside the cab was still flowing out of the broken windows which provided some cover, and Kat used the poor visibility to slide out of the truck and then start to run towards a narrow alleyway on her right.

Gunshots sounded again as this time bullets zipped around her through the smoke, a shotgun blast destroying a car windshield right beside her and making her flinch as she ran. One of the bags was proving too heavy for her to carry, knocking against her legs, and the holdall ended up dislodging the other lighter bag from her shoulder as it hit her thigh.

It fell to the concrete and she stopped to go back for it, but another sudden eruption of gunfire forced her to abandon the dropped holdall and scramble onwards towards the alleyway.

Having just gunned down the other thieves with his brother, Lupinetti covering their six, through the thickening smoke Brooks saw the woman drop one of the holdalls she'd been carrying. Real police units would be arriving at any moment so he knew they had to get clear of here right now, but not before they collected what they'd come for.

He whistled to Billy and pointed; his younger sibling ran forward through the thinning smoke and retrieved the bag. He stopped to look at the fallen truck for a moment, knowing there would be many more boxes inside, but then even his slow brain computed that neither he or his brother could squeeze through that small gap in the busted back door, and that the police would be here very soon.

He rushed back with the bag to join Brooks who was getting behind the wheel of their stolen cop car again.

'Let's split!' Billy told him, slamming himself inside too.

'Not yet,' Brooks replied, turning the car down a parallel street in the same direction that the one remaining thief had just run down.

Alone and terrified, Kat had reached a two-panel chain link fence halfway down the alley and pushed the bag through a gap before sliding through herself, looking behind her quickly and seeing the officers hadn't followed. She picked up the heavy bag again and kept going down the alleyway before emerging onto another street, but then found herself just fifty feet from the CHPD cop car which had just screeched to a halt to cut her off.

One of the large, bearded officers from East Superior was already halfway out of the driver's door.

And before she could react or think about moving, he lifted a rifle and fired at her.

Getting shot happened so fast, Kat didn't really register it. One instant she was fine, the next she was on the ground, feeling like she'd been smacked in the body with a baseball bat smeared with lidocaine. The huge CHPD officer who'd put her down her didn't have a chance to squeeze off another round as a Cleveland PD squad car braked with its tires squealing and reversed back onto the cross-street behind him. The man who'd shot Kat turned and engaged the occupants with his partner, reloading his rifle before continuing to shoot up the police cruiser. Even in her numbed, wounded state, she was confused and realized something was wrong; cops shooting on cops?

Forgotten for a few seconds in the melee, Kat managed to get back to her feet, dragging the bag behind her which suddenly felt ten times heavier. She made it to a blue mailbox, the only cover available near her, leaving drops of blood behind as she went, her ski-mask still covering her face.

She slumped to the ground, her back against the postal box, then pulled her mask off to help get her breath before looking down at the gunshot wound to her body. Blood was starting to soak through her sweater.

Archer arrived in time to see two groups of cops shooting at each other and a woman lying against a mailbox with a bag beside her, what looked like a gunshot wound to her torso. Positioned south of her and the officers firing on one another, he swung out of his rental car, drawing his Sig Sauer, and ran forward to take cover behind another parked vehicle while assessing what he was seeing and trying to make sense of it.

But Billy Loughlin had just looked around to see where Kat was, making sure she wasn't escaping, and caught sight of Archer moving up towards the parked car, at the same time that the NYPD detective saw him too; it would be hard to say which of the two men was more surprised when they instantly recognized each other from the bridge attack the previous night.

Billy shouted to his brother, who turned. Kat was forgotten as she cowered behind the mailbox, pain starting to radiate out from her side, as Archer came under intense fire from the two Gatlin fugitives now dressed as police officers. Before he'd ducked behind the car alongside him, he'd caught a glimpse of Lupinetti beside another vehicle which had just pulled up, now engaging with the police to keep them busy.

And then, one final player arrived at the scene.

Unnoticed by anyone, a car had just slid to a halt on an adjacent street, the driver having been following the sound of the gunshots, just like Archer. He got out and unseen by the Loughlins who were too busy trying to kill the NYPD cop who'd shot their brother the night before, ran across the street to the injured Kat.

'C'mon!' he told her, scooping her up. She stared up in shock and tried to say something but then sagged into him as he carried her and the bag towards his car; he ripped

open the rear door, pushed her inside and threw the bag in after her.

Despite being focused on the brothers, who were doing their best to put bullets both into him and the genuine Cleveland police officers, from his cover Archer visually identified the man who he'd just seen rescue the girl from the mailbox. He'd seen his face on the news first thing this morning, as had most of Ohio.

It was Nicky Reyes.

The two men made eye contact for a brief moment, but then Archer was forced to duck again as he came under more fire. Reyes made the most of the opportunity, jumped back in behind the wheel and backed quickly down the street away from the shootout. As he reversed then spun the car around and drove off, the Loughlins took full control of the street firefight; Archer only managed to fire a couple of shots back before being forced to withdraw behind the thicker, more solid protection of the parked car's engine block as it took the increased abuse from their weapons. The Cleveland PD officers down the street had also stopped engaging the brothers and Lupinetti, keeping their heads down under the onslaught while they waited for back up.

When the intense assault finally ceased, Archer checked through one of the shattered windows in time to see the brothers jumping into the vehicle Frank Lupinetti had shown up on the street in. As the echoes of the gunfire gave way to the sound of screeching tires, Archer immediately ran back to his rental and jumping in, turned the key still in the ignition, but the car wouldn't start, the front hood and engine shot to pieces. Swearing, he got out and sprinted down a side alleyway to try and see which direction the brothers and Lupinetti had taken.

When he made it out the other side, the three fugitives were already gone, the noise of their engine becoming lost in the city as sirens, screams and shouts for help took over.

Through a thinning haze of smoke, Archer saw a toppled armored delivery truck, four bodies lying in pools of blood and two figures struggling to get out of the door of the vehicle lying on its side, a wrecking ball from a small crane resting against it.

Half an hour ago, he'd wondered if something specific might have been taking the Gatlin Four into Ohio and towards Cleveland, or if the Loughlins and Frank going in the direction everyone was assuming Nicky Reyes was also heading had just been a coincidence.

He now knew the answer.

TWENTY

'Ten block square grid is being completely locked down,' Cleveland SWAT task force's commander told a chief deputy US Marshal and a Robbery/Homicide lieutenant thirty minutes later, the three men striding across the E Superior Avenue intersection where the armored truck had been attacked. Other law-enforcement and detectives had arrived at the scene, the bodies of the four thieves who'd been killed in the robbery still on the street where they'd been gunned down; like Craig Loughlin, back on the bridge in West Virginia, they'd been kept there for investigators and crime scene techs to assess the scene and take their photos.

Although it was just past midday, the street had been cleared of the public, much of downtown already closed off as the SWAT commander had said, two police choppers circling above seeing if they could locate the perpetrators of whatever this had been. Like an earthquake, the shockwaves from the USP Gatlin prison escapes yesterday had now reached the Ohio city; reports were also coming in that two cops had just been found murdered in an alleyway in Cleveland Heights, their uniforms, weapons, radios and squad car missing. Videos on phones that onlookers had taken showed it was their cruiser which had been used in the attack. The city's police departments now had blood in the game.

'Your office were all over this situation, right?' the Robbery/Homicide lieutenant called Richie asked the Marshal chief deputy. Richie was in his mid-forties, a fourteen year veteran with a mop of light brown hair and a pair of sharp eyes that had seen a lot and missed very little. 'Heard you had this girl O'Mara under surveillance at her apartment and she still made it out here to help pull this off?'

'My people were tapping her phones to catch a missing fugitive, not anticipating anything like this. She must've managed to slip out during the night.'

Richie's sergeant, called Glick, approached. He was eight years younger than his boss, the same height but slightly leaner with darker hair, and had almost immediately proved himself an invaluable right-hand man. The two men stepped to one side; Glick nodded over towards Archer, who was standing slightly apart from the group taking in the scene around him. 'From the NYPD. Detective badge.'

'What's he doing here?'

'Says he was at Gatlin yesterday to help transport a prisoner, but the inmate got busted out by these two Loughlin brothers on that bridge assault in West Virginia last night we heard about. Been on his tail ever since. He's the one who put an ID on Kat O'Mara and the Gatlin boys at the shootout.'

Richie moved away and approached Archer. 'Heard you were one of the first on the scene,' he told him, shaking hands as Glick went with him. 'I'm Richie.'

'First name?'

'Last.'

'Sam Archer.'

'You have any idea this was something they were planning?'

Archer shook his head. 'I wish. Sightings of them last night suggested the two Loughlins and Lupinetti might be heading this way.' He sized up the toppled truck. 'But none of us were expecting this. Or for them and Nicky Reyes to show up for a reunion either.'

'That right? All four escapees?'

'Yeah, Reyes was here too. Got the girl away from the shootout.'

'We're gonna have all of them back in shackles or shot dead before nightfall,' the SWAT commander said, joining them. 'They killed two CHPD cops. Every badge in Ohio is gonna want their heads stuffed and mounted on a wall.'

'Lieutenant, a car with some bullet holes in the side was just found east of here on St Clair,' one of the Robbery/Homicide detectives told them, approaching with a radio in her hand.

'Description?' Richie asked.

'Blue Chrysler. Georgia plates.'

'That's the one Reyes and the girl took off in,' Archer told them.

As back-up units started to arrive on St Clair Avenue where the Chrysler been located, one of the officers who'd come across the abandoned vehicle was looking at blood smeared on the back seat and on the open nearside rear door. 'Dispatch said the woman got shot,' he said to his partner, who didn't answer, instead following a trail of blood droplets on the concrete. They were leading towards a small bodega thirty feet away.

The two officers pulled their sidearms and approached the entrance.

'Katherine must've got clipped by one of the brothers,' Archer said, quickly taking the Robbery/Homicide team through his arrival at the shootout and the fugitives' eventual escapes. 'A police unit engaged the Loughlins and Lupinetti's attention, probably before they could put her down for good and take the other bag I saw her carrying,' he said, his eyes on the bullet-ridden cruiser up the street, the officers who'd been in the firefight both having been taken to hospital with gunshot wounds.

'Where were you?' Richie asked.

'Give you one guess,' Archer said with a brief smile, nodding at something behind them; the detectives turned and saw a vehicle that had very obviously taken a lot of firepower.

'Loughlins really showed you some love, huh?' Sergeant Glick said, looking at the damage. 'Damn.'

'Think they recognized me. We had a run in on a bridge last night.' Archer pointed to his right. 'During the shootout, Nicky Reyes arrived over there in that Chrysler we just heard about. He got out, ran over to Kat O'Mara and carried her clear before they took off again. It was him, no mistake.'

'A prison breakout yesterday four hundred miles away, and this morning all four fugitives show up on Superior at the same time during a robbery?' Richie said.

'They can't have been working together,' Archer said, looking at the bloodstains on the street from Kat's gunshot wound. Her abandoned ski-mask was lying there too, numbered with a card as a piece of evidence. 'The Gatlin COs said Reyes and the Loughlins hate each other's guts.'

'So what was this?'

'I'm not sure yet. Do you have an ID on the four dead thieves back by the truck?'

'We recognized two, straight off,' Glick told him. 'Arrested them before for burglary. They're brother and sister; Vaughn and Erica Till. I'll bet this month's paycheck the other two have records too. They'd need experience to attempt something like this.'

'Where were those deposit boxes headed?'

'A Morningstar bank in Public Square. The vault down there's been undergoing reconstruction, so they've been offsite for the past few months.'

'So they paid for that information, or they got someone on the inside. Maybe same with the construction site, otherwise how'd they have access to it?' Glick and Richie nodded, both of them surprised at how calm and focused the NYPD detective appeared to be, considering the sustained attack he'd just come under. 'Kat O'Mara had a bag over her shoulder. Looked substantial. They took it with them when Reyes got her to the car.'

'Witnesses back near the truck who stuck around said they saw the Loughlins take another that she dropped,' Richie said. 'My guys are going through an inventory with Morningstar to find out which ones are missing and what they made off with. Lot of boxes in the truck, but the thieves can't have lifted many considering the timeframe. Just enough to fit into two sports bags.'

Archer's eyes were still on the bloodstains on the concrete beside the mailbox.

'Whatever was stolen, it must've been worth risking all this,' he said.

TWENTY ONE

Inside the bodega across the city on St Clair Avenue, the two armed police officers who'd found Nicky and Kat's dumped car entered to find the shaken owner hiding behind the counter, the man having been the one to call 911. One cop checked the aisles with his pistol drawn as the other indicated around the store to the owner, asking the silent question. The scared man shook his head quickly.

'He took my car keys,' he told the officer as the cop's partner followed more drops of blood on the floor heading out back. 'And some medical supplies.'

'Attention all units, Loughlin brothers sighted in a red Chevrolet Blazer, West Virginia tag, near Willard Park,' the dispatcher said over the radio, giving an address south of their current position. *'Back up requested.'*

Knowing other units would respond, the officers ignored the call, following the blood trail to the back door where it stopped right by an empty space where the stolen car belonging to the shaken store owner had to have been parked.

'We need the plate, make and model for your car, sir,' one of them told the owner who'd followed them out.

With the city going into manhunt mode for the Gatlin Four and Kat O'Mara, and with local Cleveland and federal authorities conducting the search, Archer found himself surplus to requirements for the time being. After calling Shepherd to fill him in on the latest, he'd answered more questions from the Robbery/Homicide squad, given them the number for his temporary pre-paid phone, then decided to stick to his original plan and find a hotel. From there he could work on hiring a replacement car and wait for a fresh sighting of Lupinetti.

He was now in a cheapish three star place somewhere downtown, the city's layout still unfamiliar to him. He switched on the TV as soon as he entered the 1st floor room, flicking to the local news covering the interrupted heist and ongoing search for the suspects. He walked over to the window and saw the street twenty feet below was emptying, people not wanting to be out and about with armed convicts on the loose. Not a good last weekend of summer for the city.

He checked the door was locked, then undressed and showered, keeping his Sig Sauer on the ledge near the stall. The Loughlin brothers and Lupinetti were out there, maybe just a few blocks away, hemmed in by law-enforcement closing off any escape routes out of the city; it seemed crazy that they could have followed him here while trying to evade capture, but he'd learned through hard experience the consequences of false assumptions.

Once he'd toweled off and put his new clothes back on with a fresh pair of boxers and socks, he felt his empty stomach start to complain. The meal at the diner last night in Charleston had done a good job of filling him up, but his body had burned through the fuel some time ago. There was a room service menu, the limited choice vastly overpriced, but he was too worn out to be picky so used the room's phone to place an order while looking down at the street. *'It'll be brought up shortly,'* they told him.

He walked over to the bed and lay down, thinking. Four escaped felons crossing state lines, killing cops and members of the public, then each man ending up here in Cleveland shooting up sections of downtown and what looked to him to be sabotaging a robbery. He corrected himself: three of them had been shooting and sabotaging.

In those few moments he'd seen him rescuing the woman, Nicky Reyes hadn't been carrying or firing a weap…

A knock on the door jolted him awake. Archer looked at the time and realized he'd fallen asleep for almost thirty minutes. With pistol in hand, he moved over and checked the peep hole to make sure it really was room service; after putting the gun out of sight and collecting the tray, he secured the door again.

As he started to eat a burger and fries, he found a paper map in the large *Hotel Information* folder on the desk and opened it. Devouring his lunch quickly, he located where the thieves had been ambushed by the Loughlins and Lupinetti, on that East Superior Avenue intersection. He remembered Richie's comment; *a prison breakout yesterday four hundred miles away, and this morning all four Gatlin fugitives show up at the same time during a robbery?*

He was right. No way in hell was that a coincidence.

'Reyes and O'Mara are from right here in the city,' the SWAT commander told Richie and the chief deputy Marshal on a conference cell phone call, the leaders of the manhunt driving across town towards where the blue Chrysler Reyes had driven away in from the robbery had been discovered dumped outside the bodega on St Clair. The SWAT team were following in their truck, an APB out for the plates on the deli owner's stolen car. *'They'll have friends, family, places they could hide out. They'll know the streets, the ways in and out.'*

'Guy from the NYPD said Reyes has been in prison for almost twelve years,' Richie replied, as Glick drove. 'City's changed in that time. And the girl's got a bullet in her.'

'They won't hang around, instinct will be to get their asses out of town fast as they can,' the chief Marshal

reasoned. '*Same for the two brothers and this former NYPD lieutenant.*'

'That's where geography's gonna help us,' Richie said. 'Lake Erie's north between us and Canada, so to get around the water they gotta go east all the way to New York State or west into Michigan. Archer told me the Loughlins are from near Syracuse. They make it out of Ohio somehow, they've gotta be trying to head that way.'

'*What about south?*' the Marshal said.

'They just ran from that direction, Chief. Like you said, right now, with all the heat on them, they'll be working on instinct. That almost always steers people towards places they know.'

Behind the wheel of the Chevy Blazer they'd stolen after killing the couple in West Virginia last night, and stuck downtown with no way to get out in a street layout he and the brothers didn't recognize, Lupinetti saw a roadblock in the distance on the road ahead and swore before pulling a sharp left.

'The hell is this shit?' Billy said from the back seat. 'This is it?' He was looking at the contents of the bag he'd retrieved from the street; the first of two the girl had taken from the truck, but the one she'd dropped. He'd shot out the lock on the safety deposit box with the Ruger revolver, but found another smaller one inside that looked to be made of titanium with a thick Granit padlock. 'Thought there was millions on offer here, big brother. You couldn't fit five thousand bucks into this thing.'

Lupinetti glanced back at the bag. 'Must be worth something. If it was in a lockbox and the group back there chose to take it, outta everything else in that truck.'

'I heard what the bitch said to Reyes,' Brooks said, keeping his eyes on the road as Lupinetti cut down more streets, running them near what a sign said was the *State Memorial Highway*. 'The take was worth millions in cash from this.'

'So we get the wrong one?' Billy asked.

'Won't know until we get that son' bitch open.' Brooks took the titanium inner lockbox from his brother and examined it. It was then he realized Billy had been holding it upside down, and he saw the initials *K O'M* were engraved on the front.

Behind the wheel, Lupinetti glanced over and saw him smile. 'What?'

'We might not be the only ones who came away with the wrong bag.'

TWENTY TWO

Four hundred miles south in Virginia, the Gatlin laundry truck used by the Loughlin brothers to break out of the federal prison was being held in the Jonesville PD impound, soon to be signed over to State investigators for analysis. Marquez had been permitted inside to take a look after providing her credentials and explaining why she was there. Her ID had been double-checked with New York and the Marshals Office before she was supplied with protective booties and gloves.

She'd been inside the back of the vehicle when Shepherd had called, telling her that according to Archer a major incident had just taken place in downtown Cleveland with all the members of the Gatlin Four involved. He went on to tell her about the heist, the shootout, and the current lockdown in large parts of the city. 'Sam got caught up in it?' she asked.

'Why do you sound surprised?'

'Yeah, I know. But is he OK?'

'He's good, but a couple of Cleveland Heights officers aren't. Their bodies were found in an alleyway, stripped of uniforms, squad car missing. The Loughlin brothers were seen driving it at the shootout.'

After Shepherd told her the rest of what he currently knew and ended the call, Marquez switched her focus to Prez Rainey. 'You held back details,' she accused the incarcerated biker angrily on her next call as she jumped out of the laundry truck. His deal last night had been for her to call him at 1pm, but she'd jumped the gun by twenty four minutes and he'd answered. 'You could've told me your celly was planning to help Kat pull off a robbery.

Two more cops were murdered this morning. If we'd known what was coming, we might've been able to save their lives.'

'Who killed them? The kid or the girl wouldn't have.'

'You so sure?'

'I'd bet my life on it.'

She took a deep breath and started to pace. 'It was the Loughlins. They were wearing the dead officers' uniforms and driving their stolen squad car with Lupinetti acting as support. They killed all the thieves on the heist too, apart from Kat, but they still shot her.'

'*How bad?'* Rainey asked quickly.

'Don't know. She was alive last anyone saw her, but she might have bled out by now. People are dying here and you could've helped us stop this.'

'That's why the kid busted out.'

Marquez stopped walking around, standing in the sun. 'What?'

'*Nicky didn't break outta here to help the girl, Detective. He broke out to stop her.*'

*

'She's planning to hit an armored truck?' Prez asked, sitting on the bleachers in Gatlin's fenced-in yard the previous Thursday afternoon. Almost a full forty eight hours before the robbery and just after Nicky's face-to-face with Kat in the meeting hall. 'Is she missing being in a prison cell?'

'What I thought when she told me,' Nicky answered, on the bench beside the biker and staring at the ground, knowing he couldn't let the crushing anxiety he was feeling become apparent to anyone watching. You can't show any weakness in this place, *Prez had warned him all those years ago during his first twenty four hours inside.* Wrap those feelings up, lock them in a box and save it for

when you get out. *The younger man had always heeded the advice.*

'She must be working with a crew?' Prez said.

'Five, including her. The truck is returning safe deposit boxes to a major bank.'

'Which one?'

'Morningstar, in Cleveland. A downtown branch has been having its vault reinforced. The boxes have been stored off-site for the last month. This weekend, they get taken back.'

'How'd this crew know that?'

'Paid for the schedule. She's flying back to Ohio tonight and they're hitting it Saturday morning during the transfer.'

'How'd she get involved?'

'Other woman on the team is someone she met inside and now her roommate. She told her what they were planning and Kat got sucked in. There's something she wants real bad in the truck.'

'It's worth this?'

'It is to her. She told me to meet her in a town in Canada when I get out of here next week.' He swore quietly.

'You think they could pull it off?'

There was a pause, then Nicky looked up. 'No. You're right, she's gonna end up back in a prison cell. You can't attempt something like armed robbery then just hop across the border. And if someone dies, that's aggravated murder. Gets you the death penalty back home.'

'So why's she taking the risk?'

Nicky kept his voice low and told him, not wanting to risk anyone else hearing. The biker considered what he'd just heard, then rose off the bench. 'Call her right now before she's in the air,' he said, seeing one of the payphones in the yard was free. 'No details, remember.'

Nicky went with him, as the bigger man kept an eye on their backs and they walked across the yard.

Kat had just arrived at the Tri-Cities regional airport on a bus when Nicky caught her on her cell. 'Nick?'

'You can't pull this off,' *he told her flatly.* 'You're gonna get killed or end up back you-know-where.'

'What are you doing? Don't they record calls?'

'Listen to me,' *he said, not answering the question but also not giving any specifics away.* 'There's no coming back from something like this. It's gonna end badly.'

She closed her eyes, stepping off the bus and away from the other passengers. 'I'm taking back what's mine,' she told him after a deep breath. 'Don't call me again. I won't answer.'

'Kat, please, just li-'

'I'll see you next week. Go where I said. I'll be there.'

Prez glanced at Nicky as he swore before immediately trying her again. However, she remained true to her word and didn't answer. After it rang through for the fifth time, Nicky gave up and walked away, the two men returning to their seat on the bleachers. 'Turned off her phone. Said she won't talk to me until it's over.'

As Nicky thought about what Kat was planning, his eyes were drawn to two men wandering through the yard talking with each other. He knew both were convicted bank robbers who were doing thirteen years each after trying to take down a First Horizon somewhere in Tennessee. They'd almost got away with it, but now they were in here. And they were career thieves, not like Kat who was doing this out of desperation. He knew how badly she'd struggled for a long time and had seen her determination to keep fighting slowly fade to the point she'd now agreed to get involved in this crazy, risky planned heist. It was about as far as you could get from the kind of thing the old rational Katherine would do.

And there'd be no going back if she went ahead with it. He stared out at the yard, then up at the guard tower and the rolls of razor wire topping the fences.

'I gotta get out of here, Prez,' he said quietly. 'I have to stop her. She's not thinking straight.'

'Neither are you. Don't talk that kind of bullshit.'

'I mean it.'

'You're done in six days. Twelve years of your life, paid in full in a place like this. You ready to restart the clock and do it all over again?'

'Saturday's a national holiday,' Nicky continued, not seeming to listen. 'They're hitting this truck at an intersection with escape routes, but there's gonna be police all over the city for Labor Day. Even if they pull this first part off, five wanted people can't stay on the run together. They'll be too easily identifiable once their faces hit the news so they'll have to split up, then she'll be by herself trying to get to the border. And that's if the others don't kill her to get her share.'

'You know anyone else who could intervene and prevent this?'

He thought about it. 'The old family maid. Used to work for Kat's father when he was still alive.'

'She'd care?'

'She loved Kat. But I can't get her involved, even if I wanted to. I haven't spoken to her in years, and don't have a clue where she is or how to reach her. She might not want anything to do with us either, after everything that's happened.'

'I could send up some of my guys.'

'If Kat won't listen to me, think she'll listen to a couple of bikers from Atlanta who she's never met?'

'She's a big girl, kid. She knows what she's getting into.'

'I don't think she does. In her current state of mind? Her run of luck since her father died? She told me she feels like she's got no other choice anymore. That kind of thinking makes people go all-in and do stupid things. You know that.'

'What's her take?'

'Five million.' He saw Prez's reaction. 'See why she's jumping to hit the truck?'

'And these other thieves won't screw her for it?'

'She and her roommate seem tight. I don't think so. But who knows.'

'You're right. If she fails, she'll be looking at 15-to-20 for armed robbery. More as it'll be her second time inside. Or the needle if someone gets killed.'

Nicky nodded. 'She promised the way they're planning it no-one's gonna get hurt. But if things always followed a script, none of us would be stuck in here.'

'She gave you a lot with the COs standing around in the meeting hall.'

'We started using a code a few years ago. I realized pretty early here the screws listen in on what we say to visitors.'

'You try to break out before your release, they'll throw you a load more years too,' Prez said, returning to his original theme. 'And if against everything you actually make it out, you're gonna be spending the rest of your life hiding or back in a joint like this. The cops and feds will never stop until they catch you.'

'I can keep ahead of them.'

'Lot of people have thought that, kid. Almost all of them end up back inside or gunned down out on the road

somewhere. You haven't planned out a single lick of this and you got less than two days to do it. Get real. Your girl's crazy thinking is catching on.'

'Every man in here has thought about how he could break out and stay out. I'm no different.' As he spoke, Prez saw the younger man's focus switch to the fences; it was then the biker realized at the back of his mind he'd already started trying to think of ways to assist him. His celly was obviously becoming set on this, and Rainey knew he could either hinder or help.

'Even if you somehow got out of C Block without being caught, the guys in the tower would see you trying to cut through the fence,' he told Nicky. 'If it was that easy to break free, tumbleweeds would be blowing through this place. And no point trying to bribe any of them to leave a door unlocked. You'd need a helluva lot to get them to help you. Even then, most wouldn't.'

'With what money anyway? I haven't got two nickels to rub together.'

'You could try and get transferred over to the labor camp. Less security out there. Your record's good enough.'

'The screws won't bother. I'm down to less than a week left on my bid. What's the point in moving me now?'

Prez shrugged. 'I ain't got many other ideas. Like you said, guys fantasize about breaking out of a place like this without getting caught. That's where it stays, as fantasy. Shit ain't possible.'

'It's been done before.'

'Not from inside the main prison, and not planned in less than forty eight hours. Make that thirty six, if you're gonna get outta here and make it to Cleveland in time to stop your girl. That's an eight hour drive, not including roadblocks. And that's assuming you can get your hands

on a car.' Like Nicky had tried with Kat, Prez was attempting to get him to see sense, but as he spoke he noticed his younger cellmate's keen gaze was focusing on something or someone.

Rainey turned to see what had caught his attention.

It was the two older Loughlin brothers. Brooks and Billy.

'Been keeping an eye on those two for so long, I know when something's up,' Nicky said. 'They haven't been acting normal lately.'

'Look pretty much the same to me. Big and ugly.'

'They tend to hog space around the weights or walk around the yard, right?' Prez saw what the younger man was talking about. Instead of being at one of the bench presses or squat racks lifting heavy barbells or dumbbells, he saw the two brothers were jogging together and had just stopped to catch their breath; as they watched, Brooks pulled a pencil stub from his sock and wrote something on a piece of paper in his hand. 'Noticed three weeks ago they've started running. Guys that big aren't built for cardio. Why suddenly change their habits?'

Prez saw what his cellmate was talking about. He hadn't picked up on the adjustment in their behavior, but in hindsight realized the kid was right. 'Looks like they're building up their endurance.'

'So why would they do that?'

A horn went and yard time ended, one of the inmates who'd been playing basketball with a load of others sinking a final lay-up before the ball bounced dead and rolled to the edge of the court. Guys at the weight pile racked barbells and dumped dumbbells down before pulling vests, t-shirts or jumpsuit tops back on as they went to get in line.

'Not a lot of Gatlin inmates training for track meets right now,' Nicky added as they both rose off the bleachers.

'If they're planning something, you think there's a chance in hell they'll let you in on it?'

'No, but it's a start.' Nicky stepped down onto the concrete. 'Now we just gotta find out what they're up to.'

*

Two days later, with the city red hot in the search for their group of wanted fugitives, police units and Marshals' task forces with ATF support in Cleveland were searching residence-by-residence in the neighborhood near St Clair where Reyes and O'Mara had dumped their Chrysler. The area was flooded with armed cops and agents carrying out intensive searches, an APB for the bodega owner's car out over the radio, but the pair seemed to have vanished into thin air.

At the same time across the city, Lupinetti swore as he saw another police cruiser approaching from the opposite direction and turned into a parking lot, waiting for the cop car to pass and hoping it hadn't seen the car's plates. They'd found a way out of downtown, but were now stuck in another suburb called Lakewood. Sitting in a bay surrounded by other vehicles, they heard the sound of at least two choppers overhead somewhere. 'Gonna be more federal agents than people in this city in a few hours,' he muttered. 'I worked manhunts back in the day. You boys killed police and State troopers. ATF, Marshals, FBI, they'll all be wanting a piece of us.'

'Rest of that money stash you've been saying you got,' Brooks suddenly said, checking behind them from the front passenger seat. 'We're gonna need it now. Your ticket on this ride ain't free.'

Lupinetti was caught off guard. 'OK, but I gotta contact someone back home. Gonna take a bit of time.'

Brooks looked at him before taking the pistol from the holster on his stolen police belt and thumbed out the bullets on the magazine, seeing he only had three left. The rifle and shotgun were dry too; blasting their way through the second roadblock getting out of West Virginia and the shootout at the robbery earlier had eaten up most of their bullets and shotgun shells. 'We need more ammo,' Billy told him, reading his big brother's mind. As they sat there in the car, hearing police sirens and the sound of choppers in the distance, Brooks dug into his pocket; he took out the cell phone belonging to the man of the couple they'd killed the night before for this car, and switched it on before carrying out a quick search.

'Gun store, six blocks away,' he said. 'This says it's open. We gotta dump this ride anyway.'

'Right now?' Lupinetti asked.

'Yeah, right now.' They got out, and Brooks was about to stamp on the phone in case the cops had realized they'd stolen that too and could track it. But then he had another idea.

'Who the hell are you calling?' Billy asked, watching his big brother dial a number and lift the phone to his ear.

'911,' Brooks said, as the other two looked at him as if he'd lost his mind. 'They're looking for us, right?'

TWENTY THREE

After Nicky and Prez had left the yard with the other inmates on that late afternoon two days ago, they followed the line to the chow hall, the last meal of the day before the prisoners were all returned to their cells for the night. But after collecting their food, the two cellmates deviated from where they normally sat to approach an old man parked at a table by himself.

'OK if we join you, Wes?' Prez asked.

The senior inmate shrugged without looking up, and they placed their trays down opposite him before taking a seat.

'You know more than most people what's going down in here, Wesley,' Prez told him.

'So I've heard.'

Prez leaned forward as Nicky glanced around. In his peripheral vision, he thought he noticed Brooks Loughlin briefly look their way, the huge man sitting with Billy, Hoffmeier, Kattar and Lupinetti as they all shoveled what passed for dinner into their mouths. 'You heard of anyone planning a vacation outta this place anytime soon?' Prez asked, keeping his voice low. 'Say, two brothers who've been running laps in the yard.'

'Caught that too, huh?'

'My celly did,' Prez answered. Wesley looked up at Nicky, who nodded.

'If I knew something and passed it on to you, be worth some time with that tin can and string of yours,' Wesley told Rainey. 'You're the only man on C Block with a phone who I care to talk to.'

'Long as I get it back.'

'I ain't in here for stealing.'

The biker nodded and offered his hand. 'You got a deal.'

Wes shook it. 'Since those two've been working in the laundry, they've got to watching the guards at the gate checking inside the back of the truck when it leaves. Picked up the morning shift ain't too thorough. Alarms were goin' off a month back remember? The screws still didn't do it proper then.'

'They planning to take advantage?' Prez asked.

'You bet. A riot's coming in four days,' he muttered. 'While all the shit's goin' down, they're getting out in the laundry truck.' Wesley ate a mouthful of mashed potatoes. 'The screws have gotten lazy. They think no-one can break out of here.'

'How'd you know all this?' Nicky asked.

'I work in the library with Kattar. Boy struggles so hard to keep his mouth shut, surprised he don't catch flies.'

'Who's gettin' out?' Prez asked.

'Brooks, Billy and their little brother, but he's at the other place. He's only in for two years but guess he's had enough and is running with them too. Kattar said him and Hoff are also going. Their job is to start the riot.'

'What about that ex-cop? The one from New York.'

'Yeah, him too. Promised them a load of cash if they get his ass outta here. Kattar said he's got a stash hidden that he's willing to split.'

'That's a lot for one laundry truck,' Prez replied. 'Gonna be pretty crowded in there.'

'Guess Brooks has it all worked out.' Wes peered up at them briefly, then focused again on his tray. 'Or Kattar and Hoff are too dumb to see what's clear as day.'

As Wes spoke, Nicky glanced over at Hoffmeier, Kattar and the former NYPD lieutenant who'd been tagging along with them lately, bandaging visible around his arm from where he'd gotten cut last week by another couple of inmates. Lupinetti seemed to have been let into the Loughlins' circle since he got jumped, but Wes was right. For an ex-cop to be tolerated by guys like that, there had to be a lot of money changing hands and only in one direction.

Wes stopped eating the potatoes on his tray for a moment, his eyes large behind his spectacles as he focused on Prez and Nicky. 'Why you two so interested in what those boys are up to?'

'My friend here's looking to hitch a ride,' Prez said after a moment, deciding to trust him.

'So close to release? Don't be stupid, kid. Take it from me, you don't wanna be an old man in a place like this.'

'He's got his reasons,' Prez said.

'And a breakout four days from now doesn't help me,' Nicky replied worriedly. 'She's pulling this thing in less than two.'

'Don't need to know, don't wanna know.' Wesley opened a packet of cruddy margarine and started spreading it on a couple of slices of bread with a spoon. The prison didn't allow the inmates to have plastic knives. 'But I could spread a rumor. Say the guards are planning to start shiftin' people around on rotation in the kitchen and laundry, startin' Saturday. That could get Finn and Sawyer over there bumpin' up their schedule.'

'What would it take?' Prez asked.

Wesley smiled, looking at their trays. 'Your pieces of fruit.'

An hour later, when the inmates were locked in their cells, Wesley wheeled a cart of books and magazines past the cells and stopped by Prez's and Nicky's on the upper southside tier. He held out a novel through the bars; Prez moved forward to take it as Nicky stayed in the back, having unsuccessfully tried Kat several more times on his cellmate's contraband cell phone.

Prez opened the book and pulled out a small piece of paper as Wesley rolled on, quickly reading what had been scrawled on it as Nicky joined him.

vacation starts tomorrow after bfast. plan changed. ex-cop found out he's getting transferred in morning, so bumped forward anyway

need that tin cup next week to call my grandson

'Now we're talking,' Nicky whispered, as Prez checked the tier to make sure they weren't being watched.

'Yeah, but now we gotta figure out how to get you out too without the COs or the Loughlin boys noticing. And we've only got ten hours to do-'

*

Prez's voice suddenly cut off, in the present. 'Then what?' Marquez asked, having taken a seat on a bench in the sunny Jonesville police evidence compound. She'd been totally absorbed in Rainey's tale, realizing she was almost certainly the only person other than a few Gatlin inmates to get the inside details on the events leading up to the riot and the breakouts.

'*Boss is coming. Gotta go.*'

'Wait, Rainey, call me wh-' she remonstrated, but the line had already gone dead. She swore, knowing better than to dial him back; she just had to hope he'd contact her when he could. 'God dammit,' she muttered, before wandering back to the laundry truck, desperate to know what had happened next.

'*Yeah, I think I just saw some of the people from the news!*' Brooks said on a 911 call from the Lakewood parking lot, Lupinetti immediately catching on to what he was doing. *'Two real big guys and another one. They were near the stadium,'*

'*Which stadium?'* the operator asked.

'*Sorry, I'm from out of town; I think it's the one where the basketball team plays!*' Brooks said quickly before hanging up. He then dropped the phone to the concrete and stamped it to pieces before picking up the fragments and dropping them in a nearby trash can.

'They can still trace where the call came from,' Lupinetti said. 'I've done that before.'

'They'll follow the tip first. Gets them off our ass for a spell. That's all we need.'

The three fugitives then moved across the lot, carrying their bag of guns and the holdall from the heist. They waited until they saw a chopper east of them peel off, taking the bait, and once there was no sign of any police cars, the trio crossed the street, quickly making their way to the gun store six blocks away.

TWENTY FOUR

In his hotel room, having managed to get that half hour of sleep, Archer was now back on his temporary burner phone with the detective-sergeant from Robbery/Homicide, who'd been given his number by Lieutenant Richie. The man, who'd introduced himself as Allen Glick, had news.

'The four dead thieves who hit the truck were career criminals,' he told Archer. *'Three guys, one chick, lists of arrests and time spent inside. The guys were all former guests at the State pen in Elkton or at Lebanon Correctional. Dead woman served time at ORW in Marysville.'*

'ORW?'

'Ohio Reformatory for Women. Our largest equivalent for females.'

'What about Reyes' sister?'

'She's the odd one out. Girl comes from a wealthy background. Daddy was a multi-millionaire but she's done time in ORW too.'

'For burglary?'

'No, doctor shopping. She was caught with pills she'd bought illegally from faking out prescriptions. Did fifteen months when she was twenty five, five years ago. You said she got tagged pretty bad?'

'To the body,' Archer said, remembering seeing her slumped against the mailbox clutching her side after being shot by one of the Loughlins, leaving bloodstains on the concrete once she was gone. 'If she hasn't died already, she might soon if Reyes doesn't get her to a hospital or finds a doctor.'

'Search units are on it. Construction crew who've been working the site on Superior with the wrecking ball were called first thing telling them the mayor ordered no work done today. Said his office didn't want noise complaints on the holiday weekend so gave them the day off. By the time they realized it was a hoax when their foreman contacted their supervisor to doublecheck, the ball was already swinging into that truck.'

'An inside man? They'd need keys.'

'You got it. One of the thieves had been hired onto the construction team a month ago. Vaughn Till. He's Kat's roommate's brother. Two of the guys on our squad have arrested him before. The company gave him the job despite his past. Guess they're regretting that right about now.'

'News reports are saying none of the Gatlin boys have been found yet,' Archer said, watching the TV in the room.

'911 operators just got a call about the brothers being seen near the Cavs stadium so units are pouring over there. There are roadblocks choking off the city all the way out past the suburbs. We'll get your man.'

'What about Reyes and O'Mara?'

'No sighting of them since they dumped the Chrysler for that bodega owner's, but she'll be hurting real bad like you said. They should be easier to find if she's injured. Can't move as fast as the other three and we got the details of the car they're in.'

'It took Gatlin almost twelve hours before they realized Reyes wasn't in his cell. Don't underestimate him. He's proving to be just as smart as Brooks Loughlin.' Archer looked at the street below again. 'Did the bank come back on those safe deposit boxes?'

'We confirmed just two are missing. The owners are being contacted so we can find out what they contain.'

'Now we know why you helped your celly break out, Rainey,' the captain at USP Gatlin told Prez, having been grilling him for almost an hour with the prison's warden, three State police detectives and three of the US Marshals who'd been at the facility the day before. The biker had been pulled from his cell immediately after he'd dropped his call with Marquez, the phone quickly hidden in its usual place just before the COs had stopped outside his cell to collect him. 'He had to get to Ohio to help his girl out with this bank truck.'

'Bank truck? How about some details, boss?'

'Like you don't know?'

'He didn't tell me anything.'

'He's not gonna last long out there,' one of the Marshals said. 'O'Mara got shot and he dumped their first car. It had Georgia plates. We just learned that you're from Georgia, Kevin.'

'Yeah, I parked it out on the highway for him. Gave it a good wax and polish before I strolled back in through the gate in time for lunch.'

'You want him to survive long enough to wear an orange jumpsuit again, I'd start talking.'

'The kid didn't tell me shit and anything I say won't make a difference anyway. You'll catch him eventually. We all know it.'

Rainey was marched back to his cell by two waiting COs and locked inside. He was tempted to immediately retrieve the phone and pick up with Marquez in case she had more news he could pry out of her but held off, suspicious why he'd been returned here to C Block instead of being taken to the SHU after remembering the captain's threats yesterday.

He walked to the door and looked through the bars down at a lower cell on the opposite side holding Wesley. The old man was reading a book but hadn't missed Prez getting pulled before being returned to his cell.

Rainey made a twisting motion with his right arm, and Wes gave a brief nod.

A screw was lurking.

Prez lay on his bunk and waited for almost twenty minutes, then heard a door quietly open and close, the hinges creaking. He got up and looked back at Wesley again. Still holding the book, he subtly gave a thumb's up.

The CO who'd been lingering was gone.

Prez retrieved the phone from its hiding place, turned it on and waited. As expected, he had a couple of missed calls and a voicemail, but they weren't from the lady police detective from New York.

'I need your help, old man,' a familiar voice said, sounding stressed. *'If they didn't throw you in the SHU with Janks yet or find your phone, call me back soon as you can.'*

*

The night before the escape, once they'd come up with a rough plan, ironed out the kinks and Prez had sent some now-deleted messages to the outside with a couple of urgent requests, Nicky was on the top bunk studying a map of the local area on his cellmate's smartphone. He was examining the highways, the routes and other smaller roads, committing the whole landscape to memory as best he could. If he was found missing early, Lee County was going to be a labyrinth of law enforcement to try and elude tomorrow. He needed to have imprinted into his mind every possible way to get out.

His tired eyes flicked to the time on the device; almost 12:30am. It reminded him of when he was a kid, up late studying for an exam or with a deadline that he was trying to meet. At some point he had to try to sleep, and the long hours of night would suddenly be gone.

Then it would be morning and there really would be no turning back.

He powered down the phone and leaned over the side of the bed to hand it back to Prez, then saw why he'd been so quiet for the past half hour. 'What you doing'?' Nicky asked curiously, and quietly.

'Making you something,' Prez replied. 'You're gonna need the calories.'

Nicky swung his legs off his bunk and dropped down. To his surprise, he saw the motorcycle club president had separated a pack of Oreos and crushed up the cookies with water to make layers. The cream from between each biscuit had been used as icing, peanut butter in another, and he'd even mashed up a bag of M&Ms for the top layer. 'You son of a bitch,' Nicky said, looking at the correctional cake. 'You used up your supplies.'

'Cookies are out of date,' Prez lied. 'Don't feel special.' He placed the cake on the book on his bed, then used the edge of the hardback novel Wesley had passed them earlier to separate it into slices. It crumbled slightly but held together; he offered it for Nicky to take a piece, which he did, holding it on another book.

As he leaned against the wall with the slice, he glanced down at the lower tier and saw the Loughlin brothers were both lying on their bunks; he was too far away to see if they were asleep. Probably not, considering what they had planned in a few hours' time.

'You sure about doing this?' Rainey asked. 'If you're going to, now's the time to change your mind.' Nicky chewed his slice of cake; but as skilled as he'd become at

hiding his emotions, here in the cell with just Prez for company he could let the mask drop slightly. The biker saw he looked both pensive and nervous.

'She still won't answer her phone,' Nicky replied. 'She's gonna get herself killed or locked up if I don't try to do something. I spend twelve years in here, then get out and she goes down the same week? No way. I'm not letting that happen.'

'But this is what you wanna do? Last time I ask.'

Nicky took a deep breath, then nodded. So Prez let it be.

'My celly before you showed up here made me one of these cakes, night before his release,' the biker said. 'He was from some town called Barrow, in Alaska. Told me it goes dark for almost two months straight, up there in winter. At the end of spring, it stays light for another two months too. Night sun, *they call it.'*

His eyes met his younger cellmate's.

'That's what it's gonna be like for you once you get past that wall, kid. Be nowhere in the dark you can hide for long. Maybe never again, so listen to me good.' He paused to emphasize what he was saying. 'Every chance you get, you refuel, you rest up and you use that time to think. The warden, guards and State police take escapes personal. Don't matter your record in here, they'll put you down hard if they have to, and they'll hunt you day and night to get the chance.'

Nicky listened in silence.

'Assuming I can get Janks in your bunk, if the screws find him before you get to Ohio they're gonna be all over your girl in Cleveland before you can reach her,' Prez continued. 'You won't be able to contact her on the phone. Be like a conference call with police and US Marshals listening in.'

'She's not gonna pick up anyway.'

'You make it in time, is she ready to run with you? Even if you stop her taking part in this robbery? Might be so pissed at you for interfering, she won't listen to anything you got to say.'

'Maybe not, but if I can physically stop her getting involved, that's all I care about. I can handle more time inside. She can't. It'll break her for good. She's pretty close anyway.'

Prez ate the rest of his slice, then levered himself off another with the edge of the book. 'If you do get there, where you gonna go after?'

'Don't know yet. Like I told you, she's thinking Canada.'

'You get a chance to make a new life, you don't stop for a second to take it,' Prez re-emphasized. 'Even if something happens to her. You understand me?'

Nicky nodded.

'Say it.'

'I'll take it.'

The next morning Nicky and Prez were waiting, both of them on edge, the doors around the block open now breakfast was over and the inmates were on inside rec time. Nicky had tried Kat another fifteen times this morning, but the call always went to voicemail. She'd meant what she'd said.

'So if Hoff, Kattar and Lupinetti are getting out too,' he said to Rainey, who was beside him. 'How are they getting that door open?' he asked, looking down at the main entrance to the block.

They got their answer a few minutes later, when Lupinetti's two-CO escort came to collect him for his transfer to a new prison and were promptly ambushed by Hoffmeier and Kattar.

As the other inmates flooded out of their cells and chaos erupted, Prez and Nicky quickly moved through the mayhem unnoticed, Prez watching in case anyone tried to come at Nicky with the kid's release date coming up. No-one did.

Once out, they started running through the prison. Prez had kept his eyes on an inmate who'd taken the CO called Pena's keys, one of which he knew would be for the SHU block. This was the only sticking point in the plan they'd cooked up and getting those keys was a necessity; he caught up on the guy just as he was trying to unlock a door, rushing him from behind before slamming his head into the wall, knocking him out.

'Truck's gonna be outta here any second!' Prez said, taking the keys before they cut back and hurried on down the corridor where they were going to go their separate ways, Nicky to the laundry, Prez towards SHU housing. The two cellmates then stopped for a second, knowing it was almost certainly going to be the last time they'd ever see each other.

Holding several straps made from a sheet, Nicky gripped Prez's hand with the other.

'Give them everything you got, kid.'

'I'll send you a postcard,' Nicky said. A pause. 'Thanks.'

Then he turned and ran towards the laundry as the sound of the riot increased around them in the prison.

*

'I *gotta be real quiet,*' Rainey whispered in the present, a day later, going to the back of the cell. *'Screws keep coming into the block. Where are you?'*

'Hiding in a garage,' Nicky replied. *'What happened with Janks? I was all over the radio before I made it into Ohio.'*

'COs pulled another count during lockdown. From what I heard, someone got suspicious when a 911 call came in for that laundry truck driver.'

'They sweating you hard?'

'Yeah, but I'm not giving them anything. Tell me what's happened.'

'I got to Cleveland in time. But Brooks, Billy and Lupinetti showed up too.'

'What?'

'They put down the entire crew Kat pulled the job with and one of them shot her before I got her out of there. We've been running in the city ever since. I found somewhere to hole up temporarily but there are cops everywhere and she's in agony, Prez. I gotta do something.'

'How the hell did the brothers know what was going down?'

'Dunno, but we have to get out of Ohio right now, somehow. I'm running short on ideas.'

'Did she leave with anything from the truck?' Rainey asked, moving back towards the door of the cell. He got a nasty jolt when he saw Wesley trying to get his attention and doing a quick twisting motion.

A screw was back and on his way up here.

'She's got a bag of money and some expensive-looking jewelry. But it's not-'

'Good, that'll help,' Prez replied quickly. 'Can you wait one more hour?'

'Yeah, I'll try but whoever left this house might be coming back any minute. And if police lock down the street and do a sweep, we're toast. We can't hide out here forever. There are choppers in the sky too, searching-'

'Someone's coming, I got your number now. I'll call you back when I can,' Prez said, cutting him off again as he heard footsteps on the gantry outside.

Having been told to carry out random checks despite the lockdown, convinced someone on the block had a cell phone they didn't know about, the CO on the fresh shift change had heard faint murmuring coming from the upper tier in the quiet, and stopped outside Rainey's cell.

He looked inside and saw the biker was sleeping, his arm hooked under his pillow; he watched him for a few moments, the inmate turning and murmuring in his sleep.

The CO considered unlocking the cell and tossing it, but then realized that might stir things up again and the warden would have his ass. Jobs were most likely gonna go after what had happened and he didn't want his to be one of them.

Rainey waited, knowing the screw could easily be loitering just down the gantry again. Now Nicky was gone from here, they'd be suspecting him of helping the younger man to escape; they were right and his involvement wasn't about to end either. He'd asked his absent cellmate to give him an hour, so he kept waiting, counting in his head, picturing the kid hiding in the darkness of a suburban garage somewhere, police checking house-by-house and getting closer and closer to finding him.

After just over eight minutes, he heard footsteps walk off from the tier and go back down the stairs, the main door closing as the guard left. Moving fast, the biker retrieved his cell from the light housing in the ceiling then called a number saved to speed dial. '*Yo Prez, your celly's up to his neck in it,*' the vice-president of his MC chapter answered, having been bumped up when the former VP temporarily took Rainey's slot as the head of the club. Their clubhouse was just outside Atlanta, three hundred miles away. *'Some shit went down in Cleveland and cops are shutting down the city. Your boy's all over the news. He still got the ride we left him?'*

'Had to dump it. But I need you to do something else, fast as you can make it happen.'

'What is it?'

'The club's got a chapter in Cleveland, right?'

TWENTY FIVE

'How's the view?' Brooks asked, from inside the gun store in the Lakewood suburb of the city as he quickly loaded shells into the shotgun his brother had been using, his rifle already holding a freshly loaded magazine.

'No sign of PD,' Billy said from where he was keeping watch by the front window with a handgun, the sign on the door turned from *Open* to *Closed.* 'That bullshit tipoff bought us some time. Cops are dumber here than they are back home,' he added with a grin.

'Or they might be onto Reyes somewhere.' Brooks pushed the last shell into the shotgun, then whistled and tossed the weapon to his brother, who caught it with one hand and then stuffed his pistol into the holster of the belt he was wearing. Still dressed as a Cleveland Heights PD cop, Brooks tucked another three boxes of shells and six of the correct caliber rifle bullets into the backpack they'd been using to transport their firearms since they'd taken it from the dead Lee County fisherman's house, the bag from the bank truck still hooked over his brother's shoulder; then he eyed up some pistols he'd laid out on the counter. Although they'd come expressly for more ammunition, he'd decided to swap their stolen city police sidearms for fresh-off-the-rack handguns with bigger magazine capacity and less safety trigger pull. However, he and his brother were sticking with the rifle and shotgun they'd taken from the fisherman's gun safe as their primary weapons; they were getting used to the firearms by now and had sighted them in. With the bridge and truck robbery shootout, the two fugitives had made good use of the practice.

'TV just showed a map, all the roads and bridges are blocked off,' Lupinetti told them, coming through from the back of the store and wearing the owner's t-shirt; he'd taken it off him as soon as they'd arrived, having also abandoned the bloodstained jacket he'd had on since last night. He picked up one of the handguns Brooks had laid on the counter and loaded it before pushing the weapon into a holster he attached to his belt, taking two spare magazines and pocketing them too. 'I'll stay on the back exit. When we out of here?'

'Five minutes,' Brooks told him, before Lupinetti disappeared again. As the oldest Loughlin opened a box and started pushing 9mm Parabellums into a mag for a pistol he'd chosen, Billy left his post at the front door to walk behind the counter and lift a Ka-Bar knife off the wall which had caught his eye. To reach it, he had to step over the gun store's owner, who'd been gagged and restrained in the cuffs taken from the CHPD belts Brooks and Billy were now wearing. The man was looking more furious than scared; the flags on the wall and tattoos on his arms told them, if they'd been even slightly interested, that he'd served as a Marine.

Brooks finished loading the pistol magazine, slotted it into place and pulled the slide, then joined his brother on the other side of the counter. He dropped to his haunches and put the handgun to the owner's head before he pulled down the gag.

'Got a car parked outside we can take, Gunny?'

'Your friend was lying to you, redneck,' the owner growled. 'He's gone.'

'What?'

'He just took off.'

Brooks rose and quickly moved towards the back where Lupinetti had gone a few moments ago; he could hear the news still being reported on the small television, newsrooms covering the ongoing searches in the city, but was far more focused on the rear door which had been left open.

The owner was right; Lupinetti had disappeared.

'Where is he?' Billy asked, joining his brother as Brooks took a quick look around outside, but then they heard a toilet flush and the door to the can opened.

'What's wrong?' Lupinetti asked, drying his hands. 'We leaving?'

Brooks took his brother's knife and went back into the main store, realizing the owner had been screwing them around; but in the time they'd been gone the bound man had shuffled his way down to the other end of the long counter. Brooks noticed a flickering red light just above the guy's foot, next to a button which he hadn't caught before.

The owner had just activated a silent alarm.

Labor Day traffic around Cleveland had been heavy since first thing that morning, but the armored truck robbery, shootout and now the knowledge that there were armed, dangerous escaped convicts on the loose had prompted the majority of visitors to cut their Saturdays short and start leaving town.

For the troopers and officers manning the roadblocks on the highways, this sudden increase of traffic was presenting a serious headache. On Interstate 90 leading east out of the city, a group of cops and Ohio State troopers were clearing cars one at a time when what sounded like a giant metallic swarm of hornets started approaching down the inside lane; they looked over to see a mass of bikers in jeans, leather cuts and helmets on Harleys roaring up the shoulder towards them.

One of the officers stepped out to block their way, his partner joining him with a shotgun as the first cop waved at the approaching group of men and a few women to slow down and stop. 'There must be forty of them,' another officer said, looking over at the bikers after letting a car through, addressing his Cleveland PD sergeant who was standing beside him.

'Go check it out,' he said over the growling roar of the bike's engines. 'I'll cover here.'

'Not real likely our suspects joined a biker gang in the last hour,' one of the troopers ventured to the sergeant, looking at the large group in helmets and leathers. 'Anyway, they said the girl got shot. She couldn't be riding.'

'We were ordered not to let anyone pass without showing ID,' the police sergeant answered.

'Sarge, PD-' another officer called to him, but he couldn't hear the rest of what he shouted.

'What?'

'PD think they've got a fresh draw on the Loughlins!' the man repeated, louder this time.

'I can't hear shit,' the sergeant answered, his temper fraying. With the bikers, the three lanes of clogged traffic and irritable drivers using their horns, at this rate they wouldn't clear the first twenty lines before the sun went down. '*Just wave them through!*' he called to his officers blocking the bikers. '*Get rid of that goddamn noise!*'

The armed officers on the inside lane stood back and did as their sergeant ordered. '*Go!*' one of them shouted as the men and few women riding pillion zipped past the roadblock and disappeared down the highway.

Her NYPD Ford had been fixed ahead of schedule by the local mechanics, so she was ready to depart Lee County, but before she left town, Marquez had taken a detour and driven to the hospital in Jonesville one last time to see how the laundry truck driver was faring. Once she'd checked in on him, she was planning to head north to re-join Archer in Ohio and hopefully pick up on Lupinetti's trail.

She'd been admitted to the ward and found the driver in a bed in a private room with his head supported by a large frame, wearing an oxygen mask. Marquez had just passed who she'd been told was the man's wife with other members of the family in the visitor's room. Among them were a boy and girl both less than five years old.

'I can't believe he survived,' Marquez said quietly to the two doctors who'd treated him. 'My experience, a cut throat means someone's a goner.'

'Ours too,' one of the doctors replied. 'Person who did it was careless, or in a hurry. Reason we were able to save him.'

'I guess in the prison, if you attack someone you need to do it fast. Maybe it's a habit for the Loughlins.'

'He still would've bled out but the field dressing around his neck saved his life. Whoever applied it and called 911 did their part.'

'Has he managed to communicate with anyone yet?' she asked, looking in through the doorway at the driver before realizing what she'd asked. 'Dumb question.'

'Afraid not,' the same doctor told her. 'He won't be able to speak again for a while. His vocal cords were sliced.'

'Can he write?'

'I guess,' the other doctor said, glancing at his colleague who nodded. 'He's conscious. But if you're gonna ask him anything, limit it to a couple of questions only. He's still very weak and dosed up. You might not get a lot of sense out of him.'

As she looked around for writing implements, one of the doctors passed her a Bic while the other found a pad at the nurses' station and brought it over; both men then followed her to the driver's bed. Marquez saw the injured patient's eyes slowly shift to look at her. 'Hi Drew,' she said, having seen his name on the whiteboard outside the room. 'My name's Lisa. I'm a cop from New York. It would really help me if you can answer a couple questions. You feel up to that, blink twice.'

After a pause, he did.

'I'm putting a pad right here under your hand. Here's a pen.' She tucked it between his fingers. 'If you can, write your answers for me. First: do you know who did this to you?'

The driver's eyes drifted slowly from Marquez to the two doctors; then the Bic began to move, albeit very slowly, as the doctors joined Marquez on that side of the bed, curious to see what he was writing. The NYPD detective didn't need to reverse the pad to read what the man scrawled, messy but readable.

Lofl-

'Loughlins?' she interpreted. He looked at her and she thought he was about to blink, but then he wrote his confirmation instead.

yes

'How do you know it was them?' Marquez asked. He wrote again, slowly.

work

laundry

know

names

'Do you know who Nicky Reyes is?'

The pen rested on the paper, then it started to move again.

no

'Could you find the news for me?' she asked one of the doctors, nodding at the TV. The man pulled the screen around until it faced the driver and turned it on. After switching to Channel 11, they watched the main features, which were the prison escape at Gatlin yesterday, the violence that had followed across West Virginia during the night and the robbery-shootout in downtown Cleveland this morning. As footage was shown from the searches currently being carried out in the Ohio city and surrounding area of Cuyahoga County, the line of mugshots of the wanted men appeared on screen as Marquez knew they would at some point. The Gatlin Four.

'Him, on the far right,' Marquez told the driver, pointing to the face on the TV then turning to make sure he was watching. 'Was he in the truck too?'

yes

'Did he call 911 for you?'

He tapped the same word weakly.

yes

'And was he the one who padded up your neck?' Marquez asked, her last question.

The driver tapped the word again.

So it *was* Nicky Reyes who'd saved the man's life.

Fortunately for that Gatlin fugitive at that particular moment, the police and State troopers manning the roadblock on I-90 hadn't paid any special attention to one of the bikes with a sidecar riding in the middle of the large group. In it, there was a bag tucked low by the passenger's feet and also a small smear of blood visible on the left side of the bike, missed when Kat O'Mara was being eased into the seat before being strapped in, a helmet and sunglasses hiding her identity.

But the motorcycle procession was soon out of sight and heading into Pennsylvania as Ohio law-enforcement continued their searches of the lines of vehicles still jamming up the highway. Unknown to them, two of the fugitives they were hunting had just slipped through their roadblocks.

But the three much more dangerous men were still inside the city.

TWENTY SIX

After he parted ways with Prez on the morning of the riot, clutching tightly-wound straps of bedsheet in his hands, Nicky ran through C Block in the direction of the laundry but peeled off just before he got there to cut into the kitchens.

He headed straight for the stores at the back, the prison's sirens over the noise of shouting acting like a wailing heartbeat and ticking clock; he had about fifteen to twenty seconds to locate what he was looking for. He quickly found it on the shelves, a plastic container of vinegar, but it was a three gallon jug; he snatched a smaller plastic bottle of ketchup off a higher shelf and shook the contents into a sink. He rinsed out the remainder as fast as he could under the tap, then opened the vinegar and started pouring it into the bottle, sloshing some into the basin in his haste as he checked around in case anyone was sneaking in ready to jump him. The laundry truck was going to be driving off any second with or without him, but even then, he knew the guards might stop it leaving. So many things that could still go wrong.

When the bottle was almost full, he screwed the lid back on and sprinted for the laundry. He stopped dead when he got there, finding Hoff and Kattar's bodies lying on the floor where they'd been dumped beside a pile of dirty laundry and surrounded by pools of blood. I'm too late*, he thought in despair, but then saw through the loading bay that the truck was still there.*

He dropped down and crouched behind a table used to unpack and fold the laundry. The rear gate of the delivery/collection point was open, same as the back of the truck, a space of about a foot between the vehicle and the loading bay; with no sign of the brothers, and with Hoff and Kattar's bodies dumped beside him, he knew Brooks and Billy had to already be inside.

Staying low, Nicky ran to the back of the vehicle quietly, hearing a CO yelling at the driver telling him to leave immediately. He quickly slid under the truck then looped the lengths of sheet he'd brought with him over the axle before cinching up his legs.

It was as close as he could have cut it. A second later he saw the driver's feet appear and hooking one arm around the axle, Nicky picked up the ketchup bottle just as the man ran to the back of the truck. He heard the rear sliding door come down and the sound of it being locked, then watched as the driver's feet disappeared. Seconds later, the engine roared into life; the vehicle pulled out of the loading bay and rumbled past a first inner gate before heading towards the front exit as Nicky clung on, concrete speeding by just below him.

He felt the binds on the sheet straps stretch as they took the strain, then as they slowed at the gate, the leg tie came loose. He swore in panic, seeing the length of sheet trailing back on the ground like a tassel, stained with axle grease. He looped one foot around it and managed to pull the fabric back up just as he saw the shadow of one of the guards approaching, followed a few seconds later by the sight of his boots.

Nicky hooked his sneakers around the axle, the tassel out of sight again, and held his breath.

'-let us in!' *he heard someone shout.*

'-people out,' *someone shouted back, their answer broken up by the siren.*'-now!'

Nicky kept his eyes closed, praying the CO wouldn't drop down to check underneath the truck. He felt it sag slightly as the guard opened the back and stepped on board to take a look, praying the man didn't find the

Loughlins. It was the first time he'd ever wanted them to succeed in anything beyond spending more time in the SHU, and a wish he'd end up spending a lot of time reflecting on later.

But his guardian angel must have been on duty, and the boots and uniform reappeared just before the rear door was pulled back into place. There was a double thump on the back of the vehicle and seconds later, it proceeded over a speedbump which scraped Nicky's back painfully before heading out onto the road where the truck picked up speed.

And for the first time in eleven years, three hundred and sixty days, he was outside the walls of USP Gatlin.

After the Loughlins had driven away from the laundry truck in the car they'd taken off the elderly woman, the stretch of highway eleven miles from the prison went quiet again.

Wind rustled through the trees and fields, as a few birds chirped quietly from somewhere nearby.

Then a figure in an orange prison jumpsuit lowered himself down to the dirt track under the truck. His limbs were saturated with lactic acid, his arms sore from clinging to the underside of the vehicle, but the hurriedly-made straps from the bedsheet had held this time. Nicky carefully removed them before cautiously peering out from under the truck, but there was no sign of Brooks and Billy. They were gone.

He crawled out from under the vehicle, his overalls stained with axle grease, his back throbbing and bleeding from being scraped over the speedbump; he pushed himself to his feet then tried to get his bearings. The truck had stopped on a dirt track hidden from a highway by fields of corn and he could just make out a sign back on the road: Route 58.

He was free, a moment that he'd dreamed of and one that he could have experienced legally in less than a week, and it took a few seconds to adjust as he gazed around him. The sheer vastness of the landscape and amount of space was overwhelming. But a new, unrelenting invisible clock was now ticking. He hadn't escaped to admire the view and he'd just gone from due to be released, his term served in full, to a fugitive who'd already be a wanted man if the riot had been shut down and Prez hadn't managed to get Janks into their cell.

This new-found freedom was going to be short-lived if he didn't get moving, fast.

Nicky went into the back of truck, snatched a pair of jumpsuit pants from a basket, and after soaking them in some of the vinegar, dropped down and rubbed them on the axle under the truck where he'd been clinging, killing any scent of him there for sniffer dogs to pick up.

But it was as he was replacing the lid on the bottle that he heard something from the front of the vehicle. Nicky froze, then crawled back out from the truck and listened. Then he heard it again. He crept up towards the cab and as he peered through the open door, it occurred to him that during planning this escape, he hadn't spared a thought for what the Loughlins might do to the driver.

The man was slumped in his seat, blood soaking his shirt and dripping onto the floor; his pants were missing, presumably stolen by the brothers, blood all over his boxer shorts and bare thighs. The driver suddenly stirred slightly, making another quiet choking gurgle, and Nicky realized that was what he'd heard a moment ago; somehow the guy was still alive. Nicky immediately pulled off his prison jumps top, leaving the BOP-issue white t shirt underneath, turned it inside out and wadded the fabric against the man's throat. He then ran to the back of the truck and retrieved some of the cleaner overalls; he ripped shreds from another set of prison pants and going back, wrapped them around the guy's neck to keep the padding in place.

Most of the driver's shirt was soaked with blood and he was trying to say something, the fear evident in his eyes. 'Hang in there, man, you're gonna be OK,' Nicky told him. The guy blinked, as Nicky dug into the man's pockets. He found a wallet in one but ignored it and reached into the other to find a cell phone.

He held it for a moment and looked at the injured driver, before glancing at the cornfields around them again.

Right now, if Janks wasn't discovered at count after the riot was squashed, Nicky knew he potentially had a clear two days' head start. It could be the difference between getting out of Virginia or getting cornered by dogs, choppers and troopers; between getting to Kat and stopping her. The difference between staying free or being sent back to prison for at least another twelve years. Maybe even for the rest of his life, if he was a considered a co-conspirator with Brooks and Billy.

The driver's wallet had fallen open where Nicky had dropped it and glancing down, he saw a folded picture of two infants in a photo window, a boy and girl. He looked to see the man's eyes were staring at the photo before shifting up to him, full of desperation and panic.

That settled it; Nicky dialed 911.

'Operator. What's your emergency?'

'I'm on a track off Route 58,' he answered. 'There's a laundry truck here. The driver's been stabbed. He needs medical attention immediately. Get here fast.' Leaving the phone call open, he wiped the cell down carefully, followed by the wallet, and left both near the driver. 'They're coming, man. Just hang on.'

As the driver remained slumped in his seat, the escaped convict dropped out of the truck and back to the ground.

And after sprinkling more of the vinegar around where he'd been standing, then on the soles of his shoes, he took off into the cornfield and started running for his life.

Looking at the wider landscape and having seen the signpost which told him he was beside Route 58, Nicky took a guess at where he was as he sprinted through the corn, recalling the maps of the local area that he'd spent the previous night studying on Prez's phone. When he reached the other side of the field, he saw a sign showing he was relatively close, but was still three miles out from where he needed to be.

White t-shirt, sneakers and bright orange prison jumpsuit pants weren't exactly ideal camouflage, so although it slowed his progress Nicky kept to the thick cover and protection of the cornfields, dropping to the ground whenever he heard a vehicle passing nearby. He was about half a mile away from his destination when he saw blue and red lights in the distance, and waited until the patrol car zipped past on the road beside him just outside the cornfield, rightfully guessing they couldn't have been onto him so fast; but then he heard the car's brakes screech as it passed a turn to the left. He risked peering through the crops and realized the cruiser had reversed to take the road leading to where the laundry truck was parked off Route 58. The fields were too big to allow Nicky's footprints to be easily found, but now the truck with the injured driver had been located, this entire area was going to be a giant get-together for county law-enforcement very soon. A man wearing bright orange would be seen pretty quick out here, especially from a chopper.

He looked at the road signs and catching his breath, started running through the crops again, heading in what he hoped was the right direction. Twice more he had to drop down as police cars raced past on the highway, then the last thing he wanted to hear, a helicopter somewhere nearby. He prayed whoever was inside wouldn't spot him.

Finally, he came across what he'd been looking for, parked beside an old barn. The Oreo cake hadn't been Prez's only leaving gift for his younger friend; he'd also arranged for a car to be left here for him by members of his motorcycle club. Nicky hadn't known exactly where he was going to be able to free himself from under the laundry truck, but knew it would almost definitely follow Route 58 and that the Loughlins wouldn't wait for it to reach the depot. He and Prez had taken a guess, and they hadn't been too far out.

After checking to make sure the road was clear, Nicky ran out of the field towards the blue Chrysler. He found the keys hidden under a rock near the right wheel as agreed, and seconds later was inside, his chest heaving as he recovered his breath. Hidden under the passenger seat, he found a change of clothes, clippers and an Ohio driving license with a different name, date of birth and address. He and Rainey had taken a headshot on the smartphone and sent it to Prez's chapter outside Atlanta last night; not everything his MC chapter did day-to-day to earn money was entirely legal.

Nicky got out of the car and changed fast, stripping off the BOP clothing and pulling on a t-shirt, jeans and new sneakers, but he didn't use the clippers, wanting to save an appearance change for later; he was gambling that Gatlin wouldn't know he was gone yet, so his photo wouldn't be in circulation for a while. Every instinct screamed at him to get as far away from here as possible right away, but instead he gathered up his prison clothes and ran back into the corn. If he was going to stay ahead, he needed to think clearly and follow the plan.

It took him almost five minutes to dig a deep enough hole in the dry ground with his hands, the summer having been a hot one, and he dumped his BOP pants, old sneakers, t-shirt and bedsheet straps in it before pouring in more vinegar. Good riddance. He scooped and smoothed the soil back over the hole then stamped it down before brushing over and covering the earth with a couple of rocks. He tipped the last of the vinegar over where he'd been working, then examined the ground. It was a good job and would take some finding if sniffer dogs managed to track him through the fields. Even if they found his shoeprints, hopefully the trail would go cold right here when he left in the car.

Getting back into the Chrysler, Nicky took another look at his fake license. Stephen Rydell *was the name, July 4th the birthday chosen by him and Prez to make it easy to remember, the year of birth the same as Nicky's. He checked the road, seeing it was still empty, and then found a disposable cell phone and an envelope containing five hundred dollars tucked inside the center console.*

He pocketed the phone and cash, feeling an overwhelming sense of gratitude towards his celly. Without the chapter's help, the success of his escape would have been in serious doubt.

Give them everything you got, kid.

He keyed the engine, the sound of it starting like music to his ears, and pulled onto the road before heading west towards Kentucky. From there, he could then redirect north towards Ohio, but he had to get out of Virginia first before they put up blocks and checkpoints, which very soon were going to be clotting up every road out of the area with the Loughlins loose. The cops were probably already looking for them, but with any luck not him for a while. Even so, he didn't want to risk undergoing any unnecessary scrutiny.

As he drove, he saw the time was 12:06pm, which gave him just under twenty three hours until Kat was going to help pull the high-risk heist on the truck in Cleveland.

All the time he had left to get there, find her and stop her.

But twenty minutes later, he was just thinking about how he was going to locate her in the city when he hit his first big problem.

A roadblock was in place ahead.

It was on a straight stretch of highway close to the Kentucky border, but even though the block was in the distance when he spotted it, Nicky knew he couldn't pull a U turn without risking drawing attention. As he drew closer, still grappling with the instinct to spin the wheel and try to find another way out, he forced a slow, deep breath and focused on staying calm. A thought occurred to him that one of the troopers or officers here could have worked as a CO at Gatlin at some point and might recognize him, but he was committed already and moments later rolled to a stop at the roadblock, the only car on this stretch of road aside from the two Virginia State Police vehicles impeding his path.

As he waited for a trooper to approach, he realized he had dirt on his hands from digging the hole to bury his Gatlin clothing and footwear; he rubbed them under his legs quickly before lowering his window as a lawman approached it.

'License, registration.'

'Registration's at home, sir,' Nicky told him, passing over the license.

'Where's home?'

'Ohio,' he said, having asked Prez to get his guys to put an address in Dayton on the driving license, hoping it would make his passage into the state easier. The trooper took off his sunglasses, bent down and held the ID near Nicky's face.

'Why you in this area?'

'Had to drop my kid back off at my ex-wife's place,' he said. 'She moved down here last year. Thought I'd pass through Kentucky on the way home and pick up some good bourbon.'

'You got Georgia plates on your car.'

'Used to live outside Atlanta.'

The trooper sized him up for a few more moments, then handed back the license. 'Don't stop to pick up any hitchhikers, sir. Some inmates have escaped from the federal prison near Jonesville.'

'OK, thanks for the head's up.' Nicky took back the fake ID created less than twelve hours ago, and with his heart thumping drove on through the roadblock.

He was almost a mile clear when he finally felt he could breathe again, his hands clammy with sweat on the steering wheel. But he'd passed his first test and feeling more confident, drove on out of Lee County and out of Virginia into Kentucky.

His first time wearing something other than prison jumps in almost twelve years, the first time back in a car and the first time in all those years breathing air as a free man.

How long all that was going to last was now down to him.

TWENTY SEVEN

Whoever out of Prez's motorcycle club who'd brought the car up overnight had left the tank fully topped up, which allowed Nicky to get through Kentucky and up into Indiana before the sun went down. He stopped to refill at a gas station once he was over the State line, buying food and drink at the same time with some of the five hundred bucks, then parked up a few miles away in a supermarket lot to eat, making sure he was well away from any security cameras. He'd considered eating while he drove to save time but didn't want to risk doing anything to catch the attention of any passing bored cop who had tickets to fill and didn't like seeing a man with out-of-State plates doing something he could pull him over for.

His luck ran out however when, late in the evening, he was getting close to the Ohio border and the Chrysler scored a flat. Nicky pulled over to change the wheel only to discover there were no tools. Rolling slowly into the next town, his heart in his mouth when he'd passed a police car who had every right to ticket him for driving with only three fully inflated tires, he couldn't find any place still open to change it. Stealing a new car would draw unwanted attention, so he was faced with the very unwelcome fact that he would have to wait until morning.

As he sat in the Chrysler in quiet frustration, tucked away out of sight down a side road while listening to the radio, his blood turned to ice as he heard his name mentioned as another escapee from Gatlin. His luck really had just turned for the worse; Janks must've been found almost a day and a half before Nicky hoped he would be. He knew Prez would be getting sweated by the prison staff and investigators by now too, although there wasn't a chance in hell his celly would break.

He also heard that the Loughlins were the chief suspects in a prison bus ambush in West Virginia, and that members of law-enforcement had been killed as inmates on board the transport escaped. One of those freed was reported as Frank Lupinetti; Nicky had guessed that the ex-cop from C Block had to have been paying Brooks and Billy for protection inside Gatlin, but there must have been more than a few zeros on that amount of money for them to go to such trouble to free him. Lastly, he learned that the ambush had cost them their youngest brother. Whoever had put Craig down had just made two very dangerous enemies.

He tried to sleep, but only really managed to lean back in his seat with his eyes shut, keeping alert for any prowling squad car and unable to put aside the thought of the clock constantly ticking on towards 11am tomorrow morning. Hearing what the Loughlins had done already and the memory of that terrified laundry truck driver with the sliced-up neck was starting to sit heavily on his conscience. Nicky had known about the brothers' planned escape through Wes's revelations at dinner last night and used them for his own ends, but people had already been killed due to their actions. If the brothers made it to their home territory in the upper part of New York State, with the contacts they had, Brooks and Billy were going to be extremely hard to find. Nicky remembered from the news when he was a kid that the 1996 Olympics bombing suspect had hidden out in the woods in North Carolina for five years without being found; now Brooks and Billy had escaped from their cage, it would become a life or death struggle to get them back inside. Before this was over, it was likely a lot more people were going to die.

He felt the weight of that, but exhaustion won out and he finally dozed off. After snapping awake again just after 6am, he drove around the Indiana town until he found a place opening early and got them to replace the flat. The mechanic who helped him out was friendly and totally unsuspicious, and twenty minutes later Nicky was back on the road. He passed into Ohio without encountering any further roadblocks, but with the unexpected delay, time was running out.

As the morning sun came up and he made his way slowly through Labor Day Saturday traffic, Nicky tried Kat's phone repeatedly using the burner cell left in the console of the car, but she still wouldn't answer. Her phoneline most likely would've been tapped, but if she'd seen that he'd broken out of prison she'd know why, especially so close to his release. Maybe that could be enough of an incentive not to go ahead with the robbery.

With that in mind, instead of going to her apartment in Clark-Fulton which he knew would be under surveillance by now, he drove through his home city towards the intersection where she'd told him the hit on the truck was planned, remembering the familiar streets from his youth and not needing a map.

But as he approached East Superior where she'd said this was going down, the sudden outburst of gunfire told him he was too late. Kat had naively promised him no-one would get hurt; but that sound of gunshots followed by screaming immediately made it clear that something had already gone badly wrong.

When he followed the noise and pulled up to see her slumped against a mail bin a block away from the avenue, Nicky also saw a loaded black bag beside her and two separate units of Cleveland police officers engaging with each other down the street. Looking around to gauge the threat he was about to face, he saw another man holding a pistol double-handed crouched behind a car across the street from him, pieces of it being blown off as it took shotgun shells and rifle rounds.

The scene was chaotic and confusing, but as Nicky got out, intending to run over to Kat and extract her, he looked towards the direction of gunfire again and froze for a second in shock.

The three men firing at both the blond man taking cover behind the car and at a police cruiser were Brooks, Billy and Lupinetti, the two brothers dressed in police uniforms.

What the hell were they doing here and wearing those clothes?

Nicky didn't waste time trying to work it out yet, but started running towards Kat instead. 'Nick?*' she coughed weakly as he reached her. Even wounded, she looked as stunned at seeing him as he'd felt seeing the Loughlins.*

Instead of answering, he swept her up and carried her back towards his car, the bag hooked around her shoulder knocking against his leg as he ran.

After they'd swapped out their car for the one they'd taken from a bodega owner, Nicky had driven them through the eastern suburbs trying to work out what to do next when he seized on an opportunity that presented itself. He was driving slowly, not wanting to attract any extra attention with Kat writhing and whimpering in agony on the back seat, when he saw the garage door for a property on his left start to open; he pulled over to watch as a car moved out and started to head off down the street.

Hoping and praying the driver wouldn't look in the rearview and seeing there was no-one else around, Nicky quickly drove forward and turned into the drive just as the garage door was starting to lower. He accelerated and managed to get underneath as the door bounced against the car's roof and then closed behind him. He didn't know how long the driver was going to be gone, if there was anyone else in the house or if he'd been seen sneaking into the garage by a neighbor, the decision to hide in here taken on sudden impulse. But he needed a moment to see just how bad Kat was hurt and knew the cops would be out in force, prowling the streets. At least for the time being they were out of sight.

As she lay on the backseat, gritting her teeth while twisting and contorting in pain, Nicky got out, opened the back door and reached over to lift her sweater. He saw from the car's interior light that she'd been hit on her right side and figured from the damage that at least one rib had to be broken; if it was, that brought the additional, serious risk of it puncturing her lung.

He used the rudimentary equipment in the first aid kit he'd taken from the bodega to try and stop the bleeding, but knew she urgently needed expert treatment. How he was going to get that with the cops looking for them seemed impossible.

'You...broke...out,' she gasped, managing to get the words out through the pain.

'I came to stop you. I told you this was a bad idea.'

'How did you...?' She gave up finishing the question, in too much pain, but he knew what she was asking; he didn't reply, instead taking out the cell phone left for him by the Georgia bikers and calling Prez. He wasn't answering either.

'I need your help, old man,' he whispered quickly on a voicemail. *'If they didn't throw you in the SHU with Janks yet or find your phone, call me back soon as you can.'*

'You...you only had a few days....left,' Kat whispered. Nicky squeezed her arm then realized he hadn't checked the bag she'd taken with her from the robbery. He moved

over and opened the zipper, seeing a closed deposit box inside.

He looked back at her, seeing she was watching him. 'Thought I...couldn't do...it,' she said, before coughing again and arching her back.

He didn't answer.

*

Now five hours later, Nicky was in his fifth State in less than twenty four hours, but most importantly, was out of Ohio and the police heat cooking the entire area. The Cleveland chapter of the motorcycle club Kevin Rainey was a member of had turned off I-90 after riding on long past the roadblocks and were now pulling into a scrapyard down a track in the Pennsylvania wilderness, the place surrounded by tall trees, bushes and miles of woodland.

Riding his borrowed bike with a sidecar attached, Nicky followed them into a large clearing in the scrapyard which was clearly serving as a makeshift campsite tonight. There was a big bonfire already going, chairs and beer coolers scattered everywhere with another forty or so bikes already parked up. As the Cleveland MC roared in, they were greeted by members of what Nicky saw was the Pittsburgh chapter, seeing their cuts and allegiance on their worn leather jackets.

The place was humming with guys revving bikes, smoking weed or drinking booze, rock music playing from speakers somewhere. Taking off his helmet, Nicky swung his leg off the bike and went to Kat, removing her helmet too. Prez had called him back an agonizingly slow half-hour after Nicky had contacted him from the garage and told him to get to a cross-street four blocks away. A car idling by the curb had picked them up and taken the pair to an underpass where members of the Cleveland MC chapter were waiting. Prez knew Nicky had ridden motorbikes in his time and they'd had one with a sidecar ready, along with the helmets and jackets. Nicky had been informed they were heading out of the city on Interstate 90 and a short time later was riding with them, camouflaged in the middle of the group of bikers.

Nicky took off the loaned shades and leather jacket he'd been wearing. He removed Kat's too and unzipped her jacket. Her face was screwed up in pain, dried blood having stained her shirt, the bag at her feet covered by a blanket.

'*It hurts so…much, Nick*,' she groaned, before coughing. *'Oh God.'*

'Get her in the office, now,' Nicky heard a woman say; he turned to see who he later learned was the Cleveland president's wife standing there watching him with two other members of the MC. She had hair a similar shade of red to Kat's, tattoos on both arms up to her neck and was also a good fifteen years older. 'The boys by the fire see her, you got more problems,' she said, glancing back towards the Pittsburgh chapter across the scrapyard.

They helped Nicky get Kat out of the seat and carried her over towards the office for the business. There was a couch inside and Nicky threw the blanket down before helping lie Kat onto it, who was now only semi-conscious. The biker's wife checked Nicky's basic bandaging under Kat's shirt.

'Leave her with me,' the woman said, before seeing the Gatlin fugitive hesitate. 'I trained as a nurse. We just risked ten-to-twenty helping you get over the State line, guy. I'm not gonna do anything to your girl. If we wanted a bounty, we'd have sold you out by now.'

He moved back outside somewhat reluctantly but kept away from the gathering near the fire, not wanting to draw the attention of the Pittsburgh chapter. He didn't know if news of the Gatlin Four and the truck heist in Cleveland had reached these parts yet, but once it became clear Ohio

State Police couldn't locate him and Kat, the search was going to widen and their faces would be everywhere. Turning Nicky and Kat in could help a motorcycle club in many ways, like getting outstanding warrants forgotten or time clipped off sentences for friends currently locked up inside. Nicky trusted Prez with his life, but he didn't know how much sway his celly still had with the club after his fourteen years behind bars. Nicky had Kat's handgun tucked in the back of his waistband, but six shots weren't going to do much against two MCs worth of bikers carrying guns.

He decided keeping his head down and staying out of sight near the exit road was the best move right now. He then realized the bag from the heist had been left in the sidecar and hurried back to retrieve it. To his relief, the holdall was still there, and he lowered it to the ground behind the bike before opening the zip. The deposit box inside was still closed and way too heavy for what Kat had told him was meant to be inside. He looked around but the party was noisy and no-one was paying him any attention. He found a torque wrench in the bike's tool kit and broke the lock open after several blows.

There were neat rows of banded cash in the box. Lifting a few out, he found the bills were covering some smaller boxes; he opened a couple to find they contained expensive-looking jewelry. He did a quick count and it looked like there could be at least half a million dollars in money, but guessed the value of the jewels eclipsed that many times over.

Digging in further, he found another eight jewelry boxes, but instead of feeling jubilant, he swore quietly.

This wasn't what Kat had been after.

'You hear what they were talking about?' the Gatlin captain asked the CO who'd been standing closest to

Reyes and his visitor as they studied the footage from the meeting that had taken place two days previously when Kat had visited Nicky that Thursday afternoon. The shot was in color and good quality.

'Nothing interesting,' the CO replied. 'Why I walked off to listen to some others. Conversation sounded like she'd smoked too much weed on the ride over.'

'She doesn't look stoned. Check out her behavior. Girl looks nervous as hell.'

Marquez had just arrived at the control room from the hospital, wanting to see if the prison had any final news on Lupinetti before she left town, and overheard the brief exchange. She'd glanced at the screen before hearing the captain's question and noticed Brooks Loughlin had been sitting pretty close to Reyes at the next table.

She'd also noticed he was focusing all his attention on a worried-looking Nicky and fidgety Kat O'Mara.

Not on his visitor.

'Won't take too long for the cops to guess I could be hiding out in an MC,' Nicky told the Cleveland chapter's president, the man having walked away from the party across the yard with a beer in hand. 'Kev Rainey's been my only celly at Gatlin. The guards know we're tight.' Nicky pulled a $5,000 stack from his pocket and offered it to the biker; payment for his help. The burly president took the money, flicking his fingers through the wad to count the bills. Nicky noticed the man's eyes then switched to the bike; *looking for the bag,* he guessed. 'Why'd you do this?' he asked the man.

'Rainey's a legend in the club. Took a fifteen year federal gun charge alone to save three chapters' worth of guys going down with him. He wanted you helped out and we were coming this way anyway.' The huge man drank deep from the large tallboy of beer before grinning. ‘And I like getting one over on the feds. They’ve been on my ass since I was old enough to piss standing up.’

The man’s wife exited the scrapyard’s office and walked over to them, wiping her hands. ‘She’s in trouble,’ she told Nicky. ‘Bullet’s deep in there and I can’t get it out with no anesthetic. She starts screaming, the Yinzers might work out who you are pretty fast.’

‘We’ve gotta do something about the pain.’

‘One of our boys has some oxy. I’ll get some off him and dope her up.’

‘We’re gonna be here till tomorrow,’ the president told Nicky. ‘Time the sun comes up, you and your girly will be gone. Don’t care where you go or how you get there, but we never helped you. When you get caught, you and her managed to get outta Ohio by yourselves. Understand?’

Nicky nodded. ‘Get the girl to a doctor or she’s never gonna make it to wherever you’re trying to go,’ the man’s wife added. The Cleveland president put his arm around her shoulder, then they turned and walked off, the biker stopping by a cooler and collecting a drink for her as they passed.

When you get caught, Nicky thought, the biker’s words repeating in his head as he watched them walk away.

The man hadn’t even bothered to say *if.*

TWENTY EIGHT

At 7pm later that day, Archer showed his badge to an officer standing outside the Lakewood suburb gun store which the two Loughlins and Lupinetti had raided earlier, then ducked under the police tape and walked in. Richie of Cleveland PD was standing behind the counter, having called Archer twenty minutes ago inviting him to join the Robbery/Homicide squad here.

'Should've thought to put owners of places like this on alert,' Richie said, as Archer thanked the lieutenant for including him before taking a look at the scene. A small arsenal of firearms had been laid out on the counter and behind the selection, big gaps could be seen on the shelves where boxes of ammunition had been stored. 'After the shootout off Superior, might've guessed they'd be needing to resupply.'

'We know it was our boys?'

Richie's squad sergeant Glick pointed up to a camera in the corner. 'The brothers and ex-cop rolled in, overpowered the owner then raided the place.'

'Kept the man behind here but he managed to trigger the emergency alarm,' Richie said. 'There's a button near my foot.'

'What happened to him?' Archer asked. Deep down he already knew.

'Dead. Throat cut open so bad with a blade his head looks like a Pez dispenser. Lot of anger in the way it was done.'

'Probably because he managed to activate the alarm.'

Richie gestured towards the back. 'Looks like they left that way. Arriving units found no-one else here.'

Careful not to touch anything, Archer walked across the store and saw a rear exit.

'Armed teams have been doing door-to-door searches in the suburb,' Richie continued. 'Half an hour ago, the Loughlins' car was found dumped in a parking lot a few blocks south of here. Tag comes back to a thirty two year old from West Virginia. He and his girlfriend were reported missing earlier today; no-showed at a friend's house in Columbus where they were supposed to be staying this weekend.'

'Two more dead bodies dumped somewhere to find now too, then,' Archer muttered.

'Why'd they leave all this hardware behind?' one of the other detectives asked, looking at the shelves of guns. 'Taking too much would slow them down?'

'Probably, and they'll have got used to the rifles and twelve gauge they've been using,' Archer replied, remembering the accuracy of the fire aimed at him when he'd arrived at the shootout during the armored truck robbery and also in the bus on the Kanawha Falls Bridge back outside Charleston. The extradition agents Spencer and Harrington, both killed from a distance. 'All they'd need would be more shells and bullets. Anyone know yet where they got the weapons from in the first place?'

'Another missing person who got found without a pulse,' Richie said. 'Bartender who lives down in Lee County, Virginia. No-showed for work last night, wasn't answering his phone, so one of the barbacks got sent over to see if he was OK. Found the door unlocked and his body inside on the floor, back of his skull caved in from a fire-log on the floor beside him. We liaised with the sheriff's department down there, told us they found tufts of beard shaved off in the upstairs bathroom. Kitchen cupboards raided, gun safe in the basement emptied too. Had to have been the brothers, again. A car belonging to an old lady they'd killed earlier was abandoned outside the place.'

Archer swore. 'I'm losing count of the bodies these guys are stacking up, and they've only been out of prison less than thirty six hours.'

'Just got some info from Morningstar on the two missing deposit boxes and who they belonged to,' Glick said, having taken a call when his lieutenant was talking to Archer. 'One's a divorced wife of some banker doing time in Elkton, the other a woman who runs a redevelopment company in the city. Deputy over on East Superior saying both owners just got to the scene.'

'Be pretty useful to know what was stolen,' Archer said.

Richie nodded then whistled to his team to indicate they were leaving. 'Let's find out what they had in that truck.'

Every chance you get, you refuel, you rest and you think, Prez had told Nicky while they were sharing the correctional cake in his cell two nights ago, and he was currently working on doing all three.

The Cleveland MC chapter might have helped him get out of Ohio but their leader had made it very clear that this was a temporary deal, so Nicky didn't want to push his luck or attract unnecessary attention by going out to the campfire to try and find some food. But the meat he could smell cooking was wafting into the junkyard's office and making his stomach growl. Searching the room, with Kat out cold on the couch having been given some oxycodone the president's wife had scored off one of the bikers, Nicky discovered a pack of out-of-date mini-donuts in one of the drawers and ate a couple before going next door to fill a mug with water from a basin in a toilet connected to the office.

The food in his stomach and sugar hitting his bloodstream felt immediately revitalizing. Prison had taught him long ago to eat and drink fast, unexpected attacks, strict mealtimes and potential theft meaning a man needed to take any chance he got to consume calories before they were stolen or his tray of food was knocked to the floor, but Nicky made himself chew the donuts at a slower pace while he used the time to think. He'd had to do a hell of a lot of rapid planning in his cell coming up with a method of breakout and then what to do if he finally made it to Cleveland, but knew the challenges to come were going to be far more dangerous and difficult. He'd had the luxury of anonymity for a few hours but by now, his and Kat's faces would be on every TV screen in Ohio and probably neighboring States as well. He had to adapt and needed a new plan going forward. This was all just getting started.

Wiping powdered sugar off his hands onto his jeans, he went back to the drawers and dug out an old sun-faded map of the Midwest and Eastern US that he'd seen folded up under the box of donuts. As the noise of engines gunning accompanied by shouting reached the office from the fire outside, with his finger he traced the route where they'd made it out of Ohio on Interstate 90. He and Kat were now in upper Pennsylvania; from Cleveland, I-90 kept going somewhere between a diagonal and horizontal in a northeast direction. It cut across the top western edge of PA, past the small city of Erie, and then on into New York State. That roadblock they'd snuck through earlier came back to mind; trying to cross into NY on I-90 by themselves without an MC's camouflage would be suicidal, but that wasn't why he was looking at that section of the map. Almost the same length of distance away from where I-90 crossed into NY State was Buffalo and Niagara Falls.

And just north of them both, the Canadian border.

There was no TV in the office, but there was a radio and Nicky turned it on. The channel was playing some rock music on 102.9, but he waited, seeing it was almost time for the hourly news. With every passing thirty minutes, the circle which the Marshals and FBI would think he and Kat could be in would be expanding. It made him feel like a surfer on a small, beaten-up board trying to keep ahead of a giant tsunami chasing him in towards the shore.

He just needed to stay on his feet, keep balanced and focus on where he was going, not where he'd been.

On their way back to the intersection on East Superior, Archer, Richie and Glick were also listening to the news report coming in over the car radio. They were learning that another fugitive from the bus transport attack on the Kanawha Falls Bridge last night had just reached the end of his time on the run.

'Which one was he?' Richie asked Archer, as the newsreader gave a dead convict's name, the man shot dead after taking a hostage at a house in southern Indiana. Archer recognized the last name *Briley.*

'Guy who tried to kill me,' he replied.

'Seems to be a growing list,' Glick commented, drawing a smile from both Archer and Richie as they arrived at the intersection.

The three men left the car and walked over to discover a middle-aged woman with a close-cropped haircut gesturing angrily at several hapless US Marshals. '*-into that thing?'* they heard her ranting as they drew closer, seeing the truck had been hauled upright and was currently being loaded onto a flatbed with chains and a crane. 'How could you allow this to happen?' she demanded; as one of the Marshals tried to answer, she noticed Richie, Archer and the other detectives approaching. 'Who are you?' she snapped, before seeing their badges. 'You investigating this?'

'We're Robbery-Homicide,' Richie told her flatly.

'You know who did this?'

'Looks like five people were in on it. Four of them are dead.'

'The fifth?'

'She was shot during the robbery. We're searching for her.'

'She's injured that bad, you got all these people looking for her but she's still out there somewhere with my property?'

'She's been receiving some help.'

'This bitch have a name?'

'Katherine O'Mara. Is that familiar to you?'

'*What did you say?*' The group turned and saw another woman standing nearby; she was a similar age but in contrast to the other deposit box owner, was far calmer. 'Did you just say Katherine O'Mara?'

'Which box was yours, Miss?' Archer asked the first woman before anyone could reply.

'The one with my money and jewelry in it, asshole,' she snapped, before getting on her cell phone and walking off to one side.

'Kat O'Mara, yeah,' Richie said, walking over to the other woman. She was around fifty years old by Archer's guess, with sleek, long dark hair, and was dressed in a crisp white blouse and slim-fit jeans. He recalled from when he was in the gun store that she'd been described as someone with a property redevelopment company based in the city. 'You own the other deposit box?'

'I do. I'm Blair O'Mara. Kat's my stepdaughter.'

'Your stepdaughter?' Richie asked, as surprised as Archer and Glick.

'Afraid so. I was outside the city all day. Didn't hear about what happened until I just got back. I heard you tell that woman four others are dead?'

Archer nodded. 'What was in the deposit box?'

'Something personal to me.'

'Could you be more specific? It might help us understand why just two boxes were taken from the truck.'

'Some valuables,' she replied vaguely, clearly not prepared to tell them anything more just yet.

'Yeah, we sort of assumed that,' Glick answered dryly.

'When's the last time you spoke to your stepdaughter?' Richie cut in, not wanting to set this woman off too after seeing the look she gave his sergeant.

'About a year ago. Every time I think she's reached rock bottom, she gets a shovel and digs a little bit deeper.' Her eyes shifted around the intersection, the glass fragments still on the concrete, bloodstains visible from where four of the five thieves were killed. 'I can't believe she was involved in this.'

'Your daughter's the one who got shot?' the other woman snapped, still on her phone call but clearly with one ear on the conversation.

'Stepdaughter,' Blair corrected, as Richie nodded at two of his detectives who walked over to the other woman to distract her so they could continue the conversation with Blair uninterrupted.

'You haven't caught the news all day?' Archer asked.

'No, I was at a spa. Turned my phone off. No TV or radio allowed.'

'Kat didn't escape by herself,' Richie told her. 'A man showed up at the shootout and picked her up before driving off. They've both disappeared into the city somewhere.'

'She mixes with a lot of lowlifes these days. You have any idea who he was?'

'Guy called Nicky Reyes.'

Archer was watching Blair carefully to gauge her reaction to this piece of information and saw total astonishment. 'He's meant to be in prison?' she said.

'He broke out,' Archer told her. 'So if Kat's your stepdaughter, is he your stepson?'

'No, absolutely not. That young man is a murderer.'

'She gonna make it?' a voice asked and Reyes swung round on his seat, having been listening to the radio in the Pennsylvanian scrapyard office. One of the bikers from the Cleveland chapter was standing in the doorway, a black baseball cap back-to-front on his head and a bottle of beer in his hand as he looked at Katherine on the couch.

Nicky didn't answer, turning down the dial on the radio. 'How's the party?' he asked as he saw the biker wasn't alone, one of his friends on the steps behind him.

'Good.' The biker eyed up Kat. 'Wanted to see how my oxy was doing. Knocked her right out, huh?' Pause. 'We were gonna smoke up. Wanna join?'

'Nah, I'm set.'

'This weed's like nothin' you ever had, man. The Yinzer VP out there grows it himself.'

Nicky gave a nod at Kat. 'I'm looking after her.'

'Don't look like much you can do for her right now. Come take a break. We ain't gonna bite. No-one's gettin' near your girl.'

Nicky heard shouting and laughter from the campfire outside, the group currently focused on partying rather than the two fugitives hiding in the office. The Cleveland president seemed to have a lot of respect for Nicky's old cellmate and couldn't imagine that he'd let him or the injured woman come to harm under his watch. Not yet, anyway. Nicky still had six or seven hours before the sun came up and their temporary deal was over.

'Guess I could use a walk,' he said, rising from his seat. He stopped at the door, the biker having stepped aside for him to go first, but Nicky waited and the man took the lead, the other one already walking down the steps. Instead of heading over to the campfire, the bikers led the way deeper into the trees; the second man opened a beer and offered it to Nicky who declined again.

'So what's your deal?' the one who'd invited him out there asked, sparking a blunt as the other man finished his Yuengling, throwing the empty bottle into the bushes before starting on the one Nicky had rejected. 'Where you goin' next?'

'Dunno. Taking this all one minute at a time.'

'Bossman didn't tell us much, just that we were gonna help you out. But after I had some of my oxy taken, I got real curious.' He nodded to his friend. 'Pickett there told me all about you.'

'I was watching TV before we rode out the city,' Pickett said. 'You broke outta prison in Virginia, then helped your girl in there take down that bank truck this morning.' He drank the beer, his eyes remaining on Nicky. 'How much you come away with?'

'Not sure. It's her stash. I'm just holding onto it until she recovers.'

'Take a hit,' the other biker said, offering the blunt again.

'I told you, man. I'm good.'

'You don't like weed?'

'I don't smoke.'

The biker smiled and went back to the joint, but Nicky noticed he wasn't inhaling deep, just catching and releasing which meant the dope wouldn't be affecting him that much. 'They got a radio playing in the main shop,' Pickett said. 'Marshals just put a sixty thousand dollar bounty on you and the girl.'

'Changed my mind, I'll take a beer if you got another.' The biker smiled and pulled another bottle from the inside of the jacket under his cut before passing it over. 'Bounty doesn't mean much,' Nicky said, opening the screwcap. 'It ain't gonna be collected.'

'So how much is in that bag you and your girl had with you?' Pickett persisted. 'We saw you give the boss some bills after we got here.'

'I told you, that's her money, not mine.'

'We could take some of it. Like sixty grand. We do that, you might not get shipped to the Feds.'

'Not sixty,' the weed smoker said. '120. For both of 'em, remember.'

'Your president promised my celly that me and the girl make it clear of here by morning. You think he's gonna let you take us to the cops?'

'If you attacked us, he's not gonna care,' the weed smoker said.

Sounds from the woods at night and the distant noise from the campfire swelled the silence that followed.

Condensation from the still-cold beer ran down onto Nicky's hand.

'You wanted to smoke some of that wet weed,' Pickett said. 'Hit you bad and you tried to come after us. Forced me to drop you. Prez won't mind too much once we get 120 for you and the bitch. Shit, might just keep the whole ba-'

Nicky hit the first biker over the head with a wrench he'd slipped out of his pocket while they were talking; it was the same one he'd used to break open the deposit box when they'd arrived, having decided to hold onto it just in case. As the biker hit the dirt, Pickett threw his beer at Nicky and pulled a pistol from his belt, but the prison fugitive caught the second biker's hands as he tried to bring the firearm up. The hammer came down, the metal snapping into his finger, biting into the skin as Nicky stifled a shout of pain. The gun fell to the ground, ripping part of the webbing on his hand and Pickett went for it again, but Nicky picked up the full bottle he'd just dropped and smashed the biker over the head with it, the impact shattering the glass with a spray of beer and sending Pickett to the ground near his friend, both of them now laid out.

The only one left standing, Nicky quickly looked over towards the bonfire. The noise of the party had stayed at the same pitch, meaning none of the other bikers were aware of the fight. He shook his hand out, the skin bleeding from being trapped by the gun's hammer, and dropped down to check the pair for weapons, finding another pistol. He also discovered an orange pill bottle half full of oxycodone tablets, returned to the biker after Kat had been given a dose, which Nicky slipped into his pocket. Both men were still breathing, which was good; he didn't want to add second degree murder to his rap-sheet. Nicky grabbed Pickett and dragged him thirty feet or so deeper into the woods, then went back for his friend before taking a knife from Pickett's belt.

A couple of minutes later, the two bikers were bound, gagged and tied with their backs to the same tree, Nicky having ripped strips and the sleeves from their shirts and removed their jeans and bootlaces to secure them, leaving their cuts undamaged and dropped on their laps. Collecting their handguns and taking the ball cap the first one he'd hit had been wearing, Nicky rapidly made his way back through the undergrowth then stopped by an old fallen tree.

He reached inside and found the holdall where he'd hidden it earlier, the money and jewelry boxes still inside. He pulled it out, emptied the contents of the deposit box into the bag, then zipped it shut and looped the strap over his shoulder, leaving the now-empty Morningstar deposit box in the decaying tree trunk instead. He looked at the pistols in his hands, and after a moment's thought, placed them in there as well.

When he reached the edge of the clearing again, he walked as casually as he could back towards the office. No-one at the camp paid him any attention. He went inside to find Kat was still where he'd left her and just waking up. Still partially doped up, she tried to rise but fell back against the cushions, gasping in pain. Nicky moved forward to help her but as he did, saw something pinned to a corkboard that he'd missed earlier.

'What's…happening?' Kat asked quietly.

'We're leaving,' he told her, going into the bag and peeling off a couple of hundred dollar bills. He pinned them to the board with a quickly scrawled note, then went back to the couch to ease her up. 'This is gonna hurt but you need to stay quiet. OK?'

She nodded and gasped in pain as he picked her up, the strap for the bag containing the money over his shoulder and a set of car keys now in his pocket. 'Where we going?'

'The hell out of here,' he said, pulling the ball cap over his head before carrying her to the door. He checked outside briefly, but just as before, the bikers were all too busy having a good time to notice the two fugitives moving in the dark.

Reaching two cars parked side-by-side, Nicky lowered Kat to the ground then tried the key in his hand in an old, restored Mustang. It turned, unlocking the doors. He glanced back at the campfire but no shout went up. Picking Kat up, he opened the rear door and slid her onto the backseat, placing the holdall in the footwell with her, then not taking his eyes off the figures silhouetted against the flames, he moved around and got in behind the wheel.

Holding his breath, he started the engine. If they were going to be noticed, it was going to be now.

But with the noise the bikers were making, the music and several of them revving their own engines, the sound of the Mustang firing went unnoticed. Nicky slid the restored classic car into gear. Leaving the lights off, he drove it very slowly away from the campsite and disappeared into the darkness, far beyond the light of the fire.

The Cleveland MC president had demanded the two fugitives they were harboring be gone by morning.

Nicky had just made sure they were.

TWENTY NINE

'*I've been taking a closer look at the two women these missing deposit boxes belong to,*' Glick told Archer eight hours later. The NYPD detective was now standing just beyond the side of the awning outside his downtown Cleveland hotel in the morning sunshine, ready to go again after a full night's rest. The hearing in his right ear had mostly recovered, all the tiredness from the day before gone. Lockdown in this part of the city had ended and people were walking around again, seeming more relaxed on this Sunday morning. '*Remember the woman giving the two deputies a hard time? Divorced her hotshot banker husband a couple years ago when he went down for embezzlement. Court awarded her funds as part of the settlement after his estate was investigated and the money he embezzled was returned. No proof it belonged to anyone else, so altogether she's got around two and a half million dollars' worth of stuff inside that deposit box. Mixture of cash and jewelry. She's given us an inventory.*'

'Ouch. How'd our thieves know it was there?'

'*I made a call to the prison over at Elkton. The captain told me one of our dead boys, Vaughn Till, did time in the same cell block as the woman's ex-husband. The banker told investigators that he remembered bitching in the yard to Till about his wife cashing out on him in their divorce. Guess he told the wrong man.*'

'How'd they know the right bank and box number?'

'*Till got the name of the bank out of the guy and started dating one of the branch's employees when he got out.*'

'Guess she never did a background check.'

'Nope. He and his crew took their time. Didn't rush anything and must've found out about the boxes being transferred out a few weeks before. Christmas arrived early, or so they thought.'

'So this team of thieves hit the truck to only steal a pair of boxes: this banker's ex-wife's and the one belonging to Blair O'Mara.'

'Just those two. The woman told us there used to be another couple million in there, but she spent it purchasing a new home, car, clothes, vacations, stuff like that. All adds up, I guess. The ex-husband didn't know that so the thieves wouldn't have either. So an assumed 4.5 million, plus whatever was in the other box? Lot of money for five people to split. The boxes were knocked loose like busted teeth when the wrecking ball hit the truck, so it would take enough time to find the right ones from the heap without just bagging random boxes. I think the thieves would've burned up too much of the clock trying to take others, and they could guarantee what was in the two they took. Who knows what crap people keep locked up? One man's trash is another's treasure, right?'

'Anyone know yet how Kat O'Mara got involved with this crew?'

'The other girl on the heist who got shot dead by your Loughlin brothers was Till's sister. She was Kat's celly at ORW when she was in there for eighteen months. Must've hit it off because they live together across town. The other girl moved in with Kat last year.'

'What did Kat do time for? Robbery?'

'No, doctor shopping. Lied on forms and visited different practices to score prescription drugs. Benzodiazepines. Sedative meds.'

'Her stepmother was pretty cagey about telling us what was in the deposit box.'

'Legally she's not obliged to give us more details, but we ran a background on Blair O'Mara and she's clean. No record, inherited legitimate wealth from her dead husband. She's from Indiana. Last job she had before moving to Ohio was working at a casino there.'

'She might have to tell us at some point what was in that box so you know what the hell you're looking for.'

'I got a question for you too, man; how do you think your four Gatlin boys got involved in this? I can't find any ties between the Loughlins and Lupinetti with the thieves, the ex-wife with her divorce settlement or the O'Mara's. There's just one link to any of them: this guy Nick Reyes.'

'Reyes must've found out about the heist through his so-called sister.'

'But how'd the Loughlins find out about it too? You said those two and Reyes hate each other. Could he have let something slip to Lupinetti like the banker with the thief in the yard at Elkton?'

'I don't know, we'll have to look into that,' Archer said, raising his hand when he saw a familiar car with New York plates turn onto the street. 'Where's Richie?'

'Oh yeah, almost forgot; young woman called the Department half an hour ago. Says she thinks she might've seen Frank Lupinetti and the brothers yesterday afternoon.'

'It took her this long to call 911?'

'She just woke up. Passed out when she got home yesterday after drinking too much at a cookout. The lieutenant's gone to talk to her.'

'Might not be too reliable if she was that wasted.'

'I'll take it if it's a good lead.'

'Think Richie would mind if I joined him?'

'No, he told me to pick up with you again. I'll message you the address then tell him you're coming.'

Archer thanked the detective and ended the call just as the NYPD Ford slowed beside him and the passenger's window slid down, revealing a familiar face behind the wheel wearing sunglasses. 'Wouldn't park there, Miss,' he told her. 'You might get towed.'

'Jumped off any more bridges lately?' Marquez replied, matching his quick smile as she got out of the vehicle. She stretched her arms up and yawned before giving him a hug. 'Go our separate ways for one day and look what happens. We've got a lot to catch up on.'

'The journey OK?'

She nodded. 'Been listening to the news updates. Grid-by-grid searches are still happening here apparently. Extended to neighboring villages, towns and counties.'

Archer nodded. 'I've been working with Robbery/Homicide. They're a good team and willing to include us.'

'Cool, but first, I gotta take five. I was driving all night.'

'I rented my room upstairs for another day. Use the shower and get something to eat; I'll fill you in on what I find when I get back.'

'Where you going?'

Archer felt his phone buzz and saw the promised text from Glick with the location Richie had gone to. 'A woman called in thinking she might have seen Frank and the Loughlins on her way home from a party yesterday. I want to hear what she's got to say.'

'So let's go.'

He smiled. 'You just said you wanted a timeout?'

'It can wait.' She tossed him the keys to let him take the wheel. 'But my stomach can't. We're stopping to pick up breakfast on the way.'

At the scrapyard in Pennsylvania, one of the bikers from the Pittsburgh chapter woke up, having passed out beside the fire at around 4am. He opened his eyes, blinking blearily a few times, before reaching for his boots. He pulled them on and pushed himself back to his feet, scratching his beard then rubbing his eyes as he yawned.

The air was warm, even with the fire now only a mass of charred cinders; he saw he was one of the first to wake as he wandered over to a cooler. Inside, the ice had melted but there were a couple of beers floating in the cold water and he took out a can of Iron City, opening it and taking a long pull as he walked off to take a leak. He trudged into the undergrowth before pausing to open his fly and then emptied his bladder while drinking the beer with his free hand.

For a moment he thought he heard something, but deciding he'd imagined it, zipped up then walked back up towards the camp.

He stopped on the way, looking at the office where the wanted chick and her brother had been holed up last night. He'd seen the Cleveland president and his woman taking the girl into his office to try and fix her up; the president had told his boys why they were doing this, that Kev Rainey from the Atlanta chapter had asked for help, and word had spread. They all knew Rainey had taken a fifteen year federal gun trafficking charge driven by the ATF to save any guys from three separate chapters involved in the case take the heat for it. That meant the club would always help the guy out if and when he needed it.

But their president had also said that once morning came, the deal ended and that particular debt was paid. Most of them had heard about the bounty on Bonnie and Clyde last night, sixty g's a piece. He decided to check they were still there, so tossed the beer can aside and walked towards the office, but as soon as he entered, saw they weren't going to be collecting anything. The only thing on the couch was a blanket. He checked the toilet to make sure, but the wanted pair were gone.

'*YO, WHERE THE HELL IS MY CAR?*' he suddenly heard a voice bellow from outside, cutting through the morning quiet. The biker stopped and looked at the corkboard, where he knew the keys for the two cars being restored outside were normally kept.

One set was missing, some money pinned there instead, *Sorry* written on one of the bills in pen.

He moved forward, removed the pin and pocketed the money, before going back outside.

'How sure are you these were the men you saw?' Richie asked the eyewitness from the day before, passing her a printout with Lupinetti's and the Loughlins' mugshots on them. She lived in an apartment building not far from the gun store in Lakewood; Richie, Archer and Marquez were standing with her on the front stoop, the young woman wearing sunglasses and clearly very hungover. Archer had just introduced Marquez to the Cleveland PD lieutenant, the NYPD detective now munching on a danish and drinking coffee as she listened to the exchange.

'Pretty sure it was them.' The woman pointed at Lupinetti. 'Saw some tattoos on his arms. The news said they were something to look out for, right?'

'Why didn't you call 911 last night?' Marquez asked, not yet knowing why unlike Archer and Richie.

'Went too hard on the sangria at my friend's place,' she admitted. 'Left early, walked home, barfed and passed out when I got in.'

'Plenty of big guys with sleeve ink around,' Richie said. 'Pretty sure I could start mistaking their faces for someone else too after drinking too much.'

'He had some bandaging on both his arms too,' she said, tapping Lupinetti's photo again. That information wasn't something that had been released to the public, which Archer and Marquez both immediately latched onto. They glanced at each other, as Archer remembered seeing Frank getting his arm wrapped at the hospital in Jonesville just before his attempted escape.

He was about to tell Richie that but a train's horn sounded nearby. As the hungover girl groaned quietly and leaned against the door jamb, the three cops with her all looked left and saw a slow-moving freight train approaching a station fifty yards away across the street, beyond some fencing and empty tracks. A sign told Archer it was *RTA West 117th Station.*

'How often do the trains come through here?' Archer asked.

'All the time,' the woman said. 'Hear them stop and go all night. You get used to it.' The horn went again and she groaned. 'Kinda.'

'Where were our guys when you saw them?'

'Crossing the street.'

'Heading that way?' Archer replied quickly, nodding at the station.

'Sure.'

'Were passenger trains checked yesterday?' Marquez asked Richie. 'Passing through or leaving the city?'

'Yeah, carriage by carriage.'

'But not freights?' Archer said.

He paused and looked at him. 'No. I don't think so.'

Archer thought about the events of the night, police units with dogs and helicopters, intensive searches being conducted all over the city and outer suburbs with no trace of the fugitives. Men who were in a strange locality but who'd still managed to escape detection, despite two of them being easily identifiable from their sheer size.

Archer, Marquez and Richie all watched the train as it pulled into West 117th.

'They got out, didn't they,' Richie said, a statement rather than a question.

The search net had just been widened by hundreds of miles.

THIRTY

'What did Cuse say?' Billy asked, as his brother walked back into their cell after meeting with his visitor, a cousin of theirs, the day before the riot at Gatlin. 'We all set for Monday?'

'Shut up for a second,' Brooks told him, going to the corner of their cell. He looked around for paper, couldn't find any, so opened a book instead and ripped out one of the first pages before reversing it to use the blank side. Billy sat on his bunk and watched as his brother started writing with the stub of an old pencil. He was curious but managed to do as Brooks said and kept quiet.

'What you doing?' he asked eventually, curiosity finally winning out.

'Reyes and his visitor were talking at the table next to me and Cuse. I think they were using some sort of code.'

Billy turned and looked up at the higher tier, seeing Reyes in the cell he shared with Prez Rainey. 'Why do you care?'

Five to five, *Brooks transcribed, ignoring his brother, remembering what he'd overheard of the pair's strange conversation.* Right now- *no, he crossed out the w. She'd said* right, no. *Their strained body language and unusual, abrupt exchanges had caught his attention, and he'd ended up tuning out Cusick while focusing on Reyes and his female visitor, concentrating hard on what they were saying.*

USP Gatlin was a high-security federal facility, housing many inmates who were still involved in criminal enterprises on the outside, so the guards were alert to any hint of unusual conversations or behaviors, particularly during visits. As a result, some of the men in these penitentiaries had to find inventive and novel ways to get messages in and out. Brooks was one of them, which was why Reyes' conversation and his reaction to what the woman was saying had caught his interest.

He quickly wrote down the rest of what he'd heard before he forgot it then stared at the page, trying to make sense of the words. He took the paper out to the yard with them for rec time, and as he and his brother started to jog a couple of laps, something they'd been doing lately to slowly build up their cardio for once they were outside the fence, he mulled over the various possibilities.

The more he thought about it, the more he was convinced what he'd heard had been significant and not just an odd, random conversation. He disliked the guy but had to admit Reyes normally kept his cool no matter what, and was always hard to read.

Why then had he suddenly looked so wound up?

Midway through the third lap, he slowed and looked over at Reyes sitting on the bleachers beside the biker Rainey, the pair having just taken a quick trip over to the payphones to make a call. He still didn't look right. Billy stopped running too and caught his breath, as Brooks pulled out the paper and pencil stub from his pocket then started writing down a new series of words. Billy waited, knowing better than to interrupt again or maybe draw attention to what his brother was doing, then saw Brooks rise back up, looking at the sheet with a grin of quiet triumph on his face.

'I got it,' he said.

'Already?'

'Wasn't hard. Look.'

Billy leaned in, checking the paper:

five to five. that's right, no; or six to one. i will if y'all
will. i gotta change hair dye.
or not. guaranteed.
yes it is.
the time?
wanted to since I was eleven. Sharp.
day?
This saturday.

'Looks like a bunch of bullshit to me,' Billy said.

'Take the last word of four of the sentences. Put them together. Read it again.'

Billy took the paper and eventually was able to see what Brooks meant.

Five. No one will die
Not guaranteed.
Yes it is.
Time?
Eleven sharp.
Day?
Saturday.

'I got more,' Brooks said, reversing the page, having written down what Kat said to Nicky just before.

They headed out east. Her name was Superior. and. (she
paused here, i think) she died on the 22nd.
(reyes didn't answer)
been hard to take. she was only five. I wish she lived to
be a million

The two brothers read the code:

East Superior and 22nd.

Take

Five million.

'Superior and 22nd must be a street corner somewhere,' Brooks said.

'Where?'

'Could be Cleveland. I know that's where Reyes is from.'

Billy stared at the paper. 'And there's five milly on offer?'

Brooks glanced at him. 'If I'm right, then yeah.'

'What did Reyes say?'

'He wasn't happy about it,' Brook said, taking back the page. 'That part wasn't in code. Check him out on the benches. He still isn't.'

Billy looked up and casually eyed the man. 'Can we find out where she lives? If you're right, we could take it from the bitch after we get out.'

'You think she's gonna steal five million dollars and just go back home to brew a cup of coffee?' Brooks replied. He glanced over at Reyes too. 'This sounds like a robbery. We gotta work out where this Superior place is.'

'And be there?'

'Why not?'

'Cos we're stuck in here.'

'Not for much longer. Our departure date was arbitrary.' Billy gave him a blank stare. 'Means it can be moved.'

'Lupinetti'll like that. I haven't told you yet.'

'Told me what?'

'When you were meeting Cuse, the screws let the cop know he's getting shipped out tomorrow after getting cut open again last week. Warden thinks if he stays in here, he's gonna get killed. Frankie-boy was pushing Hoff and Kattar to get us to bring Independence Day forward.'

'How the hell did he find out about it?'

'Kattar told him.'

The horn went for the end of rec time, and Brooks carefully folded up the paper before pushing it into his sock. 'If this is right, we don't need the cop anymore.'

'Lupinetti's already gotten us wired nearly fifty grand for keeping his ass alive. You confirmed it with Cuse last week. And he told me he'll pay us another two hundred thousand if we get him outta here. That's guaranteed. This other thing ain't.'

Brooks looked at his brother. 'He better be for real.'

'He was a pig rolling in all kinds of shit for twenty years. He'd know where to hide it. And we'll need every cent if this Superior thing is bullshit or you're seeing something that ain't there.'

'Grab him at chow then,' Brooks said. 'Hoff and Kattar too.' He caught his sibling. 'Don't tell those two clowns about Cleveland.'

'What about baby brother? He still thinks we're rolling Monday.'

'I'll get a message to him.'

Brooks had already decided to fast-track their escape plan with this new information on Reyes and the girl, but then after hearing on their way back to their cells from chow that work rotations were being switched up early next week, much to Lupinetti's relief, bringing forward the breakout to the following morning had suddenly become a necessity. If Brooks and Billy were no longer working in the laundry, they couldn't use it to escape, so Independence Day *as they'd been calling it was kicked up.*

Unknown to them, that was precisely the result a certain other prisoner in C Block had been hoping for.

After eating what was euphemistically described as breakfast in the chow hall on that Friday morning, the two

Loughlin brothers had headed to the laundry for work detail, some essential items they'd been collecting in preparation for their escape tucked into their socks. Then right on time, the sirens started, just after Hoff and Kattar attacked Lupinetti's escort as they opened up C Block, using that as their trigger point for a riot and adapting the original plan which had been to lure a couple of COs into the block before jumping them.

Brooks and Billy knew what time the laundry truck driver arrived, when he left and that he had a routine of a cup of coffee inside the facility with some of the screws while the inmates unloaded and then reloaded the truck; that's where he was when the trouble started. However, when the COs and driver tried to open their door, they found it was jammed, a door wedge made in the carpentry shop pushed against the door on the other side. Basic, but effective.

'Where's Frank?' Brooks asked, as Hoff and Kattar ran into the laundry, the wedge buying them all some valuable time.

'His celly jumped him,' Hoff said. 'No way we were goin' back for his ass.'

'Let's get on the-' Kattar said, just before Brooks slashed his throat open to the bone and Billy shanked Hoff in the neck. They'd served their purpose; any chance of getting out with five men in the truck was slim to zero and the pair had been useful idiots. Their part in this was done.

The brothers pushed them free from the shivs as Hoff and Kattar collapsed and bled out, Brooks and Billy dragging their bodies out of sight of the door before they could start to really leak out all over the floor; if they were discovered before the truck was gone, it'd be stopped before the brothers stood any chance of getting out of the facility. Hoff was still twitching so Billy stabbed him in the eye socket to hurry things along, leaving the shank buried in there as a parting gift.

Meanwhile, Brooks had clambered over the baskets already loaded in the truck and opened up two at the back, having observed the driver's inspections in the past and knowing he only gave the baskets back here a cursory glance, same as the CO on duty at the gate. He dragged out the contents and passed them to his brother who dumped them onto a pile already heaped up ready to load. Then both of them climbed into a basket each, covering themselves with a few remaining items of laundry, Brooks making sure neither of them had left bloodstains anywhere that could be seen before the truck departed.

They'd just got into the baskets when another CO heard the noise being made by his colleagues and driver inside the break room they were trapped in, and removed the door wedge trapping them from the outside.

'What are you still doing here?' the CO asked the driver.

'Someone blocked us in!' he said, seeing the wedge in the man's hand.

'Get your ass gone,' the CO told the driver, before turning his attention to the guard who'd been trapped inside the break room too. 'They're attacking our guys back in the housing! Pena just got killed!'

As the COs took off to help deal with the riot, the driver ran to the truck, had a quick look in the back before closing the door, then leapt inside the cab and drove away from C Block towards the main gate. Despite checking several baskets, for whatever reason he was going to deeply regret and had a lot of trouble explaining at the investigation that followed, the guard at the gate didn't go all the way to the back or check under the vehicle, a mistake that ended up costing a lot of lives.

Once they were a good distance clear, and after a long wait in a queue for a traffic accident, Brooks climbed out of the basket. Then he slid open the window panel, grabbed the driver by the hair and held the shiv he'd killed Kattar with to the terrified man's neck.

*

Now, almost forty eight hours later, Brooks, Billy and Lupinetti walked out of an old, abandoned shack in the Pennsylvania woods where they'd taken shelter during the night, checked the surrounding area, then set out again. The gun backpack was slung over Billy's shoulder, the holdall from the heist over his older sibling's, one brother holding a shotgun and the other a rifle, both men still in their stolen Cleveland Heights PD uniforms which were becoming increasingly stained from grime and sweat. As the pair set the pace, the city-bred Lupinetti trudged miserably behind, totally out of his comfort zone in this new and to him, hostile environment.

As soon as they'd run from the gun store yesterday in Lakewood after realizing that silent alarm had been triggered, the three fugitives had seen a slow-moving freighter passing through the RTA West 117th Station ahead. Brooks and Lupinetti looked at each other, then clambered over the fence fast before cutting across the tracks, Billy following a few steps behind. Their jogging in the yard at Gatlin paid off; they'd caught up to the train, climbed on board and hidden away in one of the cars just as they watched flashing lights arriving back outside the gun store.

The freight train rolled into Cleveland's main station a few minutes later, but wasn't stopped or searched, and once they were through it picked up speed again, taking them clear of the city limits and heading east. They'd travelled out of Ohio, but then the train had suddenly started to slow when they were somewhere in what Brooks judged to be the northwestern Pennsylvanian woods. The three wanted men hidden on board had panicked and leapt off as the brakes screamed, then half ran and half skidded down a steep bank, Brooks keeping a tight hold of the stolen holdall from the heist as they went.

Coming to a stop, they stayed low and watched through the grass, but the train had only slowed for a signal ahead, another train passing the other way a couple of minutes later, and then picked up speed again. Its three temporary passengers waited until both trains were out of sight, the area falling quiet, then Billy had gone back up the bank to retrieve the gun bag he'd dropped in the fall.

Lupinetti stayed where he was, as Brooks scoped out the surrounding area. The night air was warm, the full moon bathing the landscape in a cold white light, the wilderness quiet. The freight had taken them just one State away from home, but Lupinetti had noticed that unlike him, the brothers already appeared far more relaxed out here than they had in the city. The three men had walked for several miles before Brooks said they needed to rest up for a few hours, each of them exhausted. They found an old shack, long abandoned, and after passing round the last of the food stolen from the Virginia fisherman's kitchen which had been shoved in the gunbag earlier, had taken turns to sleep with one of them staying up to keep watch.

Now seven hours later and after some rest, Lupinetti followed the two brothers through the woods; he was tired and every bone in his body ached from the unaccustomed exercise, but he was a free man again and would do whatever it took to keep things that way. As they walked, he saw Brooks reach into the heist holdall and take out the titanium deposit box that had been locked inside the larger one he'd opened from Morningstar, taking another look at it. They'd tried blasting the smaller box open with Billy's shotgun first thing but it had barely made a scratch, the Granit padlock sealing it proving impossible to breach.

‘Other bag must’ve held the five million,’ Lupinetti said. ‘That’s way too small.’

Brooks didn’t bother answer, thinking about the moment he saw Nicky Reyes appearing from nowhere and rescue the girl yesterday during the shootout. He hadn’t wasted any time on the guy, instead focusing on the son of a bitch cop from New York City who’d blasted Craig on that bridge in West Virginia.

But now, a day later and having had time to reflect, something that had been at the back of his mind from the moment he’d seen Reyes hit him.

‘He used us to get out of Gatlin,’ he said.

‘Who?’ Billy asked.

‘Reyes.’

‘How? We’d have seen him in the truck.’

Brooks thought about it. Reyes was nowhere near their size, one eighty at most instead of three hundred pounds. Even so, they’d have known if he’d snuck himself inside the vehicle; he hadn’t been at the back and the front baskets had been searched. Then another possibility dawned. ‘Not if he was under it.’

‘Mean, like the beaners do, tryin’ to get over from Mexico?’ Billy asked. Brooks nodded. ‘But how’d he know we were breaking out?’

‘Kattar,’ his big brother said after a pause. ‘He worked in the library with Wesley. Must’ve yapped his mouth off again. Reyes and Prez were sitting with the old bastard at chow on Thursday night. Shit.’ He considered the various pieces of the puzzle. ‘He could’ve told him what we were planning. Knew we were getting out from the laundry, so spread a lie about the work schedule to bump us up.’

Billy was giving him a blank look. ‘Reyes won’t make it out of Cleveland,’ he ended up answering instead. ‘He don’t have your brains, and you shot the bitch in the gunfight. She'll slow him down good if she ain't already bled dry.'

'Maybe,' Brooks said, looking at the deposit box. 'But now he's got the bag with the cash instead of this shit, whatever's inside.'

'Forget Reyes, the hell do *we* do next?' Lupinetti asked. 'Someone'll start thinking to check that freight train when they can't find us in Cleveland and put things together. They'll bring dogs out.'

'We got time,' Brooks said. 'Even if they realize we split town, they'll be expecting us to ride all the way up to Rochester, Syracuse or somethin'. Closer to home.'

'We've still gotta get out of PA.'

'So we find ourselves a car.' They'd almost reached a brook when a gunshot from somewhere suddenly sent all three men to the ground. As it echoed around them, Brooks slowly lifted his head as another shot rang out, further away this time.

'The hell you doing?' Billy asked, seeing him get back to his feet.

'Hunting season just started,' Brooks said. 'They're not shootin' at us.'

The other two realized he was right and got back to their feet too. 'Makes a change,' Lupinetti muttered, as he rose and trudged onwards behind the other two.

Unknown to the brothers, they were only sixty miles or so from the other two fugitives currently on the run from the Superior Avenue intersection robbery. The bell on the door of a diner outside Erie, Pennsylvania dinged as four police deputies walked in, one of them pausing to stretch out his back as the others made their way towards an empty table. The four men slid onto the Formica benches as a waitress came over, cradling some menus.

'You fellas look like you've had a morning,' a man sitting at another table opposite said, a pack of cigarettes and lighter resting beside a half full cup of coffee and an empty plate.

'Long night before it,' the lead deputy replied before removing his hat. 'Ohio's got a group of thieves they think could be heading this way.'

'Same ones who robbed that truck in Cleveland?' the waitress asked.

'That's them. Marshals think they're split into two groups; two shithead brothers with some crooked former cop and a brother-sister team.'

'TV said the woman was shot.'

'She was,' the deputy said, before ordering his food. The famished cops were too engrossed studying their menus to pay any attention to a man at the counter wearing a black ball cap waiting for a to-go order and moments later, the individual paid for his order and left.

Nicky had parked the car he'd taken from the bikers' scrapyard further down the road and out of sight; Kat was still lying across the back seat when he returned, the blanket covering her to the upper chest the way he'd left her, no police cruisers in sight. 'Where are we, Nick?' she asked quietly as he got back inside, having dozed off after he'd given her more oxycodone as a pain reliever. He hadn't slept all night, wanting to keep awake and ready to move if the Mustang drew any attention from police. He placed the bag of food on the front passenger seat while checking to make sure the deputies hadn't followed him.

They hadn't.

'Just outside Erie,' he told her. 'How is it?'

'I can't...breathe...right. It hurts real bad.'

He'd noticed her breathing had become more labored during the night. 'We have to get out of this area. They'll be widening the search net every hour. It's gonna get as hot here as Ohio soon.'

'Can you try…Rainey…again?'

'Not anymore,' Nicky said. He hadn't told her about his fight with the two bikers last night and how he'd left them lashed to the tree in the undergrowth. It was a risk to keep driving this car which was very conspicuous, nice as it was; the Pittsburgh MC would probably be out looking for him already, their deal with Prez off the table now, especially since two of their guys had been assaulted and the Mustang stolen. An advantage of driving the vehicle was the bikers were highly unlikely to report it gone but that wouldn't be much use if the motorcycle club caught up with him. The outcome of that wasn't something he wanted to think about.

However, Kat needed urgent medical intervention and all their running would be in vain if he looked back in an hour and she'd died on the back seat.

'We gotta find another car,' he told her, starting the engine.

But before that, first thing she needs is a doctor, he thought.

THIRTY ONE

'Four prison fugitives from Virginia, all showing up here when a robbery's going down, and you're adamant they ain't cooperating with each other?' Glick queried again, sitting with Archer and Marquez at the Robbery/Homicide's division headquarters. Word concerning their theory that the Loughlins and Lupinetti had managed to avoid detection and get out of Cleveland on a freight train passing through the West 117th Station in Lakewood had just been passed on to the Marshals, State police and authorities in Pennsylvania, while Richie's squad now waited for any updates.

'From what we've heard, far from it,' Archer said, as Marquez nodded.

'So how'd they all end up here? Explain the missing link.'

'Reyes was due to be released next Wednesday,' Marquez said. 'Gatlin staff said he's been behaving same as usual, staying out of trouble. Might've been edgier than normal but nothing strange about that, being so close to the end of his bid. Then after Kat O'Mara visited him late Thursday afternoon, he suddenly busted free the next morning. Couldn't wait another six days.'

'He got out the same way as the Loughlins?' Glick asked.

'Yeah, but the brothers wouldn't have known. I visited the truck they made it past the gate in and took a closer look underneath along with some State investigators at the police impound in Lee County. We found strands of white fabric in the axle joints. Looks like it could be from a sheet. A spare bedsheet, maybe.'

'Reyes lashed himself to the underside,' Richie concluded.

'Right. The Loughlins had it all planned out and he used them to hitch a ride. They can't have had any idea he was there or he wouldn't have survived. Billy's tried to kill the guy before.'

'How do you know?'

'Source at the prison,' she replied smoothly. Richie didn't push further, thankfully, but out of the corner of her eye Marquez saw Archer's head turn towards her. She pretended not to notice.

'So Reyes could've heard about their escape through loose lips in the yard,' Richie said. 'But it works in reverse; how'd the brothers know about this robbery? A man with enough smarts to smuggle himself out of prison without anyone noticing wouldn't start shooting his mouth off about a planned truck heist. Even more unlikely considering someone he clearly cared about was heavily involved.'

'All visitor meetings at the prison are recorded for security reasons,' Marquez told him. 'I watched the tape from the prison's meeting hall on Thursday. Guess who was sitting at a table near Nicky and Kat.'

'One of the brothers,' Glick said.

'Brooks. He's the brains of the two. It's gotta be almost certain that he overheard something.'

'She just told Reyes her plans with COs and other inmates in the room?' one of the detectives from Richie's squad asked. 'Doesn't sound very likely.'

'The little the nearest guard overheard made no sense to him, but they're now thinking Reyes and Katherine used some sort of a code in their conversation, or for at least part of it. Brooks was listening without them realizing. He must have deciphered what they were talking about.'

'So he heard a coded message and decided to break out the next day with his two brothers?'

'They must've already had their escape mapped out,' Marquez said, knowing from her talks with Rainey that the Loughlins' had definitely had their breakout meticulously planned, but for this coming Monday. 'What they did would take some time to plan. Maybe after hearing Reyes and his sister, they decided to bring the date forward so they could show up at the robbery.'

'Which did Frank Lupinetti a big favor,' Archer added. 'He wanted to stay in prison about as much as they did. I think he was meant to get out with them on the laundry truck but didn't show up in time. So they sprung him loose in the end on the bridge on Friday night.'

'They that keen for his company?' Richie asked.

'Frank must've promised them a lot of cash, otherwise there'd be no way they'd have lifted a finger to help him. Brooks will know if he and his brother are gonna evade capture and disappear permanently, they're gonna need every cent they can get their hands on. And there was no guarantee if there was gonna be a heist that it would go according to plan. Frank would be their backup.'

'He got away with what he was doing in our Department for twenty plus years without getting caught,' Marquez added. 'He must have managed to hide money somewhere that he's promised the brothers a share in, for them to tolerate him the way they have.'

'But they risked coming here instead of laying low somewhere?' Richie replied.

'They'd be heading north anyway. Why not stop by the city and if Brooks had been right about the code, let the truck get hit then move in and scoop up the spoils. If they got it wrong, they could just keep going. Nothing to lose.'

‘They wouldn’t worry about the extra heat that would be focused on them if they did that?’ Glick commented.

‘They clearly don’t care,’ Archer noted. ‘Their answer seems to be shoot their way out of anything. Which is why every law-enforcement officer from here to New York needs to be on their toes.’

‘The brothers and your man won’t be heading west?’ Richie said.

Archer and Marquez looked at each other, then shook their heads. ‘There’s nothing for them out there.’

‘Now we got wise to the train, we’ll pick up their trail again,’ Richie replied. ‘PA and New York authorities are putting the word out and setting up reinforced roadblocks in case our guys jumped off the freight during the night. Pretty soon an insect won’t be able to crawl over the State line without being checked for ID.’

‘If the big brother’s so smart, maybe they know that’s exactly what we’ll assume,’ Glick said. ‘They could go the other way into Indiana, Illinois or Michigan. Or further.’

‘The only freight that slowed enough at that station for them to board yesterday was heading east,’ Archer said. ‘We checked.’

‘Then that’s still not good for us,’ Glick answered. ‘You said the Loughlins are country boys. Over half of Pennsylvania is forest and woodland. They could hide out there for months.’

‘The brothers won’t exactly blend in,’ Marquez said. ‘With all the publicity this is getting, someone’s gonna catch sight of them somewhere soon.’ She smiled. ‘And Frank’s a city boy through and through. He won’t be able to take living rough for long.’

While the conversation between the group of NYPD and Cleveland PD detectives was taking place, east of their location in Erie, Pennsylvania, an Indian-American doctor was driving out of the parking lot at the city's leading orthopedic institute, UPMC Hamot.

Dr Ramesh Tejwani was a short, somewhat rotund fifty two year old consultant who was supposed to have been off-duty this weekend, but when a colleague due to perform an urgent ankle reconstruction surgery this Sunday morning had called in sick with food poisoning, Tejwani had agreed to take his place.

'*How was the procedure?*' his wife asked after Tejwani called her on the phone's system.

'Went smoothly, finished in good time. I'm leaving now but I'll stop at the store before I come home. Is there anything else we need?'

'*Not that I can think of. You still have the list?*'

'I do. Have people arrived yet?'

'Only your cousin and his wife. I'm trying to get the boys off their screens to help.'

'OK, I'll be with you soon.' Fifteen minutes later, the doctor drew into a large Wegmans supermarket parking lot on Peach Street. He locked his Mercedes Benz, took a shopping cart from near the entrance, then looked at the list his wife had given him that morning for the afternoon party they were hosting today for his twin sons' birthday.

It took another fifteen minutes to get every item, the store large and taking time to navigate, but once he was done he paid and headed back to his car with the cart of bagged goods. Just as he'd started loading his shopping, he heard someone walking up behind him but took no notice, assuming it was another customer heading to the store.

Then Tejwani felt someone take hold of his shoulder.

'Stop what you're doing,' a voice said. 'There's a gun aimed at you. Just keep acting normal.'

The orthopedic surgeon was shocked and froze, having just loaded his last bag. 'What do you want?' he asked shakily, doing as ordered and remaining still.

'You're a doctor, right?'

'I am.'

'Good. I need your help.'

'Looks like Lupinetti and the Loughlins might've hopped a freight train heading east,' Archer told Shepherd, standing in the stairwell at the Cleveland police station. 'If they were still around, they would've been found by now. These men are hard to miss.'

'The Marshals are on it?'

'Yeah, they like the lead. We have to find these three Gatlin boys, Shep. They've killed eighteen people in two days since they broke out.'

Shepherd understood what Archer was saying. *'You don't wanna drop this.'*

'No, and neither does Lis. Frank's heavily involved and we got him once. We owe Lucero to get him again. The people here would appreciate the help.'

'Then keep doing whatever you can to help track him down. I'll make sure anyone who calls wanting validation on you two gets it fast.'

'Thanks, we'll keep you posted,' Archer told him, finishing the call as Marquez entered the stairwell.

'Train we think they hitched a ride on broke down overnight after it crossed over into New York State,' she told him. 'Repaired, but was just stopped again outside Albany after resuming its journey. It's being searched, but I think our boys'll be long gone by now.'

'Shep gave us the nod to continue going after Lupinetti,' Archer said. 'You happy with that?'

'For sure.' She paused.

'But?

'You mind if I stick around here for a few hours? Just until later on tonight?'

'Why?'

'I haven't slept in almost two days; didn't get much the night before that either. Want to sneak a couple hours in to make sure I stay on-point. There's a slim chance they might have faked us out too and still be here. Another reason for hanging around the city for a bit longer.' Marquez knew he'd caught onto her comment about Billy trying to off Nicky Reyes before, and also that he was well aware she was the last person to let a lack of sleep affect her or disrupt her involvement in a case that was becoming more involved by the minute. She'd demonstrated that earlier, putting off rest to go with him to speak to the woman who'd seen the three fugitives running for the trainyard.

In return, Archer sensed she was holding something back but figured in time she'd tell him what it was, so he nodded. 'OK. I'm gonna stay on Lupinetti's heels and not let him rest for a second. He's going to be getting tired, so he and the other two will start making mistakes soon. I want to be right there when they do.' Then he paused. 'You're curious about Reyes and O'Mara too. That's another reason to stay until later.'

'Maybe. Aren't you?'

'A bit. I'd like to understand why he did what he did. But we've got our hands full with the other three right now. Frank's my top priority.'

'Then how about this: you take the Ford. I'll stay here, use a couple hours to get my head straight and make sure our boys didn't get one past us all and remain here instead or headed in another direction like Glick suggested. If it turns out they did end up going towards New York, I can use the car you rented to come meet up with you again.'

'That might be a bit difficult.' He gave her a rueful look. 'It got towed after the shootout off Superior. Took enough gunfire to write off the engine block.'

'You'll have fun explaining that to the rental company,' she told him after a brief laugh. 'I can swipe for another one. And I won't be far behind you.'

'I'll leave the keycard at the front desk at the hotel for you. Let them know you're taking the room. Tell Richie and his people I said goodbye.'

'Watch your back,' she said, slapping palms with him, but then, after he started down the stairs, he stopped for a second.

'You got a look at Nicky Reyes' visitor logs from Gatlin, right?' he asked. She nodded. 'Did Kat's stepmother ever visit him there? Blair O'Mara?'

'Not that I saw.'

Archer thought about the woman who he'd met yesterday, who'd refused point blank to tell him and Richie's squad what was in that deposit box. 'Let me know if you find anything.'

'You too. Track him down.'

In Erie, Nicky was now sitting beside Dr Tejwani in his Mercedes, having left the Mustang he'd taken from the bikers' scrapyard parked in the lot outside Wegmans, and directed the doctor to a Motel 6 ten minutes' drive away.

'Park around back,' Nicky instructed as they pulled into the small lot, checking behind them.

'How did you know I'm a doctor?' Tejwani asked nervously, as they came to a stop in an empty space.

'Saw your car leave the hospital and followed you. You left from a designated parkin-' Then the car's phone system started ringing, interrupting Nicky just as Tejwani was about to switch off the engine and pull the keys. The surgeon's hand went towards the button from habit, but then he hesitated and looked at his kidnapper uncertainly.

'Let it ring out,' Nicky told him. 'But gimme your phone.' The doctor did, and Nicky slipped it into his pocket. 'Let's go.'

Once they were out, Nicky locked the Merc and after pocketing the key he took the man to a door halfway down the line with a *Do Not Disturb* tag on the handle.

He opened it to reveal Kat lying on one of two single beds, blood staining the white sheets, the bag now containing the contents of the deposit box dumped on the floor against the wall.

'What happened?' Tejwani asked in surprise.

'She got shot,' Nicky replied shortly, closing and locking the door behind them.

'Turn that up, man,' a Penn State University student called to his companion as he sat facing a secluded lake south of Erie, eating a sandwich for lunch. Two fishing lines and a tackle box were placed on the grass by his and his friend's chairs, a Winnebago camper van behind them where the music they'd been listening to had been coming from, interrupted by the hourly news.

The two young men had been camping out here the previous night with friends from their graduating year in high school; the rest of the group had left an hour or so ago, but this pair had wanted a bit more time to sweat out the beer from the night before and try to catch more fish. His friend had just been taking a leak in the toilet on the campervan, and stopped by the passenger's side to reach in to turn the radio up, the other young man taking another bite of his sandwich before wiping some mustard off his chin as he listened.

'-cal police working with the US Marshals Office and various Sheriffs' departments, who have deployed extra resources to apprehend the wanted fugiti-'

'You hear about this?' the student by the fishing lines asked. 'There was some big robbery in Cleveland yesterday. Listen.'

-aution all residents in eastern Ohio and western Pennsylvania to stay alert. If you see anyone you think might be a suspect, do not approach them but call 911 immed-'

'When I was moving the van last night, I caught something about it,' the student by the water said, as his friend walked back over to join him. 'Some cops got killed. Marshals and police are looking for the guys who did it. Five of them. Four guys, one chick.'

A bird called from somewhere in the distance, the area around them having gradually been cast into shadow as clouds started to drift across the sun. The college student who'd returned from the Winnebago glanced around them; being out here suddenly didn't seem as much fun as it had an hour ago. 'Let's start back towards campus, bro,' he said. 'Might be roadblocks if they're looking for these people round here. It could take all day to get home.'

To his relief, his friend didn't offer up any resistance. He broke up and threw the rest of the bread from the sandwich into the water, and then reeled his line back in. He pulled up their chairs, then realized his pal wasn't helping.

'You're drivi-' he said, then looked up and his voice got stuck in his throat.

Three men were standing twenty feet behind them beside the campervan. One had a gray holdall slung across his shoulder, a shotgun in his hand, another gripping a rifle with a second bag across his shoulders. They were both dressed as cops in clothes that didn't quite fit. The third man had a pistol and had it aimed at his friend, who'd frozen where he stood.

The clouds continued to cover the sun, the remote spot remaining in shadow, and it felt a lot colder all of a sudden.

'You heard what he said,' Brooks Loughlin told him. 'You're driving, kid.'

THIRTY TWO

'How bad is it?' Nicky asked anxiously in the motel room, as Tejwani examined Kat.

'Her right lung has collapsed,' the orthopedic surgeon told him, listening to the woman's labored breathing. 'You see where she got hit?' he asked, pointing at the padding-covered gunshot wound surrounded by the heavily bloodstained material of her shirt. 'The impact smashed up parts of her ribs on that side.' He tipped her slightly. 'No exit wound, so the bullet must still be embedded in there.' He looked up. 'What fired it? Rifle or pistol?'

'A rifle, I think.'

'More power. More damage. That's not good.'

'So what do we need to do?'

'That bullet has to come out and her lung must be re-inflated.' He glanced at Nicky. 'By the way we just met, I get the feeling you won't be interested in checking her into hospital.'

'That's not an option right now.'

'Can you have her rest up somewhere?'

He shook his head. 'We gotta get moving again soon. Within the hour.'

'As she is, she's not going to make it much further. You have choices to make.'

'Could you remove it?' Nicky asked. 'Stitch her up?'

'If there's no alternative, possibly. But that's not ideal.'

'Maybe, but that's the only choice we got right now.'

The doctor looked at the gun held low in Nicky's hand, and slowly reached into his own pocket to come out with a pen. He found his wife's shopping list in the other, but reversed it and wrote a fresh list of items on the paper as

Nicky watched. 'You need to go back to the store and get these things.' Tejwani looked back at Kat again. 'And don't waste any time.'

Driving east on I-90 in the NYPD Ford, Archer had a map on the passenger seat on which he'd drawn a line following the rail-track of the *Lake Shore Limited*, the main Amtrak service from Chicago to either Boston or New York. Starting in Illinois, passing through Ohio and hugging Lake Erie until it reached Buffalo, Rochester and then other stops in New York State, the tracks were also used by freight trains like the one which had passed through Cleveland not long after the gun store alarm was hit.

Archer had asked one of the analysts at the CT Bureau in New York City to track down the driver who'd been at the controls of the long train on the previous night and had just been connected to the US Marshals' local office in Albany where the guy had been brought in for questioning. After a short wait, the driver was on the line. 'Did you make any stops last night?' Archer asked, maintaining a steady speed on the highway as he used his prepaid phone on speaker setting.

'Just told the deputies here, only for signals, not including when we broke down. No stops at stations. We ain't a passenger service.'

'So how many stops for signals?'

'Three after Cleveland until we broke down for the night. First between Ohio and Erie, second between Rochester and Syracuse, third between 'Cuse and Utica. You been talking with the Marshals here?'

'Not recently.'

'They told me their deputies are sending people to the New York State locations with dogs. Two of your boys come from around that area, I heard.'

'So you didn't stop at stations, but did you go slow or just barrel through them?'

'Depends. Went slow through Cleveland.'

'Slow enough for someone to climb on board at the West 117th stop in Lakewood?'

'I guess.'

'You see anyone?'

'If I did, I would've called it in. Company don't tolerate train hoppers. They fall onto the tracks or under the wheels, we can get sued for negligence.'

With a train weighing so many tons under his control, Archer knew the man's attention would need to be on the track ahead, not on the carriages behind him. 'How long is it from Cleveland to New York City on your schedule?'

'Should take twelve hours. Five to Syracuse.'

Would they have risked staying on the train for five hours? 'Between Cleveland and Syracuse, you think of anywhere they could have jumped off?'

'Yeah, the times I slowed for signals.'

Archer recalled his leap off the bridge in West Virginia on Friday night, doing what he had to in order to survive. Sounded like Marshals had the second two locations covered. 'Where was the first spot again?'

'In Pennsylvania. Not far from Erie.'

'Thanks for talking to me. Appreciate it.' Archer ended the call, hit the indicator and pulled over onto the shoulder to study the map.

Looking at it, he felt a pulse of adrenaline. The Lakeshore train tracks snaked through the northwestern edge of PA. The Gatlin boys could've taken the opportunity when the train slowed to leap off; according to the map, much of the area was wooded, just the sort of the place the Loughlins would choose. This would have been last night, but they'd been running non-stop ever since they broke out of prison on Friday morning so they'd need to rest.

If they'd found somewhere to hole up there was a very good chance they were still in the area.

Archer looked up at the highway ahead. The road he was on, I-90, split later on to become I-86 south but both paths led into New York State. The two highways now had roadblocks in place in certain locations and all trains were being searched, including ones with long chains of freight cars. *They could hide out,* he remembered Glick saying at the Robbery/Homicide division HQ, looking at the large areas of greenery on the map, knowing it translated to many hundreds of square miles of forestry. Not hard to go to ground out there.

But he knew Frank well and was becoming familiar with how these brothers operated. They'd broken out of federal prison, attacked the extradition bus on the bridge to free Lupinetti, shot their way through another roadblock to get out of West Virginia, then escaped with a safety deposit box after killing two CHPD officers and stealing their car. They'd steamrolled over anything that got in their way, totally unconcerned about how many people they killed in the process. Even though they'd know cops and federal agents would be looking out for them in their hometown near Syracuse, Archer guessed they were cocky enough to head to the area regardless, particularly with their run of success since they'd broken out of Gatlin. They'd be feeling confident and would want to get to familiar territory to hide themselves away, but money or not they'd need support from friends or family soon if they were going to keep evading capture. Investigators were doing the logical thing by checking the areas where the train had stopped yesterday in New York State, but Archer didn't feel that those three would have risked going all the way there on the rail-line just yet. Two of them at least were way too smart for that.

Which meant they needed a vehicle. They'd already demonstrated they'd kill without a second's hesitation, but this was Sunday daytime traffic; the main interstates out of PA would have too many potential witnesses, some of whom would be armed, as well as there being roadblocks in place too heavily reinforced for the fugitives to try and risk blasting their way through. Archer scanned the Pennsylvania-NY State border on the map. South of I-86 was *Station Road*, presumably a much quieter route, plus it seemed closest to the Amtrak rail line the brothers and Frank could've jumped off the train from.

His eyes stayed on that strip of road. He knew PA State police would be stretched pretty thin covering every route into New York right now, so most likely didn't have too many troopers left to spare for the country routes, especially as no-one had any idea where the five fugitives were at this moment. They could show up anywhere.

He tossed the map back onto the seat before signaling and getting back onto the highway. He started speeding towards the turn off to Station Road and as he drove, called Shepherd.

'Think we need to make sure Pennsylvania authorities have got people on a certain route into New York State if they haven't already,' Archer told him once he'd answered.

'Where?'

'Station Road,' Archer said, seeing a sign for the turn-off was coming up. 'South of I-86. I've got a theory.'

'Oh man, here we go. Tell me.'

Archer was correct in that all the major highways leading into NY from Pennsylvania now had strategically-placed roadblocks set up, the two States' authorities having been alerted by the US Marshals and Ohio police that there was a strong likelihood the five wanted fugitives were heading their way. Some key minor roads also had either local cops or troopers stationed on them, the deputies who knew the area concerned that their marks could slip through on the less-congested highways, and four local cops on Station Road had just checked a car before letting it through when a Winnebago campervan appeared in the distance.

Less than a minute later, the vehicle reached the barriers and stopped. Two of the officers walked forward, taking a side each, one going to the driver as the other checked the outside of the Bago and dropped to take a look at the underside. They'd heard a rumor one of the men they were after had escaped from prison in Virginia by hiding himself under a laundry truck.

'Afternoon,' the officer on the driver's side said, seeing two young men sitting up front. 'You boys are going the wrong way from campus,' he said, seeing one was wearing a Penn State football t-shirt, the other a ball cap with the university's lion logo on the front.

'Wanted to get some fishing done at the lakes up north in New York, sir,' the driver said.

'Why's the road blocked?' the other passenger asked quickly.

'Looking for this man and woman,' he said, showing the pair a mugshot of Nicky and Kat. Their old prison photos; his from Gatlin, hers from ORW. 'They robbed a truck in Cleveland yesterday.'

'Never seen them before,' the driver said.

'You?' the cop asked the passenger, who shook his head. 'What about these three?' the officer asked, showing the Loughlin brothers and Lupinetti on another paper.

'No, sir,' the driver said, shaking his head vigorously. 'Never.'

'You alright, son?'

'Fine, sir,' he replied quickly, as he looked at the other two cops standing by their cars. 'Been in the sun all morning.'

'Mind if we come aboard?' The driver nodded. 'You do mind?'

'No, I mean I don't,' the student replied quickly before glancing at his friend. The officer studied the young man for a moment before turning to the two cops at the roadblock; he made a V with his fingers pointing to his eyes then at the campervan as he moved to the side door out of the driver's view.

Lifting his rifle, he pulled open the door, the officer who'd scoped out the other side of the Winnebago joining him with his own carbine raised, the two students sitting rigidly in their seats staring ahead.

Something was making them very nervous.

The cop stepped up to check out the interior of the van, then saw a couple of coolers on the floor; he reached in and opened one of them. 'Thought you said you boys were going fishing?' he asked.

'We are.'

'You got catches here already.'

'We-um…we stopped at a lake on the way. Wanted to test out the bait.'

The lead cop glanced at his colleague, who shook his head; they both looked at the toilet door, which was closed.

The first officer nodded to the second, who raised his rifle as the lead cop stepped to one side and reached for the handle.

One of the two policemen still standing outside yawned, the effect of standing for over an hour on a quiet road in the morning sunlight, before his radio suddenly chirped.

'Unit 12, you there?'

'Copy,' he said. 'Go ahead.'

'Warning just came in the Loughlins and the ex-cop might've jumped off a train in Erie County and could be coming your way.'

As the man listened, his gaze suddenly sharpened.

There'd just been movement behind the van.

Inside the Winnebago, the officer checking the interior was about to twist the handle when an explosion of shouts and gunfire shattered the quiet outside.

The two officers inside the van swung round, but before they could react, the toilet door was thrown wide open and the lead cop took three rifle bullets to the head from Brooks Loughlin, the other cop killed a second later too. Outside, the officers by the cars were firing at Billy and Lupinetti, who'd quietly slipped out of the back of the van from the rear window moments before the cop opened the door and stepped on board.

Shotgun shells, rifle bullets and pistol rounds tore both vehicles apart, Brooks unloading with his rifle from inside the van at the two cruisers. Eventually, the smoke settled, as did the echoes of the gunshots and shotgun blasts. The silence held, as Brooks reloaded his magazine quickly.

'*BILLY, YOU GOOD?*' he shouted.

'*I'm good,*' he called back. Brooks looked down the van; the two college students had been hit in the crossfire, blood on the console and what was left of the windshield in front of them. Both were dead. Brooks gathered up the dead cops' rifles and handguns, throwing them out of the open door, then jumped out, the campervan springing back behind him, his rifle raised again as he looked down the sights.

The two squad cars had been chewed up, pieces of them all over the road. Behind him and on the other side, he saw his brother and Lupinetti appear from around the back of the campervan, both having just reloaded. Neither had been hit.

He advanced on the two cruisers to see the pair of officers beside them were down too, then looked at the road in both directions. It was still clear. Brooks opened the door of the nearest car, reached in and tried keying the engine. The cruiser started but the body was spattered with bullet-holes and he knew they wouldn't make it very far without someone reporting the shot-up vehicle.

'That noise could get someone local on their phone,' Lupinetti warned, looking at the road behind them. 'Or calling 911 if they roll up on this. We gotta keep moving.'

'We take the next car that comes,' Brooks said quickly, whistling at his brother and waving him over. The two of them gathered up all the dead officers' weapons, magazines, cuffs and radios, then dragged their bodies to the edge of the clearing, dumping them out of sight like they'd done with the old woman near Gatlin and the young couple in West Virginia on Friday night. 'Get the van off the road,' he ordered Lupinetti.

'The engine's cooked.'

'*Then push it! Just get it outta sight!*' he snapped; the former NYPD lieutenant looked at him for a moment, then turned and did as instructed.

'Unit 12, did you receive last, over?' the radio on one of the officer's belts asked, but the brothers ignored it, looking at the road behind them and waiting for the next unsuspecting driver to roll up.

THIRTY THREE

'Can I help you?' a woman in her late twenties asked, standing just inside the door of a plush-looking home in Pepper Pike, Ohio. It was an eastern suburb of the Greater Cleveland area, and one which clearly required a substantial bank balance to live in.

'I'm a cop,' Marquez said, showing her badge. 'Wanted to talk to Blair O'Mara.' She quickly assessed the woman in front of her, who was clearly too young to be Kat's stepmother; she was in sweatpants and had her highlighted blonde hair swept up in a loose topknot, Marquez having caught her on a lazy Sunday it seemed. 'You can't be-'

'*Mom,*' the girl called, cutting Marquez off. An older woman appeared a few moments later in jeans and a shirt, and the younger one turned and left. 'Keep it down, I'm watching TV,' the girl muttered to her mother as she walked into a room to her left.

'Good morning,' Marquez said.

'Morning,' Blair O'Mara replied. Marquez had found Blair's address from the details she'd given Richie earlier and before she went to lie down for an hour, the NYPD detective had decided to go ask her a few questions, her curiosity once again getting the better of her. A taxicab had brought her out here, and she had the guy waiting just around the corner with the meter running. 'You're investigating the bank truck?'

'Kind of. I'm from New York.' Blair leaned forward to look more closely as Marquez showed her badge.

'What brings you to Cleveland? It can't have been Katherine and Nicky.'

'One of the other escapees from Gatlin is ex-NYPD. He's someone we want back in custody pretty bad.'

'Did you find any of them during the night?'

'Not yet, but we will. It's tough to keep running.'

'Especially if you've been shot.'

Marquez nodded. She'd heard Kat lived in a poorer part of the city, but it had been clear as she'd taken the taxi out towards Pepper Pike that where this woman lived was just the opposite. Outside many of the impressive houses she'd passed, all of them spaced well apart, were sprinklers spitting water onto lawns so perfect you could hit a tee shot off them, expensive cars sitting in driveways, some of the properties with gates and fences to keep all unwanted visitors out. No lockdown or police checking door to door around here. 'I'm having a hard time working out the family ties. Kat, Nicky, yourself. Can you explain them to me?'

'Kat's my husband's daughter,' the woman said, keeping her arm resting across the doorway. 'We got married when she was thirteen years old.'

'Who answered the door?'

'My daughter. Alaina.' Blair gave a smile. 'We were a package deal.'

'She lives with you?'

Blair nodded. 'And works for me.'

'Is your husband here?'

'He passed twelve years ago, I'm afraid. Unexpected illness. Happened when Kat and Alaina were seniors in high school.'

'Sorry to hear that.' Marquez noticed the woman wasn't inviting her in, and it became clear the conversation was going to be conducted out here on the porch. 'What about Nicky?'

Blair's face hardened. 'His father worked for my husband. He was an alcoholic and drank himself into a car wreck when Nicholas was sixteen. For some reason, my husband decided to take legal responsibility for the boy until he turned eighteen. He had no family left to do it.'

'Kind of him. Unusual too, right?'

'My husband was a kind man.'

So that's why Gatlin had Kat down as Reyes' sister in their visitor records, Marquez thought. No blood relation. 'Why'd you move from your previous home?' she asked, looking around.

'Wanted a fresh start.'

'Must feel pretty good, living around here.'

'We've been successful. My husband made a lot of money.'

'What was his business?'

'Property development.'

'And Nicky's father was on one of the contractor teams?'

Blair nodded.

'This would be the same company you own now?' Marquez followed.

'The same.' Blair's expression was unreadable, but her eyes were cold.

'How'd you meet?'

'In a casino. My husband was on a quick vacation while Kat was away at summer camp. I worked there. We struck it off.' She smiled. 'He wasn't very good at cards, but he kept showing up at the bar inside the place where I waited tables.'

'Which casino?'

'French Lick. Indiana. Alaina and I used to live out there.'

'What happened to Alaina's father?'

'You ask a lot of questions.'

'It's my job,' Marquez retorted, but after seeing the expression on Blair's face, she softened her tone. 'I don't wanna intrude; I just want to establish some clarity. A lot of people are dying right now because of these four Gatlin fugitives and Kat.'

'Alaina's father was a waste of time. Deadbeat drug addict. Left years ago and we haven't heard from him since.'

'Katherine and Nicky seem to share a real strong bond,' Marquez said. 'Looks like he broke out of prison to try to stop what she was planning on that truck yesterday.'

'Don't get taken in. He was serving twelve years in federal prison for killing someone. That young man is a dangerous criminal.'

'Manslaughter, I heard. Not first or second degree murder.'

'So? He still took a life.'

'Kat seems to care about him. Aside from when she was in prison herself, she's visited him regularly the whole time he's been locked up.'

'Water seeks its own level.' Blair didn't elaborate further but Marquez didn't answer yet, nonetheless. Experience had taught her people tended to fill a silence if you waited long enough, and the momentum she'd built meant Blair was in the groove of answering her questions.

It worked.

'Both their mothers died when the kids were young,' Blair went on to explain. 'They lost their fathers less than twelve months apart and they each went off the rails after that happened. They could've been working decent jobs and have had normal lives by now, but Nicky got sent to prison and my step-daughter ended up addicted to drugs and found herself behind bars too a few years after him.

They've both thrown everything good they ever had away.'

'What was in that safety deposit box on the truck?'

'Something of value to me.'

'That seems clear. Which was?'

'What does any of this have to do with you finding this man you're after?'

'Me and my colleague are viewing this whole breakout as one big case.'

'Then you'll have to ask Kat that when you find her. If she isn't already dead.'

'I can't believe you're still insisting on going,' a woman said to her husband, as they drove along Station Road in Pennsylvania. The two had been arguing almost non-stop since they'd woken up and caught the news on the TV before setting out on the road for a planned short break away.

'I've got two days off, I'm not spending them stuck at home.'

'You hear that?' she asked, pointing at the radio. 'Bank robbers murdering people out there and you're taking us to a remote lake house. What are we, in a horror movie? Was this all part of the deal when you booked the place?'

'Sure, they took twenty percent off,' he bit back.

'What if some convict breaks in when we're there? What's it gonna cost us then?'

'Could that happen, Daddy?' their eight year old daughter asked fearfully from the back seat.

'No, sweetheart.'

As her parents' argument continued, the girl looked out of the window and sighed. This was shaping up to be a fun trip. 'Mom, can I watch a video on your cell?' she asked. 'Mom?'

The woman up front didn't answer, the adults' voices fading as the car slowed. Two police cruisers were positioned either side of the road ahead, but as they drew closer, the family in the approaching car saw the cruisers were riddled with bullet holes.

'Mom? What is it?'

'Don't,' her mother said to her husband; she'd caught hold of his arm as he went to unclip his seatbelt. He looked at her, then drove the car slightly closer. It was then they both saw what appeared to be dried blood on the road.

Some of it was spattered across the yellow line dividing the lanes.

'Call 911,' he told his wife immediately, staring at the cars, but she didn't answer and he saw why.

Three armed men had just emerged from the woods beside them and were approaching the car.

'You don't have to tell me what was in that deposit box,' Marquez persisted with Blair, still standing on the stoop to the woman's upper-middle class suburban home. 'But just do me a quick favor instead; explain why your own stepdaughter would try to steal from you. Seems a little unusual, doesn't it?'

'Not at all. Kat's an addict, same as my ex back in Indiana. You'll know from your line of work, these people will take anything not nailed down to get another score. I stopped tolerating behavior like that a long time ago.'

'Hitting a bank truck isn't exactly sneaking twenty bucks from your purse.'

'Kat's never been a strong character. She was sick a lot when she as a teenager. Underweight. Unhealthy. And she was a daddy's girl, which meant she learned things from him. I don't mean like how to ride a bike or shoot a basketball.'

'So what do you mean?'

'This isn't something I usually share.' She paused. 'My husband did time in prison himself when he was young. He was hustling people, working scams on the street, and got caught. Kat inherited that trait. She looks for the easy way out rather than working hard. Always has done. A weak girl turned into a lazy addict of an adult. After Thomas died, I discovered she'd started medicating with prescription drugs. She barely graduated high school and began slacking as she got more depressed; I was forced to ban her from the house and cut her off when it became clear she was stealing from me and spending the money on pills and alcohol. Now she's robbing bank trucks and committing federal crimes. Getting herself shot in the process.'

'Do you talk?'

'No, and we never will again after this. I'm done with her. This whole mess is her biggest screw-up by far, but it's not the first illegal act she's committed. Our relationship broke down years ago after she started using and getting into trouble. I don't associate with pill poppers and junkies. Like I just told you, we left that behind back in Indiana when Alaina's father decided to leave.'

'Kat hasn't been rearrested since she was released from ORW over three years ago. They'll have drug-tested her, so she must've stayed clean.'

'Or she's been using someone's else's piss,' Blair snapped. Marquez was taken aback by the woman's sudden flare of temper and coarse language, at odds with the cool elegance she'd projected until that moment. 'Even if she isn't downing prescriptions anymore, her lifestyle's finally caught up with her. She's going down.'

'You're happy about that?'

'Of course I'm not, but she needs to face the consequences of her actions. We all do.' Blair stopped talking, her brown eyes staring directly into Marquez's own. Having to talk about Kat seemed to have rattled her; she straightened and removed her arm from across the door. 'There, I've said my piece. Are we done?'

'Is this your number?' Marquez asked, showing the woman the details Richie had given her. Blair nodded. 'I'm not gonna be in town long, but might want to chat again. The police here or US Marshals are also gonna need to ask you more questions.'

Blair didn't respond and stepping back, closed the door without another word. Marquez turned and left, walking to the corner where her taxi was still waiting.

Least we can count out Kat coming here looking for help, she thought, as she got inside the cab and the vehicle drew away.

'GET OUT OF THE CAR!' Brooks shouted at the man, woman and child in the SUV on Station Road in Pennsylvania, the couple's argument forgotten, the family looking at him, Billy and Lupinetti in terror. *'OUT!'*

The two adults reached for their door handles with shaking hands while their little girl sat frozen in horror, unable to move; Lupinetti was standing guard on the road, looking both ways for more approaching traffic, but it was as he looked back up in the direction heading west that he saw a black 4x4 had appeared on the brow of the hill.

The vehicle had already stopped and there was a figure standing beside it, something in his shoulder. The car had police lights in the front fender, but it wasn't just the 4x4 that Lupinetti recognized.

It was the man beside it.

'GET DOWN!' he warned Brooks and Billy, just before a muzzle flashed followed by the report of a gunshot echoing around the area. Billy had reacted to Lupinetti's

shout but not fast enough and he shouted in pain as blood sprayed in the air, the bullet ripping through the outer flesh of his arm.

Inside the family SUV, the woman and girl screamed but the husband was suddenly galvanized into action and slammed the car into Reverse. The vehicle started to pull back fast, the man steering erratically away from the three fugitives, who were no longer paying them attention, instead separating and returning fire on the man in the distance who'd moved back behind his 4x4.

Crouching behind the Ford, a rifle from the trunk in his shoulder, Archer saw the SUV reversing wildly towards him so he kept blasting at the convicts ahead to draw their fire, giving the people in the car a chance to pull back and escape. Twenty seconds ago, he'd crested the brow of the hill in time to see the unmistakable figures of the brothers and Frank approaching the vehicle with weapons raised, Brooks and Billy still dressed as CHPD cops; but their attention on the SUV meant they'd missed seeing him arrive, get out and retrieve then load the rifle from the trunk.

He'd targeted the Loughlins first, wanting Frank alive, but now Archer was forced to duck behind the Ford as the intensity of their fire increased, two of the tires on the recently-repaired police 4x4 taking hits and sagging. '*Not again,*' he muttered, swearing to himself, knowing he needed the car. As the family's SUV drew level with him, the two adults and child staring at him in terror, he waved them backwards and shouted: '*POLICE! GET OUT OF HERE!*'

The man didn't need the order repeated and swung the vehicle around then sped away from the firefight, but then the gunfire ceased and Archer risked a look in time to see the two Loughlin brothers running towards one of two police cruisers littered with bullet holes parked across the road.

'*KILL THAT SON OF A BITCH!*' Billy screamed, clutching his wounded arm. Brooks spun the wheel of the shot-up car, the vehicle having to do for the moment until they could steal a new one, but then bullets suddenly hit the cruiser from another direction. As he ducked, Brooks saw one of the local officers from the Winnebago shootout was still alive and was leaning against a tree, blood around his mouth, his face white as he fired awkwardly with a sidearm he'd just pulled from an ankle holster.

Despite this latest distraction, Lupinetti hadn't taken his eyes off Archer, frantically trying to work out how he could have tracked them here; at the same time, he saw him run for the trees to his left, seeming to be planning to use them as cover to work his way closer while the Loughlins were distracted.

'*It's the cop who shot Craig!*' he shouted to the Loughlins, desperate to get their focus back on Archer. Hearing Lupinetti and realizing he was right, Brooks slammed his way out of the car, used the door as a shield and unloaded his rifle at his youngest brother's killer with a fresh savagery, the weapon echoing as it spat out empty shells, gun-smoke clouding the air around him. With his uninjured arm, Billy lifted his handgun to kill the officer in the undergrowth still firing on them, but rifle fire from Archer forced him down in his seat, the bullets ripping through the windshield.

Desperate to escape the NYPD cop on his tail as well as the brothers, Lupinetti saw the Loughlins were now fully engaged battling the two cops, which presented an opportunity he'd been waiting for. Billy was the first to be aware of the other cruiser speeding off.

'*HE'S SPLITTING*!' he shouted to his brother who didn't answer, too focused on killing Archer.

Down the road, Archer's rifle clicked dry and he pulled back behind a tree to reload, but by the time the fresh magazine was in, the shot-up cop car was taking off down Station Road towards NY State.

He moved back onto the road and aimed the rifle, but the cruiser was already too far away.

He kept running down the tarmac towards the officer who'd been firing from the tree-line on the other side of the road, but he'd taken another couple of bullets and was dead. Then he saw three more cops were lying there too, dumped in the undergrowth. Once he'd checked each one and found there was nothing he could do for any of them, Archer took a radio to call it in as he watched the two cruisers racing away into the distance. He'd managed to track down Brooks, Billy and Frank again, catching them by complete surprise.

But with the body count rising this fast, neither he or the local police could afford to lose them again.

THIRTY FOUR

In sharp contrast to the Loughlins' and Lupinetti's latest violent encounter with area police and Archer, Nicky was managing to keep a much lower profile. After being handed the list of items for Kat's two vital imminent procedures, he'd secured Dr Tejwani to the other motel room bed with duct tape bought in readiness, making sure the surgeon couldn't make any noise by putting a strip over his mouth. He gave Kat a quick check too; she was awake but clearly in a lot of pain and only seemed semi-aware of what was going on. He'd given her the last of the oxycodone taken from the biker but could see it was starting to wear off.

He'd then returned to the store in the doctor's Mercedes. The man's phone started going again as he was driving but he waited for it to ring out and a few seconds later a text came up on the car's interior screen: *your brother's kids already ate most of the potato chips, can you get more?* Nicky guessed from the female name that it was the surgeon's wife; no sign of her being worried yet by her husband's non-appearance at home, so she hadn't raised the alarm. Good; that gave him and Kat a bit more time. Nicky parked in the lot at Wegmans and took the phone with him as he quickly walked inside the store, glancing at the Mustang he'd taken from the biker's scrapyard which he'd abandoned here. By the time it was discovered, he hoped to be long gone.

He went from aisle to aisle, quickly collecting the items the doctor had put on the list; he wanted to get back to the motel as soon as he could, concerned that the surgeon would find a way to escape from his binds or despite the *Do Not Disturb* tag over the door-handle, a cleaner working room-to-room might unlock the door and discover them. With Kat deteriorating too, there was no time to waste. Nicky took the opportunity to collect some antiseptic zinc oxide cream as well, his back still sore from getting scraped over the speedbump at Gatlin when he was under the laundry truck. He paid for the supplies at the checkout, then when he got back behind the wheel and drove out of the lot, another store caught his eye.

'*Unless you want her to scream so loud they hear her in the next county, she's going to need something to numb the pain,'* the doctor had warned him. Nicky made a stop outside a *Wines and Spirits* outlet, Pennsylvania's strict alcohol laws recently relaxed slightly to allow sales on Sundays, and bought a small bottle of Jim Beam, showing his fake ID when the clerk asked for it. Like in the supermarket and the lot outside the Wegmans, the cameras around the place felt as if they were scorching his skin as they captured his image, but getting hold of these supplies was vital. Last of all, he stopped to buy a Leatherman multitool pocketknife from a Lowes he'd also seen on the drive over here, then drove quickly back to the motel.

'Give her some of the whiskey,' Tejwani told him once Nicky had returned and cut him free, the supplies in the bag laid out on the table in the room. The prison fugitive unscrewed the bottle, found a glass in the bathroom, and after tilting Kat's head back tipped the alcohol into her mouth; she was able to put down three pours, coughing from the first as the liquid burned her dry throat. Feeding someone with previous addiction problems oxycodone and liquor in close order wasn't ideal, but that was a problem for another day. He'd already taken the revolver from her hand and tucked it back into his pocket, before making sure the *Do Not Disturb* tag on the door outside was still in place.

In the meantime, Tejwani pulled on some latex gloves and unbuttoned Kat's shirt before using a set of scissors purchased from the store to snip away the rudimentary padding and bandages Nicky had first applied after they'd split from the truck robbery. Now the doc had scissors in his hand, Nicky wasn't taking his eye off him for a second. Twelve years in federal prison and all.

But instead of trying to stab him, Tejwani removed the last of the gauze, put the scissors down and as Nicky took them away, he saw the wound again. The bullet-hole was between two of her ribs on her right side, standing out starkly against the pale smooth skin, but twenty four hours had passed since she was shot which he knew meant sepsis could have already set in, the bacteria from the wound's internal damage spreading into her bloodstream.

'Turn that light on,' Tejwani told Nicky, pointing to a built-in light beside the bed. As Nicky flicked the switch, the doctor opened several antiseptic wipes and used them to carefully clean the area around the wound. Then he picked up two pairs of tweezers, fresh from the packet like the scissors. 'This might take some finding,' he warned. 'Get her ready.'

Nicky took a pillow and positioned it carefully so the end was over Kat's mouth but left her nose clear. She took the hint and drew in a deep breath before biting down on the fabric.

He steadied her then nodded to the doctor beside him.

Three pours of Kentucky bourbon were enough to render Katherine nicely buzzed, but she still screamed into the pillow as Tejwani pushed one set of tweezers into the bullet hole then released them in order to stretch the wound open, before searching for the metal slug with the second set.

'Nothing?' Nicky asked anxiously.

'There are shards of rib everywhere; it's making it difficult,' he said, before withdrawing the tweezers to reset, leaving the first set in place. Kat started crying; with one free hand, Nicky tipped another shot of whiskey into the glass and she drank it before he put the pillow back and Tejwani dug in for the bullet again, eliciting another muffled scream as Nicky held her still. *'There,'* the doctor said with satisfaction, his passion for his work making him temporarily forget where he was and the circumstances he was operating under. Nicky caught a glimpse of blood-smeared metal as Tejwani slowly and gently coaxed the bullet out. Once it was free, Nicky eyed the flattened piece of metal held between the prongs of the tweezers.

'Thank you,' he said, before looking at Kat and seeing she was still having difficulty breathing.

'We're not done yet,' Tejwani told him. He placed the bullet carefully on the bedside table, removed the first set of tweezers still holding the wound open, then used some clean gauze and more antiseptic to wipe around the entire area, before applying adhesive surgical tape strips and padding to patch the wound. 'Now that lung needs to be re-inflated.'

From the time he'd been a high school student over thirty five years ago, Ramesh Tejwani's parents had taught him the importance of being punctual. His wife was also a creature of habit; they both got up in the morning at the same time, ate breakfast and were out of the door heading for their respective practices at 7:45am sharp, taking turns to drop their kids off at school on the way. The end of the day also followed a routine, and on the occasions that either would be late, they always called to let the other know.

Therefore, his non-appearance from collecting the final list of groceries for their kids' birthday party was highly unusual. Waiting anxiously at their home with family members who'd already arrived, his wife had just called the hospital where they confirmed that Ramesh had left well over an hour ago. After trying his cell a few more times, she started to become increasingly worried. The tally of unanswered calls was now up to ten.

So her next contact was to the police.

'He was heading to the Wegmans in town when I last spoke to him,' she told the 911 operator.

'Could he have run into a friend, or be having car trouble, Ma'am? He's not been gone that long.'

'You don't understand, my husband is never late for anything. He knew he had to get home to help me set up. And when he's not in surgery, he always answers his phone.'

'You said he was going to Wegmans?'

'That's right, the one on Peach Street.' The call was put out to local police units, and a pair of Erie PD officers who weren't far from the large store responded before taking the turn and pulling into the lot less than a minute later. They were given the plates for the man's Mercedes but although they couldn't see it parked anywhere, decided to take a look inside the supermarket as they were here anyway.

'Like to have me one of those,' one of them said after a brief whistle, eyeing up a red Mustang they passed as the two officers walked towards the large building's entrance.

Around the same time that the two cops had told one of the checkout staff why they were there and were being taken to the security camera room with the shift manager, at the Motel 6 Tejwani searched through the bags Nicky had bought and withdrew two items: a bike pump and a two liter bottle of water.

'Empty out most of that,' he said, passing the bottle to Nicky, who hesitated. 'I'm not going to run. I'll do it myself if I have to.' He rose to follow Nicky into the bathroom and watched as he poured three quarters of the contents into the wash basin. 'Now, you need to-' Tejwani said, but Nicky was already picking up the bike pump; he cut its plastic tubing free with the Leatherman, clipped it into two lengths, one long and one short. He wiped both down with antiseptic then stuck one end of each length into the empty bottle, the longer section going into the remaining water. He then used some of the tape he'd bound the doctor's hands and feet with earlier to seal the top of the bottle.

Nicky placed the bottle by the bed as they both returned to Kat. 'I have to make an incision,' the doctor told her, taking the Leatherman pocketknife Nicky cautiously passed him. 'Can I do that?'

She nodded, her focus slightly blurry from the booze, but she was still sober enough to be frightened.

'Get her ready again.' Nicky got back into position with the pillow, his eyes still on the knife, as Tejwani used a final antiseptic wipe two inches below the bullet-hole. He wiped the blade and then used it to make a cut, Kat biting into the pillow but not screaming this time, the alcohol taking stronger effect now and doing its job to help temporarily numb the pain. After Nicky took charge of the Leatherman again, Tejwani fed the length of the longer tube into Kat's side, and turned his head to instruct Nicky but the escaped convict was already lifting the bottle.

Bubbles started to come out of the length of the tube dangling in the water remaining inside.

'C'mon, young lady,' Tejwani said. 'Let it work.'

She suddenly took a deep breath, and exhaled, breathing in and out again like normal, the lung re-inflated.

‘How did you know how to…?’ Tejwani asked. Nicky didn’t answer, instead offering his hand. The doctor, confused by this strange young man, peeled off his glove and shook it.

Back in Cleveland, having just returned to the cheap hotel from visiting Blair O’Mara at her home in Pepper Pike, Marquez entered the room Archer had booked for another twenty four hours and let the door close on itself behind her.

She twisted the lock then wandered towards the bed, her neck and shoulders sore, her eyes still dry and tired from the all-night drive. Wearing a detective badge regularly meant losing sleep and disturbed nights; she’d become conditioned to it over the years but also knew to rest when she could. Fatigue could cause her to miss important details, clues which could affect the outcome of a case or end up costing or saving someone’s life, including her own. She had plenty to think about, but could do that while she took a shower before a quick lie down. An hour’s rest and she’d be ready to rock and roll again.

She went through to the bathroom and dropped a mat onto the floor before turning on the shower, then moved back next door to remove her Smith and Wesson sidearm in its holster and place it on the bed. A back-up pistol followed, strapped to her ankle, and she kicked off her shoes before peeling off her clothes. She went back into the bathroom and tested the water before stepping under the showerhead.

She stood beneath the spray for almost two minutes, enjoying the sensation of the hot water beating down onto her tired shoulders, then started to use a fresh bar of soap provided by the hotel. Up next was her hair; despite having washed it at the motel outside Gatlin on Friday night, she’d still smelt traces of pepper spray during the ride here from Virginia, but when she looked at the small bottle the hotel had left in the stall, decided she wanted to use her own shampoo.

Keeping the water running, she stepped out and wrapped a towel around her to keep from making the tiled bathroom floor slippery, then padded through to the main bedroom. She found the bottle in her washbag and started to walk back to the shower.

Water was still splashing in the tub, the mirror in the main room misting up from the steam wafting through the open door, her feet silent on the carpeted floor. Out of habit, Marquez glanced at the main door to her room on her way back to the bathroom.

And she stopped.

The peep hole leading to the outside corridor had been showing light before but right now it was dark. A tiny detail, but something she noticed.

She stayed still, one hand keeping her towel wrapped around her. Someone stopped outside to text on a phone maybe?

Or a trick of the light?'

Or someone was standing right outside the door.

Placing the bottle of shampoo down on the floor, she took one slow step after another towards the door, holding her towel around her, keeping to the wall to avoid creating a moving shadow that could be seen under the door. She was two steps away, then one, before she heard a tiny *click.*

It was the same one she'd heard a few minutes ago when she'd used the keycard to unlock the room.

Archer? she thought. It couldn't be. He was already gone and he'd knock first, not just walk in.

The handle then started to push down very slowly. Marquez watched it just the other side of the door, but at the last moment, her hand went up and stepping forward, she eased the small security bar lock across.

The metal didn't make a sound, the hinges well oiled. She moved back silently and the door then started to open equally quietly.

Equally slowly.

It stopped when it reached the end of the security bar. The door was open now, although by only an inch. Marquez stood perfectly still, occasional beads of water dripping from her hair to the carpet with tiny, quiet *thuds*.

The door remained where it was on the end of the lock bar, then it closed again.

A few seconds later, a small length of card slid into the gap towards the lock bar and with the door now almost shut, the card pushed the lock bar away from the bolt.

Removing the last barrier.

But the moment the door had closed, Marquez had shifted rapidly. She'd pulled on her jeans and t-shirt then slipped her S&W handgun from its holster, her heart going like a triphammer as she took cover behind the bed and held her breath.

She watched as the card was slowly pulled back and lifted her pistol up with the safety off, the shower still running. The mirror by now was a complete wall of mist, the steam from the shower still drifting into the room.

She had her gun aimed at the door, held rock solid, looking down the sights.

But then her cell phone started ringing on the bed. Her eyes darted to it, then up at the door. A pause followed. Would whoever was out there think she'd leave the shower to answer it?

The answer was yes.

An instant later, the unlocked door to the room was kicked back; she couldn't shoot in that moment, not knowing who this was, but saw in the doorway the outline of two large men wearing balaclava ski masks, both carrying a raised weapon.

They saw her too. She dropped to the carpet behind the bed as a suppressed burst of bullets chewed up the cheap hotel room, smashing the window opposite the door and destroying the TV, tufts of mattress spraying into the air. The door was being held open by whoever was firing the sub-machine guns, feathers and pieces of fabric flying around Marquez like confetti as she stayed low. She moved up to the end of the bed and blasted back several times in the direction of the door, her gunshots echoing harshly unlike theirs. Another half magazine's worth of bullets ripped up more of the room, shattering what was left of the window, a few of the bullets showering Marquez with more feathers from the destroyed pillowcases as she retreated back closer to the wall and fired again at the door.

The entry point to the room was narrow and she was just managing to keep them back, but knew she couldn't for much longer. She was cornered, and in her desperation thought of Archer jumping off that bridge the other night to survive. However, there was no water beneath her room, just concrete; she looked at the almost completely obliterated window, the glass covering the carpet below it and a chair knocked over at the end of the bed.

The room was on the 1st floor overlooking the street and she remembered there was an awning directly below.

She could survive the drop.

But the glass would shred her bare feet before she could get to the window; she lunged forward to retrieve her shoes, then pulled back as whoever was firing from the door resumed with a fresh magazine, hitting where she'd been moments ago, the wall below the window now a mass of bullet holes.

With both guys firing at once, she knew they'd have to reload and waited for a pause. When it came, she pushed herself back to her feet and fired at the door repeatedly as she ran for the window.

Down on the street below, a sedan had drawn up outside the hotel about a minute ago, the driver talking to the porter when they'd heard gunshots coming from somewhere above.

They'd both gone for cover just inside the building's entrance and as they peered up uncertainly, a figure tore through the awning and hit the roof of the car hard. The person bounced onto the hood, then rolled and landed on the concrete facedown before lying completely still. The two men saw she was a Latina woman with wet shoulder-length dark hair, a handgun resting in her grip on the ground.

She lay there unmoving, blood slowly starting to pool onto the concrete around her head. Shocked, the driver looked up through the damaged awning to see where the hell this woman could have fallen from and caught the briefest glimpse of two figures looking down from a window a floor above.

But seconds later, they were gone.

THIRTY FIVE

In Erie, Dr Tejwani had just been located by the local cops. Or more accurately, an image of him recorded an hour ago had been.

On monitors in the Wegmans security room, rerunning footage from the cameras covering the parking lot, the missing doctor was watched by the pair of officers as he approached his Mercedes. They'd been told what time the hospital at UPMC Hamot had reported him leaving, so finding the doctor on the recording hadn't taken long. They'd seen him arriving and fifteen minutes later saw him return to the car with his bagged groceries.

And also what happened next.

'Oh shit,' one of the officers said quietly. But then he leaned closer. 'Yo. Is that…'

'This is 3-Charlie-10 responding to the missing doctor call,' his partner radioed in, taking the initiative. 'Looks like the doc was kidnapped at gunpoint in the store parking lot. Individual in t-shirt and jeans. Might be a long shot, but he looks close to the description of one of the wanted men Ohio said might be coming our way.'

'This is 3-Adam-23, doctor's vehicle located,' another voice then cut in, hearing the transmission over the wire. '*I'm looking at the Mercedes parked outside the Motel 6 on Schultz Road. Plate is a match.'*

'Adam-23, stay back but keep eyes on the vehicle. Code 1, repeat, Code 1,' their sergeant said, as the pair ran out of the store towards their squad car. '*Dispatch, we need SWAT deployed immediately, this could be a hostage situation.'*

'10-4. All units, please be advis…'

Inside the motel room, the tubing had been removed from Kat's side now her lung was functioning again, and Tejwani was sitting on the edge of the other bed. The girl's torso was freshly bandaged, and she'd taken some antibiotics Nicky had picked up from his trip to Wegmans with a prescription the doctor had quickly scribbled out for the pharmacy located inside the store. She was also now wearing a new plain white slim-fit collared shirt he'd bought her off the rack and was already looking slightly better.

'Relax, doc, otherwise we're gonna need to reinflate your lungs next,' Nicky told the doctor, seeing how nervous he was. Tejwani closed his eyes and took a deep breath. Nicky pulled the holdall over and counted out a couple thousand dollars from a cash brick; he offered the notes to the doctor.

'I don't want that,' Tejwani said.

'I forced you into coming here.'

'I doubt that's your money to give.' The doctor didn't take the bills, so Nicky trapped them under the lamp on the table.

'I have to tie you up again,' Nicky said. 'I'm sorry.'

For one brief moment Tejwani considered resisting, but as calm as the young man was, the doctor had recognized them both from watching the news headlines when he was eating breakfast that morning and knew what he and the woman on the bed were wanted for. Surviving this situation had become Tejwani's only goal. So he lay back docilely on the bed and Nicky taped his hands to the frame before binding his ankles and knees, the roll of tape almost gone.

'When I booked the room, guy at the desk said the maid starts cleaning around 2 o'clock, so you won't be tied here too long.' The time was just past 1pm; the doctor only had an hour to wait. Nicky taped over the man's mouth. 'Still breathing?' Tejwani nodded, surprised that the Gatlin fugitive cared whether he was or not. Nicky retrieved the money from under the lamp and tucked it into the Indian-American surgeon's pocket. 'Give it to the cops as evidence if you don't want to keep it. I gotta borrow your car but the cops will bring it back later, I'm sure.' He paused. 'Thanks again.'

Nicky went to the window to check the coast was clear, intending to carry Kat outside to the Mercedes.

But as he watched from his position on the bed, Tejwani saw the prison escapee's body language change as he peered through a small gap in the blinds.

'The Loughlins and Lupinetti lit off towards the New York line in two separate cruisers,' Archer quickly told a couple of Pennsylvania State troopers just south of the city of Erie on Station Road, several of their vehicles having recently arrived at the scene after responding to the emergency call Archer had put out over one of the dead local officer's radios. He'd also reported the incident with the family in the SUV whom the three fugitives had been about to kill and who'd been located further down the road. They were badly shaken but otherwise had escaped unscathed, the only people who'd encountered the Loughlins in the last twenty four hours to do so.

'Erie PD?' one of the troopers asked, as he and colleagues saw the bodies of the fallen officers.'

'Yeah, black and white cars, gold lettering,' Archer replied.

'The rides must've been shot up pretty bad,' a trooper stated, seeing glass all over the road as more arriving backup braked and blocked off the stretch of highway, protecting the scene. Others were in the undergrowth, inspecting the murdered cops while some were checking the interior of the Winnebago, the two dead young Penn State students slumped in the front seats.

'They were, these sons of bitches seem to have an arsenal,' Archer told the troopers. 'They're gonna blast through any-'

'Sighting of Nicky Reyes north of here!' another trooper called over.

'Where?' the man beside Archer asked.

'Outside a Motel 6 in the city, on Schultz.'

'I know the one,' the trooper speaking to Archer said. 'That's less than thirty miles away. Maybe they're trying to meet up.'

Erie's police department already had a task force on standby after they'd been contacted at sunrise by the US Marshals running the search from Cleveland, warning them about the chance the four wanted men and one woman could be heading their way and the level of threat they posed.

It meant the SWAT team reached the Motel 6 within ten minutes. Sharpshooters quickly took up positions, the keen-eyed patrolman who'd spotted the Mercedes belonging to Dr Tejwani now joined by other police units who were waiting further down the street, not wanting to give the fugitive possibly holed up in the room any hint that he'd been found.

A line of five task force officers crept down the row of motel rooms towards the one they'd been told had been paid for earlier by a man matching Reyes' description, all of the SWAT officers wearing body armor and carrying assault weapons. When they arrived outside the door, one of the men who was holding a ram moved up to the front, the team not wanting to use a shotgun for entry with a hostage potentially inside.

The Gatlin Four had created havoc since they'd escaped prison two days ago, and the local dispatcher was just reporting that less than thirty minutes prior, three of them had killed four Erie officers and two college students at a roadblock just south of the city. These fugitives needed to be taken down hard, and at least one of the four could be right here in this room, armed and dangerous.

His trigger finger ready, their sergeant who was third in the line nodded to the lead officer.

He swung the ram back and smashed it into the door before standing back, making way for the other officers behind him to breach the room.

THIRTY SIX

Almost a full month earlier, Kat O'Mara walked through the door of her apartment in the Clark-Fulton area of Cleveland, then locked it behind her. Her roommate was home and was just stirring a sauce into some pasta. Erica Till was thirty three years old and Kat's former cellmate from the women's State prison at ORW but unlike her, had found herself on the wrong side of the law since she was a kid. Erica's brother Vaughn was also a habitual criminal, same as their aunt and uncle who'd brought them up. For some, it was a calling. But despite this, the two women were good friends.

'Hey girl,' she said, before stopping what she was doing when she saw Kat's face. 'What happened?'

'I got fired.'

Erica stopped stirring the sauce. 'Again?'

'Manager said it wasn't working out.'

'How can't it, serving tables? You've been busting your ass.' Instead of answering, Kat threw her bag onto the floor and covered her face with her hands. Erica put the pasta and sauce on the backburner then went over to give her friend a hug.

'You gotta be able to complain or something,' Erica told her a few minutes later, both of them now in the tiny living room. 'They can't have a good reason not to keep you.'

'What can I do, go to Human Resources? It was a waitressing job.'

'Screw 'em,' Erica said, collecting a bottle of cheap wine from the fridge and pouring herself a glass. With her history Kat no longer drank, except on very rare

occasions, so Erica fetched her a soda. 'You'll find something better.'

Kat didn't answer, taking the can and looking at it without really seeing it. She placed the Coke down and went into the kitchen to get a glass before picking up the bottle and pouring herself a slug of wine too. Erica watched in surprise and with slight concern but didn't say anything. It spoke to her just how wound up her roommate was. 'You really think something better is out there? The way things have been going?'

Erica didn't answer for a moment. 'I don't know.'

'Nicky gets out the week after Labor Day,' Kat said, before taking a mouthful of wine. 'I've got nothing for him, after all this time. Not even a few bucks to pay him back for what he did, or help him move on into a new life. He needs a roof over his head and I'm not even gonna be able to pay the rent on this place soon.'

'You've done everything you could.'

'And I keep on failing.'

'What about your inheritance?'

'I still can't get access to it. I checked.' Erica had known Kat for five years; they came from vastly different backgrounds, Kat's one of privilege and her roommate's just the opposite, but sharing a cell, they'd had to look out for one another and had become sympathetic to the other's struggles, the basis for their unlikely friendship. After being arrested and given eighteen months for her benzo addiction, Kat had finally got clean and left prison with a simple desire to earn a living and stay out of trouble, the ultimate goal being to climb her way back to where her life had once seemed to have been heading, a successful young woman with her life ahead of her. And with the comfort of knowing she had the financial support of her father's legacy if she ever needed it.

But Erica knew Kat's inheritance had been withheld from her ever since she'd been convicted and sent to prison, the details of that situation murky. And since ORW, every time Kat had managed to find a job the place had canned her within a few weeks, or if she was lucky, after three or four months. She'd been forced to lower her sights to eventually end up where she was now, getting fired from minimum wage employment. It just never seemed to work out.

'He'll be looking at shitty jobs for the rest of his life too and getting treated like something someone stepped in,' Kat said, draining more of her wine. 'My luck'll rub off onto him. He doesn't deserve that. I don't know how he'll deal with it.'

'He's made it almost twelve years in Gatlin. Says a lot about what he can handle. And he's always sounded smart when you talk about him. He'll find something.'

'He lost over a decade of his life for me,' Kat said. 'It's my fault he's in there. I wanted to repay him and let us both live a good life, but I got nothing.' She put the glass of wine down, her hands shaking, and Erica watched her with concern. It was becoming very clear her friend had almost reached breaking point and Erica knew the temptation to fall back into addiction was growing. Things were bad. And they weren't getting any better.

But Erica couldn't provide an answer Kat wanted to hear. The reality of the world that the two women had rejoined from prison, like many other inmates before them had discovered, was that it was a bleak one. Minimum wage jobs, just enough to cover rent in bad rooms in shitty apartments in shitty parts of town. For the girl whose father had gone from serving time in the joint himself to becoming a multi-millionaire building and growing a successful business, and knowing she'd been near the top of the roll her senior year before things had fallen apart, Kat felt like she was living someone else's life, not hers.

'Blair won't help you out at all? Don't you have a claim to the estate or something?'

'No, she's long done with me. And I can't afford a good enough lawyer to fight my case and regain control of my inheritance. I'd probably lose anyway, living like this, and she's got all that money behind her.'

'What about your stepsister?'

'Alaina? We're friendlier. She's snuck me a few hundred bucks here and there when I've been desperate, but she's not gonna do anything to piss off her mom. Blair'll freeze her out too. She can be a real bitch.'

Erica didn't answer; despite the way she was feeling and her own concerns, Kat immediately picked up there was something on her friend's mind. 'What's going on?' she asked. 'Something up?'

'I haven't told you yet,' Erica said. 'I don't know how you're gonna take this.'

Kat put down her glass. 'Try me. I'm listening.'

'I remember you telling me a while back you've got something that could solve all your problems, right? A deposit box at the Morningstar in Public Square. Left to you by your father.'

Kat didn't answer at first. Whatever she'd been expecting Erica to say, it wasn't this. 'Doesn't matter. I can't get to it.'

'Why?'

'When I went into rehab before ORW, Blair was worried I'd spend everything I had on drugs, like we just said. Back when she still cared. She presented a case to the judge and everything of substantial value that I owned was signed over to her in trust until I was considered fit and

not a danger to my own health and wellbeing. I don't get access restored to any of it until they rule I'm OK.'

'But you keep getting fired?'

'That's not Blair's fault. That's on me.'

'But she has access to everything, then?'

'Except that deposit box. She can hold it but not get into it.'

'How are you so sure?'

'She doesn't have a key. I do.'

'They let you keep it?'

'Why not? It's worthless until the box is returned. They won't let me inside the vault; I tried. If she wanted to get to what's inside, they'd have to break the box open. Wish her luck explaining that and convincing a judge it was for my own good.'

'But it's at the Morningstar downtown, right?'

Kat nodded, looking at her friend curiously.

'My brother got out of Elkton a few months ago. He shared a cell block with an investment banker while he was in there. Said the guy used to bitch and moan about a load of money he'd had to give his ex in a divorce. Over four million dollars' worth of stuff in total. Cash, family heirlooms, jewelry. Just after their divorce was finalized she told him it was staying in the deposit box at the Morningstar they'd used when they were still married. They both knew she'd move it before he got out. Salt in the wound and all.'

'The boxes are held in the vault,' Kat said, seeing where this was going. 'I've got a better chance of becoming mayor than you all would of getting access.'

'The bank's been under renovation. All the boxes were moved to another location, and they're being returned to the branch on Labor Day Saturday.' She made eye contact

with Kat. 'I was gonna ask you what number your deposit box was and get it back for you.'

'What? Why?'

'We're hitting the truck. Four of us. The banker's ex has got four million plus in that box, waiting to be taken. I can get yours at the same time.'

'You'd do that for me?'

She nodded. 'I want you to get out of here like me. Score one over this bitch who abandoned you, take back what's yours and leave Ohio forever. Dump everything in the past, start off somewhere fresh. Take Nicky with you.' She smiled. 'And maybe think about giving me a cut on your way out.'

Kat rose and started to pace. 'This is a bad idea,' she said, echoing the same concerns Nicky would share once she ended up being convinced of this plan herself. 'Judge and juries go all-in on armed robbery. This could be twenty five years inside. What happens if someone dies? You could get the needle.'

'You don't get a shot like this often. We're gonna take it.'

'For a million each, split four ways?'

'Hell of a lot more than I got right now, girl.'

'You're surviving.'

'Yeah, right, look at where we are.' Erica tipped back her glass and swallowed the remainder of her wine. 'The contents of that box belong to you, not your stepmom. Risk twenty years to get it back, or spend them living in shit-boxes like this getting fired from bussing tables the rest of your days.'

Kat noticed her friend was staring at her intently, then realized. 'That's not the only reason. You want my help to pull it off, don't you?'

Erica nodded. 'We need one more person. Someone we can trust. With the chance to get your stuff back, I thought you'd be interested. Vaughn doesn't need to know how much you got in that deposit box and neither do I. But you help us out, it's all yours.' She rose and caught her friend by the shoulders, stopping her pacing so she could look her in the eye. 'We need you, girl. And you can't keep going like this. I can't either.'

Kat had slept on it badly for a few days, but after getting her final wages from the diner which, once bills were covered, didn't leave enough to eat for the month, decided she'd had enough.

She was in.

The lingering doubt and fear in her mind was outweighed by her desperation; she'd reached the end of her tether. Every turn she seemed to take in her life led to a dead end. Visiting Nicky to tell him where to meet her over the Canadian border once he got out had gone exactly the way she'd expected, but she'd made up her mind by that point. Nothing he said was going to deter her. She could finally see some light at the end of the long dark tunnel that had been the last thirteen years. It was either do something right now, or fall back into addiction, numbing herself to life and giving up on any kind of hope.

The day of the heist, the last she ever planned to be in Cleveland for the rest of her life, she'd left their apartment through the back door and rear alleyway early to get picked up, unknowingly ditching her federal surveillance positioned out front, and the thieves hit blackjack on East Superior Avenue but at a price. Erica, Vaughn and the others had all been killed right in front of her, but then she'd been chased down and shot by one of the giant men in CHPD uniform.

After she'd managed to find the strength to reach the protection of a mail bin and slumped against it, she looked down to see a small hole in her top with red seeping out around it, starting to soak her sweater, specks of blood on the concrete beside her. As she started going into shock, but still keeping hold of the strap of the bag which had just cost so dear, she suddenly felt herself being helped up. She'd opened her eyes and stared in numbed confusion at Nicky's familiar face as he'd carried her away.

She'd thought she'd been hallucinating, but she hadn't. Nicky being here was real, and then so was the pain. Between that moment and when the doctor in Erie had performed the two procedures on her, the agony between doses of oxycodone had been intensifying until she could think of nothing else, her ability to breathe becoming harder and harder. All she'd wanted to do was pass out, to make the torture stop and for this to end.

She vaguely remembered Nicky ditching a car before carrying her from one place to another. She'd had nothing for the pain until a group of bikers had shown up and one of them gave her that first dose of oxy which had helped. Their arrival had felt unreal, once again making her think she was dreaming.

Or dying.

She'd been in a daze when they'd ridden with the group, not even aware they'd stopped for a roadblock, then had lost consciousness again until she'd woken up on a couch somewhere. But post the removal of the bullet, the reinflation of her lung, more painkillers and after Nicky had told her there was a cop car parked across the highway from the Motel 6, she sure as hell was awake now.

*

'Doctor located,' the Erie SWAT team sergeant said, as one of his men pulled a knife from his vest and cut the tape binding the man's wrists, knees and ankles to the bedframe at the Motel 6. They'd carried out a quick clearance of the room and bathroom and discovered he was alone.

'Are you OK?' the officer who freed him asked as he peeled the tape off his mouth.

'It was two of the fugitives from the news,' Tejwani answered quickly, his mouth dry and ignoring the question as other officers started using keys from the front desk to clear adjacent rooms. They'd already seen the bed near the far wall had bloodstained sheets, a water bottle with two tubes connected positioned on the bedside table beside a twisted small pennant of metal. 'Reyes and the girl. She's been shot. He kidnapped me to operate on her and get the bullet out.'

'*Bathroom window's open,*' a voice called from next door. '*Broken glass in the lot outside. Car might have been taken.*'

'He was about to leave through the front door, but I think he saw you outside,' Tejwani explained quickly. 'He hauled the woman out through the back window.'

'Sweep the area and close off I-90 and 86,' the SWAT sergeant ordered over his radio as he followed another of his men escorting the shaken doctor outside to safety. 'Tejwani's safe, Lieutenant. Looks like Reyes left a car in the Wegmans' lot, before he kidnapped the surgeon and drove here to the motel in the man's vehicle. He might be going back for-'

'I heard an alarm go off, around back,' Tejwani interrupted. 'I think he already took another one.'

He was right. Now a few miles away in a hotwired Grand Jeep Cherokee, driving fast but just within the legal limit, Nicky kept driving down what he saw was called Buffalo Road, giving him a clear run east out of the small city.

When he'd seen an Erie PD squad car parked across the highway from the motel as he'd checked through the blinds, it had suddenly dawned on him that the doctor's phone hadn't rung in the last thirty minutes. Then he'd remembered that missed call in the car and seeing how many other unanswered calls there'd been.

Those cameras outside Wegmans, recording everything.

Despite seeing only one police car out there, Nicky knew they were onto him.

'Cops ahead,' Kat warned from the back seat; she was lying across it but had her head propped against the door high enough to see out of the window. Nicky picked up a cruiser parked at the entrance to a golf course and slowed slightly to ensure he maintained the same speed as the traffic around him, praying the plates on the Jeep hadn't gone out over the radio yet. He knew from talking with guys in Gatlin who'd had a lot of practice at stealing cars how modern vehicles were much harder to hotwire, but the 90s Jeep parked in the rear lot of the motel had been his saving grace. He'd already lowered what was left of the window to hide the fact it had been smashed out when he'd first broken inside with the Leatherman before using the tools to rip off the protective casing, kill the alarm and cut into the wires before sparking the ignition. More lessons from inside. At least the last twelve years hadn't been a complete waste of time.

Without moving his head he glanced at the occupants of the Erie PD cruiser as they drew nearer but the driver was talking to his partner, neither cop currently paying the passing vehicles any attention.

'We need to get into New York,' Kat said, slurring slightly, once they were safely past, her breathing much easier now, that wheezing sound gone with both of her lungs fully operational again. The Jim Beam and painkillers were clearly still keeping her woozy, but she looked much more comfortable since the rudimentary operation in the motel room.

'Yeah, but we can't take the interstate in this,' he said, as they passed more golf courses on their left, Lake Erie beyond reflecting the midday Sunday sunlight but acting as a huge liquid barrier between them and the freedom that Canada offered. It was already past the hour and he turned on the radio as another black and white police cruiser ripped past them going in the opposite direction. Unlike the one parked outside the golf club it was going fast, its lights flashing, answering a call somewhere.

The radio was playing a traffic report as Nicky switched it on. '*-on Station Road where local officers and two civilians have been shot and killed. Police are warning people to stay in your cars, do not stop for anyone looking to be picked up and stay vigilant for any sign of the fugitives described just now. Roadblocks are in place on I-90, I-86 and NY-17, and police are asking drivers to be patient-'*

'*Shit,*' he whispered.

'The brothers?' Kat asked.

'It must've been.' *So they got out of Ohio too*, he thought, and shot their way through another roadblock it sounded like, which would now put a stranglehold on every road and waterway in this region. The sons of bitches had killed more cops and another two members of the public. Nicky thought again of how he'd used Brooks and Billy to get out of Gatlin for his own ends and the weight on his conscience increased.

But he couldn't focus on that right now; time was quickly running out for making a decision about what to do next. As they headed into a borough called North East, Nicky saw signs leading to I-90 and the NY State border. They were getting almost too close to turn back, with all the roadblocks and waiting armed officers and sniffer dogs.

He took an exit onto a quieter road, needing a moment to regroup and think, and after a relatively short distance he and Kat found themselves in more rural surroundings. His fake ID had gotten him out of Virginia when he'd first escaped from Gatlin, and it had been accepted by the liquor store clerk in Erie so it had passed two tests, but with no registration, no keys in the ignition, Kat still very weak and clearly injured, a bag of money in the car, and both their descriptions now out there? They didn't have the remotest chance in hell of getting over in the stolen Jeep.

Trying to come up with a solution, and requiring more time to consider their options without having to dodge cop cars and roadblocks, Nicky continued down the road and reached a small parking lot beside a lookout spot. He stopped and put the car in Park, the engine still running. There was another vehicle parked about six or seven spaces over and a man who had to be the driver was eating something out of a foil wrapper as he sat on a bench looking out at the water, apparently admiring the view. A guy just enjoying a quite Sunday lunch.

Nicky closed his eyes; he didn't want to ruin another innocent person's day and scare the hell out of them, but this was desperation time. *Sorry for this, man,* he thought, before getting out of the stolen Jeep and approaching the stranger, who looked over and was about to nod a greeting until he saw Nicky pulling a revolver from his pocket.

THIRTY SEVEN

The guy's lunch dropped forgotten to the ground the moment he saw the handgun. He looked to be about ten years older than the two fugitives and of average height, although slightly thicker-set than Nicky; he was wearing spectacles, light blue jeans and a tucked-in casual shirt. 'Don't do that, keep your hands down,' Nicky said quickly when the man started to raise them. 'Who are you? What are you doing here?'

'B-barry,' he stammered, slowly lowering his hands as Nicky did a quick doublecheck to make sure there was no-one else around. 'My name's Barry.'

'You alone?' Nicky asked. Barry nodded quickly. 'Why are you here?'

'Eating…eating my lunch.'

'I see that; I meant in the area.'

'I work for a pet food company. I'm driving to a conference starting tomorrow. In…in Syracuse.'

'Give me your ID and cell phone,' Nicky told the man. 'Quick.' The man pulled his wallet from his jeans, extracted his driving license with shaking hands and passed it over. Nicky saw his full name was *Barrington Marsh*. 'And the cell. Unlock the screen first.'

The man did as he was ordered and handed it over. Nicky immediately removed the PIN from the phone in the settings, then snapped a photo of the ID before passing the license back. The siren of an emergency vehicle echoed through the trees, coming up from the interstate; a reminder that time was trickling away relentlessly through the sandglass.

The window of opportunity to get out of here was closing, fast.

'I'm gonna text a photo of your license to a friend,' Nicky told the frightened salesman. 'He's the president of a motorcycle club with chapters all over the country. He doesn't hear from me in an hour, you'll be getting a visit from them. But you help us out, I'll call him once this is done and it'll be like you and me never met. Understand?'

The man stared at him, his eyes almost perfect circles behind the spectacles.

'Barry?' Nicky prompted quickly.

He nodded jerkily. 'I understand.'

'Come with me.' The man got up and walked slowly ahead of Nicky over to the Jeep. 'We're boxed in on all sides,' Nicky said, showing Kat the phone after having opened a navigation map application; there were hazard triangles on every road that crossed into New York State. Blocks, barriers, dogs, guns, and State troopers. He knew they were both looking at twenty five-plus years inside, maybe even life after so many had been killed thanks to the Loughlins.

But only if they got caught.

'Can we…stay here?' she asked. 'My side hurts, Nick. I need to rest.'

'I know, but we gotta get out now. The doc's disappearance will be noticed any minute if it hasn't already and they'll be putting an alert out for the Jeep's plates as soon as the owner reports it missing.' Nicky turned to check out Barry's large white Audi. 'What storage space do you have in there?' he asked the man, who was visibly trembling now as he looked back and forth at the pair. He'd been listening to the radio before he'd stopped at the lookout point and like Tejwani before him, had just realized who Nicky and Kat were.

'Er…the trunk. Spare tire well.'

'First place they'll check,' Kat said quietly. 'And I won't…fit.'

'There's behind the front seats, too,' Barry added quickly. 'You can f-f-fold the rear seats down, leaves quite a big gap in the footwell. I use it when the trunk is full sometimes.' He closed his eyes and forced himself to breathe. 'Lying down, she could squeeze in.'

'Show me.' He and Nicky went to Barry's car, an Audi SQ8; the man opened the nearside back passenger door and released a catch on the side of the seat.

It popped out slightly, and after he folded it over, Nicky knelt to see a space underneath.

'That might work,' he said quietly, as the high-pitched wail from another cruiser on the highway reached them through the trees. 'It's gonna have to. Help me get her out, man.'

Across the border in Chautauqua County, NY, a gray SUV was approaching two police cruisers parked to one side of the highway; the officers inside checked it out as the vehicle passed but lost interest when they saw it was a woman driving. They were looking for two large, bearded men and another smaller man with tattoos covering his arms driving stolen, bullet-riddled Erie PD cop cars, not a gray seven-seater with a soccer mom behind the wheel.

But if they'd looked closer, they'd have seen all wasn't as it should be.

'Stop crying,' Brooks told the woman from where he was lying on the flattened back seats, the barrel of his rifle pushed low into her side. His brother was jammed in beside him, the two bags holding the titanium box from the heist and their guns resting between them, Billy not taking his eyes off the driver who was visibly shaking as she gripped the wheel tight with both hands.

They'd dumped the Erie police cruiser on a country road just over the State line after they'd seen the SUV driving their way in the distance and had pulled across the highway to block her. Billy had stepped out and held the terrified woman at gunpoint while his brother reversed the damaged cop car off the road and out of sight. They'd kept one of the dead officer's radios, and both brothers were listening in closely, making the most of it while they were still in range.

But the two fugitives had achieved something Nicky and Kat hadn't yet: they were now in New York State.

'Thought Frank might run on us, once we broke his ass out of the joint,' Billy grumbled, holding his upper arm which was still bleeding after being winged by a bullet from Archer's rifle. 'Lying sack of shit.'

'We'll find him later, forget about it.' Using the woman's cellphone, Brooks was looking at the border between Pennsylvania and NY near Erie. It was clogged up all over with roadblocks on the main routes out, including the one where they'd shot and killed the four officers and the two college kids in the Winnebago. He'd been reading the updates on Reyes as they came in and had discovered their fellow former C Block resident was also in the area. He'd have to be trying to get out as well, just like them.

'He ain't making it through that,' Billy said, after his brother showed him the map with the red triangles and told him Reyes was in the region. 'They'll scoop him up along with the cash if he tries.'

'The guy ain't stupid. He got out of Gatlin, remember.'

'By using us.'

'So he might end up using someone else. We better hope he makes it.'

Billy looked puzzled. 'What?'

'You want a titanium mystery bullshit box we can't open or the millions he's carrying around right now?' Brooks snapped, looking at the screen. 'I saw the bitch drop the second bag she was lugging when I shot her. It was heavy; much heavier than this one. That's the one packed with dollar bills.' His eyes shifted to the holdall they had from the heist, containing the lockbox and nothing else. 'We can't get into that thing right now without spending time we ain't got and ending up destroying whatever's inside. Even if it's worth something, we need cash, little brother. Fast. Especially now Frank took off.'

'And you think Reyes will wanna make a deal? You just said he ain't stupid.'

Brooks pointed at an engraving on the lockbox. *K O'M*, it said: Kat O'Mara. 'His girl risked twenty five to life to get this. Now we need to find him.' One advantage of the news reports was he was able to keep track of his fellow escapee's whereabouts. 'Use your brain, Reyes,' he muttered, before dialing and calling a number.

'Yeah?'

'It's me again,' he told the man who answered, their cousin Cusick, Brooks' visitor at Gatlin on the same afternoon Kat had met with Nicky a few days ago. He'd bought a disposable phone in preparation for the brothers' escape, Brooks memorizing the number, and with him calling Cusick on it from random phones, he knew the calls couldn't be intercepted or easily traced by the US Marshals or police.

'The hell are you? Pennsylvania's starting to glow red hot looking for you guys.'

'It's good, we got over into New York. We're heading north.' Brooks glanced at the woman behind the wheel; she was rigid in her seat and taking rapid, hitched shallow breaths, her vocal cords seeming to have locked as tight as the Granit padlock on the titanium box. She hadn't said more than two words since they'd taken her hostage, seeming almost catatonic with fear. 'Where are you?'

'Parked in a lot near Rochester, waiting on your call like you said.'

'Anyone watching?'

'Not right now. Made sure I weren't followed, but there's police all over the area back home. Place is crawling with cops.'

'Need you to get your ass down here to Chautauqua County and come pick us up. I'll tell you where once you're closer. Get moving.' Brooks then paused, looking back at the titanium lock box with *K O'M* on the front, the heavy-duty lock seemingly impossible to release without the key. 'Bring a can of spray paint too.'

'Spray paint?'

'Just do it.'

'Tell me the story again,' Nicky said to Barry, returning from the lake's edge at the lookout point just outside Erie. He'd quickly stripped off to scrub himself with some soap and shave, using items from a washbag he'd found in Barry's overnight bag. He'd taken the man's car keys with him, the unassuming and terrified salesman having had his hands tied to the steering wheel with Kat in the back holding the revolver on him.

'We're going to the conference in Syracuse,' Barry recited nervously, as Nicky dried off with a towel also lifted from the bag, before using deodorant and a small amount of cologne. 'You work with me in the company.'

'My name?' Nicky asked, starting to button up a shirt from a suit that Barry had had hanging off a hook in the back of his car.

'Stephen Rydell. From Dayton, Ohio.'

'And if you try to give the cops a signal?'

'She'll shoot the first officer who tries to open up the backseat. Then me.'

Nicky finished dressing; the shoes were too small but he wasn't planning on wearing them long, and although Barry was carrying more weight than Nicky, his suit didn't look too bad a fit. As he zipped up the fly, he realized he hadn't worn a suit since his father's funeral when he was sixteen. He hadn't worn anything other than prison orange for over a decade since Friday morning.

'If this works please let me go.'

'If it does, you have my word.' Nicky checked the pockets on the dirty jeans he was relieved to be leaving behind in exchange for the suit pants and saw he had sixty four bucks left from when he'd bought supplies at the Wegmans, Lowes and liquor store. It went into his pocket, along with his fake ID, the Leatherman pocketknife going into the bag of cash which he stuffed into the rear footwell. 'Time to lie down,' he told Kat.

He helped ease her across the footwell of the car beside the money and settled her in as comfortably as he could before covering her with a blanket. He folded the seat carefully over and pulled some of the boxes in the trunk forward to cover it.

'You good?' Nicky called.

'Not really,' she replied faintly. *'I'll be OK.'* Pause. *'Just hurry.'*

Nicky opened the front passenger door, but before he got in, thought of the vinegar and bleach he'd used when he'd escaped from Gatlin. When he'd passed the roadblock leaving Ohio, he'd seen sniffer dogs, and knew they were almost definitely being used at all the blocks on I-90 and 86. They were going to be his biggest threat.

Then he had an idea. Keeping hold of Barry's keys, he went to the trunk and carefully peeled back the tape on two of the boxes. He removed a couple of cans from each and picking up a rock, bashed in their sides. Then he pulled the rings, dipped his finger into each can and smeared some of the contents onto the untouched packets and other cans, before slotting the now-damaged ones back in place and resealing the boxes, making sure there was no sign they'd been tampered with.

He went down to the water to rinse his hands off and looked up at the midday sun as he did so. *Gonna be nowhere in the dark you can hide for long*, Prez had warned him, the night before Nicky's escape. Charged with nervous energy, and knowing Kat was suffering in silence in her hiding place with her pain only getting worse in those cramped conditions, the fourth Gatlin fugitive jogged back to the car and climbed inside.

He untied Barry, threw the binds out of the window, then passed him back his keys. 'Anyone asks, the cans burst sometimes. Got it?'

'Yeah.'

Nicky found a pack of gum in the inner pocket of the suit jacket and popped a piece into his mouth. 'I-90. Let's go.'

Twenty minutes later, Kat's heart was racing as she heard muffled voices; she was getting hotter and increasingly uncomfortable in her hiding place, covered with a blanket and with the A/C turned off. She knew she couldn't last like this much longer.

The excited barks of a dog had come from outside and she'd heard whoever was out there open the trunk.

Right now, she was barely daring to breathe.

She was cramped, in pain and increasingly light-headed despite having two functioning lungs again; her new shirt was damp with sweat, the gun she was holding slippery in her hands. She was gripping it too tight and relaxed her hand; having the revolver go off because she'd unintentionally squeezed the trigger would be unforgiveable, especially after all Nicky had done for her.

He'd spelt out to the guy who owned this car what Katherine would do to any officer or trooper who found her, but they both knew that was a lie. She'd meant what she'd told Nicky at Gatlin on Thursday, she'd never wanted anyone to get hurt during any of this. How naïve that hope had been in hindsight had immediately become obvious the moment the shooting started on East Superior, Erica, her brother and the other two thieves on the job all killed on the spot, and was being reinforced with every second of sharp, stabbing pain from her torso. Nicky had warned her this wasn't going to go to plan and she should've listened, but desperation had warped her thinking. She saw that now. But too late.

'If that's how much was stolen, your suspects need to rethink their business strategy,' she heard Nicky say outside. Face to face, talking with the police, but somehow staying calm. The policemen standing out there with him would have seen his old Gatlin photo, but he'd matured a lot in the years since, the decade-plus of prison life etched into his face making him almost unrecognizable from the eighteen year old who'd been sentenced to twelve years for manslaughter. He'd also pushed his hair back after washing in the lake, shaved and was wearing the suit. The doctor who'd removed the bullet out of her side would've told police what she and Nicky had been wearing at the

motel, the federal fugitive now dressed completely differently.

She hoped altogether it would be enough.

'Who said anything about money being stolen?'

'We've been listening to the radio. Heard what happened in Cleveland yesterday. Guessing that's why you guys are here.'

She kept waiting, breathing as quietly and steadily as she could, her side burning now the whiskey and painkillers had worn off. Every movement made it feel like there was a clump of barbed wire packed inside the right side of her body, slicing into her internal organs. But then after another muffled comment she couldn't quite hear, she heard the front doors open and close, seatbelts get clicked on, then the engine started again.

Once no-one disturbed the blanket, she finally dared to start hoping they were through.

They drove on for what felt like an age, Kat not daring to make a sound until they pulled over and the seat and blanket were lifted up.

'We made it?' she asked, as Nicky nodded before helping her out.

'We're over,' he told her, Kat managing to smile from a surge of relief as she breathed in lungfuls of fresh air, despite the pain it caused. Nicky shifted the boxes, put the seats back down into their usual position and helped her get as comfortable as possible, before placing the bag containing money and jewelry boxes on the floor beside her.

The bandaging Dr Tejwani had taped over the bullet-hole was keeping any new bloodstain from soaking through to her new shirt. Kat thought that was a good sign and was clinging to it optimistically. She'd been patched up, the surgeon having got the bullet out, and Nicky seemed to think she was stable, but she didn't feel any better than she had before.

In fact, she felt slightly worse.

She didn't tell him though; he had enough to worry about. They were getting closer to the Canadian border, but as they moved back onto the main road, Kat looked down at the bag beside her. They could just keep going, but the money and jewelry hadn't been what she'd needed so badly from the heist. This wasn't hers, the other box was.

And wherever they were, she knew it was almost certain because of the three initials engraved on that inner deposit box she so desperately wanted, that these Loughlin brothers would have realized that too.

THIRTY EIGHT

'She what?' Archer said anxiously an hour later, riding shotgun in a PA State trooper's car as they headed east through Chautauqua County. 'How badly?'

'She's been taken to hospital,' Lieutenant Richie from Cleveland PD told him over the phone. *'Banged up pretty bad. Like I said, she fell out of her hotel window and landed on a car below. If it hadn't been there and an awning hadn't broken her fall, she'd probably be dead.'*

'There's an obvious question here.'

'Her room was torn to shreds by gunfire. Someone sure as hell wanted her gone. Amount of spent cartridges left behind says automatic weapons and probably more than one shooter.'

'Who?'

'I don't know. Could it've been the Loughlins?'

'Impossible, I just engaged with them here,' Archer replied, imagining Marquez so desperate she'd jumped out of the hotel window, and trying to work out who could've been responsible. 'They're in New York State right now, not Ohio.'

'Lupinetti?'

'He was here too. Had Lis gone anywhere?'

'I don't know. When she wakes up, we're gonna ask.' As Archer killed the call, the trooper's cruiser sped on through the New York county with two others behind. In normal times, crossing into a neighboring state as troopers on patrol from another was prohibited, but their pursuit of the Loughlins and the threat level being so high had already been accepted as justification. They were heading for where a report had been received of another abandoned

vehicle the brothers had been seen hijacking earlier. 'Who saw them taking this car?' Archer asked, having missed further information coming through on the radio when he was on the phone to Richie.

'Guy passing by on a motorbike recognized them from the news. They were getting into an SUV, holding the driver at gunpoint. He pulled over once he was clear and called 911. One of the local deputies got a hit on the tag from an APB. Local resident, female, no criminal history.'

'Lupinetti?'

'No sign. Police are looking for him back in PA in case he went in the other direction. But when the APB scored a location the brothers were nowhere in sight. The vehicle had been dumped and they were probably long gone.'

The Pennsylvania trooper's vehicle took a turn-off to their left and arrived in a parking lot where the car had been found twenty minutes ago. Other law enforcement were already there and a chopper was circling overhead. As the PA troopers in the three vehicles pulled up, got out and caught up on the situation with their NY State counterparts, Archer immediately walked towards the abandoned SUV, seeing law-enforcement were working two K-9s around the area, looking to pick up a scent but with no apparent luck.

'Must've jacked another vehicle,' the PA State trooper who'd given Archer a lift here said.

'Or someone picked them up.' Archer's eyes were still on the gray SUV. He walked forward but was stopped by a local deputy before the NYPD detective showed him his badge. 'Been on the Loughlins and Frank Lupinetti since they broke out of Gatlin in Virginia,' Archer explained.

The deputy looked shaken and Archer's eyes shifted to the car.

'The driver?' he asked.

‘She’s inside.’ The deputy offered no further resistance and stepped aside as Archer approached the vehicle.

The woman had been left lying across the backseat, her wrists bound, and Archer saw the brothers had learned from their mistake with the laundry truck driver back in Virginia; her throat had been slit from ear to ear, but that wasn’t the darkest aspect. Her distended stomach showed she’d been about seven to eight months pregnant and there were clear signs that she’d been sexually assaulted before the brothers left, her torn underwear dumped in the footwell, blood covering the seats. They may have been in a hurry, but either one or both of them had still found time.

Two more of the PA troopers had just joined him and fell silent as they looked in at the Loughlins’ latest victim. Not just one life taken, but two. What had happened to Marquez, then this, and once again law-enforcement had lost the trail of the two brothers and Lupinetti; the situation was also looking even more challenging, now it appeared the three men had split up.

The deputy who’d let Archer approach the car walked around to the other side of the vehicle. ‘She’s not all. Come check this out.’

Archer and the troopers joined him and saw six words in large letters had been written across the side of the gray SUV, a can of red spray paint left dumped in the dirt beside a series of footprints. The lettering had run down in the afternoon heat, almost as if it had been written in blood.

‘They tagged it?’ one of the PA troopers said. ‘Like a calling card?’

‘They haven’t done that anywhere else,’ Archer replied. ‘And these words don’t make sense.’

'*Next.*' Less than forty miles from the clearing with the graffiti-strewn SUV and dead pregnant woman inside, Nicky stepped up to a counter at a Mexican takeout joint. The customer in front had just collected their food and left which meant it was the prison escapee's turn. 'Afternoon sir, can I take your order?' a teenager in the restaurant's uniform asked.

'I'll take three steak burritos with everything, two bags of chips and two bottles of water,' Nicky said. He could've stopped at a gas station or somewhere else to get food, but Kat wasn't going to start recovering on pretzels, Chex Mix or beef jerky.

'That's everything?'

Nicky nodded; he paid using the remainder of his sixty four dollars, and then stepped to one side as the workers in back started prepping his order. Once it was done and bagged up, he was just heading for the exit with the food when in a moment of sudden panic, he saw two police officers heading right for the door on the other side. He'd seen them too late to turn back and pretend he'd forgotten something, but then fate intervened in the shape of a young woman wearing a t-shirt which looked to be two sizes too small. She'd just exited a Dunkin' Donuts with a friend to their left, meaning neither cop paid the escaped convict approaching them any attention, so Nicky was able to walk right past unnoticed.

The two cops had parked six spaces away from Nicky. He got back into Barry's Audi, the man in the driver's seat with his hands taped low to the wheel, the keys in Nicky's pocket and Kat with the gun trained out of sight on their hostage, or so Barry had been told. Nicky had also stopped at a grocery store along the strip-mall before going into the Mexican takeout spot, using one of the $100 bills from the holdall to buy what he needed, and put the shopping in the back beside Kat with the burritos, chips and water. Minus a bullet and with two working lungs again, she was breathing better but her face was still white as paper, the blanket Nicky had draped up to her chest concealing the gun which was resting on her lap, the money bag still on the floor by her feet.

The two cops were now at the counter inside the Mexican place, and looking in the side mirror, Nicky saw one glance over in their direction, but realized he was getting a last look at the girl who was getting into a car on their right, not paying any attention to the two wanted fugitives and hostage inside the Audi also parked in the lot. The car hadn't been stolen so he relaxed slightly, knowing there was no reason for the cops to be looking for it.

'Keep going east,' Nicky said, passing the keys back to Barry before cutting his hands free with the Leatherman multi-tool, having used a fresh roll of tape.

After they drove on for another thirty minutes, using minor roads to avoid any unreported potential roadblocks, Nicky noticed an old farmhouse with boarded up windows set well back from the road, a large barn to its right.

'Take this turn,' he ordered. 'Park up behind the barn.'

Barry did as he was told, Nicky taking the keys again once they'd stopped. With Kat keeping the handgun on Barry, Nicky got out of the car and walked towards the barn. He pulled open the doors to find empty pens and dusty rails, some old beer cans in the grass beside it. The place looked as if it had been abandoned for a while; he returned to the vehicle.

'Can you help me get her out?' he said to Barry. Between them, they carried her into the barn before Nicky climbed the ladder to the upper level, but again all he saw was dust and cobwebs. No sign of occupancy, either human or animal. He took the chance to look through the broken window at the house the barn had belonged to, but it was clearly derelict too.

For the first time in hours, it felt as if they had a brief window to rest, regroup and consider their next move. He went back down the ladder and took the gun off Kat, then pointed at an old upturned water trough ten feet away. 'Take a seat,' he told Barry. The man did as ordered, then Nicky helped Kat over to one of the open pens, laying the blanket down before shifting her onto it. He collected the bag he'd bought from the grocery store and pulled out some items.

He ripped open a packet of straws and after carefully slotting one into the other, taped them together when he had enough to create a makeshift tube. He took the needle out of Kat's pocket that he'd removed from the bike pump bought earlier at Wegmans, thinking at the time it might come in handy for this very purpose later, and taped it to one end of the straws, then secured the other to a carton of coconut water.

He walked back to Kat, tied off a piece of tape around her bicep and tapped her forearm before isolating a prominent vein. He made a small incision with the Leatherman, wiped the needle with a tissue taken from the small packet of antiseptic wipes he'd also thrown into the bag in the motel room, then slid it in carefully and taped it down. He lifted the coconut water carton and secured it on a ledge just above the needle entry point, taping it to the wood. Without a word, he then went back to fetch the take-out food bag and passed his hostage and then Kat a burrito.

Like Tejwani before him, Barry found himself staring at the young man who'd taken him hostage.

There seemed to be a lot more to this guy than he'd first assumed.

'How's she doing?' Sergeant Glick of Cleveland PD asked his lieutenant over the phone. Inside the main city hospital, Richie looked in at Marquez lying on a bed next door, still in the clothes she'd pulled on quickly when she'd escaped the hotel room but now with some bandaging wrapped around her head. Half her hair was falling over it, making it look like a hairband; she had other minor injuries and he'd been told they'd had to shave part of her hair on the left side of her temple to stitch up a wound under the bandaging.

'She's OK. Hit the ground pretty hard, but head injuries and extremities bleed the worst. Doc says there's no swelling on her brain or anything they're concerned about.'

'She'll be hurting tomorrow. I'm looking at this drop from her window, Rich. She's lucky that car was there.'

'Suspects?'

'In and out clean. Witness from the stairs said two men ran past her carrying weapons. Wearing ski-masks, going fast. They were gone before any police arrived. Left this place looking like the O.K. Corral.'

'Hotel must have cameras.'

'Ball caps walking in, never looked up. Came in through the basement, had a sub-machine gun hidden in a holdall each, left that way on foot. No plates we can follow.'

Richie imagined whoever had come after the female detective looking down from above and seeing her lying completely still through the torn awning with blood pooling out from her head; they'd have thought she was dead. She should've been. He saw Marquez notice his presence and told Glick he'd call him back.

'You and your friend don't have a problem getting into the thick of things, do you?' he said to her, walking into the room.

'Yeah, it's known to be a habit,' she muttered, pushing herself slightly more upright. 'He's better at it than me though.'

'You doing alright?'

'I guess.' She closed her eyes. 'When I went to lie down for half an hour, didn't think it was gonna be on the sidewalk. How we doing on the manhunts?'

'Not great. The Loughlins busted through another roadblock, left us six more bodies for their count. Four cops from Erie, PA and two college kids. Your friend almost got them at the scene, but looks like they're in New York State now.'

'Is Sam OK?'

He smiled, amused at her concern for her colleague considering where she was right now. 'That's what he asked me about you. He's good. But the brothers jacked a new car. Left it in a parking lot, looks like they got picked up by a friend or stole another.' He clicked on the news on the TV in the room, which since the networks were covering the hunts had live footage patched in from local stations, reporting from the scene where the SUV had been found.

'And another victim?' she asked quietly, reading the headline.

'Two. A woman. She was pregnant.'

Marquez's eyes closed again. 'Son of a bitch. What is it with these guys?'

'We couldn't get anything on tape of who came after you either, but looks like they knew what they were doing. You get a feel for anyone tailing you from Virginia, or since you got to town?'

She shook her head. 'I went to go see Blair O'Mara at her home in the suburbs. This happened soon as I got back.'

'You should've told me you paid her a visit. I'd have come with you.'

'Figured you'd be busy.' She gave him a wry look. 'I can be pushy, but I'm having trouble seeing her ordering a hit on me. Or doing it that fast. But she mentioned a family…' Marquez then suddenly lost concentration and searched around, looking at her nightstand. After a moment, Richie saw her face and realized what was happening, then rushed to pass her a blue plastic sick bag resting on the table. Adrenaline dumping, shock, hits to the head; as she turned away and threw up, he glanced at a nurse outside who nodded, not seeming concerned.

Richie filled a cup of water, which Marquez took and rinsed her mouth out with before the same nurse came over and offered her a Tic-Tac, which she also took. 'Sorry. She mentioned a maid when we had a conversation,' the NYPD detective said, picking up where she left off. 'Used to work for the family before Kat's father died. We track this woman down and ask her face-to-face about this family's strange deal, could help us. I felt Blair was holding back.'

Richie was surprised. 'It's not connected to Lupinetti.'

'I know, but not much we can do about him right now until another sighting comes in. I wanna know why Kat's so desperate to get her hands on that bank deposit box. And who the hell shot up my hotel room.' Marquez made to get off the bed, but then nausea hit her again and she went back to the sick bag, throwing up again. After she'd recovered, she rinsed her mouth once more as the nurse this time came over and passed her the whole box of Tic-Tacs instead of just one. She and Richie made eye contact and she smiled ruefully. 'Maybe I'd better sit this one out.'

Inside the barn in New York State, Nicky, Kat and Barry were eating in silence, Kat doing her best to chew and force down a small amount of food despite her weariness, lack of hunger and the continual pain in her side. Eating was the last thing she felt like doing right now, but she knew she had to keep her strength up.

She was just working on another bite when she noticed Nicky watching something on Barry's phone. He bumped the volume up slightly. 'What is it?' Kat asked, the coconut water IV taped to her arm already improving the sunken look on her face as it slowly rehydrated her. 'Erie?'

Nicky shook his head. Instead, the shot on the network's website went to another live feed. Police cars and a Coroner's vehicle in a parking lot in the same county they were currently in, Chautauqua, NY. Nicky read the headline and saw who the suspects were.

A gray SUV was taped off by police, but he read six words scrawled on the side in red spray paint:

Gimme a call

Or you're, no friend

He put down his burrito, looking at the screen. *Gimme a call or you're, no friend.* A message to their guys further north around their home area, probably. The brothers would be needing more help by now with increasing numbers of law-enforcement seeking to close in on them.

'Could I have some wat-' Barry went to say.

'Son of a bitch,' Nicky suddenly said, but he wasn't talking to Barry. He was staring at the screen. Then without taking his eyes off it, he got to his feet, picked up a bottle of water and passed it to Barry.

'What's wrong?' Kat asked.

'I need to make a call,' he said to Barry. 'That cool?'

The man looked confused for a moment. 'Um. Sure. Go ahead.'

'Thanks,' Nicky said, before dialing a number and stepping outside the barn. He'd thought he'd been the one to use the Loughlins since he'd first planned to get out of Gatlin on Friday morning. But those few blood-red words had just told him how the brothers had known Kat was going to hit the bank yesterday.

And how they'd taken advantage of both him and her.

THIRTY NINE

Inside USP Gatlin, C Block was in its second day of lockdown and misery had company. The inmates were doing what they could to pass the long hours in their cells; some were reading or working out by doing pushups, sit ups or squats. A few were eating foods they'd already had in the cells, either from the commissary or previously smuggled out from the kitchen, other prisoners not so lucky feeling the effects of twenty four hours without anything to eat. A few were just standing with their arms resting on the bars or lying on their bunks, waiting, the clock ticking at the same pace it always did. One second, one minute and one hour at a time.

Alone in his now one-man cell, Rainey had been watching COs and law-enforcement coming and going from the gate through his barred window. He couldn't tell from this distance if the guys with badges were State investigators, US Marshals or maybe even FBI, but neither they or the guards had come into the block yet today. The total lockdown was being observed, the punishment carried out to the letter: no showers, no meals and no yard time. He was expecting a visit eventually though, being Nicky's cellmate. Especially if they'd discovered by now that a motorcycle chapter had gotten him and the injured girl over the Ohio-Pennsylvania border.

Prez had been tracking the news of the Gatlin Four on his smartphone, a text option enabled so he could watch the coverage in silence, and had just seen the report of this latest roadblock getting blasted on Station Road in Pennsylvania. He'd known it wasn't the kid even before he'd read that the Loughlins and Lupinetti were being held responsible, but Nicky had been seen in PA too, north of that location in the city of Erie, and according to the latest on the ticker had taken a doctor hostage who'd been rescued by a SWAT team, Nicky and the girl escaping just ahead of police.

So his celly had managed to source treatment for the wounded woman, which was smart, and he was getting closer and closer to Canada, which is where Prez knew they wanted to go. But now kidnap as well as armed robbery? The rising heat he was facing was only going to become hotter and wherever he was, Nicky would soon be running on empty.

Speaking of which, the battery on the phone was down to 22 percent, and Prez was about to turn it off when a number he didn't recognize appeared on the screen. The biker moved his finger to answer, but then sensed a trap; it could be the prison staff or a cop or investigator who'd somehow gotten this number and were testing to see if Rainey answered while under lockdown, which meant he definitely had a phone hidden in his cell.

But it might be the kid, he thought, remembering the desperation in Nicky's voice when he'd called from that garage in Cleveland needing help.

Rainey decided to risk taking the call, and discovered he'd guessed correct.

Inside the Gatlin guards' locker room and break area, some of the guards assigned to C Block were watching a TV while waiting to be interviewed by State investigators. '*Gimme a call. Or you're. No friend,*' one of the COs read quietly, the red lettering scrawled across the side of the gray SUV found in the lot in Chautauqua County. 'The hell does that mean.' As he spoke, the captain and warden both walked into the room. 'You see this, Cap?' the CO asked.

'No, but I just heard four more cops, two Penn State juniors and a pregnant woman got wasted by our boys.' The captain walked closer to the screen, seeing the graffiti on the car. 'They did that too?'

'Looks like it.' The CO looked at one of his colleagues. 'Williams thinks it's a code.'

'Getting a message to a friend to call them,' the captain replied. 'Don't need my high school diploma to crack that one.'

'You know these guys are always trying to communicate without us understanding what they're talking about,' Williams said. 'We've all seen the letters they get from the outside that don't make no sense. I remember hearing over at Big Sandy, one of their COs stopped a gang hit on a judge ordered by one of the inmates after decoding a message hidden in a letter.'

'So?'

'That habit of looking for word-games sticks. I catch myself looking for codes in things I read.' Williams pointed at the screen. 'Take the last word of each sentence. What does it say?'

'Call you're friend,' the captain said. 'Doesn't make sense.'

'Does if you say it out loud. And the bad spelling makes it less obvious. Not sophisticated, but it's still a message.'

'A message to who, Williams?' the warden asked. 'That doesn't help us. It could be anyone.'

'Police aren't just looking for Brooks and Billy, right, sir? The reports from Cleveland said the two brothers, Frank Lupinetti and Reyes were all at the robbery at the intersection yesterday. They broke out of prison, got past all the roadblocks, then met up to hit the truck. Now they're separated again.'

'You think they're trying to communicate with Reyes?' the warden replied. 'Through the news?'

'If they're split up and even if they got hold of cell phones, it's unlikely they have each other's numbers,' Williams answered. 'If they don't have a scheduled rendezvous point, this would be a good way of getting a message to him. I think they might be telling Reyes to *call his friend*, whoever that is. He's got too many braincells not to keep up with the news giving the latest on the hunt for him and the others. He'll see that message.'

'He didn't have a lot of visitors during his time here,' the warden noted. 'No-one apart from the girl since the very early years of his sentence. I've looked at the logbooks. He's been in this prison for a third of his life so won't be likely to have a lot of friends left, especially on the outside. And I didn't think he was close with Brooks and Billy?'

'He wasn't, but who knows what's changed if money's involved, sir?'

The captain suddenly slapped the shoulders of two of his boys, his face changing. 'Make yourselves useful. You're coming with me to C Block.'

'What is it?' the warden asked.

'I got a feeling who this friend might be.'

'How do we tell that to the Loughlins, kid?' Rainey asked, Nicky having just told him that he wanted to trade bags with the brothers. With the holdall Kat had ended up with, the other she said she'd dropped which she'd seen one of the brothers pick up as she ran from the heist shootout, and the graffiti making sense if using the same code that Nicky and Kat often employed during her visits to him at Gatlin, the kid had guessed the message on the SUV that he'd caught on the news was meant for him. 'You said you lost the cops. Don't start taking risks exchanging bags. Just run with what you got and get over the border.'

'This money isn't hers, or the jewels. We keep them, we keep more heat. She just wants what's hers.'

'You finally got some daylight between you and the police. That won't last. Make the most of it.'

'I will, but she wants back what belongs to her.'

'So how do we get a message to those two?' Prez asked, recognizing his celly wasn't going to budge. Same as this past Thursday afternoon in the yard, when together they'd first started planning his escape.

'When you got up at chow to get a message to Janks the other night, Wesley told me the Loughlins had made a deal with Boyd Hennigan to keep them posted on what was going down in the prison once they got out.'

'Why would they care?'

'Insurance. We know Boyd's been looking for payback against those two ever since they put him in the hospital last year. Wes said he'd agreed to take out Kattar and Hoff once lockdown's over if Brooks and Billy didn't manage to do it before leaving in the truck. Brooks didn't want them talking. We both know how dumb Billy is and Brooks must've been worried he might've told them about Cleveland and their plans afterward. No risks. Boyd's in C Block and he's got a cell phone. I've seen him use it.'

Prez looked out of his cell down at Hennigan's. Boyd was in for nine years for arson, having set a courthouse in Savannah on fire, but the man was also a suspect in a couple of other fire-bombings that detectives back home in Georgia couldn't make stick. Two people had been burned to a crisp in those fires, so there was a reason why Brooks and Billy would have chosen him to make sure Hoff and Kattar ended up on a slab. They knew Boyd had no problem with killing, even if cops on the outside couldn't prove it.

'Speak to him when they let you all out for a shower and chow. He can pass a message from me to them.'

'You can wait that long?'

'Can you get his attention sooner?'

Prez went to his door and managed to draw Wesley's focus; he pointed and mouthed *Boyd*. Wesley went to his bars and got the guy's attention, then said something that made him look up at Prez's cell.

The MC president made a phone shape with his hand by his ear then pointed at Boyd; the convicted arsonist nodded, before Prez then made a writing motion. Boyd understood and started signaling him his number, Prez taking a pen and book he was reading before scribbling it down on one of the inside pages. 'So if they want a trade, how you think you're gonna make it out alive from the exchange?' he asked Nicky, picking up his cell again.

But before the kid could answer, Prez heard a door below open, before footsteps echoed on the gantry leading up to his tier; Wesley had shifted focus from Boyd and was quickly making the screw motion with his hand to Prez.

'*Shit, call you back,*' he whispered, before hurrying to hide the phone.

When the captain and two guards he'd brought with him reached the cell, they found the biker lying on his bunk reading a Tom Clancy novel, only looking up at the three men when they unlocked the door.

'What happened, boss?' he asked. 'Is lockdown over?'

'Get up and step out,' the captain ordered, sliding the door back.

Rainey closed the book and did as he was ordered. Without another word the captain and CO Williams each pulled on gloves before yanking the top mattress off the upper bunk. One officer then ran his hands along the frame of the bed while the other examined the thin mattress for any cuts or incisions to serve as a hiding place.

Rainey was forced to stand still and watch silently as they began to pull apart, strip and search the entire cell.

FORTY

'Where is it, Prez?' the prison staff captain asked, once the shakedown was completed. The cell had been turned over, but nothing found.

'Where's what?'

The captain pushed him against the wall and started patting him down again. 'The phone. I know you got one.'

'You're wrong. I don't, boss.'

The captain checked him all the way to his ankles, then stopped and looked back at the cell. It occurred to him there was one final place they hadn't checked.

His eyes shifted upwards and he looked at the light fixture.

'Williams, take a look,' he told his CO, who climbed up onto the top bunk. The captain glanced back at Prez, whose expression had changed slightly. 'You wouldn't mind, right?'

Prez didn't answer, his face remaining hard to read. Williams unclipped the plastic covering and reaching up, felt around inside; a few seconds later, his hand came back, covered in dust.

But that was all.

The captain's temper snapped. 'Take him to the SHU.'

'The hell for?' Prez argued. 'I didn't do anything apart from stand here and watch you guys!'

'For pissin' me off.' Before he could say another word, the large biker was hauled out of C Block, other inmates calling out to the guards to end the lockdown already, as the MC president was taken through to the SHU. He was shoved into a bare cell, bolted in, then heard the doors outside shut. He knew they'd probably pull his now empty cell to pieces looking for the phone. They'd be wasting their time.

But throughout all this, valuable seconds had been ticking by.

Prisoners were assigned basic canvas shoes to wear when they first arrived at the prison, but could switch or upgrade to sneakers if they had them sent through the mail or carried out enough prison work to be able to buy some themselves. Prez had always stuck with the canvas option, not bothered much about his footwear, but that wasn't the only reason; right from the jump, he'd been especially interested in the flexibility of the fabric. He'd realized that with care, things could be hidden inside.

Easing off his canvas shoe, he pulled out the phone tucked under the sole; he'd deliberately chosen that particular smartphone as it was one of the smallest available, allowing it to be more easily hidden, but the screen was now badly cracked, despite him arching his foot as best he could to try to keep his weight off it. However, the phone was still working and he saw a text message had come through. After quickly saving Boyd's cell number, hoping he'd remembered the sequence right from when he'd quickly written it down, he moved away from the door to stand under the tiny window above his head before calling Nicky back, keeping his eyes and one ear on the door.

Nicky, Kat and their hostage were still in the barn in upstate New York, Barry tied to a beam now he'd finished eating, when his phone lit up with an incoming call. After Rainey had hung up so suddenly earlier, Nicky knew better than to call him back and that he'd have to wait for the biker to make contact again, if he could.

'Boyd signaled me his number and I sent him a text saying you're willing to trade,' Prez told him. *'You were*

right, kid. Call your friend *was a message meant for you. He just came back saying the Loughlins have agreed. They gave a location.'*

'Where?'

'New York State Fair, 9pm. I just checked it out online. Tonight's the last night so it's gonna be busy in there. Probably why they chose it.'

'The COs still been sweating you?'

'I'm in the SHU. They just tore our cell apart looking for the phone. I hid it under my sole. They still might find it if they strip me or take me to the showers.' He paused. *'Janks says hi.'*

'I'm sorry, man.'

'Eh, I could use some quiet time after the riot. And you got bigger things to worry about; Brooks and Billy said you bring your bag, they'll show up with theirs, but you won't just be able to walk into that place with that much cash over your shoulder.'

'I'll work that one out. Can you keep that phone off to keep it charged? I'll hit up you again later.'

'How's the girl?'

Nicky looked at her, asleep on a blanket on a pile of old hay with the coconut water IV still attached. 'Better, I think. Save that battery.' Ending the call, he rose, bagged up their leftover food, and tossed it into Barry's Audi along with their empty water bottles; he then went back and removed the makeshift IV from Kat's arm. He picked her up and carried her over to the car, covering her to the upper chest with the blanket before placing the bag of money on the floor beside her.

And then he turned back to his hostage, whose heart started hammering; Barry knew whatever this was, it was about to end. Nicky walked down on the man, who was staring at him in fright, but instead of pulling the handgun or Leatherman knife, the Gatlin escapee reached past him and tested the binds that were tying the scared salesman to the beam.

'I'll be listening to the news,' he told Barry. 'They haven't found you by later tonight, I'll drop call 911 and tell 'em where you are.' He went back to the man's Audi and Barry watched as he unloaded the boxes of pet food before placing them on the ground. 'Have to borrow your ride, but wherever I leave it you'll get it back. Sorry you missed your conference.' He reached into his pocket and took out a couple of hundred dollars, same as he'd done for the doctor earlier in the day. 'For the suit,' he said, walking back over to tuck it into Barry's pocket.

'The police will ask me about what happened. I'll have to answer. Please don't come after me.'

'No-one's gonna be coming after you. Good luck, man.' Nicky paused. 'Sorry for you that we met.'

Then he turned and walked out of the barn. Moments later, Barry watched his car leave, kicking up dust in the afternoon sun which slowly settled back to the ground before all went quiet.

As Reyes drove away from the barn, checking the traffic updates on the map on the smartphone in his hand, Archer was looking at his own primary cellphone which had finally turned back on, dried out and functioning again after his dunking in the river in West Virginia on Friday night.

Sitting on a plastic chair outside an auto-shop in a quiet area of Chautauqua County, the tires on the NYPD Ford inside being replaced, he was waiting for updates from Cleveland on Marquez. It sounded like she'd escaped her attempted killers without severe consequences, but he knew bangs to the head could be fatal with delayed hemorrhaging or swelling on the brain. Richie had described the hotel room as being chewed to pieces by suppressed sub-machine gunfire, Archer's colleague barely escaping with her life by going out of that window and landing first on an awning and then a car below. And whoever had tried to kill her had been experienced enough to get in and out without being seen or apprehended afterwards. She'd been in Cleveland less than three hours and then to be attacked like that? To piss someone off in the city that fast would be impressive, even for Marquez. Or him.

So did someone follow her there from Virginia, or New York City? He immediately dismissed the thought. There wasn't a chance that she wouldn't have noticed a tail. He rose off the plastic chair and walked across the quiet lot away from the auto-shop containing the second car in his charge damaged by gunfire in twenty four hours. He was doing nothing to dispel the reputation he'd built for himself in the Department as the last man you'd ever want to lend a vehicle to; in fact, with the two cars getting pieced up, the hotel room he'd booked back at Cleveland being torn apart, barely making it off the extradition bus alive before being forced to jump off a bridge and then getting shot at during the armored truck robbery, he was making a good run at being the most uninsurable man in America.

But all of it was the result of a supposedly straightforward assignment that was meant to have ended two days ago, involving a man who should already have been locked up in a different federal prison. Archer's hearing had been slightly affected once again from repeatedly firing the Colt M4A1 rifle on Station Road at the two Loughlins and Lupinetti, his eyes still dry and sore from the gun-smoke. He remembered the way Frank had lit off during the fight, ever the opportunist, and Archer was sure that wherever he was, even though he was on the run, he'd be feeling pretty pleased with himself at how he'd played them off against each other; his pursuer from New York and his liberators from the prison bus, too busy battling each other to keep him contained. *Enjoy your freedom while you can, Frank,* he thought. *It's not going to last.*

As the sun started to set, Archer thought again of the two extradition agents who'd been shot on the bus the other night, the various roadblocks that had been blasted to pieces and the pregnant woman raped, murdered and left dumped in the SUV with graffiti sprayed on the side. No-one was going to rest until the Gatlin fugitives were back in custody, but he knew his and Marquez's participation would either be minimized or sidelined completely soon, the US Marshals and FBI having wider and higher jurisdictional authority than two NYPD detectives; with Shepherd's approval he'd stay on it to assist as long as he was permitted, though. He hated to leave a job unfinished and was determined to get Frank back in a set of bracelets, but then there was the fact that Marquez had been forced to take a header out of a hotel window. Lupinetti aside, Shep would want Archer to find out who'd come after her and forced her to take such drastic action. And why.

The diminishing light was casting long shadows around the lot but when Archer moved back towards the garage he stopped just before he reached the open rear doors, his outline visible on the ground through the back entrance of the auto-shop.

Along with the noise of the radio, when he'd walked away there'd been the sound of the three mechanics bantering and laughing, not every day they had to change tires on a car damaged from gunfire.

But he'd just picked up on something.

Aside from the music, all was now quiet in there.

That tended to happen when people concentrated, but Archer couldn't hear the sound of any movement whatsoever inside. He turned his head slightly so his good ear was angled towards the garage. He'd heard the phone in the shop ringing as he'd walked back towards the open rear gate and now it was going again, but no-one was answering.

As he stood there, he became aware of slight movement. He dropped his gaze and saw something edging very slowly towards him from inside the auto-shop.

He remained very still, his shadow a solid black shape as he looked at the widening pool of dark red expanding from just inside the premises; but because of where he was standing, he couldn't get a better view.

He thought of Marquez again, being attacked in her hotel room, as the blood continued to spread towards him.

It glinted dully as it reached the dying rays of the Sunday sun.

Archer suddenly sprinted to his right, heading for some cars in various stages of repair in the lot. There was a rustle of movement from deeper inside the dark auto-shop, and the plastic chair the NYPD detective had been sitting on outside a minute earlier was knocked over and quickly reduced to a husk of twisted, shredded plastic as it got caught in a burst of suppressed gunfire.

Archer dove between the vehicles as more bullets riddled their sides, breaking glass, the reports of the weapon chillingly quiet. Traffic continued to move along the highway near the lot fifty yards away, no-one seeming to have heard or seen what was happening. Shaking himself free of fragments of broken glass, Archer pulled his Sig Sauer and checked under the cars, but whoever was doing the shooting was keeping out of sight.

As he looked back towards the highway, he caught sight of another armed figure moving out from the other side of the auto-shop.

His problems had just doubled.

The pair were keeping to the shadows inside the shop and not moving to anywhere the NYPD detective could get a shot off at them. Archer edged silently backwards down the aisle between the cars, remembering the ambush on the Kanawha Falls Bridge on Friday night. Craig had got the drop on him then, moving up from Archer's six, and would have killed him if he hadn't reacted so fast.

He did a quick check behind him, but then heard running footsteps from his left.

He rose slightly to take aim, but ducked back down immediately as two three-round bursts shattered windows and wing mirrors of the cars he was sandwiched between, one person firing as the figure from the left changed position to flank the NYPD detective. Again, the noise of the gunfire was suppressed and Archer still hadn't seen either shooter clearly, just shadows and the sound of running footsteps.

Noise, he thought. *Something they don't want.* He turned and remaining low, took aim and fired his gun three times, the unsilenced shots echoing around the auto-shop's garage and parking lot, but instead of trying to hit his attackers, he shot out some billboard lights that had just come on above the highway. Pieces of them showered down onto the cars and trucks passing below which he hoped would attract attention, enough at least to get a curious motorist to stop and then maybe see and hear what was going on here in the lot.

Then he heard running footsteps on his right. They were flanking him and closing in.

With a jolt, Archer realized the shooter who'd just got closer was most likely positioning himself to fire under the vehicles. The lone NYPD detective pulled open the door in front of him and just made it into the front seat of a Chevy, staying below the window level, before suppressed gunfire ripped under the rows of cars, hitting the undersides and popping tires. While taking cover, Archer checked inside the vehicle for keys, finding none, so tried to sneak a look outside but more glass from the passenger side shattered above his head, the two shooters now moving in for the kill.

Archer didn't scare easily, but he knew whoever was doing this had him covered; he couldn't get a shot off, he was outnumbered and they were advancing on his position. Local cops wouldn't make it in time either, even if any of the drivers on the highway had reacted to the shot-out lights or heard his pistol firing and had called them.

But aside from luck, one of the reasons he was still alive was the more intense the pressure, the clearer his thought processes became. Although his heart was drumming, instead of panicking he looked around inside the car for inspiration or a way out. The plastic protective casing below the steering wheel was exposed, showing the key chamber and five wires below. He didn't know if the car even still had an engine, if it worked, or which ones were the battery and ignition wires, but he rapidly started twisting pairs of them together, touching them with another which he needed to be the starter wire.

One combo didn't work, so he tried another, then another. A shred of suppressed fire destroyed the headrest above his head. They were almost on him. Out of time, he twisted a fourth pairing together, then touched them with another.

The engine roared into life. Keeping low, he jammed his hand on the footbrake, pulled the lever into Drive and then quickly pushed his hand down on the accelerator; the Chevy leapt out of the line of vehicles. It was cut up by fire from both sides, the rear windows disintegrating and three of the headrests left with bullet-holes in the fabric, but the car kept going. Archer remembered there'd been a fence ahead in the lot; he braced one hand against the wheel just as the Chevy hit it and smashed through, saving him from breaking his nose.

However, the vehicle had been in the garage to be repaired for a reason and the engine died on him. The car continued to roll and then slammed to a halt into a wall beyond the fence, no airbag fitted to hit Archer. He didn't open the door to present himself as a target, instead lifting his head slightly to check the wingmirror on the right.

It was cracked, but he could still see behind him.

The lot was empty. He waited to see if either of the shooters reemerged, but they didn't. Not yet. Most likely working out how to kill him without putting themselves in the line of fire now he'd put more space between them. He looked in the back and saw one of the headrests had been detached and was resting on the back seat. He reached for it then held it up by one of the two metal prongs below and raised it slowly.

It was immediately knocked out of his hands as the fabric took rounds from a three shot burst, one of the shooters hitting it clean.

They were still here and their aim was extremely accurate.

But then Archer got lucky again, as he was to find out later. A truck driver who'd pulled off the highway to answer a phone call had seen the lights shatter right in front of him followed by the echo of Archer's unsuppressed handgun. He'd promptly ended his call to dial 911 instead, and now the wail of sirens could be heard approaching; when the first police cruiser arrived at the auto-shop, their department on high alert after the Loughlins had killed the pregnant woman in the area earlier, the two officers found three mechanics shot dead on the floor of the shop, shell casings littering the site and a man who'd quickly identified himself as a NYPD detective, emerging from a bullet-marked Chevy that had crashed into a wall at the far end of the lot.

Once police had taken over the scene and Archer's status had been checked out, the place was locked down as he and the other cops carried out a thorough search of the site, finding nothing but a load of spent shell cartridges scattered on the ground. The men who'd murdered the three mechanics had successfully melted away into the growing darkness; but they'd made a big mistake.

They hadn't managed to kill Archer.

FORTY ONE

Several hours later, attendants at the gate for the New York State Fair were inspecting bags and the contents of emptied pockets before scanning tickets. Certainly, none of them were checking faces for the Gatlin Four, the idea that any of the fugitives would show up at an event like this so far off-center that it hadn't occurred to anyone in law enforcement as a possibility. Thankfully for him, it meant one of most wanted men in every State from here to Kentucky was having no difficulty blending in with the crowd.

Holding a ticket he'd just bought from a booth to gain him access, Nicky had given himself a quick haircut earlier with Kat's help and was also wearing glasses in an effort to change his appearance, purchased when they'd stopped at a couple of stores outside Syracuse to stock up on certain supplies, which would be necessary if what he had planned for later tonight stood a chance of going his way. He'd swapped Barry's suit for a pair of jeans, sneakers and a gray hoodie he'd also bought, knowing if the salesman had been found in the barn, APBs and BOLOs would be out there describing the clothing Nicky had last been seen wearing.

Lights from the fairground projected through the fence and unknown to him, created lines on his face almost like prison bars, his eyes half in the shade, half in the light. He slowly exhaled and took a steadying breath as the people in front of him were checked.

Then it was his turn. The gate guard asked him to empty his pockets and watched as Nicky placed some cash and his fake ID down onto a folding table along with a pen and small pad of paper. He was wanded. 'No cell phone?' the man asked.

'No.' The guard stepped back and nodded at him to go through. Nicky tucked his belongings back into his pockets and walked into the fair, breathing out again slowly. He'd made it inside, but he was also now caged in and surrounded by a lot of people who would have seen his face on the news over the past few days, some of whom could prove to be more observant than the guards. There were plenty of distractions, various stalls, rides and a music stage which was attracting a sizeable crowd, but all it would take would be someone with an eye for faces. Prez had been right; this place was busy on its last night and meant the two farmboys he was here to meet would need to be on their best behavior too. No opening fire with weapons as they'd been doing so frequently since their escape. For a while, they'd be stuck in this giant cage as well.

But Nicky knew Brooks had chosen this meeting point for a reason. He started walking deeper into the fairground, keeping his senses wired; he'd picked up the skill in the prison yard of sensing when someone was shaping to make a move on him but wasn't catching those vibes just yet. However, he knew this area was where the Loughlins had grown up and also that there was a very good chance they'd got some old friends or family involved tonight who he wouldn't be able to recognize.

He moved further into the crowds of people milling around, doing his best to become just another anonymous face while making his way towards the fences on the eastside.

Nicky might have been able to blend into a mass of people pretty easily, but when you were six foot six, weighed almost three hundred pounds and there were two of you, it presented a problem. He was also right in that Brooks had chosen this meeting point for a very good reason; three of the Loughlins' cousins were licensed vendors at the fair, and because they didn't share the family name, Brooks knew the cops would be unlikely to make the connection or have eyes on them just yet. The set-up would restrict Reyes' movements, just like at Gatlin, making it difficult for him to get away from them easily and would keep him contained for the trade. Both before, and after.

A van rolled into the fairground, Cusick up front with his permit for a hot sauce and moonshine stall, and after passing through a different gate from Nicky, he backed the Econoline up and parked inside the grounds in the inner lot, the two Loughlin brother fugitives hidden in the back. As the van came to a stop, Billy was eyeing the titanium box in the holdall from the Cleveland robbery in frustration, still pissed they hadn't been able to get it open; their lack of success and just wanting to know what the box contained was becoming an obsession with him. Brooks had taken the shotgun his brother had been using for most of their time on the run and was now loading it with shells from their bag while Billy made a last futile attempt to get the box open with a pair of bolt cutters left in the back in the van. Like Nicky, they'd had time to prepare for this, and Brooks had sawn off most of the shotgun's barrel to make it easier for his brother to hide.

'Forget it,' he said, after the bolt cutters made no impression on the Granit lock, listening to his brother cursing. 'We need quick cash, not whatever's in there. I don't want you getting doubts letting it go at the exchange.'

'What if he don't show up?' Billy replied, throwing the broken cutters aside in disgust. 'Calls in a tip to get us pinched instead?'

‘The girl was part of the heist to get that,’ Brooks said, pointing the shotgun at the titanium case. ‘It’s got her goddamn initials on it. That’s what Reyes wants. He’ll be here.’

‘You sure about that?’ Cusick said from up front. ‘Guy was dumb enough to break out of the joint a week before release to get involved.’

‘Reyes is a lot of things but he ain’t dumb. If he broke out for this bitch, he’ll make the trade for her too.’

‘How’s he gonna get the money past the gate?’ Cusick asked, stepping into the back now he’d switched off the engine to join them.

‘Both of you do me favor, let me and Reyes handle this,’ Brooks said tersely. He passed his brother the reloaded shotgun, before taking the titanium lockbox and sliding it back into the holdall from the robbery in Cleveland yesterday. ‘Billy, carry the bag. Cuse, you’re coming too.’

‘What brought your family to the US?’ Richie asked the O’Mara family’s former maid, who’d introduced herself as Marija, as he sat with her inside her small home in Akron, a city forty miles south of Cleveland. She was a short, plump woman now pushing sixty, the home decorated with a mixture of American and European trinkets. A lot of Ohioans had Croatian ancestry or were first or second generation immigrants, and judging from the flag hanging outside on the porch, she was a proud member of that club. Richie had also just met her husband; he’d been protective and somewhat uncooperative at first, concerned with what the police detective wanted with her, but Marija had reassured him and he’d gone out back to finish off some work on the deck to give them some privacy.

‘My sister. She lived here and I qualified to apply for my green card through her. Arrived in Cleveland when I was twenty, met my husband, both of us worked and lived in Ohio ever since.'

'You were a maid and housekeeper for the O'Mara family, I heard?'

'Yes.'

'So you know Katherine?'

Marija nodded slowly. Richie had already noticed she didn't have the news on the TV, despite her past connection with the still-at-large fugitives. 'I can't listen or watch anything about it,' she said, seeing him glancing at the black screen in the room. 'I'm too scared. I'm so worried for them.'

'You know Nicky too?'

She nodded. 'I love them both. They were great kids.'

'He's putting himself on the line for her, considering the only connection I can see is that his father used to work for Kat's.'

'Goes much deeper than that. The two men went back to when they were children. They grew up together; were close friends. When he was sixteen, Nicky's father joined the army. Mr Tommy went a different way and ended up serving some time in prison. They lost touch.' Marija paused.

'Tell me more.'

'You're from the Cleveland area?'

'No, Indiana. Moved here almost twenty years ago now.'

'The city's industries started suffering in the 1970s and 80s. Meant there was a load of abandoned empty properties, vacant lots, no revenue. City council bought up those kinds of places and put them in a landbank. Got offered to non-profits who teamed up with developers to rebuild affordable housing.'

Richie nodded.

‘Mr Tommy told me his story once,’ she continued. ‘Said he couldn’t get hired for a job anywhere after he got out of prison. But during the landbank program, to attract developers, the city would sell a company the land for a hundred bucks. He ended up working on the teams at one of these sites over at Fairfax and found he was real good at it. He worked his way up, saved everything he made, then bought a couple of empty lots outside the program and built two houses there. Ohio’s got no State taxes on small businesses up to $250k. That helped him get his feet on the ground. He hired guys to help him out and started turning a profit.

‘He was embarrassed about his past so had lost touch with a lot of old friends. Said he thought back then that Doc wouldn’t want anything to do with him, being in the army. But Doc was struggling too.’

‘Doc?’

‘What everyone called Johnny Reyes. Nicky’s father. He was an army medic, or had been. Tommy ran into him in a bar one night after work when he was with his guys getting some drinks. Bartender told Tommy that Doc basically lived in there. When he found out Doc wasn’t doing so good, Mr Tommy asked him if he wanted to join his team. He didn’t have any experience, but he picked things up fast. Tommy remembered that from when they were kids.

‘Doc said no, but Tommy worked on him and he ended up helping them out on a build. Mr Tommy got him to open up gradually. Found out Doc had a son and they were living in Kinsmith. He hadn’t washed out of the army either; he’d left to look after his son. His sister had been doing that for him, but she was killed in an accident while he was overseas.’

‘Kinsmith,’ Richie said. ‘It’s like our second home in Robbery-Homicide.’

'Right. He couldn't pay Doc more than his other guys. Wouldn't be fair and they'd find out at some point anyway. So instead he also offered to rent Doc and Nicky a place to live in a better part of the city. Got them out of the bad neighborhood.'

'That was generous.'

'Mr Tommy felt guilty, I think. He'd gone to prison and had managed to turn his life around, but Doc had served his country and his life had fallen apart. Tommy hired other guys who'd been to prison on his teams too, knowing how hard it was for them to find a job; most of them were good workers and grateful for the opportunity. He used to say a person could try to survive on their own, but to make something of yourself, you need to help each other.'

'Was Thomas O'Mara with Blair at this point?' Richie asked, remembering the woman who'd shown up at the intersection on East Superior the previous night.

'He was. They met a couple years after Kat's mother died.'

'And Nicky's mom? You said she was killed when Doc was serving overseas?'

'No, she died when Nicky was born. His aunt took over the job of looking after him but like I told you, she was killed when the boy was twelve. Gang shooting in Kinsmith. Bullet went through the wall of their house, hit her in the neck when she was in there watching TV with the boy. She didn't die immediately; he watched her go in front of him as he tried to help.'

That detail hadn't been on Nicky Reyes' file. Richie paused and didn't answer.

'After she died, Doc left the army to look after Nicky but he couldn't find work. When Tommy met him that day in the bar, he'd just been turned away from another hospital.'

'And Kat's mom?' Richie asked.

'Was on a phone call, didn't see a bus coming fast on the inside lane when she stepped into the street. Happened when Kat was ten years old. Meant both Tommy and Doc had lost the mother of their kids way too early. Their friendship had layers to it. They had a lot in common.'

Richie remembered the bloodstains by the mail bin from the truck robbery. The wounded girl, out there on the run, the daughter of a self-made multi-millionaire heading back down the road of crime her father had left behind.

'Katherine. Tell me more about her.'

'Sensitive. Anxious. When I was hired to help out in their home, she was thirteen years old and underweight. Mr Tommy told me she went through periods of not eating properly after her mom died and he didn't know what to do about it. Neither did Blair once she started living in the house not long after I got the job. Once they took me on, I spent a lot of time with her, started seeing to it that she ate some good food. Got her back up to a normal weight. But it was a struggle.'

'Did you live at the house?'

'No. Once she moved in, Blair didn't want anyone living there who wasn't family. Just her, Kat, Mr Tommy and Blair's daughter Alaina. I heard her telling him once it was because she was worried he was a target.'

'From who?'

'People from his old life. I told you, he was in prison before he became successful. Pretty much all the wealthy families in the suburb they lived in had hired help, but none of them were treated the way me and Doc were by Mr Tommy. He was a good man.'

'Was Doc a decent father to Nicky?' Marquez asked.

She hesitated. 'I think he tried to be.'

Nicky had gone to the far east side of the NY State fairground and retrieved the bag of money and boxed-up jewelry; he'd checked out the area an hour before and had found what he'd been looking for, a sufficient space under the fence in a quiet area where some long trucks were parked some distance from the main activity.

Just before he'd walked round through the front, he'd forced the bag under the fence. Relieved to see it was still there, he removed two items he wanted, tucked them into his pocket, then headed back towards the fair.

But he had one more stop to make first.

Brooks was the first to notice their fellow prison escapee, coming towards them from where there weren't as many people, no popular stalls nearby and some distance from the main stage where music acts were performing.

Nicky stopped ten feet or so in front of the two men, a few people walking past too focused on their night out to recognize the trio. Three fugitives of the Gatlin Four; reunited.

'Surprised you made it in here without our help,' Brooks sneered, initiating the conversation.

'I don't use you two to break into places. Just to break out.'

'You've been busy, asshole.'

'Same as you. You planning to try and kill me too?'

'Not if you do what we want.'

'I'm the one holding the bag with real value.'

'Your girl wanted this one for a reason, Reyes,' Brooks said. 'Something about this box we don't know about?'

'It's some stuff her father left her.'

'Let's just do this shi-,' Billy said impatiently, but then stopped.

The red dot of a laser had just hit his older brother's chest.

Brooks glanced down to see what his sibling was looking at, then his eyes started darting around the fairground, trying to locate the source.

'You're not gonna see her,' Nicky told them. 'Kat's on the mend. And she's got a rifle trained right on you, so don't think about pulling on me. You wanted to do this, so let's do it.'

'Nicky would come to where the team Doc was working on for Thomas were building or rebuilding homes, and he'd hang out after school,' Marija told Richie in Cleveland. 'Asked questions, sometimes helped them carry stuff. Mr Tommy took a shine to the boy, invited him to come to the house with Doc a couple times. I got to know him then. So did Kat. He was about thirteen, fourteen years old, same as her and Alaina.'

'You liked him.'

'I did. He was tough, no pushover. Had to be; he was the son of an alcoholic and that's not easy. He was getting into it with some of the other kids at school who knew his father had a drinking problem so learned to stand his ground. We thought he might be trouble, but he wasn't. He was a good kid and street-smart. He just...'

'Got a raw deal.'

She nodded. 'Doc would go through periods when he wasn't drinking, and he'd take the boy out of the city for the weekend. They'd ride his motorbike into the woods and go camping. He taught Nicky things he'd learned from the army.'

'Like treating wounds?'

'Yeah, and shooting guns, riding bikes, how to hunt and lay traps. As I said, Mr Tommy liked the boy a lot too and the two families went to some Indians games. I think Kat fell for him.'

'What about Alaina? Blair's daughter?'

'More interested in herself than boys, I think. Don't think she and Nicky ever really spoke that much. Got a lot of her mother in her.'

'You don't care for Alaina?'

'Not really. She's greedy.'

'What were Nicky's plans for his future before he got arrested? Do you know?'

'He wanted to join the army after he graduated high school. Become a medic like his father.'

'Did Doc ever stop drinking?' Richie then asked.

'He tried. He ended up dying in a vehicle crash, like Kat's mom, but unlike her, he was drunk and behind the wheel. Nicky wasn't with him and that's about the only piece of luck that boy had his entire childhood.'

'How'd he deal with it?'

'Losing both his parents before he finished high school? He was devastated. But he was used to things being shitty. Just had to accept it and try to move on. Mr Tommy took guardianship of him which helped. He was going to enlist in the army at sixteen instead of waiting two more years, but Tommy convinced him to still get his diploma first and sign up once he graduated.'

'What about Kat?'

'She was doing OK. Worried about Nicky. But then Mr Tommy died less than a year later from pneumonia and things started going wrong for her too. I was let go after he died, but me and Kat spoke on the phone a few times before Blair stopped her calling. Wouldn't let me visit her either; said they needed to move on. It was her house now so wasn't much I could do.

'Then more things started going bad. Miss Kat told me in that last call that she wasn't feeling well again.' Marija seemed as if she was about to cry, but held it together. 'Kat's father gave Nicky and his dad an opportunity. His whole life, all anyone's ever done is turn their back on that boy. No-one ever gave him a shot. But Tommy did.'

'So Nicky's trying to save Thomas' daughter in return?'

She nodded. 'He'd do anything for the O'Maras. Including serving twelve years in prison. That was for Katherine too. His kind of luck.'

'You said she fell for him. Did he feel the same way?'

'I think so, but I don't think anything ever happened. He was too busy trying to survive back then. And then he was locked up for killing another young man.'

Some cheering and loud music came from the main stage across the New York State Fairground, but the three wanted men ignored it.

'You first,' Brooks said to Nicky, looking at his bag.

'Mine's worth a lot more. Let me see.' Billy opened the zipper and showed Nicky the padlocked titanium box inside. He closed it back up and went to toss it on the ground in front of Nicky, but his brother caught his arm and looked at their fellow prison fugitive suspiciously.

'Why *does* she want this back so bad?' Brooks asked. 'Why not just keep the money and run?'

'What's in there has sentimental value to her. And I don't need a bunch of cash and jewelry that can be traced.' Nicky nodded at the bag. 'That's what she wants.'

Brooks relaxed his grip and let his brother throw the bag. 'Now you.' Nicky opened the zipper on his holdall and the two brothers saw a mass of loose bills packed in between some jewelry boxes. He closed it, then put it on the path between them and bent to shove the bag towards the two brothers. In the meantime, Brooks looked down at the red dot on his chest, then up at Nicky again. His hand was curled around the grip of a pistol hidden in his waistband under his shirt; the laser was the only thing preventing him from pulling it and blowing Reyes' head off.

But they had the money. Billy reached down and opened the bag; both brothers could see the significant amount of cash inside. The younger Loughlin then opened some of the boxes to see necklaces, earrings, and bracelets glinting up at them.

'We'll find yo-' Brooks started to say, looking back up, but in the few seconds he and Billy had been distracted by the sight of the money and jewelry, he saw Nicky had taken a couple of items from his pocket.

In one hand was a lighter, a flame already sparked.

And in the other was a set of firecrackers.

A second later, the roll landed at the Loughlins' feet, hissing as the crackers burned towards the end of a clipped, very short fuse.

Outside the Arrivals hall at Syracuse-Hancock airport just as this was happening, Archer watched Marquez approach the car with her bag in tow, and after putting it on the back seat, she opened the passenger door before climbing in slowly, clearly still in pain from her hard fall out of the window earlier in the day.

Once inside, she glanced over and saw him looking at the inch-wide bandage wrapped around her head. 'Not one word,' she told him, seeing his eyes fix on where the hair had been buzzed down, parts of it visible above and below the bandage.

'It'll grow back.'

'That's three words.'

He laughed, just relieved to see she was OK. On the doctor's advice, Marquez had planned to stay in Cleveland for at least another day or so to give herself time to recover, but then she'd learned of the attempt on Archer at the auto-shop so had promptly discharged herself from the hospital and headed straight to the city's main airport. They'd swapped notes about the attacks on them both while Marquez was waiting for her direct flight and had come to the conclusion that the same people had to be responsible. It was too much of a coincidence otherwise. The two bastards had almost snuffed them both out.

'The doc was OK with letting you fly after a head injury?' he asked.

'I didn't bash my head,' she said. 'It was glass on the awning from my window. Cut me open when I landed. Was only stunned for a few moments.'

'But you're good?'

'I'm sore,' she admitted. 'And got the mother of all headaches. But I'm here.' She'd had her gun logged and removed from her possession by cabin staff for the flight, handed back to her in a sealed bag once they'd landed. She took it out of the bag she'd placed it in to walk through the airport and ripped open the plastic before reloading the magazine and slotting it back into the scratched Smith and Wesson. 'The doc just told me to stay clear of windows for a while.' But after she made the comment, she kept the gun in her hand for a moment; Archer saw she was staring straight ahead. 'They were good.'

'They were.'

'If I hadn't stepped out the shower, I'd be dead.' She paused. 'You get a look at them?'

'I tried. Every time I raised my head they tried to put three bullets into it.'

‘We’re supposed to be the ones tracking people, not the other way around. You got any guesses?’

‘I’m thinking about it,’ he said, putting the car into Drive. ‘But wherever our Gatlin boys are, it can’t have been them. They need to be trying to keep a low profile. Whoever was using us as target practice certainly wasn’t doing that.’

Even though Nicky had successfully slid the bag full of money under the fence on the east side, he’d left the revolver he’d been carrying with Kat just in case, as protection. But to face the Loughlins he’d needed something other than the Leatherman tool knife, and that proved vital when a man who’d moved out from a nearby stall tried to intercept him as Nicky ran from Brooks and Billy, the firecrackers at their feet starting to go off and creating the diversion he’d intended.

When the stranger went to grab him, Nicky recognized the guy immediately from the Gatlin meeting hall a few days ago, the same man who’d visited Brooks when Kat had laid out her misguided plan to Nicky. The guard at the gate had checked the pen inside Nicky’s pocket, but had failed to check the inside; Nicky had known the brothers would try something so he’d already unscrewed it, the inner metal tube designed to hold ink cartridges sharpened to a point, something he’d learned from Prez who’d used an identical weapon during Nicky’s first night in Gatlin to stop him being raped by Billy and Hoffmeier.

When the guy here at the fairground twelve years later snapped forward and gripped Nicky’s collar with one hand, pulling out a knife with the other, the Gatlin fugitive was faster and stabbed the pen hard all the way through the man’s hand.

He yowled in pain. The poppers were attracting a lot of attention now, which had been Nicky’s intention, so with his attacker off-balance and focused on his sudden injury, he shoved him out of his way and ran on into the crowd. Knowing the Loughlins as well as he did, Nicky had banked everything on the fact the brothers' priority would be to get the money and jewelry out rather than come after him. Security guards were already rushing towards the origin of the noise, just as he'd hoped, and there were enough of them to overpower the brothers which was his other goal, aside from getting this titanium lockbox of Kat's back.

He left the fairground through a different stall so the people who let him in didn't see how quickly he was leaving after arriving less than half an hour ago, this time with the addition of a bag. He raced across the lot, and found Kat waiting for him inside Barry Marsh's Audi, but then the sound of the firecrackers was replaced by the much harsher sound of gunshots, shotgun blasts and screams.

'Did you…get it?' she asked anxiously.

'I got it!' he said, starting the engine then driving the Audi to the gate and back out onto the road.

FORTY TWO

Nicky and Kat were soon speeding away from the fairground, heading north on Route 690, when they saw a police cruiser approaching from the opposite direction. Kat was lying on the backseat clutching the new bag on her lap; the first time she'd had the contents of the safe deposit box in her possession since Blair had managed to establish temporary ownership of it five years ago, after her stepdaughter was convicted of drug charges and sent to prison.

Up front, Nicky watched the County Sheriff's vehicle coming towards them then pass by. *'Keep going,'* he urged the cop car, his eyes following it in the rear-view mirror.

But the cruiser didn't; instead, it pulled a U turn and moments later he saw it join their side of the road, lights flashing, now only about half a mile behind.

'How'd he…know?' Kat asked, hearing the sirens of the pursuing car. 'Someone reported us… leaving the fair?'

'Or Barry was found already and they're looking for his white Audi,' Nicky said, checking the rearview mirror. 'Shit.'

The powerful car surged forward as Nicky followed a bend in the road, briefly losing sight of the police cruiser, but he knew the officer behind the wheel would be calling for assistance. Nicky didn't know the area either which put him at a severe disadvantage but then he caught sight of a sign for a local park coming up and slowing slightly, he pulled a sharp right turn towards the open gates.

He followed the road past a baseball field on the left and parking lot opposite. The park was almost entirely empty, the State Fair likely to be attracting most of the visitors to the area tonight, but that meant the car would immediately stand out. Nowhere to blend in.

Nicky kept going, then peeled left off the track and heading over some rough ground, he swung the Audi into the relative shelter of a more heavily wooded area before switching off the engine.

They sat there in the darkness, everything quiet, looking through the trees and bushes towards what he could see of the front gate in the distance, and waited, no sign of the police vehicle.

Perhaps they'd lost it.

Then, just as he was about to start the engine and risk getting back on the road, he saw the flashing lights of the Sheriff's Department cruiser as it entered the park grounds too.

Back at the fairground, Brooks and Billy had started to run as soon as the firecrackers went off attracting all the unwanted attention Nicky had intended, but they'd only taken a few steps when they were intercepted by two members of security with another following close behind.

The guards had no opportunity to register who the pair were before Billy opened fire with the sawn-off twelve gauge, his brother doing the same with his handgun; he emptied half the magazine at them, putting down the three guards and two members of the public who were unfortunate enough to be in the line of fire as people nearby screamed and started to scatter.

The brothers ran on and had almost made it to their van, Cusick joining them nursing a bleeding hand, when the bottom of the holdall suddenly gave way. '*NO!*' Brooks yelled, as the money and jewelry cases started to spill everywhere. He and Billy frantically started scooping them back up, but the bills had been cut loose from their bricks and were already spinning away in the stiff breeze, the place suddenly resembling a ticker tape parade. Brooks hugged the bag to his chest to stop the rest of the money and jewelry tumbling out and jumped into the back of their van, Cusick climbing up front behind the wheel.

Once Billy had leapt in beside him, Brooks dragged the door closed and Cusick pulled away. Brooks put the bag on the floor and turned it over to look at the base. He saw the fabric had been cut then sewn loosely back together with thread that was bound to snap from the weight.

He remembered how Reyes had been holding the bag when he'd approached, not with the strap over his shoulder but tucked under his arm as if to keep it close.

It hadn't occurred to him at the time the real reason was to stop the bag falling apart.

Nicky had pushed the bag across the smooth path towards them, not throwing it like Billy had done with the other; it would have burst open if he had. Reyes would have known the threads would give way almost immediately as soon as the brothers picked it up.

The son of a bitch had deliberately sabotaged it.

'White Audi SQ8 stolen by male and female fugitives from Ohio located, back up requested,' the deputy from the Onondaga County Sheriff's Department said, having followed the tracks down the road into Long Branch Park. He could see the white German-manufactured car with the hot plates illuminated by his headlights, parked among some trees ahead.

The deputy drew closer then stepped out and pulled his sidearm as he saw a figure lying on the back seat. A woman, her head of red hair resting against the window.

'*HANDS*!' he ordered, his gun held in both hands, using his open door as cover. *'LET ME SEE YOUR HANDS!'*

She didn't move so he stepped out from behind the door and edged forward. As he got closer, he found himself looking at Kat O'Mara's pale face, a bag resting on her lap, her eyes squinting in the headlights of his cruiser.

But there was no sign of her accomplice.

Low on choices and fast running out of the few that remained, Nicky emerged from behind the tree beside the car as the deputy focused on Kat and cracked him over the head with a thick lump of wood, similar to how Craig had hit the Virginia fisherman two nights before but only with enough force to stun the man, not kill him. The deputy went down hard, dropping his gun. Nicky kicked it away immediately and was just reaching for the man's cuffs to restrain him before driving back out of here when he saw the lights of another police car appear through the trees at the entrance.

Not wasting any time, Nicky immediately opened the nearside rear passenger door to the Audi then pulled Kat and the bag out, and ten seconds later, with more blue and red lights arriving, he started carrying her away down one of the trails into the darkness.

Cars, trucks, bikes and people on foot were flooding out of the State fairground, the panic started by the sound of gunshots and screams proving contagious and causing a stampede; Cusick's Econoline van was just ahead of the exodus with his two cousins sitting in the back, Brooks furiously counting the remaining money left in their swapped holdall while Billy reloaded their weapons, their cousin up front driving with one hand as he nursed the other.

Ironically, their ability to escape without being challenged came at Nicky's cost. Local police authorities from various townships had just been responding to calls of shots fired at the Fair when the report came over the radio that not only had Barry Marsh's stolen car just being sighted but a local deputy in Long Branch Park had been found by his colleagues lying semi-conscious beside the abandoned Audi.

'He's saying he recognized O'Mara!' the cop who'd reached him first told units pouring into the scene. 'Must've been Reyes who hit him.'

More squad cars pulled up, Onondaga County deputies and State troopers getting out and pulling weapons. With their cars' headlights and using their flashlights, it didn't take them long to find footprints in the dirt of one of the park's trails.

'Split up and search,' a lead deputy ordered. 'The woman's injured, so he can't move with her as fast as us. Make sure they don't make it to the water.'

With weapons drawn and ready, the team of local law-enforcement separated and started to sweep the park.

Deeper in the woodland, now off the trails, Kat resting at his feet with the bag's strap across his torso, Nicky was looking around in steadily-rising panic, praying these cops didn't have dogs with them. He had his revolver but unlike the Loughlins, had no intention of firing on law-enforcement.

Then he remembered he had something else that could help.

The sound of rapid cracks and what appeared to be gunshots suddenly echoed in the air and the cops from the various departments and agencies dropped where they were standing, trying to locate where the noise was coming from.

'IF YOU SHOOT, WE WILL FIRE ON YOU!' a State trooper shouted, as birds flew up into the air from where

they'd been roosting for the night. '*PUT DOWN YOUR WEAPONS!*'

'We know what he's carrying?' a cop asked the others near him.

'Hostage found at the barn said he only saw a handgun,' a local deputy answered. 'Six shooter.'

'*How much is left?*' Cusick called over his shoulder from the front seat, his wounded hand jammed in the armpit of his other arm as he steered, careful not to speed and blending in with traffic heading down 690.

'I count forty thousand in cash,' Brooks said. 'Two necklaces and one ring.'

'*That's it?*' Billy shouted in disgust. '*That's all we got?*'

'*We lost most of it out there in the goddamn field!*' Brooks screamed back.

'We gotta get you two out of the area,' Cusick replied, passing Long Branch Park. He was too focused on the road, his conversation with his cousins and the throbbing pain in his hand to pay any attention to the mass of flashing lights far off to the right of them.

'Keep driving to Wayne County,' Brooks told him.

'I told you, they're looking for you up there. Been cops and cruisers crawling everywhere since you two broke out.'

'Better pray they don't find us,' Billy said, as his big brother threw the split bag away before punching the wall of the van in fury.

Barry Marsh's abandoned Audi was now surrounded by empty police vehicles; deeper in the park, the collective of cops and troopers had got back to their feet and were now edging their way cautiously through the trails, shotguns and rifles tracing through the quietly swaying branches and bushes.

Then another wave of cracking blasts sounded again, and they all dropped apart from the lead trooper, who just stared into the darkness in the direction the sound had come from. Reyes was said to be carrying a revolver but that noise didn't match the report such a weapon would make in any way. After the bangs died away, he waved to the two troopers closest to him to follow.

Almost a minute later, they found a strip of burned out firecrackers lying on the grass in a small clearing.

Back where the law-enforcement had left their cars, the Onondaga County deputy who'd been hit over the head had recovered enough to insist on joining the search with the others, still dazed, but determined to help out. But if he'd stayed where he was, he may have seen a shadow slip out of the trail thirty yards away, carrying a woman in his arms with a bag over his shoulder.

There were eight cars parked there, some from the Onondaga Sheriffs' Office, others police vehicles from the local towns of Lakeside and Geddes, their PD insignias on the doors. Nicky quickly checked the first three and was about to give up and keep running when he found what he'd hoped for in the ignition of a State police cruiser. The driver had been one of the last to arrive and had been in too much of a hurry to join the hunt and collar the fugitives to pocket the keys.

Once Kat was rapidly loaded into the back, Nicky slid into the driver's seat then turned the key in the engine. He quietly reversed back out, keeping the headlights off until he joined 690 again. The flashing lights of two cop cars appeared in the distance, cars speeding in the direction of the park and fairground and coming up fast as Nicky re-joined the mass departure. The trooper whose car this was had also left his hat on the passenger seat. The Gatlin escapee pulled it on and stared straight ahead as the two cars swept past in the opposite direction.

He held his breath until he saw them turning into the park.

'We don't have long,' Kat said. 'They'll realize…this is…missing.'

'We've got long enough,' he said, glancing back at her.

He was correct. It was almost thirty minutes later before the trooper who'd left his campaign hat in his car and key in the ignition returned to find his vehicle gone. The car's plates went out as the unfortunate man received a furious tirade from his corporal who'd immediately realized the only way it could have been stolen was if the trooper had left his keys in it.

'Anything?' a US Marshal asked a local police sergeant, having arrived at the scene with members of his squad.

'No,' he replied, beside his car with the radio receiver in his hand. 'Stop the search in the park. They're gone.'

The stolen trooper cruiser wouldn't be found until morning, and by the time it was located, Reyes and O'Mara had managed to slip out of their clutches once again.

But only just.

FORTY THREE

'So that message *was* a code for a meet up between our boys,' Archer said, as he and Marquez got out of their car and walked towards the entrance to the New York State Fairground that same night, Archer taking care to match his pace with Marquez who was moving slower than usual. The pair had been on their way to meet with the Sheriff's department in Wayne County, one of the local seats around the lakes and where the Loughlin boys had grown up, when the call about this latest development had reached them. 'We were right.'

'Shame we weren't on it faster,' she commented, seeing a couple of Coroners' transports and ambulances parked in the lot. Most of the site was empty now, save for a few trucks and an array of police and US Marshals' vehicles. Just before they entered, Archer slowed even further, causing Marquez to glance at him; she noticed the way he was taking in the fairground ahead. 'You good?'

He nodded, thinking back the previous year to another case which had taken him to an abandoned theme park way south of here outside New Orleans. He reassured her with a quick smile. 'Just some déjà vu.'

The two NYPD detectives showed their badges to gain access and once inside walked through the grounds, heading to where they could see most of the law-enforcement on site was clustered. But as they approached, their attention was drawn to several youngsters accompanied by two cops having their pockets turned out.

'What'd they do?' Marquez asked a passing deputy, showing her badge while nodding at the kids.

'Caught them being real helpful gathering evidence for us.' Archer and Marquez looked around and realized that what they'd assumed was litter were in fact loose dollar bills in $50 and $100 denominations scattered everywhere, some flattened against rides, others lying in the dirt or caught against the walls of stalls and attractions. Members of law-enforcement from various departments were collecting the notes and putting them into transparent evidence bags, a time-consuming task by the look of it.

'People have reported they heard what sounded like firecrackers or gunshots going off just over there,' the deputy explained, nodding to his right. 'Fair security reacted to check out the noise and came across the two brothers we've been seeing on the news. Tried to intercept but the fugitives started blasting. Three guards shot, two civilians hit too.'

'Dead?' Archer asked.

'Two of the guards are. Other one and the two bystanders are still alive. The brothers were running for where the trucks and vans were parked inside the ground, but witnesses told us the bag one of them was carrying split. Money and jewelry boxes started dropping out and the bills began flying everywhere in the breeze. Guess they decided not to stick around to try to gather it all up with more security coming after them. Just got out with whatever they could hold onto. But those boys'll be real pissed, wherever they are now. Look at how much they lost.'

About fifty feet away, Archer saw two deputies wearing US Marshal badges counting the bills already retrieved, then securing them with elastic bands to prevent the notes from blowing away again in the breeze. He could also see items of jewelry in open boxes laid out on a sheet, all of it being photographed. He remembered the woman at the scene of the robbery on East Superior who'd been ranting at detectives and Marshals. Once it made it out of evidence holding, she was going to get some of her money and valuables back, just not all of it. He pitied the guy assigned to tell her.

'How much has been collected?' he asked.

'Two hundred thousand in cash so far, on top of the bling. Some of the money we won't ever get back. People were running but some would've stuck around to pick up what they could and not with the idea of handing it in. We'll have more luck with the jewelry if any's missing though. We got an itemized list from Cleveland the owner supplied to police.'

'We heard Nicky Reyes was here too,' Marquez said.

'He was.' The deputy turned and indicated to his right. 'Got cornered a few miles up the road that way in Long Branch Park, but no word yet that he or the injured girl with him have been apprehended. We're hearing one of the trooper's cruisers from the park is missing too.'

'He escaped again?' Archer said. 'Guy's like Houdini.'

'Looks that way. Difference is, he didn't shoot anyone.' The deputy motioned towards one of the teenage boys who'd been held by local police, now being talked to by a US Marshal. 'That kid might be your best eyewitness. I'd ask him what he saw. I gotta go help out with the searches. Gonna be a long night.'

'Good luck,' Archer told him. As the man left, the two NYPD detectives approached the Marshal with the teenager.

'…gave you this?' they caught the Marshal asking the boy, holding a laser pointer. He clicked it, directing the red beam onto the wall of a stall nearby.

The adolescent nodded. 'And a hundred bucks. Told me to point that thing at the chest of one of the two men he said he was gonna talk to. Said he'd give me another hundred when he was done.'

'You got the first hundred bucks?'

The boy nodded slowly.

'Hand it over.'

'I can't keep it?'

'It's evidence, kid.'

The boy looked at the Marshal glumly, then reluctantly peeled off his sneaker and took out the bill, which he'd folded and hidden under his sole. The Marshal took the bill carefully and whistled to one of his colleagues. '*Ronnie, bag and keep this one separate, it'll have Reyes' prints on it.'*

'Can you tell us what you saw?' Archer asked the boy, after showing his badge to the deputy.

'Man who gave me the hundred was holding a bag under his arm. He met two other guys over there.' The teenager pointed at the clearing where Reyes had let off the firecrackers. 'They had a bag too but it didn't look as heavy.'

'They swapped them over?' Marquez asked. He nodded. 'Where were you?'

'Hiding behind the toilets over there like he said,' he explained. 'Pointing the laser onto one of the big guys' chests.'

'And the big men were these two?' Marquez asked, showing him a photo of the Loughlins from the original '*Wanted'* page Gatlin had printed and handed out two days ago that she still had in her pocket.

'Yeah, that was them.'

'You didn't recognize them from the TV? Or the guy who paid you to point the laser?'

He shrugged. 'I'm twelve. I don't watch the news.'

'What did the guy who gave you the pointer look like?' the Marshal asked, showing the boy Nicky's mugshot from a paper he was carrying. 'Could it have been him?'

'Yeah, I'm pretty sure. He was wearing glasses, had shorter hair. Looked older. But I think that was the guy.'

'Reyes handed over two million dollars of cash and jewelry,' Marquez said to Archer. 'What was so valuable in the bag they exchanged it for?'

'Kat O'Mara's stepmother knows,' he replied.

'But she refuses to say.'

'And now the Loughlins have lost most of that money and jewelry because of Reyes, while he presumably got what Kat wanted from the robbery. He used them to get out of Gatlin and then he does this? They're gonna rip him to pieces if they find him.' Archer saw the kid who'd had his money taken as evidence by the Marshal was still looking sorry for himself, so he reached into his own pocket, unfurled the few bills from his wallet and passed him a twenty. 'Better than nothing,' he told him, the boy taking the note. 'One more question; you didn't see this guy?' he asked, borrowing the fugitive photo off Marquez and pointing at Lupinetti's image.

'No, man. Some other dude was driving a van the two big guys left in. But it wasn't him.' The kid pointed at the Marshal's photo of Nicky. 'Before they left, the driver tried to rush this guy after he set off the firecrackers but he stabbed him through the hand with something and got away. Think he got him pretty good.' In the meantime, Marquez had stepped away to call Richie in Cleveland to update him on what had happened, but at the forefront of her mind was Reyes' cellmate down at Gatlin; with that *call your friend* code having led to a meeting which she was sure Prez was involved in setting up.

She felt nauseous at the prospect of the biker's phone being discovered in the federal prison and her number right there on the records with the length and time of their calls and conversations. She wasn't someone who made a lot of mistakes.

But this was turning out to be a major one.

'Apparently there are fifty and hundred dollar bills floating around the fairground like they were shot from a cannon,' Richie told Glick fifteen minutes later, the gang squad lieutenant having driven back to Cleveland from Akron to reunite with his sergeant. They were at the cheap hotel in Cleveland where Marquez had taken her trip through the window earlier in the day. Richie had gone out into the corridor to take the NYPD detective's call while Glick was looking at the damage, other investigators having already closed off the scene.

'The meet go wrong?' he asked, as Richie stepped under the tape and walked back into the shot-up hotel room.

'For the Loughlins, yeah. Reyes paid some kid to keep a laser pointer on one of the brothers when they met up. Boy told police he saw them swap holdalls. Reyes split right when things turned south.'

'And the contents of the other bag?'

'He left with it. Whatever's inside, it's worth more than a couple million bucks to him and the girl.'

'And the bag he gave the brothers fell apart?'

'From the underside. Ass end of it dropped out.'

Glick paused. 'Mighta been Reyes too. Slow them down.'

'Or make sure they didn't leave with squat. Police are closing off the area, but he made off in a trooper's cruiser.'

'He hurt the guy?'

'Just his pride. Didn't know it had been stolen until they got back from sweeping the park. I'll give this guy Reyes something, he knows how to improvise.'

The police tape behind them fluttered slightly from the breeze coming through the smashed window, the half-destroyed door propped open and creating a draft. 'So what now, Rich?' Glick asked. 'What do we do?'

The Robbery/Homicide squad leader looked at the room, then at his sergeant; detectives often kept certain lines of inquiry to themselves when ideas were forming, but his conversation with the O'Mara family's former maid Marija had been playing on his mind. 'Gonna leave the Loughlins and Lupinetti to the people in New York for the minute. I want to take a closer look at Kat O'Mara.'

Glick didn't answer, waiting for him to elaborate.

'Girl had a multimillionaire for a father, good grades until her senior year and a clear plan for her future, the maid told me. She threw it all away on drugs, time in the can and now she's on the run after pulling this robbery.' He looked up at Glick. 'Marquez said Kat's stepmom called the girl a quitter. That doesn't match up for me.'

'Took a bullet and still running, two days later. You're calling that one right,' Glick said, taking a final look at the damaged hotel room before lifting the police tape so his lieutenant could pass under it then going with him down the corridor. 'She sure as hell ain't quitting on this.'

FORTY FOUR

The next morning, Archer stirred then was instantly awake, still wearing the jeans and t-shirt he'd bought from the downtown store in Cleveland with his shoes kicked off onto the floor. He immediately checked the hotel room around him, on his guard after the events of the last few days, but relaxed when he saw Marquez sitting by the table across the room.

She had her phone to her ear, a cup of coffee from the room's drink machine in her hand and her Smith and Wesson sidearm in easy reach on the table. As she spoke quietly, she was looking in the mirror with her head turned. He watched as she put down her coffee and pulled the bandage away to examine the strip that had been shaved so the wound could be cleaned and stitched; seeing in the reflection that he'd woken up, they made eye contact and she pulled a face, clearly not happy about the buzzed section of scalp. He smiled and pushed himself up on the bed.

'He's good,' she said, then switched the phone to speaker and continued. 'We were at the fairground and then the park until past 2am. Rolled back to the airport and booked a room here at a hotel. One of us stayed on the door while the other got some sleep.'

'Any chance you were followed?' Shepherd asked from their police division's base in New York City. From his end, he knew it was highly unlikely his two experienced detectives wouldn't have noticed, but asked anyway, considering the attempts on their lives that both had suffered yesterday.

'No, but I wish someone had given us a shot,' she said, glaring again at the cut on her head. Archer swung his feet to the floor and pulled his light-brown boots on, looking at the time on his burner phone, his usual cell having stopped working again last night with the water damage seeming to have finally won out. It was 9:15am.

'He alive yet?'

'Just woke up,' she told him as Archer checked the chamber on his Sig Sauer then fixed the holster back to his belt before rising and walking to the bathroom. 'You're on speaker.'

'They find the trooper's car yet that Reyes stole?' Archer asked.

'This morning,' Marquez said. 'A local came across it partially concealed in a boathouse by the water a few miles south. Kayak of his is missing too, same as a shotgun that had been in the cruiser. Chopper is circling the area but they haven't found anything yet.'

'A lot of that part of the State is interconnected lakes,' Shepherd replied from his end. *'They could've come back to shore anywhere.'*

Archer had started brushing his teeth and stopped to rinse out his mouth. 'Anyone else hurt?'

'No, thank God,' Marquez said. 'Shep got on the phone with the Oneida County Sheriff's Department-'

'He contacted me first, yesterday, introducing himself and wanting to know more about you two,' Shepherd said, taking over. *'His office is leading the local effort to find the brothers. I called him this morning, told me the deputy who got cracked over the head by Reyes has got a large bump, and the trooper who got his car stolen is gonna be buying everyone donuts for the next couple years, but that's as serious as it got.'*

'A guy who got found in the barn in Chautauqua County who Reyes used to get over the line from Pennsylvania said he made some threats, but didn't act on them,'

Marquez continued, informing Archer. 'Fed the hostage, gave him water. Even left him money for borrowing a suit.'

'He could've bought him an all-expenses paid cruise, Reyes is still facing forty years plus when he gets apprehended,' Archer said. 'Prison escape, assisting in armed robbery, kidnap across State lines. He's gonna have to pay a high price for all this.'

'What about the Loughlins and Frank, boss?' Marquez asked Shepherd. 'You hear anything from this Oneida Sheriff?'

'No, they've gone quiet. The brothers were last seen at the fair and Lupinetti's dropped off the radar completely. I think the final person to see him was Archer when he took off in that cruiser yesterday.'

'Angler who found the trooper's car said there was blood on the back seat,' Marquez said. 'Kat must still be in a bad way.'

'The doctor in Erie told detectives she was. He thinks she could survive the wound, but she needs to be recuperating in a hospital with professional care. Not running from the authorities with no chance to rest.'

'Reyes has kept a step ahead this whole time, but police are getting closer now,' Archer said, returning to the main room with a glass of water in his hand. 'Sounds like he only just got away last night. They can't keep going much longer.'

'He's going to be forced to slow down if Kat's deteriorating,' Marquez continued, agreeing. 'And at some point he'll make a mistake. Same as Frank and the brothers. One slip-up. That's all it'll take.'

Archer nodded, the glass of water cold in his hand.

'What happens after that is gonna be down to them,' Shepherd added.

Neither Archer or Marquez replied.

'Thanks for getting back to me,' Richie said in the Detroit Shoreway neighborhood of Cleveland, drinking coffee from a thermos cup. He was sitting in his car with his phone resting on the dash on speaker, talking to the rehab counsellor who'd overseen Kat's recovery at ORW. 'I'm Robbery/Homicide, looking at the Morningstar bank truck job from Saturday. Wanted to ask you about the girl. I heard her poison was benzos and she served eighteen months for it?'

'That's right. Got pinched for possession and faking prescriptions. People with her family's kind of wealth tend to find ways to avoid jailtime, but the year before her conviction, city council had elected to start coming down harder on drug offenders.'

'I remember. Did some work with Vice around that time.'

'Her lawyer asked for the fact she'd lost her father in bad circumstances a few years before to be taken into consideration. First offense, so she received a reduced sentence on the condition she got clean. She had to provide supervised blood and urine tests to her PO for a year after her release, but she passed each one. Didn't seem to backslide.'

'She ever reveal when she started using?'

'Senior year at high school. Soon after her father died. Benzos, Ativan, Xanax, Klonopin. Same family, different names.'

'Sedative medication.'

'That's right. Benzos would give her release from anxiety, but drugs like that were only ever meant to be used very short-term. As in, a few days to a week. Abuse actually leads to an increase in feeling panicked and a

number of other issues, and kind of addiction level she was at, it can be more difficult to kick than heroin.'

'I've heard that.'

'Heroin addiction's more immediate. Withdrawal is very painful, but long term it's easier to stay off. But with drugs like benzos, chronic use changes your brain chemistry semi-permanently. Affects your sleep cycles, mood, anxiety, emotions. I'd say they might be the worst kind of drug I've encountered to withdraw from. Just about as close to hell as a person can get without dying. Growing epidemic of abuse of this stuff across the country in high schools and colleges. With the frame of mind Katherine was in after losing her father? She was the perfect candidate to get hooked.'

Richie thanked him for his time, then got out of the car and walked into a fast food restaurant, going towards the back where he found Glick with the manager, a squat balding man who was looking impatient and flustered. 'C'mon, Detective, I don't have time for this crap right now,' he was telling Glick. 'Morning rush is starting.'

'How long did Kat O'Mara work here?' Richie asked as he joined his sergeant, ignoring the comment. Both detectives had discovered this job was one of twelve the girl had been unable hold down in the last five years according to her tax records. This particular gig had been her first out of prison.

'Couple months.'

'Seemed to show up on time a lot for a girl who got fired,' Glick said, holding up some timecards that he'd asked to see from the office while Richie had been outside on the phone.

'She was lazy. And mouthy.'

'Not according to the guy back there working the fryer,' Glick replied. 'Said from what he remembers, the girl worked her ass off and kept quiet as a mouse.'

'Yeah, well, I didn't like her and I didn't have to put up with her bullshit. She was replaced pretty much the same day I fired her. That's all I gotta say.' He took the timecards back off Glick and walked back into his office. The two detectives understood they weren't going to get any more out of the guy for now, so walked out and headed back to their car.

'Kat's counsellor at ORW told me she kicked the habit and hadn't started using again that he knew about,' Richie said. 'She never started problems in lock-up and was always cooperative. Kicked popping pills and getting in trouble, and the maid told me yesterday when I was leaving that the girl had aspirations of going to law school.' He jerked his thumb towards the fast food restaurant. 'But our friend in there claims she was too lazy and too much trouble to hold down a job working a register or deep fryer?'

'Maybe there's some truth to it,' Glick replied. 'Addiction and grief might've killed her motivation. She grew up the daughter of a millionaire. Money was never gonna be an issue. Or so she thought.'

Richie shook his head, still looking at the diner as he started the engine. 'How'd a bright kid and the daughter of a man with an eight-figure net worth end up getting pink-slipped from serving chicken nuggets and fries? And her stepmom just abandoned her?'

'Kat wasn't Blair's daughter, Rich, remember. Blair already has one of her own to think about. Maybe she felt Kat wasn't her responsibility anymore once Tommy O'Mara was dead.'

'Maybe. You get other addresses of where Kat worked since she was released?'

Glick went into his pocket 'Yeah, a list. Where you wanna start?'

'Let's try somewhere more recent. From this year. See if we get the same story.'

'She was employed at a hardware store January to April,' Glick read from the piece of paper he'd withdrawn. 'Diner June to August. Fired from both.'

Richie looked at the paper, then tapped the store's address. 'Let's go hear what excuse this guy comes up with for canning her.'

In Oneida County in upstate New York, a deputy riding a cruiser solo heaved himself out of his car at a gas station and put his hands on his hips as he stretched his back, then walked into the store, going straight towards a food counter beside the checkout register. 'Morning Eddie,' he said to the clerk who he knew well, the young man's family from the area. The deputy had been using this gas station for years. 'I'll put in an order. Missed breakfast.'

A middle-aged woman parked on a stool watching a TV overheard him and got to her feet slowly, taking out a pad and paper. 'What can I get you?'

'You fix me up some eggs, bacon and home fries?'

'Regular bacon or maple?'

'Maple,' he said and she ripped off the piece of paper before walking into the back. The deputy saw a Bunn flask of coffee on her side of the counter and caught the clerk's attention who moved over to pour him a mug, a *hiss* coming from inside the kitchen as eggs and bacon hit the skillets. As he waited, the deputy then noticed another individual waiting at the other end of the counter, wearing a white t-shirt, jeans and ball cap. He nodded to him just as the woman reappeared with a brown bag which she placed beside Eddie who rang it up. 'What happened to your face, guy?' he asked, as Nicky swore to himself, having been hoping to get out unnoticed.

'Walked into the bathroom medicine cabinet last night.' The reality was, the Gatlin fugitive had smacked into a low hanging jagged tree branch he hadn't seen when he'd been carrying Kat and her bag through the woods after dumping the kayak they'd used to cross a lake. The impact had left some scratches and discoloring on his upper left cheek.

However, the comment seemed to satisfy the deputy, who chuckled and shook his head before parking himself on a stool and started to drink his coffee as Nicky paid for his own order, just wanting to get the hell out of here. He'd left Kat by herself in an empty church down the road where they'd broken in to sleep and hide for a few hours. Since they'd made it to shore on the other side of the lake and he'd found the church, she'd been drifting in and out of consciousness, and he'd seen the wound to her side was bleeding again.

She was deteriorating and he knew it. They'd had no food or water left, so he'd been forced to risk a visit to the gas station before getting out of the area. Stealing another car was an option, but that brought its own complications with APBs and radio call outs for a stolen ride's license plates; and after the doctor in Erie and Barry Marsh, Nicky was done taking hostages.

'That accent of yours don't sound local, son,' the deputy said, just as Nicky picked up his bagged order. 'Where you from?'

'Dayton.'

'Dayton, Ohio?'

Nicky nodded. The deputy twisted in his seat. 'Brings you this way?'

'My girl's from here.'

'Where do you live?'

'Phoenix.'

'That's my hometown. Which street you on?'

Feeling his blood pressure rising at what was turning into twenty questions, Nicky was starting to quietly panic, knowing he was getting closer and closer to having to pull the handgun from his inside pocket and take this conversation somewhere it could never recover from, when the deputy's radio chirped with a transmission. *'Howie, you there?'*

'Copy.'

'*Karlsson thinks he might've just seen the Loughlin brothers passing in a pick-up over in Oswego. He lost them on the highway but he's pretty sure it was the two brothers. Marshals want anyone in the area to redirect over there if possible. Figured that'd be you too.'*

'Can I get that breakfast to go, Ed?' he asked the clerk, rising off his stool as the young man nodded and called in to the back. *'Hey, Ohio,'* the deputy said, stopping Nicky two feet from the door. 'Forgot your change.'

Nicky stepped back to take the money from the counter. 'Thanks. Hope you catch those guys.'

'We will,' he said, and by the time the deputy's food came out, boxed up and bagged, Nicky was gone.

Outside, people were pulling in and out of the gas station to use the pumps and buy supplies, and as one local filled up his truck, dressed in hunting gear with weapons stored in the back, his cousin was sitting in the passenger seat chewing his way slowly through a breakfast sandwich he'd just bought as he idly watched a man cross the forecourt.

Then his gaze sharpened and his chewing slowed.

He'd seen the news lately and had an eye for faces.

As Nicky walked away down the street, the guy in the car didn't take his eyes off him. 'You're paying for the tank, I got the last two yesterday,' his cousin said, leaning into the car and holding out his hand for the other man's wallet. 'What is it?' he asked, seeing his companion wasn't paying him any attention.

'We're looking for your husband,' Glick told a woman standing in the doorway of a small home in Cleveland, as thunder rumbled from dark, swollen storm clouds that had gathered overhead. Rain had started falling on the ride over here and now it was coming down hard. He and Richie had found the store where Kat had worked earlier but had been told the manager wasn't in that day, so armed with his address they'd just pulled up outside his house. Richie had remained in the car, using the time to make some more calls. 'He runs the floor team at a hardware store out towards East Cleveland, right?' Glick asked.

'Wouldn't be that grand about it,' she answered sourly, drinking some coffee. 'He watches other people stack shelves.'

'Is he here? We want to talk to him about a worker who he let go a few months ago.'

'He's out. Wait here for him to get back if you like.'

'He upset you or something?'

She looked back at him for a moment, glanced past at the pouring rain then turned to lift a key off a hook on the wall beside her. 'Come with me.' She led Glick outside, then unlocked and opened her garage door. 'Take a look for yourself,' she snapped, as the detective stepped under the open door for cover and saw a gleaming motorbike in the center of the space. 'We got a leaking attic and garage roof, fall and winter coming, and he blows almost twenty grand on that.'

As he looked in at the bike, Glick saw water dripping through the garage roof into two buckets. The woman brushed past him to collect one, then tossed the old rainwater out onto the drive, followed by the other.

He watched as she re-positioned both under the leaks. ‘Yeah, you could say I’m upset,’ she said.

FORTY FIVE

'The three survivors who got shot at the fairground last night are all gonna pull through,' the chief at the Oneida County Sheriff's Office told Archer and Marquez, who'd left the Best Western at Syracuse airport and driven over to the HQ, meeting the man who'd been communicating with Shepherd. Ostensibly they were here to introduce themselves to the local police authority and explain they were hunting down Lupinetti, but were also hoping to persuade local law enforcement to keep them clued in on the latest developments. Both detectives knew small-town police were more likely to include them than federal agencies now this case was continuing to grow. 'One of them's losing his left leg below the knee, but at least he's gonna live to see his family again.'

'We saw cruisers and other vehicles going fast heading west on our way here,' Marquez asked. 'Something come through?'

'Sighting of the Loughlins over in Oswego.'

'Could it be another hoax?' Archer said. 'Or mistaken identity?'

'Possibly. Still needs checking.' The chief was visibly stressed. 'Brooks and Billy have been gone four years since they were last sent down, but they've still got plenty of people around here who'd help them out.'

'Their family network's got a long history, we heard.'

'Been a blight in these parts long as I've been alive. Involved in all sorts of bad shit. Thought we were done with those two once they kidnapped that college girl and had her tied up in Billy's basement. Shamed the entire area, what they did to that poor kid. Knowing they're probably up here somewhere after what went down at the fairground last night isn't gonna let a lot of people sleep easy.'

'Marshals?' Marquez asked.

'They're taking over the whole region. SWAT and fugitive squads in Syracuse, Rochester and Buffalo are on standby. FBI want to send people up here too after last night, but the Marshals Office said the brothers are gonna be their collar. Brooks and Billy keep dropping bodies, that might change.'

'And Frank Lupinetti,' Marquez said. 'He's who we want. He seemed to separate himself from the others but they keep getting drawn back together. We're hoping you find the brothers, we can find our guy.'

'My units get a sighting or hear one over the radio, I'll pass it on and he's all yours. One less to worry about.' He then cast a look at Archer. 'Heard you were the man who put down Craig Loughlin the other night. I knew that boy since he was knee high. He was a dipshit but wasn't a killer like his brothers.'

'Turned out he was,' Archer said. 'He just hadn't got around to it until the day I shot him.'

The chief looked at him for a moment longer, then nodded. 'Been in law-enforcement twenty seven years and I've never seen a criminal successfully ride off into the sunset with a bag of money. Not once. Never mind five from the same job. This thing's gonna end pretty soon. Highway Patrol have roadblocks in place blocking off the region. Same as out on the water. These guys are boxed in and can't escape.'

'That's what Virginia, Ohio and Pennsylvania police thought,' Marquez said.

'Hardware store manager's got a bike in his garage that looks close to my six month salary,' Glick told Richie, getting back into their car beside his lieutenant, having jogged over in the heavy rain. 'Bought it April this year, according to the wife. Victory 8 Ball, cost him eighteen and a half grand including helmet, leathers and insurance. Their roof's been needing fixing all year which is why she's so pissed about it.'

'Kat was let go April 2nd.'

'I don't know what to make of this, Rich,' Glick replied. 'People drop money on stupid shit sometimes when there are bills to pay.' He paused, looking down the street at the house. 'But that timing, man. We've never believed in coincidences.'

'When you were knocking on the door, I called the diner Kat worked after the hardware store tossed her. Waitress said the manager was unavailable until tomorrow.'

'Why?'

'He gets back from a vacation today from Key West. Been down there for two weeks. Said he's been bragging about it to the staff all month.'

'Everyone needs a vacation, LT. He might be good with money.'

'He's not, and she said none of them could work out how he was affording it. Told me the guy's paying child support on four kids and is double mortgaged on his home. That money would get pulled automatically from his paycheck. Wouldn't leave him with much.'

'So what are you saying?'

'He and our friend who bought that bike both got rid of this girl, just as she'd be settling in. We go to the managers of all the other places that have sent her out the door over the last five years since she got out of ORW, I'm starting to expect to see them walking around with diamond earrings and gold teeth.'

'You think someone's paying them off to fire her? Why would they do that?'

Richie didn't answer. Instead, a few moments later he pulled a packet of cigarettes from the glove box and got out of the car. Glick watched him for a moment, seeing him light up, then stepped out to join him, the two men standing under an awning for a corner store nearby. He'd only ever seen his lieutenant smoke on a few rare occasions; the pair of detectives stood there watching the rain.

'Case I worked just after I made detective, we had a dead kid,' Richie said, leaning back against the wall behind him. 'Young girl. Her mom and dad reported her missing and she was found three days later beside some abandoned buildings over in Glenville. She'd fallen off the top of one. Or been pushed or thrown.

'Me and my partner couldn't work it out. The girl lived with her family across town and they seemed tightknit; took a lot of care of her. She'd been sick most of her life. Hospital records had her spending over four hundred days in the ER. She was left behind by the other kids in her grade because of all the school she'd missed; didn't have any friends, so wouldn't have been playing at the site with anyone.' Richie took a drag from the cigarette, reliving the case. 'Who'd want to abduct a kid like that and kill her, right?

'Then we found a blog on a website. Back before social media and all that crap got big. It was run by the girl's mom, documented the kid's struggles and how the family were handling it, that kind of thing. Photos of the girl in the hospital, stories, the good and the bad. Fox 8 even did a main primetime slot story on the mom running a 10k raising money for the kid's treatment.' He tapped some ash from his smoke to the concrete by his feet. 'No-one else in the family had a history of consistent illness.

'Day the girl went missing, the mom said she went to the store, but when she came back found her daughter was gone. Me and my partner drove the journey ourselves, timed it, and asked locals how often the woman normally spent in the store. She was a local celebrity by now, so everyone remembered her. For some reason, the trip the day her daughter died took almost forty minutes longer than it should have done. We found tape of other times she or her husband visited the store, but this time there was an unexplained gap.'

He dragged on the cigarette, the end burning bright in the damp air.

'Some kids had been filming each other flipping skateboards not far from the site where the girl was eventually found, and one of them came in with a recording. One guess who we saw in the background of one of the videos driving past on the way to the site.'

'Momma bear.'

'She went on the offensive, played victim. Screamed and cried, couldn't believe we could accuse her of hurting her own kid. Her husband almost jumped across the interview table and swung on my partner when he suggested it as a possibility. Said they were gonna have our badges, sue the Department, go to the press. But then we showed him the skateboarder's tape.

'Never seen a man's face lose color like that. That's when the mother's armor began to crack. My partner worked her down and we got her to break. She'd been poisoning that little girl her entire life with low doses of thallium in her food. Doctors missed it because it never occurred to them to look for it. Left the other kids in the family alone for some reason, just targeted her. She used the girl's illnesses and the blog for attention. Liked being in the spotlight. Became like a drug, and she kept wanting more.

'But on their most recent trip to the hospital, one of the nurses who'd been there several years made it clear to the mother that she was getting suspicious and the woman panicked. Mom took the girl out to that abandoned lot in Glenville, told her she had a surprise for her up there, then pushed her off. Drove to the store, bought a few things to establish an alibi, got home then reported the girl missing.'

'How old was the kid?'

'Eight years old.'

After a moment, Glick stepped forward and took a cigarette from the pack too. Richie lit it for him.

'Kat O'Mara's not a quitter,' Richie said. 'She was underweight and sick a lot as a young teenager, but the maid said once she moved in and started prepping the family's food, the girl got better. But she dropped off again once her father died and the maid got fired. Ever since she's been out of prison, she's had her ass kicked out of every job, her inheritance has been kept from her and she's been stuck living in the worst parts of the city with every opportunity to climb her way back out ripped away. I took a look at the timings of all this shit and when her life started to change. Laid it out against the family history. Fits like a glove.'

'Right when her stepmom began living in the house,' Glick said, as Richie nodded. 'You think Blair was poisoning her? Making her sick?'

'I don't know. But I'm gonna find out.'

'Why would she want to keep Kat's inheritance? She's already a multimillionaire and she doesn't have a key to that deposit box. She can't touch it even if she wants to.'

Richie finished off his smoke and dropped the butt before grinding it out, looking at the rain. 'But what if the girl dies?'

In a sunnier, drier Oneida County, checking that he hadn't been followed by anyone, Nicky had just made it back to the church he and Kat had hidden in last night. The building was near some woodland which stretched down towards the lake where he'd dumped and hidden the kayak, and had felt sufficiently secluded and safe.

He slipped back into the church with the grocery bag in his hands and knelt beside Kat. He unscrewed the cap off one of the bottles and supported her head so she could drink. The holdall with the titanium lockbox was beside her, and there was also a twelve gauge shotgun from the trooper's car that Nicky had lifted from the park last night. All the possessions the two of them now had in the world.

'I'm worse...aren't I?' Kat said quietly, seeing the expression on his face and the way he was looking at her.

He didn't reply and tipped the bottle of water again but she didn't manage to drink much. 'The doc back in Erie said you needed rest. We just need to find somewhere where we don't have to keep moving for a while.'

'This...gets...' She took a slow breath and tried again. *'This gets worse, you don't...take me...to a doctor, Nick. No...hospitals. Understand?'*

'You might die if I don't.'

'You'll get...captured...if you do.' Despite her weakened state, her eyes sheened with tears. *'I should have listened...I'm...sorry.'*

'We can't change it. We just gotta figure it out.'

'So what do we...do?'

'We find somewhere to wait a few weeks until you're good enough to travel. Then try to get over into Canada.'

She closed her eyes. *'We can't...stay...here?'*

'Not for long. But it's Monday so there'll be no church service today, so we should be good until nightfall. We'll get back in the kayak on the water and go east. I saw a map at the gas station. The lake connects to rivers that can get us out of the State. We can hide somewhere east closer to New England. They'll never find us there.'

She didn't answer and he realized she'd dozed off. He quickly changed out of the jeans and ballcap back into Barry's suit, wanting to switch appearance from what he'd been wearing at the gas station in case the deputy he'd spoken to or the clerk realized in hindsight who he was. He'd have preferred not to wear the suit jacket as well, back in the clothing Barry had last seen him in and which he would've told police Nicky was wearing when he left the barn, but he felt chilled to the bone after such little sleep last night.

He pulled it on, picked up the loaded shotgun and rose, going back to the door, the bright light making him squint. He was exhausted, his cheekbones framing the black stubble that wasn't quite hiding the weight he'd lost over the past three days.

A couple of gunshots came from the distance somewhere; *hunters*, he thought. In a perfect world, the cops would have taken down Brooks and Billy by now, but he'd never had that kind of luck; it was disappointing to hear the pair hadn't been captured at the fairground, which had been part of Nicky's plan when he'd cut and resewn the bottom of the bag, and lit those firecrackers to draw as much attention as possible to the two big men. They couldn't be far away, wherever they were, and they'd be as pissed at him as they would be at whoever had shot their youngest brother on the bridge on Friday night. He'd cost them a lot of money at the fair fifteen hours ago. Nicky remembered turning and seeing those loose dollar bills spilling out of the split bag and a quick smile appeared under those hollow cheekbones. He'd always intended to make it as difficult as possible for them to escape with it all.

But then, hearing a car approaching down the track and stop outside the church, the smile vanished. Nicky swore as he stepped back, looking through the gap in the door, and saw a man in a reverend's clothing behind the wheel, wearing a white collar and black shirt.

In panic, he looked back at Kat who was lying near the altar, but as the clergyman got out, Nicky knew he'd see the splintered damage to the lock on the church's door.

Against his greatest wishes, it looked as if he was going to be forced to take another hostage.

The clergyman had stopped dead, seeing the damage to the lock, when the door suddenly opened and a gaunt, dark-haired man in a black suit and white shirt snapped into a view, holding a shotgun. The reverend was just as taken aback as Dr Ramesh Tejwani and Barry Marsh had been, and his hands went up like Barry's had at that lookout point near Erie.

'Are you alone?' the man with the twelve gauge asked.

'Yes. Yes.'

'Come inside,' Nicky told him. 'I'm not gonna hurt-'

Then he got shot.

The sound of a gunshot close by a split-second earlier sent birds who'd been congregating in the trees into the air as blood sprayed against the wood and wall of the church. Nicky reeled back and fell against the door before hitting the ground. The bullet that had come from the tree-line had ripped open the skin on the side of his neck just under his left ear, but the fact it was a rifle and not a shotgun had saved his head from being removed from his body.

As the reverend in front of him turned in shock to see who'd shot the Gatlin fugitive, Nicky clutched a hand to his neck but apart from a stinging pain found he could still breathe, his throat not torn open. From his position in the doorway to the church, he caught sight of a bulky man in camo gear emerge from behind a tree and start moving towards him, a rifle in his shoulder.

Nicky had just been found, and not by the cops.

The Gatlin fugitive let go of his neck, brought up his shotgun, and as the hunter who'd shot at him ducked behind a tree Nicky blasted a shell into the trunk, blood starting to dampen the collar of Barry's white shirt. But then in his left peripheral vision he saw another figure emerge and dropped before a shotgun shell punched a splintered hole into the church door where his head had just been. Nicky racked the pump on his own twelve gauge and blasted a shell back as the second man went for cover behind another tree, like his friend. Not cops or the Loughlins, but locals who must've recognized him when he was walking here from the gas station. And who'd probably decided to claim the bounty on his and Kat's heads.

The reverend had already dropped to the ground, his previously peaceful morning just having taken one hell of a turn. Staying low, Nicky ran over to the prone man, pulled open the rear door on the car and pushed him inside. '*Keys!*' he hissed, the rear window shattering. He swung round and fired back through the window with another couple of shells, racking the pump and riding the kick of the shotgun as blood leaked down his neck. The terrified clergyman was still holding his keys and Nicky snatched them before getting in behind the wheel.

He reversed around the building in a giant half circle, then got out and ran through a side door he'd unlocked from the inside earlier in case they'd needed a quick escape. He sprinted over to Kat, who was awake again and looking very scared.

'They found...us?' she asked, as he grabbed the heist bag, swept her up and ran back outside, her eyes on the injury to his neck.

'GET OUT!' he told the reverend, who quickly did as he was told. Nicky got her across the backseats just as the pair of hunters were reappearing at the edge of the building, and he fired at both with his revolver to force them back out of sight before getting in and spinning the wheel to drive onto the road. He took the route from where he'd walked just a few minutes ago, turning onto the main road and almost hitting another car, then sped off at high speed, just beginning to breathe again when he saw his luck had now completely run out.

A local town police cruiser with flashing lights was coming towards him, but the officers inside had seen the speeding vehicle almost hit another car and pulled a sharp turn across the road to block his path. The two cops got out and pulled weapons as they aimed them at Nicky from behind their vehicle; local officers who'd just happened to be patrolling the area, and who'd been responding to reports of the sounds of shooting at the church.

Nicky made a U-turn, but then saw a truck blocking off any hope of escape behind him, his two attackers from the church inside. He looked around desperately, his neck burning and bleeding, then saw where they'd come to a halt. He pulled the strap of the heist bag over his shoulder, the blood from his neck now soaking his shirt, and using the door as cover, got out and pulled Kat free from the back.

Ignoring shouted warnings from the police officers, who couldn't shoot with the two local hunters and other traffic in their line of fire, Nicky hustled to the railing on the side of the bridge, took a step up and with Kat in his arms, jumped.

Three nights previously in West Virginia, an uninjured Archer and the civilian driver he'd saved had landed feet first into the Kanawha River, but despite the drop being shorter, Nicky and Kat were both in far worse shape. They hit the water hard then caught by the current, immediately started to be washed downstream, Nicky fighting to keep his head above water while trying to do the same for Kat, the bag still strapped over his shoulder and trailing behind them. Gunfire came from the bridge, a bullet ripping through the bag, but neither of them were hit.

They were swept rapidly downriver for almost a minute before Nicky smashed into a rock, which stopped them dead with a painful jolt. Gasping from the sudden pain, he felt solid ground beneath his feet and fighting against the powerful flow of the water, he staggered towards the riverbank, now out of sight of the bridge. He wondered who'd get to them first, the cops or hunters.

Cold, soaking wet and exhausted, he heaved a limp Kat up into his arms again and started to head into the woods, hearing shouts from further upstream where they'd just been. Strategy had gone out the window.

This was now down to pure survival.

FORTY SIX

'*Report coming in locals and cops are engaging with Reyes!*' a sergeant at the Oneida County Sheriff's Department called out and moments later, officers and deputies were sprinting from inside the station towards squad cars, Archer and Marquez right behind them.

Neither had a radio but they didn't need directions, Archer following the other police vehicles. It wasn't Lupinetti who'd been called in, but it was two of the five fugitives, and the wanted pair might very well have a good idea about where Frank and the Loughlins could be.

So he spun the car out of the lot and they joined the others speeding out onto the road.

Downstream from the bridge which Nicky had jumped off with Kat, the local boys in hunting gear who'd first seen the Gatlin escapee at the gas station had worked their way along the riverbank, and about half a mile downstream had just found footsteps in the mud leading into the woods.

They also saw a piece of clothing, a black suit jacket held against a large rock by the force of the flowing river. The two men were cousins and had been stalking game in the area together since they were kids, so without the need to speak, one took the lead before both moved forward silently, following the trail.

But not for the first time over the past few days, Nicky had conned his pursuers. He'd carried Kat out of the water and propped her against some rocks before he ran into the woods until he reached a drier grassy spot, sheltered by trees where footsteps would be hard to track; he quickly looked around and after choosing a suitable spot for the task at hand, he'd then doubled back, taking care not to leave any obvious tracks. Lastly, he peeled off Barry's suit jacket and left it trapped against one of the rocks just to make sure the people hunting him couldn't miss where he'd come ashore. That trail leading to nothing might be enough to give him and Kat time to escape one more time.

He'd taken her with him back into the water, allowing the current to carry them downstream, and five minutes later waded out of the river for the last occasion. After moving through some thicker woodland, he reached an open hillside and saw some houses at the top where he knew there'd be a car, so he started carrying her up the slope.

The noise of police sirens in the distance were getting louder as he climbed, each step becoming more of an effort. He'd exercised in Gatlin to stay healthy and help pass the endless monotonous hours, opting for bodyweight stuff like push-ups, chin-ups and dips rather than heavy weightlifting, so had good conditioning despite the shitty food he'd lived on for the past decade, but the events of the last few days had worn him down, the mental and physical pressure taking a tremendous toll.

His arms, legs and lungs were burning, and his and Kat's clothes were sodden, making the task even more difficult. He pictured the Loughlins somewhere listening to the sirens, the focus off them for the moment, guessing that he and Kat had been located and were taking all the heat. The thought fueled his anger, driving him onwards. After all this, he refused to fail.

He'd almost made it to the top of the rise when he heard the sound of a helicopter; he looked around for cover and staggered towards a small copse to their right. He'd left the woods along the riverbank behind but these few trees further up the slope would provide some momentary shelter as long as the people in the chopper weren't using infrared. If they were, he and Kat were screwed.

He lowered her to the ground before leaning against a tree to recover his breath, but then saw she was deathly pale and shivering. He shrugged off the holdall and immediately sat behind her before enveloping her in his arms to try and share what body warmth they had.

Drawing in huge breaths, his heart thumping and needing to rest a moment before they moved on, Nicky looked out at the landscape ahead, water from lakes in the distance catching the midday light.

Night sun. That's what it's gonna be like out there for you once you cross that wall.

Shaking from the cold, he felt Kat's hand slowly move to his, something in her palm. It was the key for the padlock on the deposit box, which she'd managed to unloop from around her neck.

He knew what the small gesture meant without her having to say anything.

'We're almost there,' Nicky told her. 'Just hang on for me. We'll find a way.'

Kat didn't reply and he saw her hand had dropped limply to the ground.

It was then he realized her shivering had also stopped, her body feeling heavier as she lay against him.

On that September morning, the sun had just gone down.

But only for Kat O'Mara.

A mile away, the two hunters who'd been trying to pick up the false trail through the woodland had just been confronted by law-enforcement. Some county sheriff deputies who'd been in the area to hear the emergency callout had rerouted and they were the ones who'd located them.

'*WEAPONS DOWN!*' one of the deputies shouted, aiming his handgun. The two locals did as they were ordered slowly, then straightened with their hands up.

'We found that guy and woman!' one of them said. 'We're just following their trail.'

'So where are they?'

'Chopper's got him,' another deputy interrupted, listening to a report coming over the radio.

Stopping Kat from carrying out her plan, then keeping her alive and them both out of custody had been what had driven Nicky ever since he'd broken free from Gatlin. He'd had to fight like a junkyard dog all the way and had never felt like giving up until now.

But the torch which had been burning so brightly inside him was now almost extinguished. Still holding Katherine, he looked down at her face, pale and still, showing no signs of the pain which had dogged her for the last forty eight hours of her life. He quickly remembered first meeting her when they were teenagers, the good times together in Cleveland before he was sent to prison; how she'd never stopped visiting, the only person from the outside world who didn't forget he existed or cut ties with him after he was sentenced. The way her father had treated him and his dad, and the opportunity Thomas O'Mara had given them at a better life.

Now totally alone, he knew she'd have been furious with him if she could see him now, sitting there holding her body rather than continuing to run. *Get out of here, Nick,* he could hear her saying. *I've slowed you down enough. You can't do anything for me anymore.*

GO!

RUN!

From its position directly overhead, it seemed that the helicopter had found him but despite that, Nicky decided to make one final push; if he could make it to the houses at the top of the hill, he maybe stood a small chance.

Laying Kat down carefully against the tree, he looked at her one last time then turned and ran on up the slope.

Two minutes later, he found a back door open for one of the closest houses; desperate, he ran inside ready to confront the owner and demand car keys, but the place was empty. He checked through the windows and heard the chopper hovering, but then looked out front and saw there was no vehicle parked outside, his tired mind realizing that was only logical if there was no-one here.

The sound of sirens drew closer as he saw red and blue lights appearing on the road leading towards the houses. He slumped against the wall, his head bowed and breathing hard as he closed his eyes.

It was over.

Less than ten minutes earlier, Marquez and Archer had split up; she'd joined the officers conducting the hunt not far from the river, responding to rolling reports from the chopper's birds' eye view of Reyes' location. Then the cops she was with found Kat O'Mara's body.

As an officer called it in, his pistol drawn, another knelt beside Kat with cuffs in his hand but then checked her for a pulse before shaking his head, putting the set of bracelets away. Marquez looked down at the dead young woman. Her clothes were soaked, her white shirt stained red, some bandaging clear through the damp fabric from a wound to her right side. Reyes was nowhere to be seen, but barring a miracle, Marquez knew this was shortly going to be the end of the line for him too.

Always was a quitter, Blair had described her stepdaughter. Looking at the dead girl, who'd paid the ultimate price and given up everything for a bank deposit box, Marquez took out her phone and called Archer. 'Kat's dead,' she told him. 'She's down here on a hilltop. Reyes can't be far aw-'

'Chopper tracked him running to a house up the hill from you guys. I'm almost there. Units are surrounding the home.'

Marquez looked up to see more police cruisers arriving outside some properties near the top of the hill; she recalled Prez's descriptions of Nicky and also what he'd done to sabotage the Loughlins' bag at the fairground last night. Reyes had done a lot of illegal things in the last few days, but he and Kat had never felt like the true villains here. They hadn't murdered police officers, extradition bus agents, State troopers or slit the throats of pregnant women after sexually assaulting them.

'Think he'll surrender?' she asked. 'Or take suicide by cop?'

'Depends how desperate he is. Or what he thinks he has left to live for.' As Marquez listened, she saw the officer who'd knelt beside Kat was checking the inside of a holdall resting against the dead young woman's leg.

The bag was empty.

As blue and red lights flashed outside the house where he'd taken refuge, Nicky stepped away from the window and closed the blinds, seeing armed law-enforcement officers and deputies surrounding the home. It was then that he also heard movement from the stairs; he turned quickly and saw a terrified young woman holding a small child.

He was wrong, the house wasn't empty after all.

She stood there staring at him uncertainly, frozen on the stairs, clearly not daring to make a run for it.

Then the phone in the room suddenly rang. Nicky stayed where he was, still wet from the river and with both his and Kat's blood staining his white shirt; he eyed the landline for a moment, aware it could be a trap to draw him into the scope of a sharpshooter outside.

He stayed low, crawled across the floor then reached up and pulled the phone down to the floor before picking up the receiver.

'Reyes?' a County Sheriff's sergeant said from the fleet that had encircled the house; a neighbor had given him the number to call, the other residences on the block being quickly evacuated. 'We want to resolve this peacefully. We're not gonna come in unless we have to. But is there anyone else in the house?'

Pause. The sergeant looked down at the phone and swore.

'What he say?' a cop from Phoenix PD asked.

'He hung up.'

'Let's roll in and take down this asshole,' another deputy said, just as more vehicles arrived, Archer's Ford among them. 'We got him covered.'

'Neighbor says she thinks the woman who lives there is still inside with her kid,' another officer replied. But just as the police were deciding on their next move, the front door opened and a woman ran out hugging a child close, officers grabbing her and rushing them both to safety.

Closing the door, Nicky slumped back down again with his back against the wall, the phone in his hand; he knew police might think to look at the call log which would potentially lead to problems at Gatlin for a certain friend of his, but he needed to hear a familiar voice.

He dialed the number he'd memorized the night before his escape and lifted it to his ear, hoping for an answer.

He got one.

'Hey old man.' Nicky paused, his eyes stinging from sweat, silt and shotgun smoke as he closed them. 'Talk about a morning.'

'*Where are you?*'

'They got me in the end. I'm trapped.'

'Just you?'

'Kat's gone.'

Pause. *'I'm sorry, kid.'*

'I did all I could.'

'I know. She'd have known too.'

You can't show any weakness in this place, the biker had taught him all those years ago on Nicky's first morning inside federal prison. *Wrap the feelings up, lock them in a box and save it for when you get out.* He was out but not for much longer, back to fighting for survival for the rest of his life among some of the worst of humanity locked away from society; he closed his eyes, the muscles of his jaw under his blood-stained, stubbled face tightening. Tears almost threatened to seep through his closed eyelids, but he forced them back.

Save it for when you get out. Which now, he knew would most likely be never.

'You think they'll give me my old cell back?' he asked, trying to force a smile, his throat dry.

Outside, plans were being made to call the phone again and try to end the situation without more bloodshed when the front door opened.

A revolver was thrown out before a hand appeared, then the other.

Followed by Nicky Reyes.

Standing with the other cops, Archer stared at the prison fugitive who now had the sights and red dots of at least twenty weapons trained on him. The scene went quiet. Reyes was wearing what had once been a white shirt, suit trousers and dress shoes, the clothes blood-stained and marked with dirt. He saw the man had also been injured, with a cut on his cheek and dried blood on his neck from another injury there. Archer had last seen him in person during the heist in Cleveland two days ago and the heavy toll of his seventy two hours total on the run was very evident.

But once it also became clear he was surrendering, officers moved forward to detain the wanted man, the chopper still hovering overhead. They grabbed him and he was pushed to the ground before being frisked and cuffed.

The most inventive of the Gatlin fugitives was now back in custody, three days after his escape. Multiple state lines crossed, no-one hurt at his hands save two bikers and a local deputy who'd ended up with sore heads and bruised egos. As he was taken to an Oneida Sheriff's cruiser and put into the back, Nicky took a final look towards the hillside where with Kat, he'd made their last bid for freedom and where she'd died in his arms.

Give them everything you got, kid, Prez had told him on Friday morning before his escape attempt began.

He had.

FORTY SEVEN

'…apprehended the fugitive after he surrendered at a house in the area almost two hours ago,' the Oneida County Sheriff told some off-camera reporters, with US Marshals, a lieutenant and a sergeant from the county SWAT team standing behind him. Being the ones to apprehend a member of the Gatlin Four and the wanted thief Kat O'Mara after so many had failed in Ohio and Pennsylvania, meant Oneida's police authorities wanted representatives from their departments visible on camera. Hometown pride.

The images were being broadcast to news channels all over New York State as well as wider parts of the country. *'Nick Reyes was cornered by law-enforcement and surrendered after being surrounded,'* the Sheriff continued. *'His accomplice was found deceased half a mile away. Early indications are she succumbed to injuries she'd sustained in Cleveland on Saturday morning when this robbery took place.'*

'So the Loughlins got her in the end,' Archer said quietly, as he and Marquez both watched the announcement on a TV screen from the 1st floor inside the Sheriff's Office building, the conference being held just outside.

'*Have you recovered everything that was stolen*?' a reporter off screen asked.

'Not yet. A bag was found with the woman's body, but it was empty. The suspect has been taken for questioning. When more information becomes available, we'll let you all know.'

'What about the Loughlin brothers, Chief? And Frank Lupinetti?'

'The search is ongoing. We got two of them. We'll find the other three soon too. This area's finest law-enforce...'

Walking away from the TV, Archer went to the window and looked outside. He could see the reporters ranged behind the cameras, with rows of vehicles belonging to the news crews and curious locals filling the parking lot; but his gaze ended up shifting beyond them to a truck parked further down the street. Two men were standing beside it, their arms crossed, one chewing tobacco or gum, both dressed in hunting gear.

'A deputy told me they were the pair who first saw Reyes at the gas station,' Marquez commented, joining her colleague and seeing who he was looking at. 'Both got interviewed. They're from Wayne County.'

'Wayne County,' Archer said. 'Red Creek. Loughlins land.'

'Yeah, but same as a lot of people in the area. Probably don't mean much. Deputy told me those two are no relation to Brooks and Billy.'

'Reyes and the woman weren't the dangerous ones here,' Archer replied, shifting his eyes back to the press conference and mirroring Marquez's thoughts when she'd been standing over Kat's body. The mention of the brothers' names had reminded him of the reason they were still there. 'The three that should really concern everyone are still free.'

'I need to tell you something, while we got a moment,' Marquez said abruptly now they were alone, her change in tone catching his attention. He turned to look at her. 'It's about Reyes' cellmate back at Gatlin.'

‘You traded a lot of cash and jewelry at the fair last night for whatever the brothers were carrying,’ one of two US Marshals said, leaning over the desk with Nicky sitting in cuffs opposite him. He was being held in the same building Archer and Marquez were in but was downstairs in an interview room, still wearing Barry Marsh’s trousers and shirt.

Some of Kat’s blood had stained his chest from when he’d last carried her, the collar also a watery red from where his neck had been grazed by a bullet. The injury had been given rudimentary medical treatment, a couple of white band-aids taped across it. All he was getting right now. ‘The kid you paid to hold the laser pointer watched the whole thing,’ the Marshal continued, pressing him. ‘Told us what went down. What was in the bag you swapped for? And where is it?’

Nicky didn’t look at the two men sitting across from him, focusing instead on the wall behind them, his face and clothes caked in dried mud and silt.

‘C’mon, Nick, it’s over,’ the Marshal persisted. ‘Co-operate with us and it might not mean your whole life back inside a place like Gatlin. Whatever was in that safe deposit box didn’t belong to you or even Katherine right now. It’d been signed over to her stepmom.’ He paused, softening his tone. ‘And you look like you could use a shower. Some food. We can help you get all that. But just tell us why you made this trade. Why was that bag the brothers had so valuable to you and the girl?’

Nothing.

‘I’ve seen some dumb shits in my time but you’re champion above them all, guy,’ the second Marshal told him, shaking his head. ‘You should’ve been released in forty eight hours but now we’re gonna get you sent back for another fifty years. Hope it was worth it.’

Nicky glanced at him for a moment, but then continued to stare at the wall.

He hadn't uttered a word since his arrest.

'You've been talking to Reyes' cellmate?' Archer whispered in disbelief to Marquez upstairs, drawing her closer to the window and away from anyone who could possibly overhear. '*How?*'

'When they first grilled him at Gatlin about the escape, he saw me in the corridor when they were taking him to the SHU block,' she explained. 'Said he'd talk but just to me. He remembered us from the chow hall when we stopped the inmates from raping that female guard. We saved him too when he was getting attacked, remember? He stalled me out, but told me later he saw I was wearing a NYPD CT Bureau badge so he knew who to call to reach me. When I got back to the motel that night, Ethan got in touch from New York and said someone wanted to speak to me.'

'And it was this man Rainey? How'd he make the call? His block was in lockdown.'

'He's got a phone in his cell.'

Archer closed his eyes for a moment. 'What has he told you?'

'A lot.'

'This makes you an accessory. You've been talking with him and didn't pass it on to investigators on a federal case this wide? And with this many casualties? What if they find his phone and your number's on it?'

'I know, I was so focused on what he was telling me, I didn't think about that until it was too late. I've been trying to get in touch with him and tell him to erase my number but he won't answer.'

'That doesn't matter. If they find the phone, they can just check the records. You'll be all over them.'

'I thought it was worth the information,' she said defensively but her worry was showing, especially now seeing Archer's reaction. 'I was always gonna ask him to delete all traces.'

'He had nothing to do with Lupinetti, Lis.'

'It was Reyes. When they found that laundry truck driver and turned out Nicky saved him, I got curious about the guy. Why he risked everything to do that after he'd escaped. I had to find out.'

'What if Rainey sells you out?'

'I know he's a criminal, but he seems OK. I get how that sounds,' she continued, seeing Archer's face. 'You said it yourself, does Reyes really feel as bad as the Loughlins? Or Lupinetti?'

'No, but that doesn't mean a thing. The biker gets found with that phone, you could end up on the stand too.'

'I know,' she replied miserably. 'I know.' Below, the brief press conference ended, reporters separating to record segments or give live takes on what had been said, updating people who'd tuned in from all over several States. Archer was still processing what Marquez had just told him, surprised that his usually very professional colleague had slipped up so badly and now extremely concerned for how this might shake out for her. He was about to say something further when they both became aware of the sound of a large gathering somewhere downstairs.

They headed for the stairs and walked down to find a group of law-enforcement, Marquez hiding her worries at her lapse in judgement and thoughts of the possible repercussions, for now.

'How we doin' on the Loughlin boys and the ex-cop?' the Sheriff asked the people assembling in front of him. 'We bring all five of these assholes down, you know how good that's gonna look.'

'Brothers haven't been seen since the fairground, Chief,' a deputy told him. 'That Oswego sighting first thing turned out to be nothing. But every badge over there and in Wayne is out on the roads looking. Same in Onondaga, Madison, Cayuga and Cortland.'

'Getting reports of locals driving loops in the area with weapons in their trucks too, Sheriff,' another deputy informed him.

'To hunt down Brooks and Billy?'

'Or help them out if they get cornered. Depends who's behind the wheel. We know the influence that family has around here. Word might've gone out that Reyes screwed the two brothers out of several million dollars at the fairground last night. Could be looking to take a crack at him here too, maybe.'

'Reyes say anything?' the Sheriff asked.

'Not yet,' one of the Marshals answered. 'Think he's having trouble accepting that this is over for him. His dumb ass better get real used to the idea.'

'Some time back in the local jail might get him talking,' the Sheriff answered, echoing a similar idea of a prison captain at Gatlin a few days previously.

'Taking him to county?' a Marshal asked.

'There's a solitary wing there. Instead of keeping him here, why not lock his ass away isolated from everyone else and get him back in a jumpsuit in a cell, not an interview room. Little shot of reality and a reminder where his future's headed. How many years he serves depends on how much he co-operates, or least we can tell him that. Few hours in a cell again, he'll open up.'

‘He lasted almost twelve years in Gatlin,’ Marquez commented, but no-one paid any attention.

‘Oneida’s got a full house, Chief,’ one of his deputies added, seeing the Marshals seemed receptive to the idea.

‘Onondaga’ll have room at theirs,’ the Sheriff answered. ‘We gotta get working on finding Brooks and Billy instead. Let Reyes fester in a pair of jumps for a few hours.’ He shot the two Marshals a look. ‘You don’t want us showing you guys up and apprehending every one of your suspects, do you?’

‘Fine, we’ll transport him,’ the Marshal replied shortly. ‘I heard Onondaga’s got a bad reputation though. We need to keep him in one piece to find out what he knows.’

‘The rep’s improved. And we’ll keep him in solitary.’ The Sheriff grinned. ‘Son of a bitch has probably missed wearing orange so we’ll make him feel right at home,’ he added, as the assembled group laughed.

Archer, Marquez and the two Marshals were the only ones who didn’t.

FORTY EIGHT

'That's Bonnie and Clyde out of the game,' Glick said, watching a TV from his desk at the Robbery/Homicide unit's headquarters in Cleveland as news covered the report of Nicky's capture. Members of their squad were out working assignments related to this case, including going to visit the owner of the first deposit box to tell her part of it had been recovered last night. Two other members had gone out to Blair's home in Pepper Pike to inform her and her daughter that Kat had died.

At his desk, Richie put his phone down. 'Called French Lick PD and the Sheriff's Office over there in Indiana. Blair O'Mara doesn't have any trace of a record. Not one ticket or write-up.'

'Tommy O'Mara had a twelve million dollar estate when he died,' Glick replied, an open file on his desk that he and the rest of the team had put together. 'Blair must've inherited the majority of it. She took over his real estate business and investments.'

'What about Kat and Reyes? And Blair's daughter, Alaina?'

'Alaina got a hundred thousand apparently but she'll profit eventually through her mom too, I guess. I spoke to Nicky Reyes' defense counsel from his trial and they said he paid them almost two hundred thousand to be represented. That must've come from what Tommy had left him. Waste of money as it turned out.'

'And Kat?'

'No-one knows for sure. She never revealed what's in that deposit box, even when it was temporarily taken off her hands. Note here says Blair informed the court she suspected it was a significant sum Kat could use to waste on her addiction. How she got the hold granted.'

'So she doesn't know what's inside?' Richie asked.

Glick shook his head. 'No-one does, or did, apart from Kat and probably Reyes too, I figure. That's why Blair's danced around it when we've asked her.'

'That girl's life was sabotaged from the moment her stepmom showed up in that family home. Sick as a teenager before the maid was hired, then suddenly becoming a benzo addict with no previous issues once the maid was gone again. And all the money left from her father withheld on technicalities?'

'Kat was faking her own prescriptions to get supplies of the pills. This was a few years later too, Rich.' Glick thought about it. 'We know how she got started on them?'

'No. I'd need to talk to her prison counsellor again. See if she ever told him.' Richie paused. 'I heard a case once where a dealer slipped some of his product into the coffee of a guy who was trying to get clean. Heroin. Junkie was a good buyer, so his dealer wanted to keep him around.'

'Now we're really swinging for the fences.'

'Look at the timings. And these issues the girl developed. Tell me that isn't suspicious.'

'You don't think we're reading too much into this? Kat seemed pretty self-destructive.' Glick glanced back at the TV screen. 'Look at how it ended for her.'

Instead of answering, Richie walked over to Glick's desk and picked up the file, then found Nicky Reyes' arrest report from twelve years ago. He took it back to his own workspace to check something on his own computer, then scrawled whatever was on the screen onto a piece of paper. 'You're right, she seemed like her own worst enemy,' he said. 'But someone tried to kill her the night Reyes got arrested.' Richie rose again, folding the paper he'd just written on 'Let's go. We're paying the dead boy's folks a visit.'

'Why?'

'To tell them Nick Reyes has been re-apprehended, of course. Their son's murderer. Why else?' Glick understood the subtext, so without replying, rose and grabbed his jacket.

Outside the police station in Phoenix, NY, Archer and Marquez were back in their Ford, wanting to be able to talk freely without being heard.

On the opposite side of the lot, the local news vans had been joined by others from bigger networks, all of them hoping for the Sheriff to come outside to provide another statement, some of the correspondents still shooting segments in front of the building. The two local cousins who'd tried to hunt down Reyes and O'Mara had now left, but on their way to their car, Archer had made eye contact with the pair. Something about them had been off. He was still trying to work out exactly what it was.

But right now Marquez had sent a text to Prez to call her without fail, immediately, and as they sat in the car the phone rang; seeing it was him, she put it on speaker but kept the volume low so anyone passing outside couldn't hear. 'I need you to swap out that phone or change numbers as soon as you can, Rainey,' she told him straight away.

'Not real easy to do in here, Detective. Can't just walk to the store, you know?' A pause. *'Worried they'll find your number?'*

She glanced at Archer who was looking at her with raised eyebrows. 'Yes.'

'Relax, I'm stuck in this place because I didn't sell people out. You're good in my book after what you did in

the chow hall. Need a new phone now anyway. All you gotta worry about is if investigators on this case ever track the number and check the records.'

'I'm her friend from the hall,' Archer cut in. If they had the biker on the line, he figured he might as well use the opportunity. And something had been on his mind ever since he'd first learned of Reyes' sentence that put him inside. 'Before you go, can you tell us something?'

'Tell you what?'

'Nicky's manslaughter charge. The reason he ended up in federal prison. What exactly went down that night?'

'It's on his record.'

'We don't have it available.'

'Was about half a year after Katherine's father died. The kid was about to graduate, had plans to go down to the recruiter's office and enlist once he'd got his diploma to get out of Cleveland for good. But then he said Kat gave him a call from a party. She was upset, slurring her words, sounded all messed up. She'd taken her father dying pretty hard. Nicky couldn't be with her all the time to keep her head straight.

'He got the address out of her and drove over to the house to see if she was OK. Showed up and couldn't find the girl, then went looking around the house and found her upstairs, wasted. Some asshole was with her.'

'Taking advantage?' Marquez asked.

'*In a way. He was an older kid from Kat's high school, home from college at Ohio State. When Nicky found them, the guy was bleeding from scratch-marks on his face and Kat was on the floor. He was crushing her windpipe, looking like he was trying to kill her. Almost succeeded too. She'd already passed out. Nicky and the guy fought but the frat boy had a gun with him. He tried to use it.*

Nicky outmuscled him and College Boy got shot in the chest in the struggle. Died right there in the room.'

'So Nicky was charged with his murder,' Archer said.

'In Ohio, burden's on the defendant to prove that he killed someone in self-defense. Nick was still seventeen so should've got 3-8 years as a minor or even nothing at all under the circumstances. But the dead boy's father had influence and was out for payback. They gave the kid a dime plus two and sent him to one of the toughest federal joints in the country here at Gatlin.'

'Nicky went to prison because Kat got drunk or was too wasted on pills to act with caution?' Marquez asked.

'*She wasn't using back then. That started after. She was blood tested once detectives shut down the scene and took her to hospital. Had a high dose of Rohypnol in her system and Ohio State had some left in his pocket. Looked like the guy drugged her and was looking to score but she fought back. He got pissed when she scratched him up and started trying to choke her. Nick showing up saved her life.'*

'Even with that and testimony from eye-witnesses, Nicky still went down?' Archer asked.

'Told you, the dead boy's father had money and power. Nick wasn't an O'Mara, Kat's father was already gone so he couldn't do anything and Blair didn't want anything to do with the kid once she found out he'd killed someone. Backed off completely. He was on his own.'

As they sat in the car taking this information in, Archer saw two deputies arrive back at the station in a cruiser. He gave Marquez a *one moment* gesture and got out as she stayed on the phone with Rainey. 'You guys on a shift change?' he asked the two local deputies, approaching them.

'Who's asking?'

Archer showed them his NYPD shield. 'I helped bring in Reyes. We're still looking for Lupinetti and the Loughlins.'
'Join the club, man. Every badge in five counties wants that collar.'
'Least Reyes is being taken to county jail,' Archer said. 'What's Onondaga like? Heard it's got a reputation.'
'You mean Oneida,' one of them said. 'That's where he'll be going.'
Archer frowned. 'Oneida, Onondaga; I'm getting them mixed up.'
'Out of towners do. Names come from American-Indian tribes who lived here. But they're two separate counties. Right now, we're in Oneida.'
'Then I was right. The Sheriff said you've got a full house in the county jail here. Reyes was taken to Onondaga instead.'
'We don't often get maxed out in County. You sure he said that?' Archer nodded. 'Maybe more guys got arrested last night than we know about.'
As the pair walked off, Archer watched them go for a moment before returning to the car. 'Rainey hung up,' Marquez said. 'Someone coming. What did you want with them?' she asked, looking at the two local cops walking towards the station.
'An update. They just said the county jail here isn't usually full.'
'They might not be up to date with the intake.'
'Police have been talking all morning with each other.'
'Not to prisons though,' she replied, not taking her eyes off him. He had that look on his face that she knew all too well.
'We're waiting on a lead for Frank. Reyes might have one for us and they still haven't let us talk to him. Borrow

your phone?' She passed it over, and Archer pulled up the Onondaga County Jail facility on the map before glancing at her. She was already clipping on her seatbelt and he passed her back the cell to provide directions as he keyed the engine and took the Ford out of the PD lot. 'Let's check it out. See if we can get to him to have a quick word.'

'Nicky hasn't communicated with Lupinetti at all that we're aware of, since he broke out of Gatlin. Rainey never mentioned them talking inside either.'

'That we're aware of. Could be our only opportunity to find out if he knows anything,' Archer replied, taking them back onto the road.

Now that he'd heard what Reyes had done to get sent down for twelve years, he found Marquez's intrigue with the man's case was catching. And Archer also wanted to get a closer look at this jail in Onondaga County that the arrested fugitive had been taken to. The two local deputies' surprise about him being taken there had made him curious.

It was common knowledge that some facilities were more dangerous than others.

FORTY NINE

The O'Maras had moved to a different area of the city after Thomas had died, Blair wanting a new start, but as Richie and Glick had discovered, the family of the young man killed by Nicky Reyes twelve years ago had remained in the same home in the Westlake suburb. The rain from earlier had stopped, the air now thick and humid as the two detectives climbed out of their car. Mr McCoy answered Richie's knock, his wife joining him a few moments later as introductions were made.

'Robbery Homicide,' Brian McCoy repeated. 'Suppose that means you've been hunting for Nick Reyes?'

'Small part of the effort,' Richie answered. 'Guess you've seen the news?'

He nodded. 'Come on in.' They wiped their shoes on the mat before entering the pristine home. Richie didn't take much interest in Cleveland's politics, but knew from the file he'd read at their police squad's headquarters that Brian McCoy was a successful businessman, now retired, who was on the city council. There were degrees of wealth in every city, and this family looked to be in the top 5%.

As the two cops followed McCoy, they saw the house was expensively furnished, thick rugs covering polished wooden floors, a large living room to the left that looked as if it had come straight out of a glossy magazine. 'The last few days have been a nightmare,' Shanna McCoy said, as her husband went into a dining room and took three crystal glasses off a shelf before picking up a bottle of scotch. 'With him free out there.'

'None for us, please, sir,' Richie said as Brian opened the whisky.

'The sun's past the dial. We need to celebrate. You got the guy.'

'Another time, we're on duty. But we'll take coffee if you have it.'

'Of course,' his wife said, turning and going through into the kitchen as her husband continued to pour himself a glass of scotch.

'Who got him?' Brian asked.

'Police in upstate New York. Marshals are taking over custody.'

'So you're sure he can't escape?'

'He caught everyone by surprise once. That's not gonna happen again.'

'I've been counting down the days that son of a bitch was serving. Shanna and I were dreading the day he was being released. I knew it was coming up on Wednesday.' McCoy swallowed a mouthful of the whisky. 'He won't be getting out after this, I assume.'

'Not a chance,' Richie said, and the man nodded.

'That's great. Come take a seat,' he said, leading Richie into the living room to continue the conversation. Glick wandered off to his right, intending to follow Shanna to the kitchen, but slowed when he reached the stairs.

There were family photos running all the way up the wall to the next floor. Curious, Glick walked up a few steps to get a closer look and saw the McCoys had originally been a family of five. He could tell by who was missing in the latter photos that it was the eldest child who'd been killed by Reyes. The guy was muscular, even as a late teenager, with light hair and a square jaw. Glick could see from other photos that he'd played football and in a couple of studio photos where the family were all dressed up and smiling together, he looked uncomfortable.

Definitely more of an athlete than a politician like his father.

Glick reached the last photo at the top of the stairs as he heard Richie small-talking with Brian in the living room, Shanna still preparing coffee. He glanced to his right and saw a bedroom door open, but there was a stillness about the room that told him it hadn't been occupied for a long time. He walked to the doorway and saw photos on the wall of the dead boy.

This had been Luke's room. He understood why parents of a child would keep a bedroom as it was before their kid died, even after all this time. The room was probably a lot tidier than the young man would have kept it when he was alive but Glick could picture the guy hanging out in here. Games consoles in the corner, posters on the wall of several famous sports stars long since retired. Medals were pinned to the edge of several shelves, with a few framed photos of Luke at wrestling meets or playing football. He'd been a strong, athletic young man, killed in his first year at university at Ohio State.

On a shelf by the wall, a yearbook caught Glick's eye, in particular the name on the spine. *Cleveland Catholic High.* It was the same school that Kat O'Mara had attended, he recalled. Glick entered the room, picked up the yearbook and started flicking through the pages. The year's date told him Luke had been a grade ahead of her, so there was no entry for the girl.

Glick was about to close the yearbook when he saw the edge of a photo, tucked between the back pages.

He pulled it free and turned the image over to look at it.

'Detective?' a voice suddenly asked, and he turned to see Luke's mother in the doorway, looking at him standing in her dead son's room. 'Coffee's ready.'

'I'll be right down,' he said. 'Sorry for coming up here uninvited. Cop curiosity.'

She looked at him for a moment, then nodded, but didn't join him in the room; Glick sensed she probably didn't venture in there often. She turned, not waiting to see if he followed, and walked downstairs to join Richie and her husband. Glick stared at the photo in his hand and considered pocketing it, but then took out his smartphone and snapped several photos of the image. When he was done, he put it back in place, returned the yearbook and headed downstairs, his cell still in his hand.

'LT, we gotta go,' he told Richie, who was sitting with the couple as Shanna was pouring Glick his coffee.

'A call?' Richie asked, immediately catching on that it was time to leave.

'New lead on the remaining fugitives,' Glick replied. 'Marshals want to meet with us.'

Richie placed his cup down and rose. 'Sorry to show up then have to leave so soon. We just wanted to tell you in person that Nicky Reyes is back behind bars. Felt you were owed that.'

'Thank you, Detectives, we appreciate it,' Brian McCoy said. 'You two come back when you're off duty sometime and we'll have that scotch. I'll keep a bottle ready.'

'We will.' The detectives left and walked to their car. 'What's going on?' Richie asked, once they were inside. Instead of responding, Glick took out his phone, went to the photo he'd taken of the image he'd found tucked in the yearbook and passed the cell to his lieutenant.

Richie looked at it, then zoomed in.

'*What?*' he whispered quietly.

'Bet your ass we got a new lead, LT,' Glick said, starting the engine as Richie studied the photo.

The US Marshal in the interview room at the Oneida Sheriff's Office had promised Nicky he could get a shower and something to eat if he told them where he'd hidden the contents of the empty holdall found beside Kat's body, but Nicky was still refusing to speak. Just as the Sheriff had suggested, he'd been taken to the neighboring Onondaga County Jail to be held awaiting further questioning, moved without the media outside the Oneida Department's base catching on.

Nicky was uncuffed and then ordered to strip, just like the day he'd arrived at Gatlin all those years ago. He did so slowly, feeling numb and completely drained. Barry Marsh's clothes were collected up and bagged, and Nicky was then led naked to the showers, relieved to find them empty; he didn't have the energy to deal with other inmates right now. He was so tired, he felt as if he was walking using someone else's legs.

'Get to it or you can share the space with some of the other boys,' the CO with him said, throwing a bar of soap onto the tiled floor by Nicky's feet.

Outside, the front gate to the jail buzzed open and the NYPD Ford rolled in, Archer having driven there quickly following Marquez's directions. Transferring Reyes to this jail without any of the press picking up on it meant there were no cameras or reporters hanging around outside the gates of this facility; not yet anyway. They probably assumed he was still at the Sheriff's Office or heading to Oneida's lockup instead. For that reason alone, sending him to another county's jail was a good choice.

Marquez checked behind them as Archer slid the car into an empty space, and then realized not everyone had been fooled. As they arrived, they saw a familiar Ford 150 truck parked on the far side of the lot on the other side of the fence; Archer instantly recognized the two locals in hunting garb who'd been in the parking lot at the PD station, both currently sitting in the front seats.

‘Dammit, how’d they know?’ Marquez asked, as Archer pulled the keys from the ignition, studying the pair.

‘Maybe they’ve got a contact inside the Sheriff’s Department.’ Archer paused. ‘Or they want to make sure they get credit for their involvement after the reward the Marshals put out for Reyes’ and O’Mara’s capture.’

‘They don’t need to sit outside the jail for that. So what are they doing here?’

The two NYPD detectives could see both locals were staring in their direction. The driver had his window down and spat some chewing tobacco to the concrete, not taking his eyes off the two cops.

Archer and Marquez got out and walked to the entrance; she pushed a buzzer and after a couple of seconds, the door was opened for them. Behind her, Archer glanced back over his shoulder again before they walked in and saw the two men had now got out of their Ford, both still staring at him and Marquez.

Like Brooks and Billy on the bridge the other night, they moved pretty fast for men their size.

The shower inside the county jail pummeled Nicky’s exhausted body, the captured fugitive ignoring the CO standing there watching him, no stranger to a lack of privacy after twelve years of incarceration. The water swirling down the drain at his feet was a light shade of brown from all the dirt and silt he’d picked up since jumping into the river. Only a few hours ago, but now what seemed like a lifetime away.

The scraped injury across his back from the speedbump outside Gatlin on Friday stung from the water and a stream of red beaded down his chest, the pressure from the shower causing some bleeding from the wound on his neck under the two band aids. The water slowed to a trickle then stopped, and Nicky turned just in time to catch an old scratchy towel, another guard bringing in a set of jail jumps, canvas shoes and handcuffs.

'We've been involved in the manhunt for the fugitives from Virginia from the start,' Archer told a guard working desk duty inside the county jail. 'We were told Nicky Reyes was being brought here.'

'You were told wrong,' the CO replied quickly.

'We were at the Sheriff's Office in Oneida County half an hour ago when it was decided to bring him here,' Marquez added. 'We know he's here, man. Why deny it? We're not media.'

The CO's eyes narrowed. He took their badges, looking at each in turn slowly and deliberately, before handing them back. 'So what do you want?'

'To ask Reyes a few questions before more investigators arrive. Three of the Gatlin Four are still out there. One of them's a person of interest to us. We need to get him back alive.'

'Can't let you see Reyes. This is a federal case, not NYPD. Don't concern you.'

'Speaking of that; where are the Marshals who brought him?' Archer asked.

'Strong lead on the Loughlin brothers came in over in Wayne County. Tip said they're hiding out in a house over there. Marshals left to check it out but they'll be back pronto. Reyes is locked in nice and tight.' He gave a smile that was more of a sneer, seeming to be enjoying the authority he had over the two NYPD detectives. 'Like you said, load more investigators are gonna be here within the hour. You two aren't even close to the front of the queue.'

'We've earned the right for a five minute conversation with the guy,' Marquez persisted. 'The man we're after killed one of our colleagues. And my friend here put down Craig Loughlin. Did all of you a big favor there.'

There was an adjustment in the CO's attitude. 'That was you?' he asked Archer. He nodded and the correctional officer leaned back in his chair, taking a better look at them both. 'What happened to your head?' he then asked Marquez, looking at her bandage hairband.

'I fell out of a window. Enough questions, man. You letting us in or not?'

'If I do, you're not going in with those guns.'

'We're law-enforceme-'

'Save your breath, lady. In here, you follow our rules. Cops from other counties don't come in here with weapons. I buzz you in with them, I get fired, and what's to say you won't just plug Reyes in the head if we let you see him? Your man here's already bagged one fugitive in the last few days, right?'

The two detectives glanced at each other. 'OK. We need to fill out any forms?' Archer asked.

'Yeah.' The desk guard dug out a couple of sheets and passed them over, waiting while the two detectives wrote down their details. Then they pulled their holsters and placed them in two plastic trays the man brought out. 'Cell phones too.'

'Why?' Archer asked.

'Because I said so.'

After a moment's hesitation, they added them to the tray; the CO then rose and walked around from the desk, not taking his eyes off the two city detectives. He dropped and patted them both down, before lifting Marquez's pant leg.

There was a rasp of Velcro and he came up holding her back-up piece, a smaller handgun.

'Our house,' he said, giving her a look. 'Our rules.'

Nicky was now dressed in orange jumps and locked inside a solitary cell in a secure, quiet wing of the county jail; although it was slightly larger than the one he'd shared with Prez back at Gatlin and he was the only inmate inside, the space somehow felt much smaller. That was partly due to the freedom he'd experienced over the past few days, seeing vast landscapes and fields that went on beyond the horizon, but was largely down to the fact he knew there wasn't a chance in hell he was ever getting out again. As he'd speculated while still on the run, breaking out of federal prison, assisting in armed robbery and kidnapping across State Lines was an easy twenty five to life, and it wasn't his first offense either.

But if you'd waited, you'd have walked out of Gatlin in two days to find Kat in a coffin. The Morningstar truck robbery would have gone ahead without him last Saturday, the Loughlins would have shown up there unexpectedly anyway and Kat would have died along with the other thieves, finished off by the brothers who would have taken both bags and split. Nicky would have been a free man, but he'd have had to live with the thought that he might have been able to prevent it.

Brooks and Billy had been responsible for the deaths of a lot of people, and for that Nicky felt considerable guilt, having known about their planned escape and using it for his own ends. But he hadn't killed anyone; all he'd wanted to do was stop Kat, knowing her desperate plan was going to end badly. In a way, his escape had given her an extra two days of life, as difficult as they'd proven to be. She hadn't died alone either. But perhaps he'd just prolonged her agony. Maybe it would have been better for her if she'd been shot dead at the shootout instead.

He felt the cell's walls closing in, constricting and confining him in a way they hadn't since the early days at Gatlin. A fresh count of many thousands of days ahead, but this time any hope of release and the chance to build a normal life again one day, gone forever.

His jaw tightened, just as it had in the house on the hill before his surrender; he stared blankly at the wall, his eyes glistening, fighting down the sudden surge of emotion that hit him as he faced his new reality. He knew if he gave way to it, he'd be done.

But he'd never felt such gut-wrenching despair.

Now inside the block and being taken towards where Reyes was being held, Archer and Marquez were stopped by another CO, *Pruitt* the name on his tag. He was pudgy with thinning ginger hair and by the expression on his face, wasn't exactly thrilled to see them. 'Cap just heard you two showed up,' he said, nodding to their escort who turned and walked back the way he'd just come. 'Told me to pass on, Reyes is off limits. Feds want exclusivity with him when they get back here.'

'You guys are killing us, man,' Marquez said. 'Radio your captain again. We earned a quick talk with the guy.'

'No. You need to go, right now.'

'We're not going anywhere yet,' Archer said bluntly. 'Let us talk to your captain.'

'He left to go to D Block. He'll be back in twenty. You'll have to wait. Go do it out front.'

'We already signed in and handed over our possessions,' Archer replied, looking straight at the man. 'We'll wait here.'

Like pieces on a chessboard, some of the people whose lives had become interconnected since the USP Gatlin breakout in Virginia on Friday were being drawn together once again. Nicky in a single cell, Archer and Marquez in the prison block wanting to see him. Even the two local hunters in the pick-up parked just outside the fence; they had more of a history in this than either Archer or Marquez could have suspected.

And at the back of the county jail, two more powerful pieces on the board had just arrived.

A CO had driven into the facility in his own truck with the sliding canopy cover over the bed. 'Thought you were on duty?' the guard at the gate said, having just taken over in a shift change. 'Where you been?'

'Wife called, remembered she'd left a heater on at home,' the CO replied with an eyeroll. 'Had to go switch it off.'

The gate guard smiled and made a comment, why the CO's wife would need a heater during a warm September morning not occurring to him, and the truck re-entered the prison, swinging around towards the back of the facility. The driver reversed the truck up to an intake point out of sight of the front gate and waited; he wasn't getting out to return to duty just yet.

Instead, he was looking up at a camera positioned on the wall above.

Its red light suddenly went dark. He got out, walked around and opened the rear gate to the bed of the truck. The pair of giants hiding in there had already changed into the XXXL jumpsuits the CO had brought from the prison when he was sent to collect them thirty minutes ago. They'd shaved their heads, Brooks his beard too in order to adjust their appearance as much as possible. There was nothing they could do about their size, however they weren't intending to be here long enough for that to become an issue. The brothers had just come full circle.

But this time they were breaking into a prison, not breaking out.

'He's in solitary,' the CO who'd driven them in and opened the gate told the brothers, before passing them each a shiv from the confiscation locker. He wasn't related to Brooks or Billy, but like so many in the lakes area, their families went back a long way and he'd known the Loughlin clan all his life. 'How'd you grease this?'

'Oneida Sheriff was a friend of our pa's since they were kids,' Brooks said, the look he was giving the CO making the smaller man nervous. He'd been ordered to help them get inside, but just wanted to get this done and them gone; he knew how dangerous these two men were.

'Wondered why he pushed to get Reyes sent here,' the CO replied nervously. 'You got a window we carved out. False tip sent the Marshals and other investigators heading to Wayne looking for you, but we got a problem. Two more cops just showed up wanting to see him.'

'Marshals?' Brooks asked.

'No, smaller fry. We're stalling them out but that won't work with the Feds. You gotta get this thing done fast then I'll get you back outta here. Cut up the wrists. Need to make the scene look like Reyes did it himself.'

Brooks took one shiv and Billy took the other. The extended Loughlin family had contaminated this area for years, like an infection that had survived repeated treatment and which proved impossible to eradicate; the current members had influence in several counties, established mostly through fear and intimidation, which meant they'd built some very useful contacts over the years. As well as the sheriff at Oneida and a couple of deputies, they had the captain here at Onondaga and three COs in their pocket.

Unknown to Nicky, he'd been sent into the very mouth of the beast.

With their fellow Gatlin escapee trapped in a cell, the man who'd used them to escape from federal prison, ripped them off by sabotaging their bag trade at the fair and who they'd had a vendetta against ever since his first night in Gatlin all those years ago, the two brothers were about to make sure the guy didn't get to face a life sentence. He'd cost them millions of dollars. His time to pay for that and all the other crap had finally come.

The CO from the truck unlocked the entry point and the two fugitive brothers made their way into the facility. They may have finally just got back to familiar territory where they'd been born and raised.

But in a place like the county jail, the two brothers felt like they were truly back home.

FIFTY

'Cameras?' Brooks asked the guard, as he and his brother stopped just inside the Onondaga County Jail's corridor, waiting for the CO to secure the entry point behind them. The prisoners in the block were all currently contained, making it possible for the two fugitives to slip into the building unseen. Even if they were noticed, they weren't the only big men in here so being immediately identified wasn't likely, particularly as everyone thought they were still hiding out somewhere; like at the State Fair last night, the prison would be the last place anyone expected to see them. And unlike the fair, they could get out clean, as long as they left fast after doing what they were here to do.

'Hinckley's controlling them; he's closing down the ones that could cause us trouble,' the CO said. 'We'll wipe the tapes, say the system failed. He'll get you out; his truck's the one in the lot beside mine. You can hide in the back. His shift finishes in twenty and he'll drive you clear. We don't get checked.'

'We got a couple of our boys waiting too, case he is,' Billy said. His brother had arranged for two of their longtime friends to park just outside the gate in their truck, the same pair who'd been eyeballing Archer and Marquez. The men also had a change of clothes, weapons and supplies for Brooks and Billy to help them disappear into the wilderness for months afterwards.

The CO passed the brothers a set of keys. 'These'll unlock the solitary wing and surrounding corridors. You only need Hinckley for one access door, just before you reach Reyes' wing. He'll see when you're ready.'

Inside the guard control center for A Block, Archer and Marquez had been trying to reason with Pruitt and another CO about letting them see Reyes, but as Marquez was continuing to argue their case, Archer happened to glance at the camera feeds.

His curiosity, suspicion and sense that something was wrong had been slowly escalating since he and Marquez had arrived from the neighboring county. *Sheriff said you've got a full house. Reyes was taken to Onondaga instead;* a statement that had come as a surprise to the two Oneida cops who'd told him their lockup was rarely full.

So why transfer Reyes to another jail when theirs more than likely had space?

The wrong thing said to the wrong man. Archer latched onto details like that. And as he took the opportunity to look at the screens, his attention suddenly snapped to one in particular.

'Are these cameras static?' he interrupted, cutting across the ongoing argument. Marquez and the COs looked at him as their back-and-forth stopped momentarily.

'Why?'

'I think I just saw someone.' He tapped the screen. 'Coming down that corridor.'

The other CO, a man with a pinched face whose nametag identified him as *Hinckley,* walked over and looked. 'Probably a guard. Can't see nothing.'

'Can you show me where the entry point on that side of the facility leads?'

Hinckley shot a quick glance at Pruitt, then after selecting the correct camera with controls, he tapped a screen and swept the lens across from the left to right and back again, moving it as far as its field of vision would allow.

The corridor it was covering was empty.

‘What did you see?’ Marquez asked as Archer frowned, looking at the screen.

Who he thought he’d seen was the question. It wasn’t possible.

Or was it.

‘I’m not sure,’ he told her. ‘But it looked like-’

‘You two look like you haven’t slept so good in a while,’ Hinckley interrupted. ‘Might be time to leave and let us handle our prisoners. Reyes isn’t going anywhere. You can talk to him after the Feds do. Maybe.’

Archer ignored him, checking each screen in turn before focusing on one corridor in particular. After studying the shot for a moment longer, he turned and without a word, left the control center, realizing from the layout that the hallway in question was very close to this one. ‘*HEY!*’ Pruitt called.

Continuing to ignore him, Archer made it to the window in the door in time to catch the back of a huge man on the other side, passing across a T cross-section of the corridor ahead. A second later, another appeared and glanced behind him just before following the other individual, quickly moving out of sight; they were the same pair he’d glimpsed in orange jumpsuits on the cameras.

Both men were huge and although they’d changed their appearance by buzzing their hair and shaving their beards, Archer immediately recognized them. He’d also seen that neither man was in handcuffs.

They were roaming free.

‘Send personnel to protect Nicky Reyes right now,’ Archer said to Hinckley and Pruitt after running back into the control center. ‘It’s the Loughlins,’ he told Marquez. ‘They’re in the block.’

‘*What?*’ she said in shock.

'The hell are you talking about?' Pruitt said. 'Those brothers haven't been captured, they're still out there.'

'Enough of this shit,' Hinckley added. 'Time for you two to go.' He stepped forward to usher them out but then Marquez looked at the screens too and saw Archer was right.

Brooks and Billy appeared in shot, moving down another corridor. They stopped at a locked door and looked straight up at the camera, just as she and Archer had done during the riot at Gatlin three days ago.

Waiting for the door to be opened for them.

In that instant, she understood why she and Archer had been blocked from seeing Reyes; why the captured fugitive had been brought here inside of the jail a county away.

And why these two COs had been doing all they could to get the NYPD pair out of the control center ever since they'd shown up.

Hinckley quickly drew his baton while Pruitt kicked the door shut to keep Archer and Marquez inside, but before they could turn on the two detectives Archer swiped a mug of coffee left on the desk near his right hand and threw the contents into Hinckley's face. It wasn't hot but still momentarily blinded him, the CO yelling and dropping the baton as he tried to wipe the liquid out of his eyes. Archer abandoned him for the moment to help Marquez, who was fighting to keep Pruitt's arm down.

Unlike his friend, he hadn't drawn a baton.

He'd pulled a handgun.

A few corridors away, the Loughlins suddenly heard a gunshot while still waiting at their penultimate access door. Brooks checked behind them as Billy tried to use the keys on the lock, but they were just for the SHU area of the prison, not here, and none of them fit.

Shouting started to echo down the corridors, inmates reacting to the gunshot.

'*The hell they waiting for?*' Brooks hissed.

When Archer had gone to Marquez's aid, the firearm discharged as they fought Pruitt for control of the weapon. Still trying to clear his vision from the faceful of coffee, Hinckley managed to reach the controls for the cameras on the console and started to quickly tap some buttons; realizing what he was doing, Marquez left Archer to deal with Pruitt, scooped up Hinckley's dropped baton and brought it down hard on his arm before hitting him again over the head, knocking him away from the controls and to the floor.

Meanwhile, Archer wrested the pistol out of Pruitt's hand, then slid his right arm around the back of man's neck, the fingers of the right hand going into the sleeve of his left. He brought his left forearm around quickly to apply a judo Ezekiel choke; Pruitt panicked and tried to fight Archer off but five seconds later went limp, temporarily unconscious, allowing Archer to release the hold and cuff him, Marquez using her own set on a dazed Hinckley.

As soon as he was secured, she went back to the screen but saw Brooks and Billy were no longer standing there waiting for the door to open.

Hinckley had managed to open it before she could stop him.

Nicky had also heard the gunshot from his cell and was kneeling to look out through the food slot in his door, wondering what was happening. This place wasn't familiar to him like Gatlin and with no time to adjust to the various noises and rhythms of the jail, the unexpected sound made him far more uneasy than he would have been in territory he knew.

Then to his surprise, the electronic locks on his door suddenly buzzed and it slid open. He rose and stepped forward uncertainly, checking outside.

No-one was there; no guards, no federal agents, no other prisoners.

The hell was going on?

Sensing a trap, he took a couple of wary steps out of the cell. It was then, through the bars of what he suddenly hoped was a locked door at the end of the corridor, he saw Brooks and Billy.

Walking towards him in solitary, with only that door between them.

'They're gonna kill him!' Marquez said from where she and Archer were watching in the control room, having found the screen for the solitary wing corridor. Someone else had just unlocked Reyes' cell and they saw the captured fugitive emerge just as the two Loughlins appeared down the corridor.

Both detectives watched helplessly as the three inmates from USP Gatlin came face to face, almost certainly for the last time. However, the three men were still separated by one more locked door, but not for long apparently, as they saw Brooks yelling something at his brother who one-by-one was trying keys in the lock.

'OPEN IT!' Brooks shouted, seeing Nicky and gripping the shiv he'd been given as Billy fumbled through the various keys. He finally found the right one, feeling the mechanism turn, but Nicky had already taken off down the

corridor in the opposite direction, other inmates in the solitary wing peering out through their food slots and calling out, wondering what was happening.

Nicky reached the barred door at the end, frantically pushing at it, but it was secured. Behind him, he heard the other door get slammed back and swung around to see the two Loughlin brothers running towards him, both of them carrying a shank. He didn't have anything to fight them with and backed up against the door, the two huge brothers closing in on him.

He remembered looking out at the landscape earlier when Kat had died in his arms. Now just a few hours later, his own life was about to end. He hoped it would be quick.

But then the door behind him buzzed and clicked open.

'I got it!' Marquez said, having found the control for the right door. Beside her, Archer watched Reyes turn and push his way through before slamming it behind him, the door locking automatically a fraction of a second before the brothers got there.

They'd bought him a bit more time.

'We gotta go help him,' Marquez said but Archer was already checking the fire exit map on the wall of the housing block, looking to see where they were and how to reach Reyes.

But unknown to them both, the A Block control room was being monitored by the main control center in the facility, the county jail's captain watching in frustration as Reyes passed through another door that had just been opened for him by the detectives from New York City, only the actions of the two cops keeping the fugitive alive.

Their arrival and Hinckley and Pruitt being overpowered had just created a major complication. There'd been a brief window here, the timing quickly but carefully arranged, the captain aware that US Marshals and cops had been drawn away off-site for another twenty minutes to half an hour, but then this pair from the NYPD had showed up. And once they got out, they were going to start talking.

The captain had already sent two other COs who'd been in here with him on an errand to another block, not wanting any potential witnesses for what was going to happen to Reyes. That meant no-one was there to see as he shut down all the cameras, knowing he needed to change this from just an apparent suicide in Reyes' cell to something much bigger.

About to set off in the direction of where he'd last seen Nicky, carrying Hinckley's keys, Pruitt's gun and with the facility's layout in his head, Archer had just left A Block's control room when an alarm started sounding.

He stopped and looked up, and saw the red light on the side of the camera lens was gone.

Then the door down the corridor ahead clicked open and it wasn't alone. Behind him, Archer saw the one at the other door had just been released too.

Having stayed behind to open more doors to help Archer if any were blocking him from reaching Reyes, Marquez looked at the bank of screens and goosebumps prickled over her body, her blood turning to ice.

Every inner door inside the facility had just been opened.

Which meant all the prisoners in the county jail had just been set free.

FIFTY ONE

Nicky hadn't registered all the doors had opened, as he had something far more urgent to deal with; he'd just been caught up on by Billy, who was ahead of his brother and who moved very fast for a man so large. Nicky already knew that from Gatlin and his previous encounters with him. The college girl Billy had abducted, tortured and murdered four years ago had learned it too.

A few seconds earlier, the brothers had been distracted by two inmates, who suddenly finding themselves free to roam the county jail had taken quick advantage; Brooks had turned to deal with them as Billy kept going after Nicky. The younger Loughlin chased his fellow Gatlin fugitive down and tackled him to the floor. He intended to use his weight to pin the smaller man before stabbing him, but dropped his shiv as Nicky fought back. He scooped it up again, but Nicky managed to twist an arm free and buried his thumb into the huge man's eye socket. Billy screamed and reared up, allowing Nicky to fight his way out from under him. He scrambled back to his feet and ran on through the next open door, pushing it shut behind him and hearing the lock re-engage just as Brooks reached it. Three hundred pounds slammed into the door but the lock held.

Punching the wire-enforced window in anger, Brooks looked back at his brother who was bent double covering his face, blood dripping off his cheek to the floor.

The other side, Nicky had no idea where he was heading, the county jail's layout totally foreign to him, but he continued to run.

The moment the alarm sounded and Archer had realized what was happening, he'd raced back to A Block's control center. The screens had all gone black, but he and Marquez didn't need them to know how much danger they were in, the rising level of noise from elsewhere in the building sounding just like Gatlin on Friday morning when the two NYPD detectives had arrived on what they'd presumed was going to be a simple transfer from prison to prison.

Now three days later, after going through so much, they found themselves trapped in another facility where a riot appeared to be breaking out.

But this time they were alone with no support.

'We gotta get the hell out, Sam!' Marquez said quickly, looking down at the two COs they'd overpowered lying on the floor, both restrained in handcuffs.

'The cell block's entrance point is between us and the way we came in,' Archer said, looking up at a camera trained on the room, its red light black too like all the others. 'We're cut off.'

'So what do we do?'

Archer glanced at the two COs then across the room saw a large metal closet with a key hanging from the lock; passing Pruitt's gun to Marquez, Archer opened the doors, threw the shelves with their contents to the floor, then with his fellow detective's help maneuvered Hinckley and Pruitt into the closet one a time. 'Better keep quiet, fellas,' Archer warned them both, before closing and locking it, pocketing the key. The two COs might have tried to take on him and Lisa, but he knew that if inmates found the pair of cuffed guards, they'd be killed and not necessarily quickly.

As Marquez picked up the room's landline and started dialing, Archer searched the drawers in the desk. He found a roll of scotch tape then snatched a couple of magazines from a pile off a stack on a small table near the door. 'We're two cops stuck inside Onondaga County Jail,' Marquez informed the local operator, having called 911. 'A riot's breaking out and we need immediate back up. Someone in here opened the doors to let the inmates out and shut off all the cameras.'

'Lift up your shirt,' Archer told Marquez quickly, who looked at him in surprise before realizing what he intended to do. She pulled the hem of her shirt free from her beltline, then held two of the magazines in place over her stomach and back as he started to pull the tape around her. 'Lower down too, over your kidneys,' he said and started quickly winding more tape around the magazines, strapping them to her body over her internal organs. Some sort of protection. Two minimally-armed cops locked in a county jail with over a hundred freed inmates. They were going to need it.

As he went to fetch more of the magazines and strap up his own body, someone slammed the gate back down the corridor outside and they heard the sound of approaching footsteps.

Archer happened to be standing out of sight of the door, but Marquez wasn't. A tattooed white prisoner in a vest with a large beer gut saw her and cut into the control room, drawing breath to yell to others in the corridor, but instead of a shout it came out as a gargle as he was caught from behind in a chokehold and pulled to the floor by Archer, who didn't take his eyes off the door.

It would take seconds for the man to lose consciousness, but seconds would be all his friends would need to get to Marquez if they weren't far behind. She was trained, but in a fight to the death with nothing but her bare hands these guys would win, and both she and Archer knew it. With their weight of numbers, it wouldn't take long for them to kill Archer too.

The inmate went slack, and Archer let him go just as another burst through the door.

Across the cell block, having just missed Nicky, Brooks went back to Billy to find him still bending over, clutching his face. He pulled his hand away to see his brother's eye socket was bleeding heavily.

'I can't see out of it,' Billy whimpered. More gunshots suddenly sounded from somewhere across the prison, and Brooks knew from past experience the chaos was only going to build. With blood now staining his jumpsuit and bare arms after killing the two inmates who'd rushed him a minute ago for his shiv and keyset, he hauled his brother to his feet and dragged him deeper into the prison with him, now even more determined to finish what they'd come here to do.

This time, Reyes couldn't hide under a truck to escape.

The second inmate who'd just burst into the control room with a shank in his hand ran at Marquez, but she was holding the pistol Archer had passed her and the prisoner dropped as she put a bullet through his shoulder.

Then two more inmates appeared, the gunshot attracting their attention, a taste of how totally outnumbered the pair of NYPD cops were. Archer tackled the closest into the desk but not before the prisoner slashed at him with a razor and cut his arm; Archer connected with a hard step-in elbow on his jaw in return, causing the prisoner's knees to buckle and sending him to the floor but Archer didn't have time to prevent the second inmate making contact. The guy stabbed Archer in the upper back a split-second before Marquez fired, putting the prisoner down, not a kill shot but enough to disable him.

Seeing the shiv sticking out of Archer's shoulder blade, she rushed forward to help him, but before she could do anything he quickly pulled her back out of sight, easing the door almost fully closed after hearing more people approaching. The prisoners they'd put down were all either groaning from being shot or coming round. Time was short.

The footsteps faded and no-one else appeared. Checking each way and realizing the corridor was clear, although almost certainly not for long, Archer pulled the door shut behind them and moved with Marquez out into the hallway before quickly cutting into a small break room for the guards.

'Pull it out,' Archer told her, easing the door almost fully closed and turning his back to her so she could get hold of the shiv.

'I can't, it'll make the bleeding worse! Like we told Lupinetti at Gatlin.'

'I fall back, it could do more damage.'

Instead of withdrawing the shank, she gripped the handle of the toothbrush, a razor blade attached to the other end, and quickly snapped off the end as Archer cursed fluently under his breath, the pain radiating through his entire body. Not ideal, but it meant the wound would stay packed and avoided the risk of the razor slicing any further into him. He was also bleeding from the slashes of the other man's shiv, the cuts more superficial but still open wounds.

'More prisoners are gonna appear; they'll be drawn by the gunshots,' he said as she nodded.

'So we've gotta move.'

'You want to just leave Reyes to the brothers?'

She shook her head.

'Me either,' he said, closing his eyes for a second, trying to ignore the pain, adrenaline helping as it kicked in. 'Let's try to find him.'

Running for his life, this time not in the outside world but in the closed confines of an unfamiliar prison, Nicky knew the Loughlins wouldn't be far behind him. To go to all this trouble to show up here and kill him, they weren't going to give up that easy.

As he heard shouts getting closer from some of the freed inmates, he spotted a door to his right and tried the handle. It opened and he squeezed himself into what was a storage closet. Quickly pulling the door shut, he held the handle tight, chest heaving, waiting for the inmates he could now hear in the corridor to run past his hiding place, praying they were too fired up to start trying doors.

He could see their shadows in the light under the door as they ran past. Once it went quiet and praying they were gone, he pushed the door open slowly then checked up and down the corridor. It was empty so he slid out then looked around, trying to locate an exit.

As he made his way along the hallway, it occurred to him that someone had unlocked that door when the Loughlins had almost been on him in the SHU block. Not the door to his cell, but the one that had allowed him to escape.

If it wasn't a mistake, then he had to hope that at least someone in here didn't want to see him die.

A few corridors away, Archer and Marquez rounded a corner and bumped straight into three inmates, two of them already bloodied from attacking other prisoners. The same two were each holding a shiv, the other a baton stolen from somewhere, and seeing Marquez's gun they immediately went for her and Archer.

She raised the pistol and put the one with the baton down, the weapon flying out of his hand and skidding down the corridor as he fell, but the front man who'd rushed Archer managed to stab him in the thigh as they fought. The NYPD cop punched the shiv holder hard, knocking him to the floor, but then Marquez felt a sharp pain too as the third man stepped forward and stabbed her in the body. The magazines taped there partially blocked the attack, though she felt the shock of pain as the tip of the blade pierced her skin; she shielded her face and neck with her arms as he caught her gun hand and used his other to slash at her again, trying to get to her throat, her forearms taking the punishment and being cut open as she kicked out at him desperately.

Her attacker then changed tactic and tried to tear the pistol free from her grip but Archer was already on him and tackled the inmate to the floor, beginning to feel increasingly light-headed from blood loss. He trapped the man's shiv arm in a keylock and wrenched downwards, the inmate shouting in pain as his arm was twisted from the torque. Archer punched him a couple of times for good measure, the guy's arm broken, and kicked the shiv away.

'Response team will be here soon,' Archer panted to Marquez, blood starting to dampen his sweater, another shiv now sticking out of his leg. 'We just have to …'

But instead of answering, he heard her take a sharp intake of breath and turned.

Brooks and Billy Loughlin had just walked into the corridor.

Just like at Gatlin when the riot took hold, the inmates were fighting anyone and everyone they came across in the euphoria of unexpected freedom, attacking the COs, each other, whoever. They didn't care. So far, Nicky had managed to avoid other prisoners and had just made it towards what he thought could be a way out.

But as he passed a side corridor, he saw a CO splayed out on the floor, blood pooling slowly from a wound to his head. Nicky assumed he was dead, but as he was about to run past, stopped, thinking of that truck driver from outside Gatlin three days ago. He went to the injured CO and felt for a pulse, finding one. He'd already worked out that if the Loughlins had been able to walk into the solitary wing the way they had, then some members of staff here had to be working with them. But if the newly-freed inmates found this guy, the man could be raped, tortured, killed or all three; an unconscious or badly-wounded screw was a dream for some of these guys who had a lot of pent up fury to vent.

Swearing under his breath, Nicky pulled the man towards the relative safety of some toilets he'd just passed so the guard would be hidden from immediate sight, but after a quick search, to his intense disappointment found the man didn't have either his baton or keys. Someone had already taken them.

Over the last few days, although he'd been heavily occupied with avoiding arrest and getting that bag of money off Nicky, the memory of his youngest brother getting gunned down on the bridge in West Virginia on Friday night had never strayed far from Brooks' mind.

And just like on Station Road in Pennsylvania when they'd split from Lupinetti, the man who'd killed Craig was right here in front of him once again. This time though, Brooks saw the cop was wounded, blood staining his jeans and sweater, some of it dripping over the police badge on his hip. When Billy had kidnapped that student from Maine and locked her in their basement before enlisting his brother's help to kill her, just before she'd died the woman had started praying. Brooks was a godless man but now, seeing the man responsible for his brother's death served up right in front of him, he knew it was fate.

However, no higher power was going to deliver justice.

That was going to be down to him.

Archer got the gist of these thoughts from the murderous look on the man's face and watched as the older Loughlin brother started to advance down the corridor towards him, his bulk seeming to almost fill the entire space. Billy was a bit slower to realize who they'd got cornered, but then also recognized Archer and his eyes widened in anticipation, blood streaming down the left side of his cheek as he moved forward to join his brother.

While Archer tried to clear the dizziness that was beginning to affect him and focus on how to try to survive what was about to happen, Marquez aimed the gun in her hand and fired, but it clicked dry, the small magazine empty. The pair of detectives backed up into the wider space of the chow hall to their right, looking for something, anything, to defend themselves with; Archer saw two fallen inmates, one with a knotted-off gym sock lying beside him weighed down with something heavy and picked it up quickly, keeping Marquez slightly behind him who was frantically searching for another weapon or way out.

Billy fanned out slightly to make sure the two cops were being backed towards the wall.

Then he and his big brother went in for the kill.

Archer swung the weighted sock sideways and fast towards Billy as he rushed in, the Gatlin fugitive dangerously quick and almost getting to him first. It hit the younger Loughlin in the side of the head and caused him to stumble, his sheer size and weight knocking Archer backwards as he crashed into him. The NYPD cop smashed into a table bolted to the floor but managed to stay on his feet; using the table as leverage, he shoved Billy backwards hard with his feet but then at the last moment threw his other arm up to try and deflect Brooks' shiv, seeing the second attack coming. It missed his chest but another wave of pain scorched through his body as the razorblade sliced into his arm, the power behind the stabbing attempt immense. Archer felt as if his forearm had almost been broken from the force of the blow.

He didn't have room to swing the sock again with Brooks so close but as the much larger man made to grab him, Archer jumped forwards and upwards instead, sending the top of his head crunching into the older Loughlin's lower jaw and snapping his head back. Billy meanwhile had got back to his feet, his head now joining his eye in bleeding profusely, and with a roar of rage slashed wildly at Archer who reacted fast and jumped back, the razor slicing open some of the fabric on his sweater and cutting across his chest. In the meantime, Marquez had taken advantage of being ignored and slammed a shiv she'd found on the floor by the second body into Billy's torso in a desperate attempt to put him down, but all it did was enrage him further. He roared again, this time in pain, and swung, Marquez scooting back, the slashing blade in the giant's hand missing her throat by centimeters.

Brooks had dropped his keys and shiv, the headbutt having cracked two of his teeth and sending pain radiating through his skull, but now he had two free hands. He stepped in when Archer tried to swing the sock again and lifted the smaller man into a bearhug. The sheer power of the giant convict's arms was immense and he squeezed so hard Archer thought his back was going to break, the weighted sock falling to the floor; unable to breathe and hearing the sound of some of his ribs cracking, he lunged forward and bit into Brooks' face as hard as he could, feeling his teeth break the flesh.

Brooks yelled and let Archer go, blood now leaking down his face. Billy however, had just caught Marquez with a hard punch and one shot was all it had taken. Archer saw she'd been knocked out cold and was now slumped on the floor, defenseless, her bloodied shirt sticking to the magazines taped underneath in that attempt to protect her vital organs. As Brooks rushed Archer again and this time dumped him hard to the floor, the NYPD detective saw Billy grab Marquez by the hair and pull her head back, the bandage from her hotel room fall still in place, his shiv in the other hand to cut open her throat from ear to ear. No words were being spoken, the silence highlighting the primal savagery more than anything else could possibly have done. This was just about killing.

But then the weighted sock was picked up and swung by another hand. It swept through the air so hard the end of the fabric stretched out almost another half a length, and when it connected, the impact shattered Billy's skull and killed him instantly. Brooks was too intent on killing Archer to notice and was now astride him trapping the NYPD cop with all three hundred pounds of his weight. Archer was trying to use every grappling technique he'd ever learned to escape being pinned, but was too weakened from blood-loss and the sheer size and weight of his assailant for anything to work.

Brooks scooped up his shiv from the floor, and as he grabbed Archer's collar with his other hand, glanced to his right and saw his brother's dead body.

He twisted slightly and looked up.

Nicky Reyes was the one holding the sock.

In that second of hesitation, with no other weapon within reach, Archer realized he actually wasn't unarmed. The shiv from where the Latino had stabbed him in the corridor was still buried in the side of his thigh. He brought his leg up just as Brooks turned back, but his hand slipped off the grip. As the huge man brought down his blade to slit Archer's throat, no chance of going shallow as he had with that laundry truck driver, Archer lunged for the handle again.

This time he got it.

And just like with Brooks' youngest brother Craig on the bridge, he beat Brooks with speed. He pulled out the sharpened screwdriver from his own leg then in one smooth movement, slammed it deep into the giant man's neck as hard as he could.

He left the shiv buried there as Brooks' eyes bulged in shock and terror. The giant Gatlin fugitive swayed and seemed as if he was still going to try and cut Archer. But then he toppled sideways, clutching at his neck; in the slipperiness of the blood, Archer managed to get out from under and push himself back to his feet. The oldest Loughlin slumped beside his brother's body and stared up at the NYPD cop in shock, fighting for breath, before his eyes eventually dulled and his face went slack.

Then, as shouting and alarms continued to sound around the county jail, Sam Archer and Nicky Reyes were left looking at each other. Nicky standing with the weighted sock in his hand, Archer now unarmed. Nicky immediately recognized the man in front of him from the shootout at the robbery in Cleveland on Saturday morning. And although he didn't know who he was, except that the guy must be a cop judging from the blood-stained badge on his hip, Nicky also realized this guy and the woman lying unconscious on the floor were most likely the pair who'd been trying to help and keep him alive in here.

As the two men continued to weigh each other up, details he'd learned over the past few days of Nicky Reyes' life returned to Archer; his rough childhood, the premature death of both his parents. Given twelve years in federal prison for saving Kat's life. Breaking out six days before his release to try and save her again.

Neither man moved as two inmates ran into the chow hall behind them, saw the bloody scene and immediately took off.

But then Nicky's gaze lowered to the floor.

To the set of keys that had been dropped in the fight and were now resting near Archer's foot.

The emergency lighting was flashing on and off, casting the two men's shadows onto the wall beside them. A riot response team and armed back-up would be here any second, but Nicky still made no attempt to go for the keys, his eyes going back to Archer's. The sound of prisoners' shouts continued to echo as more blood was spilled elsewhere in the county jail, the cameras off which meant nothing was currently being recorded.

After a long moment, instead of reaching down to pick up the keys, Archer gave Nicky a slight nod. Over the years, the Gatlin fugitive had been conditioned to hide any emotion, but that small movement caught him completely by surprise.

For a brief moment, his expression lightened.

Then Archer turned his back on Nicky and went to check on Marquez who was starting to regain consciousness. As he shifted her against the wall just behind them, the blood loss from the open wound on his leg was increasing now the shank was gone, and he found himself joining her on the floor as the room began to spin, clamping a hand to his thigh to try and stem the flow.

He looked at the battle scene in front of them as they sat side by side, hearing the sound of doors opening and shouts from a riot squad breaching the facility.

Apart from the bodies of the two inmates and the Loughlin brothers, he and Lisa were alone again.

Nicky Reyes and the keys were gone.

FIFTY TWO

A week later in Pepper Pike, Ohio, Blair O'Mara was with her daughter Alaina in their kitchen. Alaina had her cell phone in her hands, constantly refreshing the homepage for new headlines.

'He's one man,' she said to her mother in frustration. 'There are what, hundreds of thousands of cops in this country? How can't they find him?'

'Stop worrying about it. He's not going to come here.'

'He can't get away with this. With what he did. He breaks out from prison twice? Are you kidding me?'

'He'll end up making a mistake. They always do. People don't survive out there on their own.'

'Most people, maybe.' Blair didn't answer and watched as her daughter rose and snatched her jacket from a hook near the front door. 'I'm going out.' Alaina slammed the door behind her and continuing to check her phone, walked off down the street, cutting into a nearby coffee shop a couple of minutes later. She was a regular, turning up around the same time every day, the money and business her mother had inherited from Thomas O'Mara ensuring she didn't have to work for a living, so her time was her own. She ordered at the counter then took a seat, looking at her phone once again while she waited for her drink.

She willed Nicky, wherever he was, to make the mistake that would get him caught. Kat had always had a thing for the guy, but Alaina had taken against him almost from the first moment she'd met the teenage boy when he'd shown up at their old house, that initial dislike bolstered when she'd found out where he and his father lived, confirming him as trash in her eyes. Her dislike of Nicky had only increased when she'd never caught him checking her out or given her the chance to rebuff his advances. In fact, he'd pretty much ignored her, which to a popular girl used to being the center of attention was unforgiveable; she'd told herself it was because he knew she was way out of his league but deep down, knew it was because he was totally disinterested in her. His attention was all for her junkie stepsister.

The waitress brought Alaina's coffee over and moved away to start clearing and wiping down some other tables. 'Never give you enough, do they?' a voice said to her right, and Alaina realized the speaker was talking to her.

She looked up and saw a brown-haired man in a sports jacket, shirt and loose tie sitting at another table nearby. He had the day's newspaper spread out in front of him, a mug in his hand.

'Enough what?'

He nodded at a pack of Domino she was picking up. 'Sugar.' She gave him a look that should have told him she wasn't interested in anything he had to say, and tore open the packet to pour the contents into her coffee. But it seemed the guy wasn't perceptive or just chose to ignore the signal. He folded up his paper. 'My wife keeps a dispenser at home, same shape as the salt-shaker. Learned my lesson to check.'

'How interesting,' she said, making her boredom clear. But the man wasn't deterred and kept looking at her. Alaina was about to pick up her coffee and move to another table when the guy lifted his paper and what she saw caught her by surprise; underneath was something she recognized. It was the yearbook from Cleveland Catholic High, the year printed on the front the same that she'd graduated. Beside the book was a police badge too. Both kept her in her seat as her eyes flicked back up to the man's face.

'How well did you know a kid called Kyle Choh, Alaina?' the man asked.

The question and the use of her name took her completely by surprise. Off-balance, it took her a moment to answer. 'We went to high school together. I don't really remember. Hung out in different groups.'

'He remembers you. Said you bought some benzodiazepines from him just after you graduated. Told us his father was a chemist, so Kyle would go to the pharmacy and sneak supplies without his father being any the wiser. Sold the pills to the kids at school, right? Well, he did before his father noticed the discrepancies in his pharmacy records and his son ended up getting caught. Fessed to all of it to try and avoid going to prison.'

'Kyle never sold me a thing. I don't do drugs. Didn't back then, either.'

'He's got no reason to lie.'

'He asked me out on a date a couple times and I said no. Obviously he never got over it. Guess this is his way of getting back at me.'

'See, Kyle told us he sold you one pill bottle, but then you went back to him for more before he got caught,' another voice said, and Alaina turned. A second man had taken a seat at a table the other side of her, this guy younger and with a darker complexion. He had a Cleveland PD badge and gun too. Both were on his hip. 'Hit him back up another half dozen times. That's a serious amount of pills for someone who says she never popped one. And you don't look like the type who'd waste your time playing dealer. So where'd they all go?'

'My stepsister probably stole them. Heard the name Katherine O'Mara? If you haven't, check the news from the past two weeks.' Alaina stared at this second cop arrogantly to show she wasn't intimidated, but he saw a flicker of fear in her eyes.

She'd realized she might have just slipped up.

'So you bought six full pill bottles and just had them sitting around the house?' Richie said, rising and taking a seat directly across from her. Glick brought his chair over too, so they were both at the table. 'Even though you didn't want them for yourself? Doesn't that strike you as odd?'

'Kat's rehab counsellor said your stepsister started hallucinating when she was getting off the pills before she started her sentence at ORW,' Glick continued, before Alaina could answer. 'She was screaming your name a lot. Doc asked her afterwards if she could remember why. Kat told him you were the first one to give her a pill. Limited dose though, just to get her through. Senior year stress and losing her father? Being a high-strung girl already, she must've been a nervous wreck.'

Silence.

'I worked a case once where a woman was poisoning her kid,' Richie told Alaina. 'When I took a closer look at this, I thought your mom was responsible for doing something to Kat. Crushing up pills and hiding them in her food or drink. Kind of thing you'd do with an unsuspecting pet dog, right, to get it to take its medication? From what I heard, Kat was in a pretty bad way around the time you all graduated. Father gone, the guy she was falling in love with sent down for twelve years for saving her life after some asshole who happened to have a gun in his waistband tried to choke her to death at a party. And no guarantee her guy would survive in prison, considering where he was sent. You lived in the same house and had money Kat's father left you; I don't think he'd have been quite as generous if he'd known what you planned to do with it. Or the kind of person you really are. Do you?'

Alaina remained totally silent.

'We've been trying to work out why you did what we're pretty sure you did. Jealousy? Greed? Because her father stuck around in her life and yours didn't? Whatever it was, I figure you thought if Kat was gone too, your mom would inherit the girl's probably very significant share of Thomas' estate. That would make it much easier for you to access it. You couldn't kill her without attracting suspicion, so you thought the next best thing would be to get her addicted to something destructive. She was already suffering bad from depression, so it wouldn't have taken much, right? And you weren't in any hurry.'

'Around that time was when your stepsister developed the benzo addiction,' Glick continued. 'But she never pointed the finger at you. Only thing she ever told her counsellor was that you gave her that small dose early on and that you had them to help you sleep. We checked your medical records and found that was a lie. You were never prescribed benzos. We called PD from Orange County in Indiana too to check out your mom a while ago, but then we got them back on the phone again yesterday. Wanting to know more about your biological father.'

'Turns out he's been a Xanax abuser for years,' Richie said. 'Same family of drugs. You knew very well how addictive and destructive they were. Kat was on the edge of the cliff, so you stepped up and gave her a good kick off the edge.'

'So how'd I do that?' she asked neutrally. She was still maintaining a dismissive, *I can't believe this bullshit* expression, but the eyes didn't lie. And the young woman's were still telling the two detectives she was rattled.

‘Probably by mixing the contents of the pills into Kat’s food and drink,’ Glick replied. ‘Otherwise, where’d six bottles worth of benzos go, Alaina? Thomas and Kat’s maid Marija had been fired by that point too, so it’d be easy enough to slip it into her meals; slipping that crap into Kat’s portion to get her physically addicted without her knowing.’ Both detectives watched the color drain out of her.

‘She started spiraling once high school was over and Nicky Reyes had gone to prison,’ Richie said. ‘It was going to take a while, but you figured if she fell hard enough, you could get your mom to temporarily take control of the girl’s inheritance which would be a step towards making it permanent once she died. Kat ended up in prison too but she kicked the habit, unfortunately for you. She was getting better. Your plan was going up in smoke.’

Glick opened a folder and laid down four photocopied documents with signatures at the base, spreading them out. ‘These are copies of signed confessions from four local managers in the city area from where the girl worked. They each say you paid them ten thousand dollars to fire Kat from the job and to stay quiet about it. That’s a lot of money but we checked; Thomas left you a hundred grand and I’m sure you get plenty coming your way from your mom too. You must’ve thought it was worth the outlay, right? Considering how much more you were expecting to get in the end? Like an investment.’

‘Sure Kat’s father would be real pleased to know how you used your inheritance,’ Richie continued. ‘And beside these four, other people who employed her told us you ran a campaign of badmouthing her to them. These guys ended up getting rid of her without you having to pay out. I guess the other four were harder to convince.’

Then Glick reached into his pocket and withdrew a photo in an evidence bag. He placed it down in front of her.

'Know how we got onto you? I found it when we went to visit Luke McCoy's family. It was tucked into the kid's yearbook in his room.'

He tapped the photo as she looked down at it silently. The untouched coffee in the mug in front of her was starting to go cold.

'That's you with Luke McCoy at his prom,' Richie said. 'You two dated for a while there, when he was a senior and you were a junior. Kyle told us all about that too. People missed that though, right? Too busy throwing the book at Nicky Reyes for killing Luke, the guy you'd persuaded to murder your stepsister at a house party. You convinced him to drug then kill her, didn't you? Love-bombed him so hard he wasn't thinking straight. I wonder what you promised him to get him to do that.'

By now Alaina's bravado had disappeared; she looked terrified, the two detectives' plan to catch her off-guard working perfectly. 'I learned something a long time ago, doing this job,' Richie told her. 'Crime scenes talk to you, but sometimes so quietly you almost miss it. This one was so spread out over the years and hundreds of miles, and it was shouting at me that your mother destroyed Kat's life. But Blair had nothing to do with this, did she? She was totally unaware of everything you were doing. Thought Kat's problems were all her own fault, probably because you'd convinced her. But in fact, her own daughter was responsible for all of it.'

Alaina was clearly panicked but as the two detectives watched, she managed to pull herself together, her face readopting its habitual, bored expression. She shook her head before laughing briefly. 'Nicky making clowns of all of you. Those robbers breaking into a truck and killing people with you guys too inept to catch them. Desperately fumbling around for anything to make sense of what happened, so now you come at me with…with this bullshit. I'm gonna see to it you're both fired for harassment and slander.' Her eyes dropped to the photocopies of the sworn statements. 'I don't know how you persuaded those guys to give you these fabrications; but if you're lucky, maybe they might hire you both to work a fryer or sell wiper blade fluid when you're out looking for a job.'

'You're under arrest,' Richie replied bluntly.

'For what?'

'Illegal purchase of prescription drugs, solicitation of murder for hire, and bribery.' He tapped the signed confessions from the managers who'd sent Kat out the door. 'That last one we have you nailed down for.'

'You can't prove any of this.'

The Robbery Homicide lieutenant smiled and rose, pulling his handcuffs from his belt. 'Maybe not. But let's see, shall we.'

*

'The Loughlin clan are a bigger problem than anyone outside the region could've guessed,' a US Marshal explained to Marquez, standing with a colleague in the visitor's room serving one of the hospital wards in Syracuse, NY as he passed her a folder. She was in a hospital gown sitting in a chair, bandaged and strapped up with lines feeding her antibiotics and painkillers.

'How bad?'

'We're helping build a case, but every time we turn over a rock, something else crawls out. If you have a prison captain, a county sheriff and three county jail guards willing to do what the men at Onondaga did at the snap of

Brooks Loughlin's fingers, it shows the influence he and his family had.'

'Were they related to any of these guys?'

'A couple distantly, but not all. Also helps explain some of the stuff that's happened in Onondaga County over the last ten years or so.' He dropped another file in front of her. 'Remember the two boys who sent you through the window and tried to kill your friend at the auto-shop?'

She opened it and read the first lines of the report inside. 'You gotta be kidding me.'

'They're the same pair who were waiting outside 'Daga County, day you and Archer almost got killed and Reyes escaped. Sheriff sold them out to try and pitch for a deal. They're local boys, sent to waste Archer after he shot Craig Loughlin on that bridge in West Virginia. Brooks set it up.

'They were in Cleveland to get your colleague, not you. Which must've been why they didn't finish you off when you fell out the window. Kept trying to track Archer but couldn't find him. Then his cell came back on and they tracked him to that auto-shop.'

'They're childhood friends of Brooks, Billy and Craig,' she read from the arrest reports and confessions.

'Guess they didn't anticipate how hard it'd be to kill you and Archer. Catching sight of Reyes on the morning he was apprehended was just a stroke of luck for them. Day before, they used a dump-car with two suppressed sub-machine guns in the trunk and left it in a lot in Rochester after they tried to knock you off in Cleveland and then Archer on their way home. Attempted to torch it, but a passer-by saw the car on fire and reported it before the flames really took hold.'

'A passing cruiser got them on camera leaving Chautauqua County,' the other Marshal said. 'The ballistics match the bullets dug out of the walls at the motel and mechanics' shop. When we arrested them and broke them down, they confirmed the Sheriff sent them after Archer on Brooks' orders. They almost bagged you instead.'

'We were working with the Oneida Sheriff's Office when we came to town.'

'Good thing you and Archer didn't spend a lot of alone time with the chief,' the first deputy replied. 'He'd have been looking to set you two up for another shot and they'd have got you eventually. No-one's that lucky.'

'Those brothers seem to have had a lot of pull.'

'Brooks headed up the family after his father died and even though he was stuck doing life down in Virginia, he still called the shots. Put him, his two brothers and a load of other relations together, and no-one was ever brave or dumb enough to go against them. Piss one off, you got all of them on your case, so just because someone was on the outside didn't mean they were safe from Brooks and Billy inside Gatlin. People seemed to have always believed that the brothers would escape one day. Just didn't expect it to be the Friday before Labor Day weekend.'

'But how'd they find us? Archer was at an auto-shop in the middle of nowhere. I was back in Ohio at a motel.'

'Sheriff called your Bureau in New York pretending to be working with you guys. Your sergeant checked his credentials and had no reason to suspect a trap; told him Archer was holing up in a hotel in the city. Once we found the chief was dirty, we ran a search on all the computers he had access to. He used one to do a cell ping trace six times on Archer's phone. How they found him again at that auto-shop in Chautauqua County.'

As he said that, Marquez went cold and felt her mouth go dry; she was suddenly picturing herself in an orange jumpsuit too, something all too easy to imagine. The speed the tech search had produced results unsettled her, knowing they could do exactly the same with Prez Rainey's cell phone records if they ever found his number. The Marshals had wanted to meet with her today to give an update on what had happened, but she'd been in their position before and knew they could be feeding her information to see how she reacted.

Perhaps they already knew about her communications with the biker. Or maybe she was just getting paranoid.

'How long did the riot at Onondaga actually run for?' she asked.

'Almost until sundown. Riot team got you and Archer out, but by then the entire place had gone crazy. Police and federal agents didn't have a chance to find out Nicky Reyes was missing until they regained full control and could do a count.'

'He just walked out past you all?'

'One of the COs was found injured and handcuffed in a toilet in his underwear and socks. No uniform. That's when they realized Reyes must've slipped through at some point, straight past the response team.'

'He's getting good at that.'

'Whatever. We got him once. We'll catch him again.'

Marquez looked at the two Marshals carefully, keeping her face impassive. 'I'm being investigated too, right?'

'For what?'

'Firing a weapon in the prison.'

'You didn't bring the piece in, and you two were trapped in the block with criminals who were intending to murder you. Don't think you're gonna have any issues with State investigators about that.' The Marshal leaned forward. 'But what's the last thing you can recall?'

'Brooks and Billy rushing me and Sam in the food hall.'

'You don't remember how the younger brother was killed?'

'No.' Pause. 'Why?'

'We've been trying to work out how someone your size managed to get around him, pick up a weighted sock and found enough power to brain him over the back of the skull. Guy had a head like a slab of concrete.' The two Marshals were watching her very closely.

'His eye was damaged. He couldn't see properly which would've made it easier. Archer must've got him.'

'While trying to fight off three hundred pounds of Brooks Loughlin? So someone else didn't do it?'

'You'll have to go by what Archer says. I told you, Billy had knocked me out.'

'You're sure you didn't see anyone else?'

'Like who?'

'Someone with a grudge against them, maybe. Who they'd broken into the jail in the first place to kill.'

'We were hoping you could confirm that for us,' the other Marshal said.

There was a pause.

'Nicky Reyes never killed anyone while he was on the run, did he, Deputy?' she suddenly asked, reversing the questioning, knowing full well what they were driving at.

'No. What's your point?'

'I got smashed out of a motel room window and was stabbed in the jail. Archer got cut up way worse than I did and was attacked on a prison transport bus. He was also shot at in Cleveland, on the road and at the auto-shop. We spent three days tracking these fugitives across State Lines and watched good people die on the way. But it feels like you're trying to say we might've stood by, watched Reyes kill Billy Loughlin then let him escape? I'm catching that right?'

The deputy Marshal licked his lips. Trying to get clues and tells was a lot harder when the person you were interviewing was a detective with Marquez's experience.

'I know every badge from here to Ohio wants the Reyes collar,' she continued. 'And how you must've gotten chewed out by leadership for trusting local law enforcement and Onondaga County with him once he was caught. But you want to pin someone for inside help, take a look at the Oneida Sheriff's Office or the local police all over this area. Because you got real problems here. Not with us.'

'We're low on leads on Reyes,' the other Marshal said. 'We came up with a theory.'

'After all that happened to us, why the hell would we help him?'

He looked at her but didn't answer. He couldn't; he didn't have one.

'You run this past your Chief?'

'No.'

'I wouldn't.'

Also wearing a hospital gown and robe, Archer was sitting in the ward's communal room staring out of the window, bored and frustrated with his enforced inactivity when he saw Marquez walk in, slowly wheeling her IV drip stand.

'How'd it go?' he asked.

'They won't be back anytime soon,' she said, and Archer understood the hidden message without her needing to elaborate. 'Pointed out some facts of life.' She touched the stitching on her head. 'The assholes who gave me this and went at you at the auto-shop were those two boys we saw loitering in the parking lot outside the Sheriff's Office and County. Childhood friends of the Loughlins, sent after you by Brooks because you put down Craig. They're hunters.'

'Explains how good they were.'

'Yeah, but this time they were after you, not the local wildlife.'

'How'd they find me at the hotel?'

'CT Bureau in New York got a call from the Sheriff who said he wanted to contact you. Shep made sure he was legit, then gave him your cell number and let him know you were currently at that hotel in Cleveland. These two were dispatched-'

'But you'd taken over the room instead of me,' he said, looking at the stitched cut on the side of her head where the hair had been shaved. 'Sorry, Lis.'

'Like you said, it'll grow back soon.' Her smile turned into a grimace. 'It better.'

'But how'd they find me at the auto-shop then? Shep didn't know I was there.'

'GPS. The area you were in was mostly warehouses, so you weren't hard to find. After you went into the river, your phone was dead until you got to Chautauqua County on Sunday, right?'

'And they showed up a few hours after I turned it on again. I get it. The sheriff tried to get us killed.'

'On Brooks' orders. When we find Lupinetti, he and the Sheriff can fight over who gets top bunk in a cell.'

Archer went quiet for a moment, Marquez's comment reminding him that their man was still out there. 'Marshals any closer to finding Reyes?'

'Still no trace of him, or the contents of Kat O'Mara's deposit box. One of the locals who lives near the woods where Kat died phoned in to say he thought he might've seen a man in uniform moving through the area later that day. Took him to be another investigator, so didn't take any more notice.'

Archer didn't respond as Marquez looked at him. She'd told the Marshal the truth when she said she'd been out cold when Billy had been killed, and Archer had told her later he'd been the one to hit him. He'd held her gaze when he said that, but they both knew he'd been trying to fend off Brooks Loughlin just before she was struck by the knockout punch. When consciousness returned and she'd found herself leaning against the wall with Archer beside her holding a stab wound to his leg, she hadn't noticed anything other than the bodies of the two brothers. It took until later when someone had asked how the Loughlins had managed to get through the various doors inside the county lockup that she realized no-one had mentioned finding the keys Brooks had been holding when they'd cornered them in the chow hall, which would have answered the question. And Nicky Reyes happened to have disappeared from the jail at around the same time.

Archer had told investigators during his own questioning that he'd been in and out of consciousness from blood loss, and with the cameras in the block shut off, his was the only account they could use on the report. She'd never pushed it, in the same way he wasn't pushing her about her phone-calls to Prez during the manhunts. This entire situation had been complicated. Nothing black and white, with good and bad on both sides. And some things were better left unsaid.

But she was concerned about her fellow detective. Archer had been unusually subdued since they'd been admitted to the hospital, which was understandable considering the injuries he'd sustained. However, she knew from long experience how resilient he was and that he'd definitely suffered worse in his time, so she felt that getting stabbed was unlikely to be the cause of his uncharacteristically low mood. She guessed that Lupinetti still being out there was eating away at him, just as it was for her. The other members of their team had driven up to visit a couple of times, Shepherd now working with the Marshals Office on tracking Lupinetti down, but she knew Sam was as frustrated as she was by being stuck in the hospital, both of them wanting to be the ones to find him and complete their task. Archer didn't take failure or unfinished business easily. Neither did she.

The Marshals' questions had her reliving that situation in the jail, and she remembered how when they'd been locked inside Onondaga, Archer's first concern had been to strap up her torso with the magazines to protect her, then the punishment he'd taken to help keep her alive. Without him, she would've been shanked in the liver and be dead by now.

But before she could say anything more, she saw him look past her, surprise on his face.

'What are you doing here?' Archer asked as his sister appeared in the doorway, getting to his feet slowly as his brother-in-law pushed her wheelchair into the ward.

'Decided to take a drive to Niagara Falls.' She glanced at Marquez. 'This was on the way.'

'You called them?' Archer asked Marquez.

'Heard you've been recovering. Again,' Sarah answered instead, smiling as she stopped beside them in her chair.

'We've got to stop meeting in hospitals,' Archer said. 'Don't want these injuries becoming the story of our liv-'

But then Marquez saw his expression change. He went from looking subdued to almost as if a light had suddenly been switched on inside him.

'*Son of a bitch,*' he said quietly.

'Come again?' his brother-in-law Jack said, as Sarah stared in surprise at her brother.

Archer turned to Marquez, excitement back in his eyes, that bored and frustrated look he'd been wearing a moment ago gone. ‘I think I know where we can find Frank; if we’re not too late.’

EPILOGUE

As Marquez had proven in her interview with the two Marshals at the hospital, trying to trip up an experienced detective during questioning wasn't easy and neither was tracking one down if they wanted to remain hidden. Since he'd split from the Loughlins on that road by the NY-PA State border, Frank Lupinetti had successfully evaded capture in the ten days since. He'd quickly dumped the car and after travelling by night and laying low during the days that followed, he'd eventually ended up back in New York City, the place where he knew best how to hide.

He hadn't lied to Brooks and Billy Loughlin when he'd told them he still had plenty of money hidden, cash he'd accumulated during his years as a corrupt cop in the NYPD. After making contact with an old and trusted former colleague of his who'd been the one to wire the Loughlins money when Frank was still in Gatlin, desperate to keep himself alive and to ensure he got protection after the last attack, Lupinetti had borrowed money from the guy, bought some clothes, a smartphone and a ticket out to New Jersey on the promise that when he returned, his friend would be repaid in full with interest. Dressed in his new threads with his tattoos covered, wearing an Islanders ballcap and now with a burgeoning beard, Lupinetti wasn't easily recognizable and didn't attract any attention. Up to that point, things had gone to plan and he was beginning to feel pretty confident.

But when he got off at his stop, Bloomfield, and walked another twenty minutes to his destination, he swore quietly and repeatedly to himself as he stared at a new housing development, in the process of being built on what had been a totally deserted tract of land two years ago. The site was busy with workmen and with all the activity, there was nothing he could do until night fell to check the place out properly. He walked back to the nearest town, bought a shovel and gloves then waited impatiently for the sun to go down before returning to the now empty development site.

With the sound of traffic passing on the nearby highway, but confident he was almost invisible in the dark despite the moonlight, Lupinetti took out his cell phone and checked the coordinates he wanted, pinpointing the specific area he was looking for. It was on the left side of the development and to his intense relief, although the area had been marked, the land was still undisturbed.

He found the spot, pulled on the gloves, stamped the shovel into the ground and started to dig.

After almost twenty minutes of hard work, he went to scoop more earth when the shovel hit something. He was about to clear the space around it, but stopped when he thought he heard the sound of an engine, closer than the cars on the road. He waited for a few moments, but hearing nothing else, he returned his attention to the hole he'd just dug and with his heart beating even faster, quickly uncovered a dirt-covered strap.

He cleared the soil around it until he could see a large bag and pulled it free.

He dumped it onto the pile of soil on the edge of the hole, then knelt down and opened the zipper, letting out a quick laugh of relief when he saw rolls of money secured in elastic bands, still curled up in there just as he'd left them a few years ago. Seven hundred thousand dollars, his emergency fund built up over his twenty year-plus career, money his fellow former cops, the guys who'd exposed him and those who'd locked him up had no idea existed. His *get out of jail free* card, kept out of bank accounts where it could be found. He'd won after all.

It took much less time to refill the hole, and when he smoothed it back over, saw in the moonlight that it had clearly been disturbed. Not that it mattered; no worker finding it could possibly guess that this was where one of the most wanted men across the eastern United States had hidden a cache of cash. He'd dump the shovel with the gloves somewhere before heading out of the Tri-State area for good.

He smiled again, remembering again how he'd escaped from the Loughlins when Archer had distracted them back on the road leading out of Pennsylvania into New York two weeks ago. *Couldn't have done it without all three of you boys*. The smirk remained in place as he picked up the bag, shovel and gloves and turned to walk back into the night.

But then the entire area suddenly became flooded with light.

'DROP THE BAG AND PUT YOUR HANDS UP!' a voice shouted as Lupinetti stopped dead, dropping the shovel and gloves and throwing his forearm up to shield his eyes from the headlights blinding him. '*RIGHT NOW, ASSHOLE! DO IT!'* In total shock, he shook the bag off his shoulder and raised his hands, as figures wearing vests and badges appeared out of the darkness with their weapons up, having been lying in wait. Lupinetti closed his eyes as he felt himself grabbed, pushed to the ground and cuffed, before being hoisted back up. When he was moved out of the direct glare of the headlights, he recognized the three detectives surrounding him.

They were all Sam Archer's teammates.

He stared at them, stunned, his shock at being caught clear in the glare of the lights. Matt Shepherd stepped forward and pulled up the sleeve of Lupinetti's sweater. 'Hospital near Gatlin took a photo of your arm when you got cut. It was added to your transfer folder.' He tapped several digits tattooed there, the co-ordinates for where the money had been hidden. 'Had the numbers inked down in case you forgot, right?'

Lupinetti stared in dismay at his arm then at Detectives Alice Vargas and Josh Blake who'd just opened the bag to check the contents. He looked at Shepherd, who gave him a smile just as broad as Frank's when he'd found the cash a few minutes ago.

'You're gonna really love to hear who figured that one out,' he told him.

Inside USP Gatlin earlier that same day, Prez had walked back into his cell after just having a visit in the meeting hall with the temporary president of his MC. The man had been on damage control with the Pittsburgh chapter after Nicky had attacked two of their members then stolen one of their cars during his escape from Pennsylvania, police pushing hard to find out how the fugitive had ended up with the bikers in the first place. '*When you get out, the gavel is all yours again, boss,*' the temporary president had told Rainey. '*I can't deal with this shit.*'

As he returned to his cell, now with less than ten months to go on his sentence, Prez found a postcard waiting for him, mail having been left in the cells during his absence.

It was blank, but he saw the card was from Mesquite, near Dallas, Texas.

As he looked at it, a smile on his face, there was the rattling of chains from the concourse and he turned to see a white-faced young man being led into the cell. The CO called Anderson unlocked his ankle chains and cuffs and nodded at Prez.

'Meet your new celly, Rainey.'

The doors closed behind him, and the young man stood there uncertainly staring at the older man. Prez lay down on his bunk, looking again at the postcard. 'Welcome to prison, kid.'

On a road just outside Vancouver, Canada, far away from Virginia and the place which had held him for eleven years and three hundred and fifty nine days, a man with a shaved head paid for some items inside a gas station, the bored attendant barely paying any attention to him.

He got back into his car, a bag under his seat containing almost a million dollars. Nicky had bought a phone with some of the cash, using a fake name, and had learned from checking the news that Alaina, Kat's stepsister, had been arrested and was being charged in Cleveland for a list of crimes. A reporter for the Cleveland Plain Dealer newspaper had done a full in-depth piece surrounding the young woman's arrest, her charges and the accusations made against her. He'd been shocked when he'd read the news; Nicky had never taken to Alaina, but would never have suspected that she could have been responsible for Kat's downfall. Any suspicion he'd had that Kat was being mistreated in that household had always fallen on Blair, not her daughter, and even then he'd never imagined things could have gone that far.

But Thomas O'Mara had been wise enough to plan ahead for when he was no longer around, determined to protect his daughter and her future, which had led him to taking measures to ensure Kat would always remain financially secure, measures known only to the two of them. The deposit box within the box being shipped back to Morningstar hadn't held money or jewelry as everyone had suspected. Instead, the titanium box had contained six separate items: five of them were $1,000,000 government treasury bearer bonds, issued in February 1977 and redeemable until 2047, rolled into a single, tight scroll.

The bonds served as Kat's additional inheritance and insurance from her father, which she'd so cruelly been refused access to, all due to Alaina's malign influence. Neither mother or daughter had ever had a clue what the box contained, just that it had held something of great value. Gambling had been Tommy's hobby, the reason why'd he'd met Blair at French Lick in Indiana, but he'd been much more successful at the tables than he'd ever let on. The bonds came from funds he'd earned playing cards over the years, a secret only he and his daughter knew about until Kat had shared it with Nicky that fateful Thursday at Gatlin, two days before the heist. Untraceable cash, converted into the bonds and left for her to do with as she saw fit.

Nicky had been in prison long enough to know how to trade in bonds; he'd received a slightly lower price, but that had ensured the trade was kept quiet and he still had the remaining four for the future. He'd used some of the cash to source a new set of fake documents, and crossed the border without any difficulty on this side of the country after a pitstop in Texas to mail that postcard to Prez; sent to let him know he was OK and also in the hope he could convince the mass of law enforcement looking to recapture him that he was heading south into Mexico.

The second item in the box had been a photo, from a day Thomas O'Mara, Doc Reyes, Kat and Nicky had gone to an Indians ball game. Nicky tucked it onto the sun visor in front of him before he moved back onto the road, making sure to stick to the speed limit as he continued along the highway, almost five million dollars in the car in various forms of currency.

He thought of his mother who'd died giving birth to him and the loss of his father. Then Kat's father's passing. The almost twelve years in prison, followed by Kat's death, a direct result of her desire to try and give them both a chance at a better life. The Loughlins who'd wanted him dead and the cops who he knew would be after him until the day he died. Save one, the man whose name he'd never know, who for whatever reason had given him that smallest of chances back at Onondaga County Jail, an act he'd never forget.

He glanced at the photo on the visor, the three people he cared for most, no longer here but who in their own individual ways had done so much for him. By the time darkness had fallen, the car with Nicky Reyes behind the wheel had disappeared into the night.

We got him once, the US Marshal talking to Marquez at the hospital had said confidently. *We'll catch him again.*

He was wrong.

They never would.

'Blair O'Mara wasn't involved in any of this,' Richie told Archer over the phone, that same night on the other side of the continent at the hospital in Syracuse. *'We all assumed she was the one blocking Kat from getting to that deposit box, but it was her daughter.'*

'Bunch of managers we've sweated put down in writing that Alaina paid them off to fire Kat,' Glick continued, the call on speaker at their end. *'And the college student who Reyes killed in self-defense had been in a relationship with the girl when they were at school together. She must've convinced the frat boy to try and get rid of her stepsister.'*

'Why would she do that?' Archer asked. 'Had they fallen out?'

'Not that we can find out. Probably motivated by greed. Jealousy. Spite. All of the above. We all know teenagers act irrationally which can lead them to do some dumb things. Looks like she took it to another level and never let the grudge go.

'We know too her mom inherited a huge amount when Thomas O'Mara died as well as taking over his company; but that wasn't enough for our girl. She wanted Kat's share too. She guessed there must be something of great value in that deposit box and knew if her mom could get control of it, it would make it much easier for her to get her hands on it. Set about ruining the girl's life, drip-fed poison and negativity in her mom's ear about Kat to turn her against her. She's a real snake in the grass, this one. Much stronger personality than Blair.'

'So what was in the box? You ever find out?'

'No, but wherever it is, we're pretty sure Reyes has it,' Richie answered. *'If it was worth something, gonna make it a lot easier for him to disappear, that's for sure. Going back to Alaina, it looks like she targeted Kat from the moment they started living in the same house. We're thinking she was slipping stuff into her food to make her ill.'*

'Would explain why Kat was suddenly sick so much as an early teen,' Archer said, having heard about the girl's past.

'Then getting her killed at that party didn't work, so Alaina got her hooked on substances instead once Kat's father and the maid were gone,' Glick said. *'Gave her a free run.'*

'She started mixing small amounts of benzos into Kat's food and drink,' Richie continued. '*But when Kat got out of prison clean Alaina had a problem; she knew she couldn't keep trying to get rid of her without people getting suspicious.'*

'So she paid off her employers to fire her, keeping her jobless, desperate and away from her inheritance,' Archer said. 'If Kat's life was still a mess, Alaina banked on the fact that she'd end up on drugs again. Ensuring the court would allow Blair to keep control of that deposit box.

Then only a matter of time before Kat ended up back inside or dead.'

'The way her life was unravelling, Kat was on a downward spiral which is what her stepsister wanted.'

'And Nicky tried to save Kat. Wanting to pay back what her father did for his.'

'*Yeah. That's what we think.*'

After talking for another ten minutes or so, the two Cleveland detectives wished Archer a swift recovery and said they'd keep him posted as the case against Alaina progressed. He knew Marquez would want to be updated, but that could wait a few hours until morning. Then, as the night drew in and darkness fell, Archer realized he wanted to be somewhere he wouldn't be disturbed. He left his hospital room and found a bench outside the building, sitting slightly gingerly, his stitches healing and his body still recovering from that brutal, close-to-fatal fight with the Loughlins.

He looked up at the dark sky. After his friend Lucero's funeral, his close friend and the detective whom Lupinetti, among others, had helped kill, Archer remembered watching a sunset so fiery it had seemed as if the sky was burning. But tonight in contrast, it was totally black save for the cold white moon and a few stars. No shades of gray, unlike down here on Earth.

Cops and prison guards trying to keep him and Marquez alive, while others had done their best to get them killed. Convicts on the run trying to take their lives, as another fugitive helped save them. A man and woman with no relationship aside from their fathers' friendship risking all they had for each other, while a stepsister who'd had almost everything she could ever wish for doing her utmost to destroy the other girl's life.

How things can change, Marquez had said the night before they'd gone to Gatlin, when so much had later turned out to be far different from what it had first seemed. Good to bad, and bad to good. The Marshals would never let the case drop, however with the certainty that night was dark and day brought light, Archer knew they'd never see or hear anything about Nicky Reyes again. The man had more than paid his dues for the mistakes in his life.

But one thing held no shades of gray. It burned and shone in Archer, the same as it did for the escaped fugitive who was Archer's opposite in so many ways, and yet in others, so similar. A kindred spirit; like the sun and the moon taking their turns in the sky.

Sometimes a person had to venture into the darkness.

But the darker the night, the brighter the dawn that followed.

THE END

###

About the author:

Born in Sydney, Australia and raised in England and Brunei, Tom Barber has always had a passion for writing and story-telling. It took him to Nottingham University, England, where he graduated in 2009 with a 2:1 BA Hons in English Studies. Post-graduation, Tom followed this by moving to New York City and completing the 2 Year Meisner Acting training programme at The William Esper Studio, furthering his love of acting and screen-writing.

Upon his return to the UK in late 2011, Tom set to work on his debut novel, *Nine Lives*, which has since become a five-star rated Amazon UK Kindle hit. The following books in the series, *The Getaway, Blackout, Silent Night*, *One Way*, *Return Fire*, *Green Light, Last Breath* and *Jump Seat* have been equally successful, garnering five-star reviews in the US and the UK, France, Australia and Canada.

Night Sun is the twelfth novel in the Sam Archer series.

Follow @TomBarberBooks.